MANDARIN GATE

MANDARIN GATE

ELIOT PATTISON

MINOTAUR BOOKS ❈ NEW YORK

MANDARIN GATE. Copyright © 2012 by Eliot Pattison. All rights reserved. Printed in the United States of America. For information, address St. Martin's Press, 175 Fifth Avenue, New York, NY 10010.

www.stmartins.com
www.minotaurbooks.com

Design by Kelly S. Too

ISBN 978-0-312-65604-1 (hardcover)
ISBN 978-1-250-01208-1 (e-book)

First Edition: November 2012

10 9 8 7 6 5 4 3 2

*To the people of Tibet,
wherever they may reside*

MANDARIN GATE

CHAPTER ONE

The end of time was starting in Tibet. Shan Tao Yun's old friend Lokesh had told him so repeatedly in recent months, reminding him just the day before as he had pointed a crooked finger toward an unnatural cloud lurking on the horizon. More than once during the past year Shan had listened, chilled, to Lokesh and their lama friends solemnly recount the ancient prophecy. Humans had been given their chance and had failed, had let their civilization become more about inhumanity than humanity. They were spiraling downward, biding their time until a more intelligent, compassionate species arose. The evidence was everywhere in Tibet, and it seemed perfectly logical to the lamas that the process was starting there, at the top of the world, the land closest to the homes of the deities.

Now, as he watched Lokesh clearing an old pilgrim path, murmuring prayerful apologies to the insects he disturbed, Shan realized he cherished the old Tibetans not just for their gentle wisdom but for the joy they showed despite the approaching clouds.

"Jamyang frolics with a goat!" Lokesh suddenly called out.

Shan saw that his friend had paused and was cocking his head toward the opposite slope. He looked across the small, high valley in confusion, making out now a running figure clad in the maroon robe of a monk. He glanced in alarm toward the road in the larger, main valley beyond. Only an hour before they had seen a police patrol. Jamyang was an unregistered monk, an outlaw monk, and it was reckless of him to show himself so close to a public road.

"He'll be late for his own festival," Lokesh declared with a grin, reminding Shan that the lama had asked them to join him in an hour for a meal at the little shrine by the remote hut he called home. The rest of the day was to be devoted to celebration of Jamyang's restoration of the shrine.

Shan stepped to his truck, pulled his battered binoculars from the dashboard and focused them on the opposite slope. "Not a goat," he reported a moment later. "He's chasing a man." The figure in front struggled to balance a sack and a long object across his shoulders, running with a bent, uneven gait.

With a worried, confused expression, Lokesh raised a finger and traced in the air the course of the path the running figures followed. "It is the way to that new Chinese town!" he warned, pointing to where the trail disappeared over the crest of the ridge. "He doesn't realize where he's being led!"

With sudden alarm, Shan studied the slope again. He had carefully avoided the town, one of the new immigrant settlements that were sprouting in the Tibetan countryside, and had warned his old Tibetan friends to stay away as well. The government had begun paying a bounty for information on unregistered monks, much more for their capture, encouraging a new breed of bounty hunters who did the work of the police in ferreting out hidden lamas. "Bonecatchers," the Tibetans called such reviled men, for those they brought in were usually dazed, emaciated hermits who were little more than skin and bone. The bonecatcher who lured Jamyang into government hands would earn more than most Tibetans made in a year. There would be a police post in the town, with a jail. Once in the town the bighearted lama would never get out.

Shan frantically consulted the worn map on the front seat of his truck, then leapt behind the steering wheel. He called out for Lokesh to meet him at Jamyang's shrine but as he turned the pickup truck around the old Tibetan leapt into the cargo bay.

He drove with reckless speed down the mountain, the decades-old truck bouncing and swerving in the loose, uneven gravel, fishtailing around the base of the ridge where Jamyang ran, then up the rough switchbacks of the far side to cut the fleeing man off. Shan could hear the clatter of the loose buckets and shovels in the rear, and above it the laughter of Lokesh, the gentle laughter that had helped keep Shan alive during the first terrible months when he had been thrown into a gulag barracks years before.

The old engine groaned and coughed as the truck climbed the dirt track that stretched up and over the ridge ahead of Jamyang, at last shuddering to a stop by a long defile of boulders where the trail intersected the road. Below them were open pastures and, less than a mile away, the small grid of streets that marked the new settlement.

The running man was so pressed with carrying his heavy load and watching the path behind him that he nearly collided with Shan. He gasped and tried to avoid Shan by jumping onto a ledge stone at the side of the trail. But his limp threw him off balance and he fell heavily, cursing as he twisted on his ankle, sprawling in the grass, the objects in the sack he had been carrying scattering around him.

"He's a lunatic!" the stranger groaned with a fearful glance down the trail as he rubbed his ankle. "Raging at me like some crazed yak!" He began quickly gathering the objects in the grass.

Shan studied the man a moment. He was a tough wiry figure in his thirties with a long scar over his left eye that disappeared into shaggy black hair. His tattered fleece vest and cap seemed to mark him as a shepherd, but under the vest the Tibetan wore a black T-shirt with the image of a skeleton holding a sickle. Shan took off his hat.

The stranger stiffened as he recognized Shan's Chinese features. "He's not registered, Comrade!" the Tibetan cried out in a thin voice as he retrieved a small copper offering bowl. "He can't be, hiding in that hut like some wild animal." He pulled himself up, wincing as he put weight on his foot, then inched toward the largest of his burdens, two planks, as long as his arm, tightly wrapped with the ribbons used to tie together the wooden plates carved for printing Tibetan scriptures.

Shan took a quick inventory of the other objects the limping man gathered. A rolled deity painting, a small bronze figure of a *dakini* goddess, two sections of a ritual trumpet, and a silver *gau*, one of the amulet boxes devout Tibetans wore around their necks with secret prayers inside. With the printing blocks, such antiques would fetch enough on the black market to feed the man for weeks.

The shepherd began to lift the blocks to his shoulder, then gasped and stepped backward as he saw the tall lean man in the maroon robe who had materialized beside him. Jamyang smiled. *"Lha gyal lo,"* he said to the thief. "May the gods be victorious."

The stranger raised the blocks in front of him like a shield. As Jamyang put a hand on the blocks he pulled them back, struggling to wrest them free of the lama's grip. "There'll be a bounty for the sorcerer!" he cried to Shan, then gestured to the settlement below. "There's a police post in town, right there in Baiyun!"

The man, Shan realized, was genuinely afraid of the gentle middle-aged lama. Jamyang had appeared at his side, not from the trail, but as if out of thin air, without being in the least winded. Tibetan tradition included many tales of lamas who could magically transport themselves.

"What is the bounty for thieves?" Shan asked the stranger.

The man turned his makeshift shield toward Shan, then toward the end of the truck where Lokesh now stood. He sagged and lowered the blocks but as his gaze settled on the faded insignia on the truck door his chagrin faded. "You're just a damned inspector of ditches," he said.

"I am the damned *official* inspector of ditches," Shan replied, "and that is the closest to the government of the People's Republic you want to come today."

The Tibetan stared at Shan for a few heartbeats then frowned and looked up in confusion as Jamyang, one hand still on the blocks, extended the little bronze dakini with the other. He released the blocks, grabbing the figurine and stuffing it into his pocket before placing the other stolen objects on the tailgate of the truck. After a moment Lokesh began to help him, then good-naturedly directed the thief to sit on the tailgate and pushed up his pants leg to examine his ankle. Lokesh sighed and glanced at Shan. The man may have sprained his ankle but his leg had already been twisted from a fracture that had not properly healed.

"You should have a crutch," Jamyang declared, and glanced about the slope. The nearest trees were far below, along the stream that ran by the new settlement.

"I will drive him," Shan said.

"Of course you won't," Lokesh quickly rejoined. "You will take Jamyang back and begin the celebration. By road it is miles to the town but by this sheep path it is a short walk. I will be his crutch, then meet you at the shrine later."

Shan gazed with foreboding at the old Tibetan, knowing it was futile to argue. "You have your papers?" he asked his friend. Police were appearing with alarming frequency in the valley, checking and rechecking registration cards, even laying unexpected traps on back roads. The people of the valley were steeped in Tibetan tradition, which made them inherently suspect to the government. Lokesh gestured to his shirt pocket and nodded, then pressed his fingers on the gau that hung from his neck, as if to indicate the real source of his protection.

Shan gave a hesitant nod. *"Lha gyal lo,"* he offered. "We will wait for you before the evening meal."

The shepherd held up a hand as Lokesh helped him onto his feet. He reached into his pocket and extended the bronze goddess to Jamyang. "No," the lama said, "I gave it freely. It is an auspicious day," he declared.

The thief's face clouded. He remained silent, watching the lama with wide eyes as he limped away, one arm braced over Lokesh's shoulder. Shan too gazed in confusion. The little dakini had been one of the oldest, most valuable pieces from Jamyang's shrine.

Without another word the lama moved around the battered truck and climbed into the passenger seat. By the time Shan settled behind the steering wheel, Jamyang was staring at his prayer beads, working them with a strange intensity as he murmured a mantra, a long repetitive invocation that Shan did not recognize.

The silence between them was strangely brittle. Shan began to wonder whether the lama felt Shan had unnecessarily interfered with the thief, whether he grasped the new threat raised by such a man knowing the location of his hut. "You don't always understand how dangerous it is," he offered in an apologetic tone.

Jamyang turned and tilted his head at Shan as though surprised at the words. A tiny smile flickered on the lama's face and he ran his hand through his short black hair. "You don't always understand how dangerous it is," the lama repeated in a whisper, then resumed his mantra.

After several minutes the lama seemed to relax and as they edged along a long ledge he raised his hand in a tentative motion. His voice was as light as a feather. "I think I should say words at your pilgrim shrines. Just a few moments."

They had reached a sharp curve at the edge of one of the steep switchbacks, with an unobstructed view of Yangon, the sacred mountain that reigned over the long valley, the majestic peak that was believed to anchor the local people to the old ways and the old, sleeping deities. Four rock cairns, restored by Lokesh and Shan, rose up from near the road. Built with *mani* stones, rocks inscribed with prayers, they marked not only the road's intersection with one of the valley's many pilgrim paths, but also a semicircular flat above a steep drop-off where the earth was packed hard. The overlook had been used by pilgrims for centuries to pay homage to the land deities.

The lama was out of the truck before Shan brought it to a stop, an energetic bounce in his long stride as he stepped to the rim of the ledge, throwing his arms out as if to embrace the mountain. As Shan watched he spoke in a low confiding voice toward the peak, then turned to visit each of the cairn shrines.

It was a day of rare beauty, the mountain's snowcap shimmering under the cobalt sky, its slopes alive with the hues of early summer. Shan's anxiety began to fall away, giving way to a new contentment as he watched the lama. It was not the first time they had saved Jamyang from detection by the authorities, and today had been the closest yet. Each time it happened, Lokesh would later explain that the lama was not destined for bonecatchers, that he and Shan had been chosen by the deities to help save Jamyang for a greater destiny, to help keep the old ways alive.

Shan plucked a sprig of heather and set it on the cairn next to Jamyang. He wasn't certain the lama knew he was at his side until Jamyang suddenly spoke. "I read once about the age of the planet. It has taken us four billion years to get to where we are," he said with a melancholy smile.

Shan had grown to deeply care for the lama in the months since he and Lokesh had first encountered him, restoring a wall of mani stones along a lonely track in one of the high side valleys. Jamyang was in his late fifties, a few years older than Shan, not nearly so old as Lokesh. Like many of the lamas he would never speak of his background but it was obvious he was highly educated, not only in the Buddhist scriptures but in history and literature and the ways of the world. Shan knew his old friend had begun to regard Jamyang as something of a bridge, as one of the rare independent, untainted teachers who would survive another generation after Lokesh and the others of old Tibet were gone. Jamyang never joined in when others spoke about the end of time. He still nurtured hope, Shan knew, even though that seed was beginning to dry up and die in so many other Tibetans.

"Lokesh and I climb up the slopes some nights," Shan offered, "just to sit with the sky. Last month we watched showers of meteors. They all seemed to land on Yangon, as if they were being called in to the sacred mountain."

Jamyang nodded. "The mountain and its deity have always been there. They will always be there, long after all of us. Man cannot change that, can we?"

Shan studied the lama a moment, not certain if he understood. "No," came his tentative reply, "we can't." He watched in silence as Jamyang walked to the truck and retrieved a copper tube, one of the trumpet sections the thief had taken. He pulled away a plug of wood and extracted a small roll of cloth tied with string. It was a line of prayer flags, handmade flags, each bearing a sacred image and an inscription in Jamyang's own hand. He gave Shan one end and silently they fastened the line between two of the rock cairns, anchoring the ends under the cap rocks. Each flap in the wind would renew the prayers.

The lama offered a grateful nod when they were done, then gestured toward a cluster of crumbling structures in the distance, on the floor of the main valley. "There are probably signs of visitors on such a day," he said. It took Shan a moment to realize there was inquiry in Jamyang's tone. He retrieved his binoculars and trained them on the ruins. The local farmers and shepherds had begun restoration work on the ancient, abandoned convent a few months earlier, working in their spare time. Others, like Lokesh and Jamyang, usually worked there under the cover of night.

"Yes," he reported, "I see a truck."

The lama offered another silent nod. "I will join you in a moment," he said, motioning Shan to the truck. Shan climbed behind the wheel and watched as the lama paced along the prayer flags, touching each in turn, murmuring the words to empower them in their task, then turned to the mountain and abruptly dropped to the ground, prostrating himself to Yangon as a pilgrim might.

It was late afternoon by the time they had parked the truck and climbed the half-mile trail to the lama's hut. The little structure where Jamyang slept, originally a shepherd's shelter, was as spare as a hermit's cell. The lama spent most of his time in the shallow cave above, where he had restored an ancient bas-relief depicting several deities and sacred signs.

Shan coaxed the smoldering embers in the hut's brazier back to life, adding some of the dried yak dung the lama collected for fuel. They silently shared some tea, then Jamyang filled a small wooden pail with water and they moved up the trail to the shrine.

Jamyang had arranged two crude benches like altars below the old rock sculptures, which were now covered with offerings. No special prayers would be offered, no celebration begun, until all the offerings were cleaned. Jamyang returned the items recovered from the thief before filling an offering bowl with water. Then he produced a rag and began reverently wiping the objects on the altar. Shan emptied the ashes from a small ceremonial brazier and walked down the slope to collect some of the fragrant juniper wood whose smoke attracted the deities. As he worked he puzzled over the somber, unsettled mood that had settled over the lama on the drive back. Jamyang had seemed eager to say something to Shan yet he had never found the words. But now the lama was home, at his secret shrine, and serene once more.

It was indeed a day for celebration. Now that rehabilitation of the simple, elegant shrine was complete, Shan knew Jamyang and Lokesh would begin bringing local Tibetans to worship there, to show them that the old ways were not forgotten. The risk to the lama would become ever greater. Shan would have to make them understand that they should never bring more than a handful of worshippers at a time. To assemble more would risk attracting the authorities. Beijing worked hard to scour all vestiges of Tibetan tradition from the land but it would never succeed as long as men like Lokesh and Jamyang existed. In recent weeks devout Tibetans elsewhere in the valley had taken to defying the police by holding impromptu prayer gatherings, marking them by sounding the long, deep-throated *duncheng* horns that once had summoned worshippers to temples. The daring group that was doing so would no doubt come to Jamyang's shrine and no doubt taunt the authorities with their horn from the site. He found himself studying the landscape like a soldier, considering where he might stand as an unseen sentinel when worshippers came, marking routes where Tibetans might flee when police began climbing the mountain.

Half an hour later, as the fragrant smoke drifted upward into the calm, clear sky, Jamyang sat, legs crossed under him, and began reading scriptures to the stone-carved deities. As he spoke all vestiges of worry left the lama's face. Shan sat beside him in the position of the novice, keeping the long loose pages in order, holding them down when the breeze freshened. His eyes wandered along the makeshift altars. Jamyang was an accomplished artist in the traditional style, and he had taken to adorning everyday objects with religious signs. Along the rim of a tea churn he had painted a conch, a leaping fish, a vase, and the other Eight Auspicious Signs of Tibetan ritual. A large eye stared out from a copper pitcher. The handle of a small barley scythe sported a vine with lotus flowers.

Suddenly Shan froze. At the center of the bench nearest Jamyang was something new, a black and alien object. A small automatic pistol. It was impossible that Jamyang would have such a weapon, but then he saw that it too had been adorned with a flower and the mantra to the Compassionate Buddha was painted along its barrel. Shan struggled with the urge to leap up and fling the treacherous, ugly thing down the slope. He told himself that this was just another of Jamyang's ways of pacifying the world, that to the lama the gun was one more of the everyday objects that could be purified with sacred words. Once purified, the old ones believed, such a weapon would never cause harm again.

Shan fought against his impulse, tried to quiet his pounding heart. More than once in his imprisonment he had seen a monk executed with just such a pistol, kneeling and reciting mantras as the executioner hovered over him. He reminded himself that others would be visiting the shrine, others who knew possession of such a weapon was a serious crime, others who might not understand Jamyang's ways. Where could the lama have found the weapon? Shan pushed down his fear, reminding himself that Jamyang's naïveté was in its own way a gift, part of the pureness of the teacher. He settled back, deciding not to disturb the ritual but resolving to return in the small hours of the night to dispose of the pistol.

They sat in the pool of late-afternoon sunlight, watching as the shifting shadows gave movement to the deities on the rock, the sweet smoke wafting over them, the only sound now that of Jamyang's low mantra and the occasional song of a lark. Shan relaxed again, letting his consciousness embrace only the reverent words as the lamas had taught him. A door in the back of his mind opened and he began hearing the chanted prayers of the monks of his former prison barracks, the sound once more soothing his troubled spirit. For the moment it did not matter that there were brigades of Chinese police seeking to ferret out men like Lokesh and Jamyang, two of the gentlest, kindest humans he had ever known. It did not matter that bonecatchers roamed the hills, that outsiders were settling in the valley, pushing out Tibetan families who had been rooted there for centuries. He could forget for now the nightmares of death that increasingly disturbed his sleep. He would not even let thoughts of his son, locked in a gulag camp thirty miles away, cloud the day. Shan had been learning from his friends to accept that what mattered was the here and now, the experience of this moment. And this moment, in the company of the prayerful lama, his heart filled with anticipation of Lokesh's arrival and more reverent hours to follow, was perfect.

As if reading Shan's mind, Jamyang looked up from his meditation. "The gods are content enough," the lama declared with a serene smile. He reached through the fragrant smoke and squeezed Shan's hand. "I take strength from you being here now," Jamyang whispered, and wrapped his rosary around his fingers.

Then the lama picked up the pistol and shot himself in the head.

CHAPTER TWO

The nightmare of death had seized Shan once more. He had to be having one of his soul-splitting visions that haunted his sleep with images of tortured lamas and executed monks. A low sobbing moan echoed in the shallow cavern and he glanced frantically about for its source before realizing it came from his own throat. Then he saw the crimson rivulets rolling down his hand where blood had sprayed on him. He leapt to Jamyang's side.

The lama's eyes were open, aimed at the carved deities above the altar. But he was beyond seeing. The bullet hole in the center of his forehead was neat and round, like a third eye. The place where the bullet had torn out the back of his skull was a bloody knot of bone and tissue.

Tears ran down Shan's face as he cradled the dead lama in his lap, "Recognize the radiant light that is your death." He had heard the words of the Bardo, the traditional Tibetan death rite, so often that they left his tongue unbidden. Jamyang's soul would be confused, would be terrified at the difficult journey it was so abruptly beginning, and the living had to comfort it. "Recognize that your consciousness is without birth or death." The words came in tiny choked breaths, lower and lower until finally they died away.

He did not know how long he sat, paralyzed with his grief, did not know how long Lokesh had been there, but when he looked up his friend was standing a few feet away, staring at the dead lama with a stricken expression.

"We had cleaned the offerings," Shan explained in a forlorn whisper. "I had never seen this pistol before. I was going to get rid of it tonight. But he picked it up and pulled the trigger so suddenly I couldn't—" Lokesh stepped forward and knelt by the body. Shan's question came out in a hoarse croak. "Why, Lokesh? Why? We were going to celebrate his gods . . ."

With a trembling hand the old Tibetan lifted Jamyang's head from Shan's lap and they laid the dead man out on the earth before the shrine. Lokesh stood motionless, staring at the body, then, as if the reality finally struck him, he sagged and fell onto his knees. Shan's heart wrenched as he watched his friend press the dead man's head to his breast and rock back and forth. Backing against the stone face he slid to the ground, numb with the horror before him, as he began reciting anew the words of the Bardo chant. The old Tibetan did not bother to wipe at the tears that flowed down his leathery cheeks.

At last Shan rose and stepped to the pail, splashing cold water on his face before stepping away, out into the cool wind, lifting his face toward the sky. The souls of the purest lamas were said to ascend toward the sky in a rainbow stream of light. But there would be no rainbow for Jamyang. At the end of his pure life he had committed a grave sin, an impure act that would condemn his soul to be reincarnated among the lowest of life-forms. In their prison the old Tibetans had called it "taking four," finding release from the agony even though it meant reincarnation as a four-legged creature. Shan choked away another sob. What had been Jamyang's agony? He had had so much to live for. Impossibly, inexplicably, Jamyang had taken four.

He had to push his fear and grief away, he knew. There was much to be done, and grave risks to be taken.

"The farmers and shepherds could come anytime," he said to

Lokesh. "It will be impossible to hide this." Word of an unregistered monk dying of a bullet in his head would attract too much attention. "The knobs will learn of it," he said, referring to the dreaded Public Security bulldogs, the elite of Beijing's many enforcement arms. They both knew that if the knobs discovered that one of the monk out-laws had been living here protected by the local Tibetans they would use it as an excuse to round up two or three dozen and ship them to one of Beijing's new pacification camps.

Lokesh looked up from his task with query in his tear-soaked eyes.

"We have to carry him to the hut so he can be cleaned," Shan con-tinued. "I will go and bring back help from the hermitage." The her-mitage of nuns, five miles away, was tiny but he knew its inhabitants had shared Jamyang's secrets. "We have to remove him quickly, be-fore word leaks out. If the knobs discover the shrine they will destroy it." Shan looked at the little bas-relief deities with new torment. Only a week ago Jamyang had said they had to treat every such shrine as if it were the last in Tibet, the last in all the world, for someday one of them would be. Beijing did not abide such secret places of worship. The knobs had special teams, godkiller squads, who used dynamite, even portable air hammers, to destroy them. "Jamyang would not want that. He was the opposite of a godkiller."

All this time Lokesh had not stopped whispering the Bardo, mouth-ing the ancient words as Shan spoke, but now he paused. "The old convent ruins are closer," he said in a hoarse voice. "Nuns from the hermitage are likely there, working on the restoration." He lifted Ja-myang's shoulders, and gestured for Shan to take his feet.

Shan eased his truck to a stop by a wide, sloping ledge and quickly climbed to the edge, checking to be sure there were no new vehicles at the abandoned convent, largely destroyed fifty years before. He took one look toward the ruins below and shrank back in alarm. Quickly he retrieved his binoculars and crept back up the ledge, dropping to a prone position as he reached the top.

The site was alive with activity. He had expected to see the truck he had seen from a distance earlier in the day, and perhaps some of the tractors and donkeys used by the local Tibetans. Instead, parked beside the truck by the front gate were an ambulance and three of the utility vehicles favored by the police. Uniformed figures were gathered in the courtyard inside the front gate.

He turned onto his back and gazed toward the southern horizon, toward the distant mountain that marked the gulag camp where his son Ko, his only flesh and blood, was imprisoned. Shan had long ago given up on his life as a high-level investigator, had declined offers to return to Beijing even after serving years in the gulag himself. But he would never give up on his son. He lived in two-week intervals, for the first Sundays of each month on which he was permitted to visit Ko and the midmonth letter he was permitted to write to him. Colonel Tan, the ironfisted military governor of the county, had made it clear that Shan would lose all visiting rights if he stirred up new problems for Tan. He would never give up on his son, but he would also never give up on the old Tibetans.

There could be any number of reasons the police had descended on the ruined convent—the most likely one being that they suspected smugglers were scavenging it for artifacts—but if the officers chose to interrogate any of those helping to restore the old buildings, the frightened Tibetans could well tell them about Jamyang's shrine. A new and terrible possibility occurred to Shan. If the police found Lokesh with the body and an illegal pistol, it would be the end of the gentle old man, a thought that Shan could not bear. He had to know what the police were doing, had to keep them away from the ridge, had to find a way to keep Jamyang's irreplaceable relics out of the hands of the godkillers. He slipped down the ledge to his truck and began brushing off his clothes.

Half an hour later he stood in the shadows at the rear of the ruins, having left his truck in the rock outcroppings behind the complex. Quickly he recalled his mental map of the old convent. Although it had been small, it had rigidly adhered to Buddhist tradition in its construction. Below the courtyard was the *dukhang,* the main assembly hall with ancillary chapels arranged along the walls. At the rear had been two *kangtsang,* residence halls, and the small, somber chapels reserved for protector demons, where the restorers had been sheltering some of the most important artifacts recovered from the rubble. In the center of the courtyard was a chorten, one of the ancient relic shrines resembling an onion topped with a steeple, which had been the first structure to be restored. Only a few weeks before, by the light of a rising sun, he and Lokesh had helped Jamyang whitewash the chorten. He ventured a glance from the corner of one of the crumbling buildings toward the front of the compound. Nearly a dozen figures stood on the opposite side of the courtyard, most in uniform, facing away, looking into the shadow of the shining white chorten. He stepped purposefully across the open ground separating him from the closest of the old demon shrines, his heart pounding as he reached the rear of the little stone building. Leaning against the wall, calming himself, he glanced back through the gap in the rubble that used to be the rear gate, wondering whether he should try to rescue some of the artifacts secreted in the building. Anything the police found would be declared property of the state, destined for destruction or removal to some dusty warehouse in the east.

"They say these old ruins are filled with ghosts."

He spun about to face the woman who had spoken. Her uniform looked freshly pressed, the red enamel star on her cap recently polished.

"More and more all the time," the Public Security lieutenant added absently as she glanced up at him then returned to scanning the ground near Shan's feet.

Shan struggled to keep his voice steady. "People lived here for centuries. Lived and died."

The woman, in her midthirties, glanced up again long enough to cast him a cool grin, as if he had made a joke, then bent and studied the patterns of shadows in the dirt around them. "Even a shallow footprint can speak to you when the light is right," she declared in a professional tone.

As she knelt Shan saw the latex gloves folded into her belt, beside a small automatic pistol. He fought the compulsion to bolt toward the outcroppings, then retreated a step toward the corner of the stucco-walled building and found his hand resting on a faded religious symbol, painted in another century. An all-seeing eye.

"You'll never lift prints from a wall like that," the officer said as she rose, straightening her uniform.

"But rough surfaces can snag a fiber from a passerby." Shan felt a flush of shame that the words of the former Beijing investigator would leap so readily to his tongue. He had forsaken that life, left it far behind after finding his new incarnation in Tibet.

The woman cocked her head at him, assessing him, studying for a long moment his tattered clothes and scuffed boots, then offered a hesitant nod of agreement and reached into one of the deep pockets of her tunic. With a chill he watched as she produced several cellophane bags and handed them to him. Each was imprinted with a single line along the bottom: Public Security Bureau Evidence. "Major Liang is a stickler for procedure," she stated as he took the bags, then she moved on, scanning the ground again as she disappeared around the corner.

Shan stared with foreboding at the bags in his hand. The woman was not there to destroy the convent, not looking for smugglers. And why had she accepted him so readily? She had assumed, despite his shabby appearance, that he somehow was helping with an investigation. He stepped away from the building to study the figures gathered in the central square fifty yards away. Beyond the cluster of uniformed men, plumes of dust rose from the road. More vehicles were approaching. He wanted to run. He had to run. Then he remembered

Lokesh, waiting at the shrine with the body of their friend. Jamyang had seemed unusually interested in the ruins that afternoon. Shan pressed his hand against the eye of the deity again, murmuring a quick prayer, then began a slow, deliberate circuit toward the police gathered in the square.

He feigned interest in the ground as he walked along the stations where large prayer wheels had once been spun by pilgrims, pausing at a pile of carpentry tools left by the restorers, lingering again at a small circle of red paint drops by one of the few remaining wheels where a paint pot had apparently rested. Someone had been painting the cradle of the wheel and been interrupted. On the wall behind it red paint was spattered. A worn brush, its bristles congealed with paint, lay on the ground at the base of the wall. The spatters formed a high arc, except for one patch in the center that was a slightly different hue, the identical color of a small drying puddle six feet from the wall. He covered a hand with one of the bags and used it to insert the brush in another bag, then dropped the brush back into its original position. As he looked up he felt the stare of a Public Security officer sitting on a bench in the shadows by the front gate. His cold, flinty expression did not change when Shan offered him a nod. He kept staring at Shan as a subordinate trotted to his side, kept staring even as he listened to the junior officer and snapped out a curt reply that sent the younger knob retreating like a frightened courtier.

Shan fought a shudder as he broke away from the man's icy gaze and walked around the end of the chorten. Then he froze at the butchery before him.

He had seen death in Tibet more times than he wished to recall, had seen it that very day, but he had never seen anything like the death that had come to the old convent. Three bodies lay sprawled on the ground in a pool of red. They were arranged in the pattern of a U, the two largest lying beside each other, four feet apart, the third lying perpendicular to them, under their feet. The head of the man farthest from Shan lay against its owner's shoulder, nearly severed, the flesh chopped and sliced with repeated blows of a heavy blade.

The body closest to Shan had no face. The man's head had been hacked at, so that his face and the sides of his head were nothing but raw, torn flesh. His skull glinted white between shades of red. Most of the red wasn't blood, Shan realized. The two bodies were nearly covered in paint. In the center, their hands, one left, one right, were held down by a stone. The worn hiking boots of the closest man lay on the belly of the third body, which Shan now saw was a Tibetan woman wearing a wool cap. The expensive athletic shoes of the second man lay on her legs.

The mechanical click of a camera stirred Shan from his paralysis. Two officers were taking photographs of the corpses. He stepped behind them then circled the bodies, forcing himself to look at the gore. The woman had a bullet hole in her chest. He saw now that it was not simply a pool of red the men lay in, it was a rectangle, and the killer had not just used red paint. In the upper-left corner there was a large yellow-spiked blotch with four smaller ones, in an arc at its lower right. The brown eyes of the man whose face had been sliced away gazed lifelessly at the chorten, a pool of blood under a bullet hole in his neck. The figure whose head hung by a few ligaments lay with his face toward the shrine, locked in a brooding, angry expression. He was Chinese. A Chinese man, a Tibetan woman, a faceless monster; all three murdered in the shadow of the mountain where a lama had just killed himself.

One of the police taking photographs suddenly clutched his stomach and darted away to retch up his last meal. A young officer scolded him and shoved him back toward the bodies. "We must have complete images of the murder scene!" he barked at the cowering policeman.

"Scenes." Shan had whispered the word to himself, unmindful of the silence in the courtyard.

"You dare to correct me?" the officer snarled. "You . . ." He studied Shan in confusion.

Shan turned to retreat and found himself looking into the thin face of the female officer he had encountered earlier. She returned his gaze expectantly, then broke away to address her colleague. "I am not sure jurisdiction has been established," she declared, as if to defend Shan. The officer winced at the words, and for the first time Shan took note of the different uniforms. The young officer who had challenged him wore the olive of the People's Armed Police, the thugs of Chinese law enforcement. The green apes, many Tibetans called them. The woman wore the grey of the Public Security Bureau. Two other men, both Tibetans, wore the blue of the local constables, still others the light green of medical attendants.

Jurisdiction. The woman was savvy enough to understand that those who wielded the most power in the People's Republic wore no uniforms at all. It was the slender thread by which Shan's freedom now hung. He would be arrested in an instant if he were found to be there on false pretenses. Those who impersonated police were shot.

The lieutenant turned back to Shan with a questioning look. He had no choice but to continue with the charade. Shan took a deep breath, then pointed to the man with the mangled face. "Only this one was killed here. He was bleeding from a bullet that pierced his jugular. Only he has a pool of blood under him." Shan pointed to the woman. "She has a bullet hole in her chest but no pool of blood."

The woman looked unconvinced. "But it's all red. How can you know?"

"Look closer. The blood is darker. It dries differently." He pointed to where the two shades of red met. "The difference is subtle for now but noticeable. In another hour the blood will be nearly brown. The wounds on the other two did not bleed out here. There would have been marks showing where they were dragged from but—" He shrugged and gestured toward the feet of the assembled police. The ground all around the courtyard had been trampled by their boots.

Shan's gaze lingered for a moment on a pot of red paint at the base of the chorten, then turned back to the red rectangle with its pattern of yellow spots. The killer had gone to a lot of trouble in arranging the scene, as if for a message. A chill crept up his spine as he at last recognized the rectangle constructed under the bodies. It was the Chinese flag, red with one large and four smaller yellow stars in the upper-left quadrant.

"Fools!" the young officer barked at the others, then he quieted at the sound of footsteps behind him, the anger on his face suddenly replaced with fear. The gaunt older officer had risen from the shadows. For a moment Shan thought the man in the green uniform was going to drop to his knees.

"Everyone back!" the older knob growled. "You and your men," he declared to the officer in the olive tunic, "will have site security. One at the gate, the rest to set up a roadblock half a mile up the road." What had the knob lieutenant called the senior officer? Major Liang.

The young officer shrank back, then murmured hurried orders to his men. The men in blue, the local constables, retreated toward the gate without another word. As the men in green marched away, two more men in grey appeared out of the shadows. The question of jurisdiction was resolving itself.

"Her hands," Shan said, gesturing to the dead woman. "That is red paint on them, not blood. She was painting the old prayer wheel by the wall. The paint is spattered in an arc where her brush went flying. Under the arc is a pattern of blood. She was shot there, taken by surprise as she worked, facing the wall. I think you will find that bullet went through her back. It came out her chest and is probably in the wall. Unless the weapon was a revolver there will be a bullet casing on the ground nearby."

The female lieutenant spoke in quick, clipped syllables, and the knob soldiers moved toward the wall. Major Liang shot Shan a warning glance, then followed the squad.

Suddenly Shan was alone with the bodies. He gazed for only a moment as the police retreated around the far side of the chorten, then moved quickly, letting old instincts take over. He knew from experience that such officers could do strange things with the truth of such killings, could make inconvenient murders disappear. Worse still, they could use murders at such a holy place as an excuse to destroy what was left of it. He owed it to Jamyang, to Lokesh, and all the old Tibetans, to understand what had happened.

He ran his fingers over the dead flesh, lifting limbs, testing for rigor mortis and temperature. They had been dead for four or five hours. He stooped over the faceless man, clenching his jaw at the butchery. The face had not been simply sliced off, the flesh and skin at the front and sides of the skull had been hacked away, like bark being chipped off a log.

The pockets of the man with the nearly severed head held only car keys and a package of unfiltered cigarettes. A bird, perhaps a crow, clutching a snake in its talons was tattooed inside his forearm. The savage blows that had nearly taken off his head had ripped apart another tattoo at the base of his neck, a creature with scales that might have been a dragon. Shan saw now the dirt caked on the heels of the man's expensive shoes, bent to study the direction of the trail made by the heels before it disappeared, stomped away by police boots. The man had been dragged from somewhere near the front of the compound, perhaps even from the gate. He lifted one of the shoes that lay on the woman to examine the dirt embedded in its heel, then felt something more at the ankle and pushed up the pant leg. He paused in surprise. He had not seen an ankle holster for years. It was a subtle, hidden thing seldom seen outside the big cities of the east. There was no subtlety about the use of guns in Tibet. The holster held nothing but a piece of folded paper jammed in the bottom. He glanced back to confirm the police were still out of sight then stuffed the paper in his pocket. He rose and leaned over the body once more, pushing his fingers deeper into the pockets. He tapped the half-empty cigarette pack and felt a hard, unyielding surface. A piece of iron slid out of the pack, an intricately worked trapezoid with Buddhist prayers etched around two large holes in its narrow end. A flint striker. The dead Chinese wearing expensive clothes was carrying a primitive Tibetan tool for lighting fires.

He stuffed the striker back into the pocket then looked more closely at the two hands at the center of the flag. It wasn't a stone that held them down, it was a weathered fragment from the ruined carvings that had been scattered around the grounds before the restoration had started, an image of one of Tibet's Eight Auspicious Signs. He bent and saw the lines that represented stacked garlands of cloth. It was the Banner of Victory, which hailed the triumph of Buddhist wisdom over ignorance.

Shan moved hesitantly to the woman, knowing likely he had no more than another minute before the knobs returned. She appeared to have been in her fifties, with a delicate face, though her tattered brown frock and rough hands were those of a farmer. The necklace strand around her neck had been severed, probably when the killer had dragged her body. With two fingers he gently closed her unseeing eyes and murmured a prayer.

Quickly he found the bullet hole in her tunic, over her heart. It was a large, ugly wound, the hole of the bullet's exit. She had indeed been shot in the back. The bullet's exit had pushed out threads of other fabrics, red and white. He pried at the fabric and found that her chest had been bound with a length of cotton. A small stiff rectangle the size of an identity card extended from underneath. With a guilty shudder he lifted the cloth and extracted the rectangle, quickly stuffing it inside his pocket without taking the time to look at it. If they knew who a Tibetan victim was, they could make life very uncomfortable for the family, whom they would have always assumed hid information about the dead. He was taking a terrible chance.

The knobs would be back at any instant, furious if they found him interfering with the bodies, but he did not trust them with the evidence, and felt strangely unable to leave the woman. He pulled at her frock, awkwardly trying to cover her grisly wound. For the first time he saw that her frock had dried paint on it, in several colors. It was a just a work frock. She had put it on over her dark red dress.

Run, a voice screamed inside, *flee into the maze of rocks. Lokesh needs you.*

With another anxious glance in the direction of the knobs, he bent to study the severed necklace. It had been made of tightly braided yak hair. He tugged on one end, releasing from under her shoulder an ornate silver box. A *gau.* She had been wearing a traditional necklace with a traditional amulet box.

Another siren rose in the distance, rapidly approaching, but still he did not move. With a shudder he pushed off the wool cap on her head and saw the short brush of black hair, then he pulled back the work frock.

A small choking sob escaped his throat as he recognized the maroon cloth. It was a robe. At the ancient, ruined convent, a Buddhist nun had been murdered and placed under the feet of two Chinese men. He grabbed her gau and fled.

CHAPTER THREE

He drove the truck wildly, over low ridges, up narrow tracks that were little more then dry washes, sliding to a stop where it intersected the old pilgrims' path. Even after stopping he gripped the wheel tightly, knuckles white, head bent low, unable to control the dry sobs that wracked his chest. The day that had begun so reverently, so serenely, had turned into a waking nightmare. Jamyang had not simply died, he had killed himself, a grave sin for the devout. The old convent that had become a symbol of hope for the battered Tibetans had been turned into a butcher's ground, and was in the hands of the knobs.

Jamyang had died. Then the nun and two men had died. No, he forced himself to admit, the bodies he had seen had been dead at least four hours. Those at the convent had died first. A new wave of despair swept over Shan as he considered the horrific possibility that Jamyang had done the killing then had been driven to suicide by his guilt. He frantically tried to reconstruct the day, hour by hour. The murders had occurred perhaps two hours before they had seen Jamyang on the slope chasing the thief. He recalled now that Jamyang's appearance there had been unexpected, even perplexing. If he had been chasing the limping thief all the way from his shrine the lama should have caught him long before reaching the slope.

Shan climbed out of the truck and stepped to the ledge where

Jamyang had lingered, strangely emotional, hours before. Shan had thought he had stopped to gaze on the sacred mountain, but there were many overlooks that afforded a view of the mountain. What made this one unique was that it also overlooked the old convent. Jamyang had asked whether Shan could see signs of visitors there. *No,* a voice inside shouted, *it was impossible.* The lama had spoken prayers, had prostrated himself before the mountain, and gone back to clean the offerings. Shan had tried to ignore the melancholy tone in his words. Jamyang had been saying farewell to the deities. He had somehow known about the murders.

Lokesh was alone with the lama's body when Shan reached the hut, sitting at Jamyang's head, still intoning the words of the death rite. He fed the coals in the small brazier and made tea, then placed a cup at his friend's side, dropped some juniper on the brazier, and waited.

When at last the old Tibetan paused in his recitation, he had trouble rising, as if his grief were too big a burden. Shan helped him to his feet and handed him his tea. The hot brew revived Lokesh, and as he sipped it he cocked his head this way and that at the dead man, as if listening for something from Jamyang. He was, like Shan, still totally perplexed about what had happened at the shrine.

"We can't stay with him here for three days," Shan said, referring to the traditional period observed by most Tibetans for the rites. "There are police in the valley. There will be many more."

Lokesh nodded solemnly. "Shepherds were here." His voice was dry as sticks. "They will return with horses and a mule before midnight. It is nearly a day's ride to the bone flats," he said, meaning the clearing secreted high in the mountains where the *ragyapa,* the traditional flesh cutters, readied bodies for consumption by the vultures. The ancient tradition of sky burial, reviled by the government, had, like so many other Tibetan practices, been pushed into the shadows.

"You must go with them," Shan said. "Stay up there to finish the rites."

But Lokesh was not listening. He was wiping at the bullet hole in Jamyang's forehead. "It isn't the way of things," the old Tibetan said, wiping again, watching the wound expectantly. "We should send for some of the wise ones. They would know how to call him out."

Shan studied his old friend, who had been an official in the Dalai Lama's government before the Chinese invasion. Lokesh communicated more in not speaking than any man he knew, and when he did speak it often seemed to be in riddles. As he watched Lokesh cup some of the fragrant juniper smoke and hold it over the bullet hole he finally understood. The old Tibetans believed that when a man died his soul lingered inside the lifeless husk, confused, and eventually found its natural path out through a tiny hole on the crown of his head. Old lamas would often pluck hairs from the top of a dead man's head to clear the way. But Jamyang's skull had two new, and unnatural, holes.

"His spirit was well focused," Shan offered.

"No," Lokesh replied slowly, with great conviction. "He killed himself. Which means something had taken over his spirit. Something wrapped around it like a serpent. It is still there. We have to pry it off." His fingers gently touched the side of Jamyang's face, lingering over the birthmark on his jaw that looked like a lotus blossom, one of the sacred signs.

Shan opened his mouth to argue, to find some way to comfort Lokesh, but he knew that no matter what he said his friend would suffer this anguish for weeks to come. And perhaps Lokesh hit close to the truth in suggesting an evil spirit had possessed the lama. Certainly something evil had tormented him, had driven him to his abrupt suicide. Evil had also swept over the ancient convent that day, and now four people had suffered violent deaths. The logical part of Shan told him it was impossible that the events were connected. But the instincts of the former inspector said they had to be.

"More police in the valley?" Lokesh suddenly asked, as if just hearing Shan's warning.

Shan closed his eyes a moment. He was not sure he could summon the strength to tell Lokesh what had happened at the old convent, wanted more than anything to not add to the pain the old Tibetan already felt.

He realized his friend had stopped his ministrations to the body and was staring at him. "You were going for the nuns," Lokesh said pointedly.

Shan felt a great weight bearing down on him. "I went to find help at the convent. Instead there were bodies." The words seemed to tear at his throat as he spoke them. "Three people were killed there."

Lokesh did not speak, only stared with moist eyes at one of the little bronze deities by Jamyang's pallet as Shan described what he had found at the convent. Lokesh and the oldest lamas had always been pools of serenity amid the horrors of the gulag, had told new prisoners that the inhuman conditions at their prison were nothing more than a test of faith, had stood like rocks against the torture and deprivation. But even stone can crack against a torrent that lasts for years. For the first time since Shan had known him, despair clouded his friend's eyes. He still had no words when Shan had finished, only lit some incense on Jamyang's little altar and took up the death chant again. Shan's heart broke as he watched the old man, seeing the tremor in his hand where none had been before, hearing him falter in remembering words he had recited countless times before.

The moon was high overhead when the shepherds arrived. They would not speak with Shan, would not accept his help in rolling Jamyang's body into a shroud and tying it to the back of the mule. Lokesh had withdrawn deeper and deeper inside himself. He had become an aged, frail creature who needed help in mounting the horse the shepherds offered to him. He made no reply to Shan's words of farewell.

Shan found a perch on the ridge above the hut and watched the forlorn caravan as it traversed the moonlit valley then looked toward the stars, struggling to control the emotions that raged inside.

Eventually he curled up on a blanket outside the little hut but found only fitful sleep, beset by hideous dreams. Truckloads of troops were pouring into the valley in response to the murders. Farmers were being violently ejected from their homes. He awoke with a groan as a baton hovered in the air, about to slam into Lokesh. Shan gave up on sleep and stared into the sky. By dawn he was back at Jamyang's shrine.

The mystery behind the suicide began with the mystery of the pistol. He set the weapon on a flat rock in a pool of sunlight. It had been painted, not just with a lotus flower but also with images of a sacred conch shell and a fish. But why? Had Jamyang really meant to pacify the weapon somehow, as Shan had first believed, or to sanctify it for its intended mission? It was a small semiautomatic, the kind issued to police officers and soldiers. Private possession of such a weapon was a serious crime anywhere in China but a Tibetan who possessed one would be treated not just as a felon but a traitor. It seemed impossible that Jamyang would encounter such a weapon without being arrested by its owner, just as impossible that another Tibetan would have given it to him. It was almost as unlikely that he would know how to use it, yet in the last instant of his life he had lifted the gun with the alacrity of one trained in weapons, flipping off the safety and pulling the trigger in one fluid movement. Shan lifted the pistol and released the magazine. It was empty. Jamyang had kept only one bullet.

When Shan had tried to warn him of the dangers in the valley, Jamyang had repeated his own words back to him. *You don't always understand how dangerous it is.* Only once, just the week before, had Jamyang probed Shan's background, showing a surprising interest in his years as an investigator. Had that been why Jamyang had wanted Shan there in his last moments? Had he planned the celebration to be certain Shan would be with him? Had he been inviting Shan to unravel the mystery of his own death and those below? Jamyang's face rose before him, wearing the cryptic, questioning expression he had shown at the pilgrim shrines. For a moment it was so real Shan could have reached out and touched the smudge of dirt where he had prostrated his forehead to the mountain. *It has taken us four billion years to get to where we are,* the lama had said.

Suddenly the vision was gone and he saw only the pistol. He stared at the gun with a desolate expression, then finally rose, walked a hundred feet from the shrine, and buried it under a flat rock by a clump of heather.

The deities carved on the rock wall seemed to return his gaze as he settled before them, looking at him with melancholy question in their eyes. He recalled the first time he and Lokesh had encountered Jamyang, surprising him as he had been trying to restore a crumbling wall of mani stones along a lonely path in the upper valley. The lama had been as skittish as a wild animal, darting away before they could greet him. Lokesh and Shan had spent an hour working on the wall themselves, hoping he would understand they intended no harm, and had felt his gaze the entire time, but he had not reappeared. A week later when Shan had responded to the screams of a shepherd girl by leaping into a pool of quicksand to save her lamb, Jamyang had suddenly appeared to help Lokesh haul Shan and the lamb out of the pit. He remembered the shy smile on Jamyang's face and his laughter when Lokesh had quipped that Shan looked like one of the offering figures shaped in mud by the nomad families. They had seen him more often then, on high trails, sometimes waving at them like an old friend, sometime watching them in silence as they cleared ditches, even stopping to meditate near them. Shan had seen it before. Tibetans, especially those of a certain age, sometimes grew to know each other through shared silences. He remembered the contentment on the lama's face when he had finally taken them to meet the deities he was so reverently restoring, and the greater joy when Lokesh had described how a similar carving had once existed outside a private chapel of the Dalai Lama's in Lhasa, long ago destroyed.

Lokesh had suggested they might clean the faded, grime-covered paintings on the rock face above the sculpture and the three of them had begun the task together. They had spent many hours there in the following weeks, the air sometimes filling with cries of glee from the two Tibetans as their delicate brushes uncovered images of nearly forgotten gods. The benches used as altars had come later, to hold the offerings brought by shepherds and farmers. So many had been brought that Jamyang had stored some in the rear of the shallow cave, under a piece of canvas.

Shan walked along the offerings, touching several, pausing as one, then another, brought back a memory of Jamyang or Lokesh exclaiming over its workmanship. An old silver pen case inlaid with turquoise. A little jade dragon that looked more Chinese than Tibetan. A bronze figurine of the Compassionate Buddha set with jewels along its base, a *purba*—the short spikelike dagger of Tibetan ritual, a thick disk of jade with a wide channel cut through its center and flowers carved around its edge that looked strangely familiar, no doubt the base of a missing statue. He picked up the purba. A narrow brown ribbon had been tied around it. The purba had been on the altar for weeks, but not the ribbon. He fingered the ribbon uncertainly, wondering why it looked familiar. He suspected Jamyang had tied it on while he had cleaned the offerings just before dying, had tied it to the implement that was supposed to ritually cut through consciousness. He set it down uneasily, then moved to the canvas-covered pile in the shadows. Eventually the knobs would find the shrine, and the thief surely would return. The treasures would have to be taken away for safekeeping.

He lifted the canvas. On top of the pile were the ribbon-bound printing blocks Jamyang had recovered from the thief. Shan had never seen the boards before. The ribbon. He glanced back at the purba. The ribbon tied to it had been taken from the blocks, as if the lama had wanted to draw Shan's attention to them. It had been two weeks since his last visit to the shrine, when he and Lokesh had helped clean everything, including the objects in the little cave. The printing blocks had not been there then. He brought them out into the early morning light, laid them on the end of a bench, and untied the ribbons. He turned them over to reveal their inscriptions, then stared in shocked disbelief.

They were not printing blocks. They were indeed old, indeed sacred, but they were not Tibetan. His hand trembled with excitement as he ran a finger along the carved characters. One of the two slabs was inscribed with a single vertical line of Chinese ideograms, of a very old style, the second with the identical characters plus small legends on either side of them. He looked up at the altar, realizing now why the jade disk had seemed familiar, then retrieved the disk. With an action that had been familiar in his youth, he pressed the two boards together, the writing facing outward now, and slid their ends into the channel on the disk. They fit perfectly, held erect by the heavy base. It was, impossibly, a Chinese ancestral tablet. In the distant, lost world of Shan's childhood he had visited family shrines that had been lined with such tablets, each inscribed with the name of a dead ancestor, each reverently cleaned and prayed over by living relatives on festival days. The tablets, the old Taoist priests had explained, enshrined the souls of the dead. Shan had not seen one for years, for decades. He would never forget the day when the Red Guard had raided the family shrines of his neighborhood and made bonfires of all the tablets. An old widow down the street had been inconsolable, saying the Communists had incinerated the souls of her ancestors.

Yuan Yi, the tablet said, mandarin of the third rank, died this fifty-ninth year of the Kangxi Emperor. The opposite side recorded the site of his burial, in Heilongjiang Province. Shan did a quick calculation. The mandarin, of very high imperial rank, had died in 1721 and been buried in the cold mountains of distant Manchuria. Jamyang had given up his most precious Buddhist artifact for a three-hundred-year-old Chinese spirit tablet. Shan replayed in his mind's eye the moments on the slope with the thief. The man had held tightly to the tablets, had acted ready to fight for them. Perhaps Shan had misunderstood. Perhaps the limping shepherd had not been intent on luring Jamyang to the police for a bounty but to get the tablets to town. When he had overtaken the thief, Jamyang had been more interested in recovering the tablets than the objects stolen from his altar.

It seemed impossible that the gentle, reverent Tibetan who hid from the Chinese authorities would hide and protect a Chinese artifact. What else had he misunderstood about Jamyang? The unregistered monks lived like a network of spies, each deliberately blind to the whereabouts and background of the others, for fear of being arrested and forced to divulge the information. The knobs had taken to calling such monks traitors. If they did not cooperate with the Chinese government they were by definition splittists—reviled supporters of an independent Tibet. It was always understood that such men kept secrets, but Jamyang's secrets had led to violence and death.

Shan stared at the ancestral tablet. Surely the spirit board of a Chinese official dead for three centuries had nothing to do with Jamyang's death. The lama had planned his death carefully, wanting to spend his last hours in acts of reverence. Yet he had interrupted those plans to race after the thief, as if he had to recover the tablet before dying. Shan's confusion was like a physical pain. The more he considered Jamyang's last day the less sense it made. He wrote down the inscription from the ancestor tablets and returned them to the storage chamber, then paused to lift the little jade dragon. Carved into its base was an elaborate seal. He dipped it into the water bucket under the bench and pressed it onto the dry wood. Yuan Yi. The wet imprint was the name of the long-dead mandarin. He set the dragon back on the bench, strangely disturbed by the little jade creature.

The lama's hut was that of a true ascetic. A shelf above his pallet held a tin cup with a toothbrush. Beside a small personal altar with a plaster Buddha and incense burners was a worn plank, on which Jamyang had sat for hours in meditation. In the corner that served as a makeshift kitchen was a chipped enamel basin, the brazier, a nearly empty sack of barley, a small brick of tea, and one of the small wooden pails used by the shepherds for transporting butter.

The shepherds. One of them had first taken Jamyang to the remote, neglected shrine, overgrown and nearly covered with vines and weeds. It had been mostly devout shepherds, singly and in families, who came to visit and receive a blessing from the lama, sometimes even asking him to bestow a name on a new infant. But another shepherd had stolen the artifacts, a bitter shepherd with a limp and a scar on his forehead. Had the thief indeed been more interested in getting the ancestral tablet to the new settlement than in collecting a bounty on Jamyang? He understood nothing of Jamyang's death but now he began to realize he also understood nothing of the lama's life.

He lowered himself before Jamyang's altar. The lama had left a single sheet of scripture, like an offering to the Buddha. It was a verse from the Diamond Sutra. "Thus shall you think of this fleeting world," it said. "A star at dawn, a bubble in a stream, a flash of lightning in a summer cloud, a flickering lamp, a phantom, and a dream." With new despair he stepped outside, and faced the sacred mountain, ablaze in the early light. A bank of clouds below gave the impression it was floating in the sky.

His fingers touched something in his pocket. He pulled out the piece of paper he had taken from the secret holster of the man who had nearly lost his head. It was a list of places and dates, each named at least twice, with dates over the past year, except for the last two, which were in the coming weeks. The names were all Tibetan towns. Tawang. Zayu. Zhangmu. Yadong. The writing was in Jamyang's hand. He recalled that the paper was not the only thing he had recovered from the bodies, and reached deeper in his pocket to retrieve the bloodstained card from the nun's body. The bullet that had killed her had pierced the bottom, leaving a half circle. The back was covered with prayers in tiny, cramped Tibetan script. His breath caught as he turned it over and saw his mistake. It was not an identity card. It was a photo of the Dalai Lama, covered in the dead nun's blood.

During his months in the valley Shan had carefully avoided the immigrant settlement, often adding half an hour or more to his trips in the upper valley by taking old roads that circumvented the small town. A Party official writing in the *Lhasa Times* had recently praised the Chinese immigrants who populated such new rural centers as the "frontline troops" in Beijing's war on the past. WELCOME TO BAIYUN said an already fading sign at the edge of the town. The name meant White Cloud. It had the sound of a tourist destination. Above the name were the words PIONEERS OF THE MOTHERLAND, beneath it another Party slogan: THE FRONT WAVE IN THE TIDE OF MODERNIZATION.

The wave had crashed over several traditional Tibetan farms that had sat at the intersection of two country roads. The farms were gone, the houses at the intersection replaced with a gas station, a teahouse, and a small grocery store, the outbuildings and fields replaced with a few blocks of nearly identical cinder block and stucco houses with corrugated metal roofs.

He drove slowly past a squat building constructed of cement panels in the center of a fenced compound where the Chinese flag rattled on a metal pole. Parked beside the pole were two police cars, a battered sedan bearing the insignia of the local constables, the other one of the grey utility vehicles favored by Public Security. The center of town seemed almost abandoned, its small dusty square populated only by one of the fiberglass statues of the Great Helmsman that were being erected all over Tibet. Shan stared, wondering at the unnatural air of the town. No children could be seen anywhere. The only inhabitant of the park was a solitary dog, sitting, staring at the statue.

Shan slowed the truck to a crawl then parked it along the last block of houses. He had begun walking back toward the square when he noticed a gathering in the field behind the houses. Sheep and yaks were being sold under an open pavilion, a long tin roof raised on cinder block posts. A dozen Tibetan vendors were selling their wares from blankets spread on the grass beside the pavilion. On the far side of the field stood a weathered stable of stone and timber, the sole surviving structure of the old farming community.

He worked his way along the edge of the crowd, studying the Tibetans in the makeshift market. An old woman with a face like wrinkled leather sold noodle soup. A nearly toothless man in a tattered jacket sold yak butter in old tin cans and inch-high deities molded of clay. Shan paused to buy some incense and two of the little deities, then leaned against a post of the pavilion to survey the grounds. A woman wearing a wide-brimmed hat sat on a blanket selling long spools of spun wool. As Shan watched, a man with shaggy hair, wearing a dirty fleece vest, emerged from the crowd beside her, leading a young ewe toward the stable. Shan quickly retreated, circling around the building.

He waited until the shepherd had tied the animal in the rear stall before he stepped from the shadows, blocking the entrance. "You're not limping as badly as when I saw you last," he declared in a casual tone.

The shepherd's eyes went round with surprise. He glanced back at the square hole in the wall that served as the stable's window, as if thinking of fleeing.

"Jamyang had other artifacts. A jade seal. Some figures set with jewels," Shan said. "But you left them and shouldered those heavy tablets. Why?"

"Black market," the man said, looking at Shan's feet. "Tourists buy such things."

"In Tibet, tourists want Tibetan things," Shan observed, "small things that can be stuffed in a suitcase."

The man shrugged. "Some outsiders need other things. Cans of food. Blankets."

Shan studied the man in confusion. Outsiders. Foreigners were strictly prohibited from entering Lhadrung County. "What is your name?"

The shepherd took a step to the side as if thinking of charging past Shan. "I am a loyal citizen."

"I can go out into the market," Shan said, "and have your name in five minutes. Of course then everyone will know someone from the government is seeking you."

The man's eyes were smoldering now. He was taking on the air of a cornered wolf.

"Tenzin Gyalo," the man offered.

"No. You are not the Dalai Lama." Shan took a step closer. "You are a shepherd who has misplaced his flock."

The words seemed to unsettle the man. He looked back at the animals in the stall with what, for an instant, seemed like longing. "Sometimes I help out on market days. It's good to work with the animals again." He took another step to one side as he spoke, made a feint to the left, then darted past Shan on the right.

As Shan spun about, ready to pursue, a shovel handle appeared between the man's legs and he tripped, sprawling on the ground. He quickly sprang back up but just as quickly a hand grabbed his collar and swung him about, propelling him back into the stable.

"You can cooperate here," came a level voice, "or you can cooperate in my detention cell."

Shan's throat went dry as a uniformed knob entered the stable. He glanced at the window himself, instinctively thinking of fleeing, then recognized the woman. It was the lieutenant he had spoken with at the convent. As she approached the shepherd her hand touched the manacles on her belt.

"Jigten," the shepherd said in a stricken voice. "Jigten is my name."

The lieutenant extended her hand, palm upward, and the man unbuttoned his shirt pocket and extracted his registration card.

"Do you enjoy your new home at the relocation camp, Jigten Somala?" the officer asked as she read his card.

"The people of the motherland have been generous," he murmured. Every Tibetan Shan knew had rehearsed lines they used when confronted by an official.

"No need to dirty your hands with all those animals," the lieutenant said. "You even have electricity."

"We strive to repay the people's kindness," Jigten recited.

"Electricity. Free food. Free shelter. A paradise on earth."

Shan looked at the lieutenant. It almost seemed that she too had her rehearsed lines.

"Paradise on earth," Jigten repeated.

"You were about to speak with Comrade—" she looked at Shan expectantly.

"Shan."

"You were about to answer Comrade Shan's questions," she continued.

As Jigten looked back at Shan, fear was in his eyes. Once, in Tibet, people had feared demon deities whose slightest touch could destroy them. The demons had returned in the twenty-first century, wearing the grey uniforms of Public Security.

The lieutenant offered Shan a conspiratorial smile, then retreated out the door. Jigten sank onto a milking stool. "They don't give us money in that camp. Just give us a little food and tell us to sleep in those damned boxes they call houses."

"You're not from Baiyun?" Shan asked.

"That's for Chinese pioneers." He gestured toward a low ridge beyond the town. Shan followed Jigten's hand and saw several thin columns of smoke beyond the ridge, like distant campfires. "A hundred nomads taken out of the *changtang*, nearly our entire clan. The Chinese are teaching us what it means to be civilized."

Shan fought a shudder. One of Beijing's newest campaigns was to clear away the *dropka*, the nomad shepherds from the changtang prairie, the vast grassland wilderness that dominated much of central Tibet, and put them into camps. Shan fought the temptation to help Jigten to the window and follow him out. The lieutenant would not have gone far. He spoke in a low whisper. "Which explains why you might steal. But I asked you about those tablets."

Jigten lifted a clump of wool from the dirt floor. It was the season for shearing sheep. When he pressed the wool to his nose his eyes took on a melancholy expression.

"This is a town of professors," Jigten explained. "They like old things, especially old Chinese things. They speak of dead emperors like they were old friends. Sometimes they have medicine I can trade for. That's all I want. Medicine. They refuse us any real medicine in our camp. There's a professor with wire-rimmed glasses who has a daughter with lung sickness. Sometimes he has extra medicine. Those tablets would have meant a week's worth at least." He seemed to sense Shan's hesitation, did not miss the worried glance Shan shot toward the entry. He rose and took a step toward the window, then another.

"Did Jamyang know these professors?" Shan pressed.

"Jamyang was a ghost," Jigten said, taking another step. "People don't really know ghosts. You can't really steal from a ghost." He put a hand on the sill, paused to see if Shan would stop him, then climbed outside.

Shan stared after the forlorn, limping shepherd, watching him disappear back into the marketplace crowd.

"Interesting technique," came an amused voice behind him. "I heard about it in a seminar once. Yo-yo style. Reel them in and terrify them, then release them when they least expect it. When you pull them in again, when you really need them, they'll be begging to help you."

As Shan turned to face the knob lieutenant, she reached into a pocket and produced a bag of salted sunflower seeds, which she extended toward Shan before gesturing him to the bench against the outside wall.

He stole a long look at the slender woman as she sat down beside him. The lieutenant had probably been with Public Security for years but she did not have the brittle features and frigid eyes of most knob officers Shan had known. There was an unexpected softness in her face, an intelligent curiosity in her eyes. In another place, out of uniform with her hair loose over her high cheekbones, she would have been attractive.

But her reflexes were that of a knob. "I'll try to arrest him for something soon," she said in a distracted tone as she watched the throng. "Let him spend a night in my holding cell, then tell him I'm releasing him as a favor to you." She sat down beside him. "A favor to Comrade Shan," she added pointedly.

He returned her steady gaze as he took some of the offered seeds, struggling not to betray his fear. Tibet was rife with secret Chinese operatives. She had decided he was some kind of undercover officer, building a network of informers.

"To whom do I owe my gratitude?" he asked.

"Lieutenant Meng Limei, local liaison for Public Security," she offered, then went back to watching the market. With a shudder Shan saw that two Public Security vehicles had arrived, parked on either side of the market. As he watched, a truck of armed police eased to a stop on the road. "At headquarters they always say the only way to round up the traditionalists is sending out teams to scour the mountains. Then Major Liang arrived. 'Don't be so clubfooted,' he said, 'haven't you ever heard of letting the flowers bloom first?'"

It was one of Mao's most infamous campaigns. Let a Hundred Flowers Bloom. Mao had told intellectuals and other rightists that they could criticize the government with impunity, even encouraged them to gather in protest and paint walls with democratic slogans. Public Security took months to secretly photograph them and record their identities, then closed in and arrested thousands.

"'Let them come down on their own,' Liang said," she continued. "'Find a way for them to feel comfortable with their traditional ways. Announce some kind of Tibetan festival,' he suggested. I told him this market already attracts much of the local population every week."

Shan gazed out over the gathered Tibetans, reminding himself that the roundups of Tibetans he had expected after the murders had not yet started. An old man with sparkling eyes sat with a plank on his legs, writing short prayers and handing them out to passersby. A child squealed with delight as another man, fingers extended at his temples, chased her like a wild yak. "These are but the early flowers," he said, his heart like an anvil. "Arrest them and the ones you really want will burrow so deep it will take years to dig them out."

Lieutenant Meng studied him. "You know more about the local Tibetans than you're saying."

"You know more about the murders at the convent than you are saying."

Meng chewed on her seeds. "That's being handled by our specialist from outside. Major Liang is in charge." She meant, Shan knew, Liang was an elite troubleshooter from Lhasa or even Beijing. "As the senior local officer I am just assisting."

"You mean your main assignment is pacification."

The lieutenant did not disagree. "There was a new memo. We are supposed to speak of it as assimilation now. Embracing the indigenous population with the open heart of the Chinese motherland." She spoke the words with raised eyebrows. For a moment Shan thought he detected sarcasm in her voice.

"Liang's solution will no doubt make some political officer proud," Shan observed. "Solving a murder by throwing a grenade in a crowd."

"I'm not sure I follow."

Shan watched with foreboding as the big Chinese men in plainclothes positioned themselves around the market. "Beijing expects bold responses to murders. In Tibet it's always simple. Round up a couple dozen Tibetans, sweat a few in interrogation so accusations of disloyalty start flowing. Collect enough statements to arrest a dissident and close the file with a press conference and an article in the *Lhasa Times* that warns about the ongoing dangers of splittists," he said, using the Party's euphemism for those who sought Tibetan independence. "It may sound good in Beijing but it doesn't stop a killer. It will make your job a hundred times more difficult, Lieutenant."

Meng frowned. "People in Beijing went into a blind fury when they saw those crime scene photos. A Chinese flag in red paint and blood. Two dead Chinese men with their boots on some peasant woman. Of course it was a dissident."

"You mean they want it to be a dissident. And in doing so they become the murderer's puppet. You're in charge of local assimilation. Special troubleshooters sent by Beijing come and go. You'll still be here. You're going to let them set things back by years. And set your career back."

She lowered her sunflower seeds. "I'm listening."

"They haven't thought it through yet but eventually they will. It will begin like a little bell ringing down a long tunnel. In a case like this it could take weeks before anyone even stops to listen to it. But eventually it will be heard. Eventually the clapper on the bell feels like a hammer on the skull to some of those involved."

Meng's mouth twisted in a half frown. "Do you always speak in riddles?"

"The truth will come back to haunt you. No matter what public label is put on it, those in Beijing will eventually realize this could not have been an act of political resistance. It was too clumsy, too inconspicuous, too simple."

"These are simple people."

"They are simple. Not simpletons. Arresting a few random agitators may feel good today but eventually those in Beijing will see it has caused a bigger problem. There's a new term used by the Party, civil unrest with physical manifestations. The kind of problem it takes a battalion of troops to solve. Colonel Tan runs this county. They will be his troops, led by him personally. Do you know him?"

"Tan the sledgehammer. He chews bullets for breakfast."

"When he comes he won't care if you're Chinese or in a uniform. If you are in the way of his machine it will roll right over you."

Meng studied Shan as if for the first time. "You speak like someone wise in the ways of Beijing."

"I spent twenty-five years beside those who define those ways."

The announcement seemed to worry Meng. "Everything I do is consistent with guidance from Beijing," she quickly explained.

"Guidance from Beijing is kept intentionally vague. That way when some remote cadre makes that excuse she can be blamed for misinterpreting it, even abusing it." He glanced at the distant mountains. Lokesh was up there. He had to keep Lokesh safe, had to keep Jamyang's secret life safe. He gestured toward the market. "Of course, you can round these people up today. But that will just light the fuse. It will be weeks before the powder keg explodes, before the folly of it becomes apparent. Then more weeks of meetings, even secret hearings. I used to prepare scripts for such hearings. In the end it will be the field officer's mistake. The senior local officer always should have known better." Shan spoke in a slow, level voice. "You're going to need political reeducation, Lieutenant Meng, at one of the big institutes back east. Living in a dormitory, reciting Party scripture for hours every day, sitting for more hours in criticism sessions, looking over your shoulder for the one who is going to make you the subject of the next session. You will be expected to volunteer for one of those patriotic brigades that wave banners in parades. Some cadres find it quite invigorating. Like taking an extended vacation with the Great Helmsman."

She returned his steady gaze without expression then broke away to study the Tibetans once more. He was not sure he had scared her so much as piqued her curiosity.

"I need more," she said at last. "I need a reason to talk to head-quarters, a reason to change their orders."

Shan nodded toward the Tibetans. "The market is where the truth gets told. You are doing your job, always sifting for local intelligence. You picked up a rumor. People know about the dead woman."

"Know what? Whoever she is, she has been abandoned. No one has reported her missing. No one has asked about the body."

Shan stared at her a moment. "No one told you? She was a nun."

Meng's hand crushed the bag of seeds. Her face clouded.

"Explain that it changes the entire interpretation of the crime scene," Shan said. "The flag, the boots pressing down on the woman, the cap covering her short hair was all a pose for police photographers, a ruse of the killer to point suspicion at a dissident. You realize that now because no dissident kills a nun."

After a long moment she rose and took several steps before lifting the small radio on her belt. The truck of armed police, still waiting in the street, drove away. The men in plainclothes began retreating back toward the grey vehicles.

The lieutenant watched the police drive away before turning back to Shan. "Fine. I have done what you asked. It's going to cost me several unpleasant hours back at headquarters."

Shan heard her expectant tone and cocked his head. "Is this a negotiation, Lieutenant?"

"Of course it is," she shot back. "North. South. West. I need the fourth to go with the others. I've heard the prayer horns that mock us from the heights. They sounded again the night after the murders."

"Now you are speaking riddles."

"You're going to tell me about that lama who slinks around the hills like some damned outlaw."

CHAPTER fOUR

When Shan did not respond, Meng turned and pointed down the dusty street, toward the center of the town. They walked in silence, past another gas station, past a post office in a prefabricated building, then into the small structure that appeared to be Baiyun's main food store. One of the Tibetan constables sat by the front door. A matronly clerk at the counter saw them and fled into a rear corridor.

Meng led Shan into the same corridor, into the back storeroom. A door leading outside hung ajar. The clerk had not only fled from the counter, she had fled the building. Meng stepped to the closetlike meat locker, opened the heavy metal door, and gestured Shan inside.

The freshest meat lay outstretched on three long tables, with frozen chickens tossed in a pile at the rear of the metal-lined chamber. Two tables were against the walls and the third so filled the center of the locker that Shan barely had room to squeeze between the tables. The bodies were covered with sheets. Adhesive tape around their thumbs identified them only according to their positions at the crime scene. *Bei. Nan. Xi.* North. South. West.

"These should be in a forensics lab," he said uneasily.

"Don't be ridiculous. We're hundreds of miles from a lab. Such a valuable resource would never be allocated to"—she paused, searched for words—"a local crime."

Shan studied the knob officer. They were both treading on dangerous ground now. "I think we are here, Lieutenant, because you know this is not some local crime. Because you know about special troubleshooters called in from afar, you know their priority isn't to dig into the truth but to dig into the politics. But can it be possible that you are actually interested in the truth?"

Meng ignored the question. "Nan and Xi died elsewhere and were dragged to the chorten. You were right. The woman Xi died at the wall, where a nine millimeter bullet was recovered. Bei was shot and bled out after being dragged to the chorten. The man Nan had an empty holster but no pistol has been found. He was attacked at the corner of a building by the front gate. His blood stained the wall and pooled on the ground."

As she spoke Shan stared at the body of the woman. On the sheet covering her lay a sprig of heather. "Who was here?"

"No one," Meng said. "We are watching the place." She pushed the heather onto the floor.

Shan glanced at her. She meant the constables were watching the place. Her Tibetan constables.

"I asked you about that lama," Meng pressed.

Shan returned her steady gaze. "Lamas don't commit murder."

The lieutenant frowned, then stepped to the side of the body marked Bei, the faceless man. "That first night the bodies were here Liang came in with a doctor. As far as the major is concerned my job as local liaison means I am his escort, charged with keeping locals out of his way. The doctor was interested only in this one. Liang stepped to his side and ordered me to my station to write a report for him on the local political situation. The next morning I came back. The owner was terrified. He didn't object when I came back in here. I found this—" She lifted the sheet over the man's naked thigh. His skin was paler than that of the others. There was an incision eight inches long, closed with fresh sutures.

Shan bent over the incision. There was no swelling, no bruising, no scabbing. He pointed to the ridge of tissue above the incision. "He cut open the dead man's leg along an old scar."

Meng silently nodded.

He stared at her warily, sensing a trap. Knob officers were not permitted to be so headstrong. It was unthinkable that one would seek to intrude on the secrets of her superiors. She was only a lieutenant, he reminded himself, when most officers her age were of higher rank. "If you were to cut open these sutures it would be insubordination," Shan concluded. "So you want me to."

There was mischief in Meng's narrow smile, but also a certain nervousness Shan had not seen before.

"Do you have the times of death?" he asked as he lifted a knife from a wall rack.

"Of course. Sometime during the past week, give or take a day. I admire your faith in our abilities. We have their personal belongings, two shell casings and a timber ax that was found with tools stored near the front gate that is consistent with the weapon that severed Nan's head. No blood on it. Liang took the bullet we dug out of the wall. We're pretty certain the victims are two males and a female. That, Comrade, is the extent of our forensic investigation."

"But Liang has resources, access to labs. You said he brought that doctor."

"As far as I can tell what the major is doing is reviewing the files on every inhabitant of Baiyun."

The incision was deep, all the way to the femur. Except there was almost no femur. The bone had been shattered long ago, replaced with a prosthetic. As he stared at it Shan felt his chest tighten.

"I don't understand," Meng said as she bent to the incision, prying the flesh apart with her hands.

"Titanium," Shan explained. "This was not done in China." He quickly moved to the man's mouth and pried it open. At least half a dozen teeth had been extracted. "Bodies will speak of their home if you look close enough."

"A foreigner!" Meng gasped.

It changed everything. Her curiosity was gone, replaced by fear. She grabbed the sheet and covered the body, her movements suddenly frantic. "We must leave! Now!"

"No," Shan replied. "You must leave. Go outside. Forget we were here." He stepped to the other man, Nan, the Chinese whose head had nearly been severed.

"Not him!" Meng said. "No point."

He began to pull away the sheet. The second man's head had been crudely sewn back in place. Even so the man was short, Shan realized. Short and stocky and dark-complected.

Meng paused as she reached the door. "Major Liang is expected today. It won't matter whom you work for if Liang finds you with a murdered foreigner."

"All the more reason for you to leave."

She eyed him coolly, then turned and left without another word. Shan quickly pulled away the rest of the sheet from Nan. The holster on the man's ankle had been removed, like everything else. He looked at the black bird tattooed on Nan's forearm. With his expensive clothes the man had seemed like an affluent businessman, perhaps even a senior official. Now, as he returned the sheet, Shan was not so sure. Meng had known him, had seemed oddly dismissive of the man, and of his death. But Jamyang too had known him, and given him a paper with a list of Tibetan towns. He paced slowly along the man, lifting his appendages, even examining his long black hair and scalp, then sniffed at the black deposits under his fingernails. Motor oil.

Meng was nowhere to be seen as he stepped outside. The sleepy little town of Baiyun was coming to life in the late afternoon. Trucks were pulling off the valley's only paved road into the gas station. The smell of steamed rice and onions wafted from the little tea shop. In the square, two pairs of Chinese men, all older than Shan, were playing checkers. He pulled a newspaper from a waste barrel and sat on a bench, pretending to read as he studied the checker players and the buildings beyond.

Baiyun, in the remote mountains of central Tibet, had nothing of Tibet. It was a Chinese town, or some distant bureaucrat's notion of what a Chinese town in Tibet should look like. White Cloud town. A pretend Chinese town in a pretend province of China. Someone had tried to plant gingko and plane trees along the edge of the park but the plants were nearly all dead or dying. The park benches that had been placed along the square were falling apart. Some of their planks were missing. The fiberglass statue of Mao, meant to be the focal point of the town square, was already being corroded by the harsh, dusty winds that often roared up the valley. Scores of such statues had been assembled in government warehouses, destined to replace the centuries-old stone chorten shrines that had once been fixtures in Tibetan villages. There was a new political slogan favored by the Party head in Tibet: The Communist Party Is Your New Buddha. When he had first heard it, Shan had actually thought it was some kind of joke. But now the slogan was emblazoned on public walls and banners all over Tibet and offered up for Tibetan schoolchildren to recite like a militant mantra.

Shan looked back at the statue. The only Tibetan writing he had seen anywhere in Baiyun was inscribed along the top edge at the front of its pedestal: PRAISE THE GREAT LEADER TO WHOM WE OWE OUR LIVES AND PROSPERITY.

He gazed absently at the words as he forced himself to reconstruct the grisly scene in the store's refrigerator. Liang's special doctor had opened Bei's leg up, and extracted his teeth. They had suspected him of being a foreigner but finely worked teeth were becoming less reliable an indicator of foreign origin in modern China. The titanium rod was unquestionable proof. They had closed up the scar then pulled the teeth for good measure. He looked up, surveying the streets again. He still had the sense of something unnatural about the pioneer town, and not just because it was one of Beijing's prefabricated formula settlements.

Folding the paper under his arm he wandered around the square, sitting again, closer to the checker games that had been set out on upturned crates. Once more he surveyed the park and the modest windblown houses beyond it. There was another slogan on the back edge of the pedestal, in Chinese. It was faded, barely legible even though the statue was probably no more than a year old. He found himself rising again, trying to read the words. They were carefully written, in a very light hand that gave the impression of an official inscription that was weathered. But it was no official slogan: *Superior leaders are those whose existence is merely known.*

He stared at the words in disbelief, reading them again. It was the first verse of the seventeenth passage of the *Tao Te Ching*, written more than two thousand years earlier. The chapter explained how the best leaders were those barely known to their people, the worst were those who interfered with daily life. They were words that Beijing would choke on, the words of dissidents, though not of Tibet.

As he turned back toward the checker players he sensed movement, as if they had all been watching him. He slowly walked among them. Curiously, the players all had books beside them. A book of European history, in English. A book about the bone oracles of early China. A book of rites from the last dynasty. All but one of the players glanced up, nodding absently at Shan. The fourth man, an older, refined-looking gentleman wearing a grey sweater vest and wire-rimmed spectacles, seemed to studiously avoid acknowledging Shan. In his lap was a book of Sung dynasty poetry.

Shan moved on, pausing under one of the trees to look back. There were professors in Baiyun, Jigten had explained. He had been taking Jamyang's spirit tablets to sell to a professor. A young man walked by, carrying a cloth sack of rice on his shoulder. He was compact, his skin almost olive-colored. Most of the town's inhabitants were tall, long in the face, with prominent features, people of the distant northeast, of Manchuria. This man had the features of China's tropical southwest, not far removed from the tribes of the rain forest. Shan watched the figure as he disappeared into an alley. He had seen the features before, on the tattooed dead man.

He looked back at the men in the square, trying to understand his odd discomfort, feeling more than ever the urge to flee, to find Lokesh and take him to safety. But he also felt a growing need to understand this strange, unreal town with three bodies in a refrigerator.

A cry of pain broke him out of his paralysis. Low, rushed voices rose from the alley off the square. A woman cursed from the shadows, then gasped. Figures ran away, between buildings.

Meng was on her knees when Shan reached her, retching onto the ground.

"I'm all right!" she growled when Shan put a hand on her shoulder.

"You're not all right," Shan said. "You were attacked. I should find a doctor." He quickly scanned the shadows. Rice kernels were scattered around her, the bag they had been in on the ground a few feet away. He looked warily about. A figure in the shadows turned and ran as Shan took a step toward him.

"No doctor!" Meng snapped. She leaned over, shaking the rice from her hair, then, bracing herself on the building, rose unsteadily. Her hand went to her upper lip. Blood was dripping from her nose. "I'm prone to nosebleeds," she said. "You know, the altitude."

"You were just attacked, Lieutenant." He handed Meng her hat. "A Public Security officer was attacked."

"Nonsense. We . . . collided," Meng said weakly. "Not looking where I was going."

Shan looked up the alley, out to the square. "You were watching me. Following me."

"I strive to learn from my elders. Like I said, you are wise in the ways of Beijing."

He stared at her. The more he interacted with Meng the more of an enigma she became. There should be urgent radio calls, plans for a sweep of the town. People were sent to prison for years for lifting a hand against a knob officer. He considered her words. Which ways of Beijing worried her?

"You knew who they were," he said. It was not a question. "Just like you knew who that other man was. The one labeled south. His tattoo was like the banner of a gang."

Meng fished a napkin from a pocket and held it to her nose. "They describe themselves as more of a social club. The Jade Crows they call themselves, a group of undesirables from Yunnan. Someone there decided to give them transportation to Tibet instead of prison."

"You mean they bribed some court official."

Meng acted as if she had not heard. "It's part of the model for pioneer towns. Mix the populations. Don't let one group take over the town."

"They show every sign of having taken over the town, Lieutenant. Your town." He turned at the sound of footsteps in the alley. The Tibetan constables were running toward them.

Meng seemed about to argue, then looked at her bloody napkin. "It's late. I have a long drive to headquarters," she said, then turned and disappeared around the corner of the building.

Headquarters. She meant the district Public Security headquarters, twenty miles north of the Lhadrung County line. Shan reminded himself that she did not report to Liang but to other officials, officers who had set pacification as her primary duty. He was tempted to follow her, but outside the county Shan's meager protection would not exist. Outside Lhadrung he was no one, a former gulag inmate who had ignored the rules requiring former prisoners to remain in the county of their registration.

He looked back at the square. The checker players had all disappeared.

The responsibilities of the Irrigation Inspector for the northern townships of Lhadrung County were far-reaching. Shan's district

encompassed nearly a thousand square miles. His first annual reck-
oning to the county seat had reported two hundred and twenty-five
road culverts, twenty earthen dams, and three hundred and fifty
miles of ditches used for drainage. In a lighter moment he had once
mentioned to Lokesh that his was an honored post, an office that
had existed in the old Chinese empires, and for the next week the old
Tibetan had addressed him with imperial honorifics. In reality it was
a job that kept Shan covered in mud much of the time. His assignment had been the clever, and cruel, inspiration of the county governor, Colonel Tan, who had grudgingly accepted the obligation to
protect Shan after he had saved Tan from a false accusation of murder
the year before. But Tan had wanted Shan as far away as possible, and
so humiliated he might be tempted to flee. The appointment, and moving Shan's son Ko to Shan's former prison camp in Lhadrung were,
Tan had sternly warned, the last favors he would ever do for Shan.

The silver lining to Shan's cloud was that he had no direct super-
visor, and could travel anywhere he wished within his district in the
battered old truck that came with the job. He leaned on his shovel
now, watching the convent ruins below. A police barricade, manned
by two officers, still blocked the road into the murder scene but there
was no sign of activity inside the convent compound itself. He lifted
his shovel like a badge of office and set off down the path that led to
the ruins.

There had been only one vehicle at the gate when he had looked
with Jamyang. The nun, the foreigner, the Chinese man, and their
killer had been there, and surely they had not all arrived together.
Above the convent there were several old pilgrim paths but as they
approached it they converged, so there was one main path from each
direction that reached the old walls.

Half a mile from the compound he stopped at an intersection with
another path, looking up the trail that arrived from a narrow hanging
valley above him. It was the route to Thousand Steps, the nuns' hermitage. The murdered nun had no doubt come to the convent down

that path. It had been a beautiful early summer day. The birds would have been singing, her step would have been light. Once at the ruins she had taken up her restoration work on one of the old prayer wheels. Once one or two of the wheels were done and being spun by the devout, Lokesh had told him, the convent would be invincible, as if the wheels would defend it as surely as great guns.

He slowly turned in a circle, surveying the landscape. The nun had come from above, the Chinese man had driven, but what of the foreigner, what of the killer? The convent had once been the hub of the upper valley. Other trails converged from the shepherds' homes high in the mountains, still others from the farms and even Chegar *gompa,* the monastery at the mouth of the valley miles away. Keeping out of sight of the police at the roadblock, he found the other trails that led into the ruins of the gates along the side and rear walls. They were all intersected by a line of heavy boot prints where police had circuited the building, but all the tracks leading up to the walls were those of the soft, worn footwear of Tibetans. At the rear wall, where the trail was soon lost in a tangle of brush, Shan discovered the track of a single bicycle. It had been ridden to the convent and hidden among the boulders, then later ridden away.

Bicycles were becoming more common among the people of the valley floor, who were being pushed away from using yaks and donkeys, but he never recalled seeing one anywhere but on the roads. Few paths were in good enough condition to allow any kind of wheeled passage. He studied the rocky landscape where the trail disappeared. The path might lead to the trails of the upper slopes but he doubted a bicycle could be used on those trails. Much more forgiving would be the large path that ran along the lower part of the ridge, the more heavily used pilgrim path that connected the convent and Chegar monastery.

As he began to climb over the crumbling wall he heard a sharp cracking sound. He spun about to see a robed figure standing fifty yards away, frozen, staring at Shan.

Shan ran, but the monk was faster, weaving around boulders before disappearing into the field of outcroppings. Finally halting, panting for breath, Shan watched the rocks, hoping for another glimpse
of the stranger. He saw him only for an instant, a close-cropped head
wearing a pair of sunglasses that peered out from behind a rock,
then disappeared. The monk had not been there for the restoration
project. Shan ventured to the point where the man had first appeared, starting for a moment at another cracking sound under his
own foot. He bent and picked up a black piece of plastic, then saw
another, and another, then small shards of thick glass. Behind a boulder the ground was strewn with more, dozens of pieces. Gathering
several of the biggest, he laid them on a rock and tried to reassemble
them. A camera. Someone had smashed a camera against the rocks.
A very expensive camera, judging from the pieces he saw. It had not
been done by the monk, who had inadvertently stepped on the plastic. Had this too been the work of the killer?

He returned to the compound, hugging the shadows now, moving
from one building to the next, pausing often to watch behind him.
Yellow tape had been hung near the chorten, cordoning off where
the rectangle of red paint, still faintly visible, showed where the bodies had lain. Shan paced around the tape, oddly loath to step over it,
then headed to the prayer wheel station where the nun had been
killed. Without conscious thought he pushed the wheel, then paused,
watching it. It was a reflex he had acquired during his years with
Lokesh, something most Tibetans would do whenever they were near
such a wheel.

The nun had probably been the last to push the wheel. Now, as
Lokesh would say, Shan had picked up the chain of prayer, adding
his link to the dead woman's, as nuns and pilgrims had done at this
spot, with this very wheel, for centuries.

He kept the wheel moving, the low grinding sound his accom-
paniment as he pictured the nun at work. She had been shot in the
back, though at an angle. There had been a separate pool of blood. The

Westerner had been with her, helping. The killer had shot him in the neck, then quickly shot the nun as she had begun to turn.

Shan spun the wheel again, watching it with a forlorn expression before facing the courtyard, forgetting for the moment that it was a murder scene. He had visited many such places with Lokesh, and the old Tibetan always somehow gave him a sense of their former grandeur, of the elegant reverence that had dwelt there for so many years. But today, alone, Shan felt small and empty, just another wandering pilgrim who had lost his path.

He hesitantly stepped toward the chorten. Only a few weeks earlier there had been much laughter in the dawn as Shan had helped Lokesh and Jamyang whitewash the shrine. Its loose stones had been relaid, and a fresh coat of stucco applied, and as they prepared their brushes the two Tibetans had described to Shan the many types of chortens in the old teachings. Marking in the sand with sticks they had drawn images, naming each for him. The enlightenment chorten, the lotus chorten, the wheel chorten, the miracle chorten, the descent from heaven chorten, the victory chorten, the nirvana chorten. Shan recalled now how Lokesh had paused as he had discovered a stone at the base that had pushed through the new stucco, as if something had forced its way out from inside. The old Tibetan had not said anything then, simply jammed the stone back and painted over it, but Shan had seen the worry on his face. He knew there were other chortens that were constructed to trap and subdue demons.

Shan stepped now to the far side. The new stucco was cracked. The stone had fallen out again.

He found himself backing away, staring uneasily at the dislodged stone, then turned and moved to the front gate. The smudge of color marking another pool of blood was clearly visible at a corner of the building closest to the gate, where the third victim had been nearly decapitated. He looked inside the little alcove near the front gate where the Tibetans had been storing tools. Meng had reported that a woodcutter's ax had been discovered there and was being held as the likely butcher's tool. But surely such a long-handled tool was too clumsy. It seemed unlikely to Shan that an ax had been responsible for the broad, clean slices that had cleaved away the flesh from the foreigner's skull, but the meager inventory of tools presented few alternatives. A crude spade. Two hoes. A rake. A small and very dull sickle. He paused, remembering now a crew of farmers who had begun clearing brush from along the back wall.

It took him several minutes to locate the farmers' store of equipment, inside the little chapel where he had first encountered Meng. Under a piece of tattered felt lay a chain, a rope, a small pry bar, and a heavy brush hook with a long curving blade mounted on a rough handle as long as his forearm. Carrying the hook into the sunlight, he ran a finger along the edge of the blade, recalling now that he had seen the farmers at work, using the blade to slice through branches as thick as his thumb. He held the blade close, examining it in the sunlight. Its pockmarked surface held rust but flecks of something darker also stained the metal. He tore off a piece of the felt, wrapped it around the blade, and leaned the hook inside the doorway of the chapel before studying again the tracks outside the building. Meng had been studying the ground when he had first seen her there. There were now at least half a dozen other tracks. Two or three sets were from police boots, two sets were his own, but two more sets were of soft rope-sole shoes, leading back over the wall. One of them led to where the bicycle tracks began, which led in the direction the monk had fled, in the direction of Chegar gompa, the monastery, at the head of the valley. He paused for a moment, debating whether to follow the tire marks, then picked up his shovel where he had left it and turned back to the trail he had arrived on. He could not risk having his unattended truck discovered by the police.

Half an hour later he stood at his truck, gazing in frustration at the ruins below, as he endeavored once more to piece together the movements of those who had been in the convent the day of the murders.

"Maybe it doesn't want to come back to life yet."

Shan turned slowly to face the stranger, gripping his shovel tightly. It took a moment for him to discern the young woman, for the brown robe she wore blended with the hillside. She sat, legs crossed under her, by a clump of heather.

"There was an old lama who used to come to our tents when I was a girl," she continued. "He said at such places ancient spirits are slumbering. You can't force them awake, he said. They will wake at their chosen time. He said when they do they could walk among us and look just like another man."

She was barely out of her teens, but the girl's face, half of which was heavily scarred, the other half fixed in melancholy, said she had seen much of life. Her robe marked her as a lay nun, an unofficial companion to, and a student of, ordained nuns. It had become one of the ways that Tibetans evaded the ever-more onerous restrictions on donning a maroon robe.

"I have learned to trust a lot of what old lamas say," Shan replied, and loosened his grip on the shovel.

"Abbess Tomo isn't coming back, is she?"

"Abbess?" Shan asked in surprise.

"The head of our hermitage."

The woman had not been just a nun, she had been the senior nun of the valley. He shook his head slowly. "She's not coming back."

"No one wants to talk about her. They act like maybe she just went on a retreat somewhere."

"I saw her body."

The woman bit her lip. "She raised me since I was ten. Since—" she pointed to the ruin of her face. "My father borrowed a truck to take our sheep to market. It was going to be like a holiday, my mother and grandmother were going with us. No one told him the brakes were bad. We went off a mountain road. There was an explosion and fire when the truck crashed at the bottom. Only a lamb and I survived. Not even all of me," she added, gesturing again to her face.

"My name is Shan," he said.

"I am Chenmo. Some of the older nuns are reciting death rites in secret, in one of the old hermit huts. I thought they were for Jamyang so I went last night to sit behind the hut and join in. When I heard them say her name the grief seized me so hard I could barely breathe."

"There are many ways to say good-bye."

Chenmo offered a small, sad nod. "They started the death rites for Jamyang after Uncle Lokesh stopped to speak with the nuns. He carried the body of the lama hermit on a mule. Now they say rites for two. I do not understand the day of blood." She paused and scrubbed at the tears on her cheeks. "He said to watch for a Chinese with eyes like deep wells and mud in his fingernails. He said that the man would wear purple numbers on his skin. Uncle Lokesh said we could trust him."

Day of blood. The terrible afternoon of murder and suicide would be marked indelibly in the mental calendars of the local people for years, maybe generations.

"I see everything but the numbers," Chenmo said, forcing a smile. "What did he mean?"

Shan rolled up his sleeve and extended his forearm.

"Oh!" Chenmo said with surprise in her voice, then again "Oh," more darkly, as she realized what they were. "Lokesh said you see secrets in deaths. Were you a murderer then?"

"No. Some ministers in Beijing felt safer if I was sent away. They didn't understand the blessing they were bestowing on me by sending me to a prison full of lamas and monks. I didn't either for the first few weeks. But eventually I was reincarnated."

Chenmo nodded, as if she understood perfectly. "We know Uncle Lokesh but we have never seen you before."

"I do not wish to disturb the tranquility of convents." Lokesh would always be welcome in such places, he knew, but not necessarily a Chinese with a government job, however menial.

"Not a convent. A hermitage for nuns. Not a place for visitors."

"But I was going to come. I have something to leave there."

When Chenmo did not respond he pointed to his truck, parked near the ledge above them. She rose and warily followed him, staying several steps behind. Her uncertainty disappeared as he reached under the dashboard and pulled out the gau he had retrieved from the dead woman. Chenmo's hand trembled as she accepted the silver amulet box, then she sobbed and clutched it tightly to her breast.

The gau seemed to release the tide of grief that had been swelling in the young novice. Tears began streaming down her cheeks. She let Shan lead her to a large flat boulder, where she sat weeping, staring at the gau in her hands.

After a few minutes he brought her a bottle of water from the truck and sat beside her as she drank.

"I am sorry," Chenmo said. "I tried not to cry in front of the nuns."

"I am sure they cried too, just in their own way," Shan said.

The young woman offered a melancholy smile.

"Did you ever help Abbess Tomo in the old ruins?" he asked.

When she nodded, he continued. "There were two other people with her, two others who were killed with her in the ruins. A Chinese man with tattoos and a foreigner. Did you know them?"

"No Chinese came, not to the ruins."

"But there was a foreigner."

Chenmo stared at the gau as she spoke. "Mother Tomo said not to speak of it. They were secret, brought in by secret people."

Shan weighed her words. There was more than one foreigner. "You mean the resistance. The purbas." The local Tibetan underground had taken to calling themselves after the dagger used in Tibetan ritual.

"They don't use any names. Dharamsala, is all. They say it like a password." It was the town in northern India that was the capital of the Tibetan government in exile. "Sometimes they come across from India. They work in the shadows and go back in shadow."

Shan had seen the secret ways. There were prayers brought from senior lamas and secret letters carried for families separated by the closing of the border. But there were also fuel trucks that mysteriously caught fire and pylons for remote power lines or phone towers that toppled in the night. Public Security might be obsessed with finding renegade monks but when they caught scent of such operatives they became rabid hounds. The most aggressive of the young resisters did not always adhere to the pacifist ways of their elders.

"She said think of them as phantoms, protector demons who can't be seen. Is that what you are?"

Shan shrugged. "I am just a former convict, here for all to see." As he digested her words, he grew more alarmed. "You mean the purbas brought in the Westerners?"

Chenmo stared at the old gau again, as if consulting it. "Jarman. Amerika," she said, using the Tibetan terms for Germany and the United States. "They make films. They told us if they could film the restoration project and show the film in the West it would protect it, that Beijing couldn't destroy it then."

"Why you?"

"Because it was ours. I mean the hermitage was part of the convent once. We are where the spark is kept alive, after the convent was bombed."

"And the foreigners were filming the restoration?"

"Yes. Using little cameras. Doing interviews."

"You mean video cameras?"

Chenmo shrugged and made a circle with a thumb and a finger and held it to her eye. "Little cameras." There were still many Tibetans, Shan reminded himself, who had little or no experience with modern technology, and little or no inclination to gain any.

"Were these foreigners staying at your hermitage?"

"These are dangerous times, the abbess would warn us. There are Chinese in the hills. Bonecatchers, and others who beat up farmers. We couldn't risk bringing them to Thousand Steps. Only a few of us at the hermitage were to know. She said if the government discovered we were harboring illegal foreigners they would destroy the hermitage, ship us all to prison." The northern townships of Lhadrung County were one of the regions of Tibet that were still off-limits to foreigners, because of their many prison camps.

Shan knew the young woman was still wary, that there were layers of secrets in places like hermitages, which had to be carefully peeled away one layer at a time. "Lokesh says we can learn much about what goes on inside Tibet by listening to those from outside. What were their names?"

"Rutger and Cora. They were never apart," she murmured, then quickly looked up, frowning, as if she had not intended to reveal the names.

"Rutger," Shan said. "Dark hair. Three or four inches taller than me. A square jaw."

"If you have met him, why ask?"

"I only met him briefly," Shan said. Without his face. Without his teeth. Without his life. "He is gone too, Chenmo, with the abbess."

Chenmo replied with a somber nod. She knew the German was dead.

"I worry about the woman Cora. All alone now. Do you know where she is?"

"Pray her screaming in the night stops. Pray for the silent," Chenmo replied. "Silence is how she must live now."

Shan did not understand. "You mean she is at the hermitage?"

But Chenmo just pointed to a butterfly. Without another word she rose. Only after she had followed it, drifting away, did he grasp what she had told him. Cora and Rutger were never apart. Cora was having screaming nightmares. She had to stay silent to stay alive. The missing American woman had witnessed the murders.

CHAPTER FIVE

Months earlier Shan had seen the trucks transporting people and equipment into the low hills beyond the Chinese settlement. But in a land of many prisons and constant military operations you learned not to make inquiries about strange convoys and stayed away from the dust clouds that marked new construction. He remembered pulling over for such a convoy and grimly reading the insignia on the escorting vehicles. Bureau of Religious Affairs, Beijing's favorite arm for turning Party dogma into ethnic propaganda. Public Security. The Institute for Tibetan Affairs, responsible for distributing the swelling ranks of Chinese immigrants and redistributing native Tibetans.

Clear Water Camp was one of the new relocation facilities, Lokesh had reported after he had encountered some of its residents digging for roots to eat. The government abhorred the nomads of the changtang, the high wilderness prairie that comprised much of central Tibet, for out in the vastness of the grasslands they were almost impossible to locate and even more difficult to control. They were, according to government fact-finding missions, hotbeds of Tibetan tradition. Settlements like Clear Water were built as transition communities, temporary stopping places where Tibetans were processed into lives that would be more aligned with the socialist cause.

As his truck crested the hill a gasp escaped Shan's lips. He halted, hands on the wheel. He had traveled across the changtang, had befriended some of the joyful, free-spirited nomads whose clans had called that wild land their home for hundreds, probably thousands, of years. The nomads had been corralled like sheep in a pen. Scores of small identical square buildings lay in rows before him, all with the same corrugated metal roofs and metal doors, the same single window and steel pipe chimney.

As he left his truck by the entrance a plump Chinese man bounded out of a long cinder block structure that apparently served as the camp's office.

He greeted Shan as if he were a long-awaited guest. "Comrade! Welcome to Clear Water Resettlement Camp!" He paused, glancing at Shan's truck, parked far enough way so that its faded government insignia was visible, but not the words underneath. "How may I assist?"

"Just a quick look on my own," Shan ventured, then turned to the man with a stern air. "How many do you account for here?"

"We accommodate one hundred and twenty-seven citizens, with room for dozens more. One of the great successes of redistribution."

"Successes?" Shan asked.

"Of course. We are able to administer medical care, provide dry sleeping quarters, provide two meals a day. Schoolteachers may arrive any day. None of which they had before. Sixty percent have already taken Chinese names, qualifying them for electrical feeds, so electrical distribution into households of reformed nomads is at unprecedented levels. Nearly half are taking the Chinese history modules sent by Beijing. Very encouraging statistics. We are passing out new bedding," he added, pointing to a pile of tattered sheets by the door of his office. "Historic breakthroughs."

Shan saw the empty stares of the Tibetan men and women who sat before the little huts. The encouraging statistics.

"Where do they work?"

"No need. They are provided for. Employment will be found for them in a few months, after they graduate from my finishing school," the manager explained, grinning at his own wit. "Some have found a few sheep to tend to. More like pets." The man gestured toward the administration building, the stuccoed wall of which was adorned with a mural of ebullient factory workers. "I have the numbers if you wish to review them. We are ahead of our quotas. Best performance in the entire prefecture."

Shan fought a shudder. "I think I will just look for myself," he said.

"Let me just lock up," the manager said.

"Alone."

"I don't usually let—"

"You would rather have me tell Colonel Tan you impeded my report?"

The man shrank back and shot a nervous glance up the road before retreating into his building.

None of the displaced shepherds would look at Shan as he walked down the first of the narrow streets. The little prefabricated structures, each the size of a small garage, had metal frames into which sheets of plywood had been inserted. Only a handful of the metal chimney pipes showed any smoke. Several of the inhabitants were cooking at small braziers by their doors. Electric wires dangled low between buildings. A woman carrying towels herded three children from a long squat structure at the end of the block, apparently the community washhouse. Half a dozen other women waited with buckets in a line at a spigot that was spitting up brown water.

Shan tried to look into the faces of the shepherds. Most turned their backs on him. An old man, sitting on a bench made of cinder blocks and planks, looked up from the block of wood he was carving. Shan sat beside him, offering the man a roll of hard candy he found in his pocket. The man accepted the token with a nod and returned to his work. He was whittling the figure of a sheep.

"Tell me, Grandfather, what became of your flocks?"

The man rubbed his stubble of whiskers before replying. "They waited until we had the flocks all gathered. We were preparing for our clan's lambing festival. Two sets of livestock trucks came that day. One set took the sheep, one took the shepherds. At some camps they just machine-gunned the animals, even the dogs. My granddaughter managed to get her puppy on the truck. The next day a soldier killed it with the butt of his gun. He told her it was just the right size for the army stew pot."

Shan glanced back at the administration building. The manager was watching him through a crack in the door. "I am sorry."

The man nodded again.

Shan studied the man's leathery, wrinkled face as he whittled. He was old, in his eighties or even nineties. "I traveled in the changtang once," Shan said. "For as far as I could see it was a sea of grass, rolling like waves in the wind. I don't think I ever felt so free."

"Some in our clan ran away that day. I was their headman. Rapeche they call me. They need me. I am worthless here. The soil of our lands flows in my blood. I tried to go back. Last month I started walking down the road but a day later the knobs picked me up." The old shepherd paused, then shrugged. "They gave us papers that say we have to stay in this county, unless we get their signature on a pass. Except they never give their signature."

They were in a prison without bars. Shan looked up and down the track between the houses. "Where are the young men and women?"

"The Chinese from the relocation office told all the families that their young had to serve the people. Sent to factories in China. I said to them we were people too, and they laughed. My granddaughter is in Guangdong now. She writes us once a month. She makes socks for sale in America. Works twelve, sometimes fourteen hours a day. Sleeps in a dormitory with two hundred other girls. She says she found an old temple and borrows a bicycle to ride there on her day off. She lights incense for us."

Two young boys ran past, kicking a tin can, then stopped near the spigot. One of the women had fallen to her knees, crying, as another kicked the spigot.

The headman frowned. "The fools who built this place knew nothing about campsites. No protection from the wind. Hardly any water. They drilled half a dozen wells and they all went dry but that one. Clear Water, my ass." He shrugged again. "They say they will leave a tank truck in the parking lot."

"I am looking for a man named Jigten. He has a limp."

"Which is why they wouldn't take him for the factories," Rapeche said. "His mother hardly has the strength to get out of bed. Her lungs are rattling. He does things to help her that she would never approve of, if she knew." He shrugged once more and kept whittling. "We do what we have to do to survive."

The hut the old man directed Shan to, the last in the northernmost row, appeared unoccupied. There were no coals in the brazier by the door, none of the carefully tended vegetable shoots that grew along the front walls of other huts. But from a rope fixed to a nail on the rear corner bits of cloth fluttered in the wind. Someone had turned their new sheet into prayer flags.

The flimsy door was ajar. Shan warily pushed it, and when there was no response he stepped inside. He passed through a small cubicle of a kitchen into the room that comprised the rest of the hut. Under the solitary window Jigten lay slumped against the wall, apparently passed out in exhaustion. Before him, an old woman lay on a pallet. Her leathery face spoke of great strength and determination, though it seemed to take great effort for her to move her head toward Shan. Despite her obvious sickness, her smile was welcoming. "We don't get many visitors to our tent," she said in a hoarse voice.

Shan offered the traditional greeting. *"Tashi delay."*

"I should make tea." Her voice was like sandpaper.

"I have had tea, Grandmother," he replied. "I like your prayer flags."

"Jigten worked on them all night, asking me to bless each one as he finished. I said that fat goat of a manager will be upset. But my son said once the flags were up the gods would make them invisible to officials."

Shan reached into his pocket to extract one of the little clay deities he had purchased at the market in Baiyun and pressed it into her hand.

The woman's grateful smile was broken by a series of hacking coughs. For the first time Shan saw the beads of sweat on her brow. She had a fever. On a stool beside her was a bowl of water and a cloth. He soaked the cloth, wrung it out, and wiped her forehead.

"I was on the changtang once," Shan said. "I saw herds of antelope. They moved like the wind across the grass. On my last day a big one, an old male, came up to me. He looked at me with an apologetic expression, like he was saying what a poor fool I was to have only two legs, then he sprinted away. I swear his hooves never touched the ground, he was just flying over the grass. I still have dreams about him."

"A chiru. His spirit mixed with yours. A good sign," the woman said, then began speaking of her youth, when the herds of antelope numbered in the tens of thousands.

Shan was wringing out the cloth for a third time when suddenly he heard a sharp gasp and Jigten leapt across the room as if to strike at him. His arm was already raised for Shan's jaw when he froze and looked down. His mother's bone-thin hand was wrapped around his ankle. "We have a hearth guest," she said in a chiding tone, as if Shan had just entered their yurt on the prairie.

"He's a Chinese!" Jigten protested. "An official!"

"No, he's something different," his mother insisted. "He saw the prayer flags. The spirit of a chiru dwells in his dreams."

Jigten sagged. He glanced upward, and for the first time Shan saw a plank laid over two cement blocks, the family altar. Sitting on it was the old bronze dakini Jamyang had given the thief. With a look of great sorrow he straightened and lifted the little statue, extending it to Shan.

"No," Shan said, refusing the altarpiece. "This is her place, watching over your hearth. A protector demoness."

"I think he came to speak with you, Son," the woman said.

The crippled thief gently tucked his mother's hand inside her blanket. "I could make some porridge," he said stiffly, for his mother's sake.

"I would be honored," Shan said. "On my next visit perhaps. Why did you go to Jamyang's shrine?"

Jigten's head snapped back toward his mother, his eyes wide in alarm. He did things the old woman would not approve of. "Sometimes things just appear when you need them," he said awkwardly.

"Why that day?"

The shepherd glanced at his mother, who stared expectantly at him, then frowned. He was not going to be able to lie in the presence of his dying mother. The shepherd's words came out in a whisper. "There was an old cairn by the highway. A truck had hit it. I saw him down there, rebuilding it."

Shan looked back at the old woman. He stole for medicine. If Jamyang had known, he would have given him most of the items on his altar. He gestured Jigten toward the kitchen before asking his next question. "You talked about outsiders buying cans of food and blankets. You were selling things to foreigners. A German man and an American woman. Where did you meet them?"

Jigten frowned. "We were working at the old convent, hauling debris. Two or three times I saw them there. Once on the hills above, taking photographs. There's a shepherd girl with a scarred face who wants to be a nun. She watches over them."

"Where were they staying?"

"They always came from the direction of the hermitage, with that girl acting like their guide."

"What did you sell them?"

"Some ropes and food. Some blankets."

"Where would you get such things?"

"Mostly from the Jade Crows. I do odd jobs for them. They deliver supplies to the pacification camps. Sometimes I drive or do repair work for them."

Shan looked at him in surprise. "But the camps are run by the People's Armed Police. You mean they have a contract with the police?"

"Sure. The green apes. They run the camps, they provide the trucks."

He considered the shepherd's words. "The Chinese men who disturb the farms in the hills. It's the Jade Crows, doing the work of the police."

Jigten shrugged. "Like I said, they have some kind of arrangement. The police prefer not to go up into the hills. They get bitten by dogs. They hear the phantom horns. They get hounded by ghosts."

"An arrangement with the Armed Police," Shan said, thinking out loud. "But not with local Public Security."

Jigten offered no reply. Shan needed none. Those who had attacked Meng in town held Public Security in contempt. Meng had not only been attacked, she had lied about it as if she feared reporting it. He hesitated a moment, puzzling again over why she had been attacked. Not even the most arrogant gangs would risk assaulting a knob without a good reason.

"Our headman Rapeche made a protection charm for the manager," Jigten said abruptly, speaking toward the shadows at the back of the room. "That fat one at the gate. He gets frightened sleeping alone in that concrete building. Old Tibetan ghosts rise up in the night to haunt the Chinese in this valley," he added with an air of satisfaction. "He confided in Rapeche after that, said we won't stay here forever. More trucks will arrive. They will break us up and take us away to Chinese cities. They say there are entire blocks where nothing green grows, where the wind is full of grease and chemicals. Then we'll look back at this place as a happy time. At least here we still have most of the clan together."

He cast a worried glance at Shan, as if remembering who his visitor was.

"*Lha gyal lo,*" Shan whispered in a pained voice.

"You don't know what's happening in Tibet. Before long, Tibet will be nothing but camps and the keepers of camps." Jigten's voice grew hollow. "They converted an old army base to a pacification camp on the other side of the mountain. The police bring in another truckload of Tibetans almost every week. That don't call it a prison but that place has razor wire and guards with guns. It's a cage with no way out. Last month they started a graveyard there."

As he spoke voices were raised in alarm outside. Jigten shot up and ran out the door, Shan a step behind.

A man on the low ridge above the camp was shouting frantically, pointing down the valley. The Chinese manager was at the front gate now, crying out in his high-pitched voice, ordering everyone to return to their huts. The shepherds ignored him and ran up the ridge.

Shan arrived at the top of the ridge panting, his gaze following the arm of a nearby shepherd as the man pointed first to the line of dense, black clouds rolling off the sacred mountain and then to the red and blue flashes in Baiyun. The town was more than a mile away but the blinking lights of police cars were plainly visible. A line of shadow was moving across the fields. Half the population of the town seemed to be fleeing their homes.

Shan ran to his truck.

He saw more than a dozen police cars as he reached the town, and half a dozen big trucks, all troop carriers of the People's Armed Police, the green apes who did the heavy lifting for Public Security. He didn't have to look for Meng. She stepped in front of his truck, then climbed into the passenger seat, as if for protection. Police were swarming in and out of the buildings, herding the few remaining inhabitants into the central square, while other officers stood at the edge of the field, blowing whistles at the retreating residents.

Meng gestured to the chaos. "Welcome to our model Pioneer community," she said. "If Major Liang had his way he'd probably burn the town down."

"I don't understand."

"The bodies. Late yesterday someone stole the bodies."

Shan considered her words. "Late yesterday," he pointed out, "someone attacked you. The constables came running, leaving that meat locker unattended."

"The owner of the store has fled. Only one thing keeps Liang from arresting the whole town."

"Officially the murders haven't taken place," Shan inserted. "Hard to explain arrests for stealing murder victims when no murder has been reported."

"Exactly." Meng was watching the dark clouds that were rapidly overtaking the town. "We don't want to put a blemish on the heroic faces of our Pioneers. We just—"

At first Shan thought Meng was interrupted by someone throwing stones at his truck. Then the sound was more like rifle shots, accelerating into a machine-gun staccato. People began crying out in pain, flinching, clutching at their arms and shoulders as if they were being stung. Some of the immigrants dropped to the ground, curling up with their hands over their heads. Others ran, dashing for the nearest cover.

Hailstorms in Tibet came quickly and left just as quickly but they always brought with them destruction and terror, sometimes even death. Shan looked back toward Clear Water Camp. The ridge was empty. The dropka might ignore the orders of their camp manager but they knew how to read clouds.

Shan pulled his wide-brimmed hat low on his head and leapt out of the truck. He grabbed two of the buckets from the back and ran toward the fields. He pulled up an old man who had fallen to his knees, blood running from the hands that shielded his face, then held a bucket over the man's head. The man gasped in confusion, then grabbed the bucket and pointed to a woman who had fallen a few feet away.

"I have her!" Shan shouted over the roar of the storm, then pulled the woman to her feet and covered her head with the second bucket. They ran, like most of the people in the fields, toward the open-walled pavilion that had been erected for the market. As Shan pushed the woman inside and turned back toward the field, the hail abruptly stopped.

People were crying. A donkey brayed. Dogs were barking. The police seemed to have forgotten their search and were climbing back into their trucks. Several stared dumbfounded at their cars. Most of their rooftop light fixtures were in pieces. Three windshields had been shattered. Voices, some frantic, crackled on their radios. One constable, a Tibetan, stared somberly toward the huge mountain that hovered over the valley. The angry storm had come from Yangon, home of the deities who protected the valley.

Shan searched the crowd, spotted the grey-haired man with the wire-rimmed glasses he had seen playing checkers and followed him to a small bungalow on the side street behind the town's modest teahouse.

As the man paused at his front door to speak with a neighbor, Shan quickly circled the house and entered the rear door. He was sitting in the kitchen when the man entered. He did not seem surprised to see a stranger in his house.

"Your men already searched here," the man said in a level voice. "You can see we have few possessions and even less space to hide anything." His voice trailed away as he noticed Shan's muddy boots and tattered work clothes.

Shan did not speak. He reached into his pocket and set the little jade dragon from Jamyang's altar on the table in front of him. "You can buy these from stalls off Tiananmen Square for forty renminbi. A genuine relic from the Kang Xi emperor, the vendors will say, and the tourists never know any better. But my instinct says this is not a reproduction."

The man sank into a chair, his gaze fixed on the little dragon. "So you're here to tell me it belongs to the state," he declared in a tight voice. His long, thin face seemed to grow weary as he spoke.

Shan studied the man for a long moment, his eyes were deep, uncertain pools. There was great intelligence in them, and also a hint of fear. "My father had a small collection of seals from the imperial times," Shan explained, "which he cherished. When I was very young he would take me in the closet and show them to me with a candle, exclaiming over the history they must have witnessed. Sometimes he would visit antique stalls in the market, hoping to find a document with a seal print that would match. But by then the Red Guard had burned nearly all the imperial documents. When we were sent for reeducation in the country he buried them in a field and never was able to recover them. Probably long since destroyed by a bulldozer."

The man stared at Shan. "It was one of a matching pair," he ventured at last. "I had to trade the other years ago for medicine when my daughter first became ill."

Shan pushed the intricately worked seal across the table to the man, who stroked it with a gentle hand, gazing at it with a sad smile. He pushed it back to Shan as a police radio barked from the street outside. "It is not safe here. If those goons had found it today they would have stomped it under a heel and laughed. It has a new guardian in the mountains."

"Jamyang is dead," Shan stated.

The man's eyes widened in alarm. "No. Not Jamyang. He knows how to survive."

"I was with him when he killed himself."

The man's face twisted in pain, draining of color. He pressed a fist against his mouth as if to stifle a sob, then dropped his head into his hands. "I think I shall make some tea," he declared with a sigh.

"I am called Yuan Guo," the stranger explained as he waited for his hot plate to boil water. "I raise goats."

Shan paused a moment. There had been another Yuan, on the tablet in the mountains. "I am called Shan Tao Yun," Shan replied. "I inspect ditches, which means mostly I dig mud and manure. I didn't always inspect ditches. You didn't always raise goats."

Yuan's expression began to warm. "In Harbin," he said, referring to one of the large cities of Manchuria, "I was a professor of history, ever since the university was reopened twenty-five years ago. I decided to join the Pioneer program. The state promises me land rights if I stay five years. And meanwhile"—he gestured about the sparse, cold room—"I get all this." He lifted a fork and began chipping leaves from a brick of tea. From a room down the darkened hall came the sound of coughing.

"I met an old relative of yours, Yuan Yi. I want to bring him back to you."

Yuan's hand froze in midair as he spun about to face Shan. "You mustn't!" he cried out, then he seemed to collect himself and turned back to silently sprinkle the leaves into two chipped cups before joining Shan at the table. "Please," he said in a low, plaintive voice. "He must stay on the mountain. He too is in exile."

Shan waited until his cup was filled, then spoke through the steam of his cup. "Perhaps you should start with Harbin."

Professor Yuan Guo had lived most of his life in Harbin, he explained, and had been a graduate student at the university there until it had been shut down by Mao, then worked at a locomotive factory until the university had reopened. He had helped establish the Chinese history department and had married another professor, who had worked in a chemical factory during her reeducation. She had died of cancer ten years later. Yuan had raised his daughter alone, then had retired four years earlier and enjoyed a peaceful existence reviewing old manuscripts in the university library until his daughter Sansan had been arrested for antigovernment activity on the Internet. "She faced a few months imprisonment but Public Security asserted what they called aggravating circumstances. She was identified as ringleader in a group of prodemocracy advocates. All were children of the retired professors in our building. There was a meeting, the kind we used to call criticism sessions. We were found to be politically irresponsible. If Mao had still been alive we would have been branded hooligans and paraded in dunce caps."

Shan sipped his tea. "My family was sent to the rice paddies for being in the Stinking Ninth," he said, referring to the most reprehensible of Mao's infamous list of bad elements, the intellectuals.

Yuan grinned, leaned forward, and began his tale in more detail. They were two old soldiers sharing stories of the war. Yuan had specialized in the history of Imperial China, his wife in Western history. Their daughter had graduated from the university with a degree in anthropology and had been working for a Western computer company for two years when she had been arrested at an Internet café. The café owner had been arrested the week before for failing to record the identification cards of all the Internet users in his café and negotiated his freedom by agreeing to help Public Security snare his customers.

"We were told we could have our children sentenced to long prison terms or we could all join the Pioneer program. Each family in our building was told to report to the train station at three A.M. with no more than a hundred pounds of belongings."

"Surely not the entire building?"

"We were a special case, a building of professors or retired professors, with children who had grown up well educated and well versed in Internet democracy." Internet democracy. It was one of the

terms of the new age, for those who practiced dissidence anonymously over the Internet. Except the government had learned ways
to make sure no one could use the Internet anonymously. "We were
contaminating the educational environment, someone in the Party
said. They wanted us gone. From the university. From the city. From
Manchuria. Some of my colleagues tend to think it was because a
land developer in the Party wanted to level the building and erect a
high-rise."

"Everyone agreed to go to Tibet?"

Yuan offered his sad grin again. "We were put on a train. We had
escorts. We had no idea where we were going. Nostalgic in a way.
Like old times." He meant the years under Mao when entire city
blocks were simply ordered to the new Chinese cities being built in
the Muslim and Buddhist lands of western China.

Shan cocked his head in disbelief. "You're saying the government
kept a cell of dissidents intact and just transplanted them?"

"They knew where we were going. A high-altitude wilderness.
Barely enough for us to subsist on. They were confident Tibet would
break us. We could do no harm here. And the Party had set ambi-
tious goals for the number of new Pioneer settlements. They were
having trouble filling their quotas."

"But the life of a retired professor in Harbin . . ." Shan's voice
trailed away. Both men knew what he meant. Professors labored
their entire careers at low pay because of the privileges they were assured at the end, the comfortable housing, the open access to university resources, the ability to study and write what they wished, the
appointment to prestigious committees.

"My daughter Sansan has always been frail. She never would have
survived prison. Now we have daily walks in the fresh air. The goats
give us milk. She gets stronger every day."

"Professors and Jade Crows. Quite the socialist experiment."

"More than ninety percent of us are from Harbin. The others are
from the jungles of Yunnan Province."

"Criminals who bribed their way into exile instead of prison," Shan suggested.

A sliver of a smile creased the professor's face. "We prefer to think of them as a tropical social club with wanderlust. The prisons of Yunnan are quite overcrowded I hear."

"But already they have begun to—" Shan's words were cut off by new shouting in the street. Yuan darted to his front window.

More police were visible now, pushing apart a stack of trash cans, opening the backs of vehicles. As an officer in grey began walking toward his front door, a small gasp escaped Yuan's throat. He quickly stepped to his dining table, grabbed a roll of paper, and sank into one of the two easy chairs in the room, hiding the roll in the small of his back as he picked up a book to read. As he did so a thin woman in her late twenties ran out of what Shan took to be a bedroom. A computer screen lit up at her touch and keys rattled as Yuan's daughter quickly worked the keyboard, then withdrew what Shan took to be a memory card and darted back into the bedroom.

The knob sergeant did not bother to knock or announce himself. He threw open the door and glared at the professor, his eyes full of challenge. "Our house is open to you," the professor said as he looked up from his book, then went back to reading.

"Of course it is," the officer spat, then gestured two companions inside and down into the other rooms. He began roaming the main chamber, lifting books, pulling back cushions stacked against a wall. Faint martial tones rose from the darkened corner. Sansan had brought up one of the patriotic Web sites of the Party, where soldiers and factory workers paraded twenty-four hours a day.

The officer opened the closet by the door, then kicked up a corner of the carpet as if he might discover a trapdoor. As he stepped into the kitchen he tapped walls, even opened the refrigerator. "It's broken," he announced, lifting out a box of salt crisps and a book.

"It's never worked," Yuan said cheerfully. "But it's a great status symbol. Tibetans never have them."

The officer nodded his approval. His men appeared. As the three marched out the kitchen door, the officer gave orders to search the little toolshed at the rear of the yard.

"They searched your house twice today," Shan observed as Yuan stepped to the door, watching the knobs as they entered the shed then, moments later, left his yard. "Was it Public Security both times?"

"I don't know," Yuan said with a worried glance back toward the bedroom. "No. The first were just some of those Armed Police. They ordered us all out on the street with megaphones. They're not as subtle."

"Bodies from a murder scene were stolen from the store's meat locker. The first time they were trying to find them."

The professor returned Shan's gaze without expression. He knew about the murders. Shan looked back to the grey vehicles on the street, then surveyed the room again. "The Armed Police were looking for dead bodies," Shan observed. "But these knobs were looking for a live one."

The professor said nothing, just frowned, opened the door, and gestured Shan out of his house.

CHAPTER SIX

Shan watched the high ridge with worry as he walked back to his truck. The night before, Lokesh had not been at the little house in the hills they had claimed for their home. He should have returned by now. Had his old friend stayed with the flesh cutters to perform more rituals for his dead friend? Or was he back at Jamyang's shrine now, purifying it after the stain of suicide? Shan prayed that he had stayed with the flesh cutters. The upper valley was overflowing with police. Meng had reported that Liang was already dispatching patrols into the high valleys. The long prayer horns had sounded again at dawn, as if taunting the searchers. They would keep expanding their search. The gentle old Tibetan would be like fresh meat before such hungry dogs.

He was lost in his worries as he opened the door and settled behind the wheel, was not even aware of the youth waiting beside him until the tattooed hand seized his wrist.

"You're taking me for a ride," the stranger growled. A long folding knife, a switchblade, appeared in his other hand. He did not bother to open it. "Exactly where I say, Old Mao. No questions."

Old Mao. It was slang of the Chinese cities, used by street gangs for grey-suited bureaucrats.

Shan turned toward the stranger. He was barely out of his teens, not much younger than his own son, who had once led a street gang. He had seen him before, carrying a sack of rice. "If you raised your sleeve," Shan asked conversationally, "would I see a black bird?"

The back of the stranger's hand slammed into his jaw. It was answer enough. Shan shook off the pain and started the truck.

Like so many others in the county, the old farm compound had been abandoned years earlier, a victim of the early campaigns against landowners after the Chinese army had arrived. The fields had gone to brush and small trees, the stone stable at the top of the old pasture above the house had weeds growing out of its roof. A crib for storing grain had been partially dismantled. To one side a tall roof had been raised on poles, under which the cabs of two heavy trucks were parked. A man with grease on his face looked up from an open engine compartment as Shan pulled to a stop.

The house, built in the traditional style with quarters for animals below and humans above, also seemed to have been untouched for years. Its windows were cracked, the protector deity painted on the wall by the entry so faded as to be almost unrecognizable. But inside, a fresh coat of whitewash reflected the light of several hanging lanterns.

Two Chinese youths at the end of the chamber looked up as Shan was pushed toward the staircase. One, with a cigarette dangling from his lips, held a knife in his hand, the other was extracting a knife from the wall. An old cloth *thangka*, a painting of one of the sacred female dakinis elegantly rendered in shades of blue and gold, had been hung as a target. She was torn and sliced into fragments. They had been throwing their blades at her head. For a moment Shan forgot everything else as he stared at the scene. He fought the temptation to dart forward and pull the painting from the wall. Lokesh would have stood in front of the dakini to protect her.

One of the youths noticed Shan's expression. His lips curled in a sneer. "*Cao ni mai!*" "Fuck your mother."

His escort pushed him up the stairs, into what could have passed for a brothel in any eastern city. The plank walls of the upper floor were covered with gaudy silk screen hangings, images of fighting dragons, fighting roosters, fighting serpents, and scantily clad women frolicking with pandas. The scent of onions and steamed rice mingled with incense, not Tibetan ritual incense but a cloying mix of jasmine and cinnamon. A bright lantern was suspended over a table where four men played mahjong.

"They say you know that lama who lives alone up on the mountain." The man who spoke waved the others from the table. He was in his forties, a compact figure with long black hair and the hard, small face of a jungle warrior.

Shan took a seat across from him before replying. "Since when do the Jade Crows care about hermits?"

"Back home we count monks among our best customers."

"You're a long way from Yunnan." Shan glanced at the other men, who stood in the shadows as if awaiting orders.

"Fresh mountain air. It does us all good." The man lit a cigarette.

"The lama was a friend of mine. He died."

The stranger hesitated. "Died? Jamyang died? When?"

"The same day as those at the convent. I didn't know the others."

The man's eyes flattened as he studied Shan, like those of a coiling snake. "You only got to know them after they died. You stood over them at the convent, sought them out in that meat locker, sought out naked dead people. Back home we could arrange for you to do it on a weekly basis. Big money in fetishes." He exhaled a plume of smoke in Shan's face. "Except it was my brother you treated like a piece of meat."

"I do not know what happened to the bodies if that's what you want to know."

"The head of our clan deserved better."

The head of the clan. The dead man had been the head of the Jade Crows. "No one deserves to have their head cut from their neck," Shan replied.

The words brought a snarl to the man's face.

Shan glanced at the cold, expectant faces of the men who watched him. Early in his career Shan had pursued an investigation to Yunnan, where much of the population was only two or three generations removed from the warrior tribes who once ruled the province's jungles. His case had been dropped after his informant had been tortured and killed. Bamboo splints had been pounded under the man's fingernails before his throat had been slashed. Shan had insisted on seeing the photographs of the dead man, and paid for it with several sleepless nights. "I am not the killer."

"You?" the gang leader spat with a cold laugh. "Three competitors jumped my brother once and he sent one to his grave and the others to the hospital. I am Lung Tso. My brother was Lung Ma. People in Kunming quake at the name of the Lung brothers." Lung studied Shan in silence, taking in his tattered clothes. "A man like you doesn't take out a Jade Crow."

"What kind of man does?" Shan asked.

Lung's hand reached below the table. There was a blur of movement and his fist hammered a dagger into the table an inch from Shan's hand. Shan did not move. "You were not brought here to ask *us* questions! I want what is ours returned!"

"I am the ditch inspector for the northern townships. You have me confused with someone else."

Shan braced himself as Lung sprang from his chair. He pulled the dagger from the wood then aimed the point at Shan's throat. "You may wear the clothes of a ditch inspector and drive the truck of the ditch inspector but I can see your eyes. And you were at the old convent with those bodies. We can see you talking with that damned knob lieutenant. You are no ditch inspector. Why would a ditch inspector be at the murder scene? You're a fucking informer. Who do you work for? Not the Armed Police, I know that much."

"I take that to mean the Armed Police told you I was at the convent," Shan replied. He remembered now, with new worry, that Liang has sent one of the olive-coated men to stand at the gate. Shan had been seen while he had been examining the bodies.

Lung Tso flipped the dagger in the air, catching it by the handle without taking his eyes from Shan.

"I have a certificate of appointment signed by the county governor. Colonel Tan. Surely you are acquainted with him." Shan could not imagine Tan allowing such immigrants into his county without a personal introduction, to gauge his new inhabitants and demonstrate the tight reins he kept on his county.

Lung winced. "Ironfist Tan they used to call him. The prick came to town and ordered us to stand before him in the square like we were new recruits. He looked old. More like Rusty Fist now."

"He could still pound you into the ground without even blinking."

Lung's nod was so subtle Shan barely saw it. He did not see the stick that slammed into his cheek from over his shoulder. He gasped, unprepared for the stinging pain, and turned to see the youth who had escorted him from town holding a thin length of bamboo. As Shan watched, he reached to a wall hook and pulled down a leather-bound baton that ended in a cluster of wires bent into jagged angles at their ends. Pioneers were not allowed much baggage, but the Kunming settlers had managed to bring their tools with them.

"You met Genghis," Lung said with a thin smile, gesturing to the youth.

Shan struggled to keep his voice level. "He doesn't strike me as Mongolian."

"He just likes the name. A bloodthirsty bastard who made sure everyone in the known world respected his clan."

As if on cue Genghis slammed the end of the baton against the back of a chair. It splintered the wood. Shan did not bother to wipe away the blood that dripped down his cheek. He watched the wires of the baton. If they hit his face they could take out an eye.

Lung muttered a curt syllable and suddenly hands were all over

Shan, pulling him up, searching his pockets, turning down his socks, then dumping the contents of his pockets on the table. His truck keys. His pocketknife. A blue stone he had rubbed smooth during his years of imprisonment. Short sticks of incense. The remaining clay deity he had bought in Baiyun. Lung Tso picked up the figurine, then the stone, studying each for a moment before setting it down. It was as if, Shan realized, the gang leader didn't know exactly what he was looking for. "Perhaps if you told me what you seek," he offered.

Lung slapped him. "Who the fuck are you?" he demanded. He slammed his fist down on the little deity, smashing it into dust, then hooked a finger toward the men behind him and strong arms slammed Shan back into his chair. Genghis pulled open Shan's shirt then paused, lifting out the small gau Shan wore around his neck. It quieted the gang for a moment. A spirit box, many Chinese called such amulets. The people of Yunnan were known to be superstitious.

"There were three bodies in the refrigerator," Shan stated. He tried to appear unconcerned about his gau. The only thing he had taken from Lung Ma's body was inside the amulet box.

"I know of only two. I want what is ours returned," Lung repeated.

He knew of only two. Meng had been attacked and the constables had come running to her, leaving the bodies unguarded. If he sought something belonging to a murder victim the first place to look would be with the body but Lung knew it was not with the body.

"I don't care what kind of arrangement you have with the Armed Police. Those bodies are the concern of a special Public Security squad. They will declare war on the Jade Crows if they think you have their bodies."

Lung stared in silence.

"And there *were* three," Shan repeated. "Your brother. A nun. And a foreigner. Find out what they had in common and we will find their killer."

"We?" Lung spat.

"I told you. My friend also died that day. He is dead because of those murders. He died unsettled. I told him I would find a way to resolve things."

The men holding Shan released him and backed away. Lung shot a nervous glance toward them. The dark, thick forests of Yunnan were famous for their ghosts. "You told him?" he asked uneasily. "He's dead."

"In Tibet the spirits of those who die violent deaths wander forlornly until there is resolution." His captors did not object as he began to return the items on the table to his pockets. "They are called *jungpo*. Hungry ghosts. They like the night. They like to hound those who owe them something."

The words brought another long silence. Genghis cursed under his breath and retreated another step.

Only Lung seemed unaffected. "A Chinese helping some dead Tibetan? I don't think so. More like a goddamned informant scavenging for loot."

"My friend Jamyang. The abbess. Your brother. They're all jungpo now. The old convent isn't so far from here. Lung Ma will probably wander back this way looking for you. What will you tell him when he asks why he had to die? What will be your promise when he demands his killer be found?"

Lung glanced again at his men. Shan's words had clearly unsettled them. The dagger in his hand shot forward again, embedding in the table against Shan's hand, raising a trickle of blood. "It's you my brother will come after if you keep interfering," he growled, lifting the blade. Shan went very still as the point touched his wrist and pushed up his sleeve as though searching for a blood vessel. It stopped at the tattooed number on Shan's forearm. A cruel grin split Lung's face. "*Lao gai?*" he asked, using the term for hard-labor punishment, the worst of Lhadrung's prisons.

Shan silently nodded.

"How long?"

"Five years."

"Where?"

"The Four hundred and fourth People's Construction Brigade. Thirty miles south of here."

Lung grinned. "Perfect. Good as an admission that you are a killer and a thief."

Shan watched in surprise as Lung withdrew the blade then produced a pencil and scrap of paper and wrote down the number. "If you had something to do with my brother's death I will see that you take days to die," he growled.

Lung tucked the paper into his pocket, then tilted his knife and sliced a long, wide splinter off the edge of the tabletop, and then methodically cut it into five smaller, flat splinters that he lay in front of him. As he did so one of the men behind him gripped Shan's wrist and forced it open, spreading his fingers on the table. "This is what I will tell my brother we are doing if he comes asking. This is how Jade Crows deal with informers." He looked back to Genghis. "Vodka," he barked, as if settling in for the evening's entertainment.

The gang leader stared at Shan until the youth brought him the bottle and poured him a glass. He downed half of it in one swallow before speaking again. "The sun has gone down. We have all night. First," Lung said in a matter-of-fact tone, "you will tell me where it is, what that damned lama gave my brother." He opened the drawer in the table, extracted a small hammer and lifted one of the long splints, then paused, looking up in confusion. One of the hangings with the dragons was pulsing with red light.

Genghis pulled the hanging back to expose a window. He cursed. "The knob bitch!"

Lieutenant Meng was leaning against her car when they brought Shan out, a police radio in her hand, held like a weapon. Over her shoulder a portable police strobe was flashing. Another car, with two constables, waited down the lane. Genghis shoved him toward Meng and retreated.

"Follow me," was all she said.

His hand shook so badly he had trouble inserting the key into the ignition. He sped out of the farm compound, fishtailing in the gravel. As the farm disappeared behind a hill he stopped, clenching the wheel, and a sob escaped his throat. Jigten was right. He did not understand what had been happening in Tibet. The Tibet he knew did not have Chinese gangs living in remote valleys, did not have Chinese intellectuals living in tracts of shabby cottages. Like his Tibetan friends he had lived on the fringes too long, trying to ignore the long convoys of immigrants, the opening of the rail line to Lhasa that was bringing in colonists by the thousands. The Tibet he had come to know was occupied Tibet, with millions of Tibetans controlled by small armed pockets of Chinese, where there had been no doubt that Tibet could step forward with its own culture once those pockets had been removed. But that Tibet was being consumed from the inside out.

He realized that Meng's car had also stopped, waiting for him. The Tibet he had known also did not have Public Security officers who helped him. He pressed his hands on the wheel, calming himself. "When the world has turned upside down," Lokesh had once told him, "just turn a somersault and find a new way to stand." He wiped the blood from his hand and put the truck back into gear.

Meng led him back to town, into the gravel lot beside the police post. "How did you know I was there?" he asked when they climbed out of their vehicles.

"One of the constables said that Genghis was in your truck. He's the little prick Lung sends to summon people." She took a step and pointed him toward the teahouse on the corner that served as the town's sole café.

"I need a map of Tibet and a flashlight," he said, reaching to open his gau.

She frowned, not hiding her impatience, then stepped back to her car and handed him a map and a light.

Shan quickly located the towns on Jamyang's list, the paper Lung Tso had meant to torture him for. They were all border towns, on roads that led across the Tibetan border to Nepal, India, and Bhutan. When he looked up, Meng was standing at his shoulder. "I've been ordered to arrange for more pressure in the hills," she declared in a tight voice as she gestured again toward the teahouse.

"Pressure?"

"Reconnaissance in force they call it. Anyone who does not co-operate gets detained. The owner of the teahouse has been held for questioning."

"Why?"

"Failure to maintain a complete record of those who use the Internet connections at his tables. New patrols are going out. Someone is knocking down the new road signs in Chinese. Yesterday an Armed Police patrol stopped a farmer and when he couldn't produce his papers they shot the yak he was taking to market."

"Those four-legged splittists are particularly troublesome."

Meng frowned again. "The constables were ordered to go out and bring it back, for the kitchen at district headquarters. They reported that they couldn't find it."

Shan stepped to the beat-up sedan parked beside Meng's car, the vehicle used by the constables. He ran the flashlight beam along the body of the car, then plucked a tuft of long black fibers from the seam where the trunk met the body. Meng said nothing as he raised the hairs in the beam of light, then let them drift away in the wind. She had known the constables had found the yak, and probably returned the meat to the farmer. She had known and wanted him to know she knew.

For a few heartbeats they stared at each other, then she nodded toward the rear door of the teahouse. "And I have been ordered to find those who are playing those damned horns in the hills. We have decided they are unpatriotic."

Shan hesitated as they reached the building. "And ordered to find me?"

Her answer was to open the door.

The little café was dark except for a single table in the center, under a naked lightbulb hanging from the ceiling. Major Liang sat in front of a file on the table, staring at the ember of his cigarette. Meng settled into the chair across from the major and looked up at Shan. *He should run. He should find Lokesh and hole up in a cave for few months' meditation.* With every instinct screaming against it, Shan sat down.

"I only get assigned to very special projects," Liang declared, speaking to his cigarette. "Three years ago a monastery went on strike five days before a scheduled visit by some foreign diplomats. The monks thought the visit gave them some leverage over us. They tore up their loyalty oaths, put up a picture of their damned splittist leader. So I was called in. By the end of the first day, the monks were en route to ten different prisons, never to see one another again. By the end of the second, bulldozers had leveled the monastery. By the end of the fourth day, all the rubble was hauled away and I had new highway maps printed showing a blank space where the monastery had been. When we intercepted the dignitaries we apologized and explained there had been a foolish mistake, crossed wires in the planning. We showed them the empty map and took them to a tame monastery where the monks greeted them by singing patriotic songs. After everyone was gone I brought in ten truckloads of salt and covered the old site. Nothing will grow there for decades." He finally looked up at Shan. "I got a medal and a promotion for that."

"Surely a man of your talents belongs in Beijing," Shan observed in a flat voice.

"But I so deeply enjoy what I do. I am a field commander, not a paper pusher. I am due in a week to address some new problems in Rutok," he declared, referring to the county in far western Tibet whose number of prisons and internment camps rivaled even those of Lhadrung County. "Another damned monk immolated himself. A clear sign of poor discipline on the part of the local authorities," he added, his eyes lingered on Meng, who would not meet his gaze. "I don't have a lot of time. Let's say six days."

"I asked for help with forensics from Lhasa," Meng began. "They won't—"

Liang raised his hand to cut her off. "I am ever aware of your district's failure to efficiently deal with evidence, Lieutenant. No matter how long we give you, you'll just complete your analysis and declare there's not enough to go on." Liang blew twin jets of smoke from his nostrils. "The murders were committed by a Tibetan lama named Jamyang. A renegade living alone in the mountains, seeking ways to advance the splittist cause."

Shan could not bring himself to meet Liang's gaze. He spoke toward the ashtray at Liang's elbow, filled with crushed butts. "The murders were not a political statement."

"You're wasting my time then. Lieutenant Meng said you know about the Tibetans." The major reached behind his chair into an open briefcase and laid a stone of the table. "Tell me what it is."

Shan clenched his jaw. He had seen the stone, pressing down on dead hands at the convent. "An old weathered rock."

Liang repeated his words like a rifle shot. "Tell me what it is."

"A decorative stone, probably from an old temple or shrine."

"You truly are worthless, Meng," Liang spat. "You would have me waste time with this—"

"A carving of a sacred sign," Shan inserted.

Liang slowly nodded. Shan realized the major had been testing him. Liang lifted the stone, staring intensely at it now as if it were about to reveal all the dark secrets of the valley. "This murderer had a complex mind, Comrade. Starts by laying out the signs of dissent, dead men on a Chinese flag, boots on a Tibetan. The first reaction of anyone would be that it was a dissident. But then he left just enough evidence to identify the woman as a nun. Once that was known it couldn't be a Tibetan. So we must find a lunatic Chinese killer. Except, Comrade," Liang said, looking at Shan over the stone now, "except for this stone. He couldn't resist the temptation, like a private little boast. The police would never see the point. Too subtle. He had to gloat, had to seek out the stone. Did you know there is an old building at the rear whose floor is covered with fragments of carved stone? He went all the way back there just to fetch his stone. Not any stone. Why this stone, Comrade Shan?"

Shan was filled with foreboding over the strange game Liang played. "It is one of the Eight Auspicious Signs."

"Which exactly?"

Shan hesitated. "The Banner of Victory. To celebrate the triumph of Buddhist wisdom over ignorance."

Liang offered a thin smile. He had known already, Shan was certain. He had to admit that the major at least had hit upon the conundrum of the murders. No Tibetan would ever kill the abbess. No Chinese would ever leave the banner stone.

"And except for you there's probably not a Chinese within a hundred miles who knows that. It was a sign for Tibetans. The killer was Tibetan. You still haven't told me about that renegade lama. This splittist Jamyang who lives like an outlaw in our mountains. The enemy of our motherland. We would have paid a rich bounty for him even before this tragedy."

The major held his gaze on Shan. It was not an official explanation yet. Liang was testing his story. Shan returned the stare without blinking. "Jamyang is dead."

"You speak with some confidence, Comrade."

"He is dead."

Liang stared at Shan for a long moment. "How convenient for him."

"I doubt he felt that way." Shan broke away from the grip of Liang's eyes, and watched the headlights of a passing truck. A new warning burst into his consciousness. If Colonel Tan walked through the door at that moment, while Shan was stealing confidences from Public Security, he would be back inside one of Tan's prisons by the end of the day.

"I want his body."

Shan shrugged. "Bodies have a way of disappearing in this valley. They say the bodies of certain lamas get lifted on a rainbow into the heavens. These Tibetan gods work in mysterious ways."

The fire in Liang's eyes flared red-hot. "I already know who the gods of this valley are. Do you have to be taught that like one more stubborn Tibetan?"

Shan glanced back at Meng, who gazed uneasily into her folded hands, then out the window again, this time looking at the high ridge above the town. In his mind's eye he could see the familiar image of Jamyang brimming with joy as he found a new patch of spring flowers. The lama would laugh to know that his death might be used to rid the valley of a man like Liang.

"There is no reason for you to miss your engagement in Rutok, Major," Shan suggested. "The Bureau's perpetrator is dead. Case closed. Political discord once again ends in tragedy." It was the parable-like ending that Beijing always coveted.

Liang's lips curled into a thin, frigid smile. He studied Shan as if trying to decide if Shan was goading him. They both knew there was another reason the major could not leave. The Jade Crows had taken two bodies. The knobs had secretly taken away the body of the third, a foreigner, but his American companion was unaccounted for. Shan clenched his jaw so as not to betray his sudden realization. Liang could deal with the murders in any number of ways. But no matter which way he chose, the American woman still posed a direct threat.

"Of course if there were loose ends because of possible conspirators." Shan shrugged and lowered his voice. "Then you should consider going north."

"North?"

"Any foreigner involved in this mess would know they had to flee the county, run as fast and far as possible. Everyone would expect them to head to the nearest border, to the south. Which is why if someone like that needed to get away quickly, with minimal notice, the train would be the answer," Shan explained. "No one would expect a foreigner to flee deeper into China. The army patrols against saboteurs, but on-board security is said to be lax. There are stories of stowaways. Or someone could bluff their way right through the gate with the right paper."

"Paper?"

"Say a big currency note and an American passport."

Liang leaned forward. Shan had his attention.

"Getting to the station in Lhasa would be the difficult part for a foreigner. The road to Lhasa runs the length of Lhadrung County, where Colonel Tan maintains permanent security checkpoints. The only safe answer is to wait for night to slip around the roadblocks. But that adds two or three days to the trip. So a theoretical conspirator would be arriving in Golmud," he said, referring to the northern terminus of the railway, "tomorrow night or the night after. Theoretical," he repeated. It was tempting bait, Shan knew. The Armed Police, not the knobs, were responsible for security on the train. If a fugitive escaped there would be another government office to blame. "Of course, if there is a foreigner involved, no doubt it's best to let them go. If someone is here illegally, there's no need to account for them. Good riddance, right?"

Liang inhaled deeply on his cigarette, frowned, crushed out the cigarette and left the table in a cloud of smoke. As Shan watched him leave the room, a new question occurred to him. How could Liang have known Jamyang's name?

Shan looked up to find Meng gazing at him. She touched Liang's file. With a single finger she lifted the top flap. The passport photo on top was weak and grainy from having been faxed and scanned multiple times, but finally Shan had a face for the phantom he sought. Her thin face had high cheekbones and a strong chin. MISSING PERSON read the caption in English. Under the photo was the name Cora Michener. The notice was from the American embassy.

The Thousand Steps that gave the name to the nuns' hermitage were worn and cupped from centuries of use. Shan had climbed half the long stairway before pausing, breathing heavily, to study the little complex. The old buildings clung to the steep hillside as if part of the mountain. The narrow tower and slanting walls of the outermost structure hung at the edge of a cliff, evidence that the little compound had started life as a *dzong*, one of the hilltop forts that had once dotted the Tibetan landscape.

He had left his truck out of sight far below so as not to frighten the nuns, and as he neared the buildings he paused at each of the little shrines erected along the final flight of steps, reciting mantras in the traditional fashion.

His prayers were to no avail. The first nun who spotted him was kneeling with a bucketful of water over some sprouting plants at the edge of the courtyard. She rose in alarm, backing away, then turned and ran around the corner of the nearest building. Shan halted, resisting the urge to follow. This was a hermitage, where nuns made vows to meditate or chanted mantras for hours every day, sometimes not breaking the cycle for weeks or months. He would not be the one to disturb such reverence. Stepping to the little garden plot, he lifted the ladle in the bucket and continued watering the plants. By the time he had finished he felt unseen eyes on him. He settled in front of the little chorten in the center of the yard, legs turned under him in the lotus fashion, then extended his right hand downward in what was known as the earth-touching mudra, a traditional hand prayer that called the earth as witness. Out of the corner of his eye he saw movement on a path higher up the slope. Several nuns were hurrying away. They were fleeing because of him.

More than a quarter of an hour passed before a middle-aged woman with hair cropped close to her scalp appeared at the base of the old tower, staring at him in cool appraisal before stepping closer.

"You are the Chinese who helped Jamyang," she declared. Her voice was not welcoming. Another woman approached, hanging back like a retainer to the nun. Shan recognized Chenmo, the young dropka who had been raised by the abbess. Three more robed figures appeared from the tower, following uncertainly.

"I was a student at the lama's foot," he replied. He paused, unable to hide his surprise. The three other figures were monks.

"You are the Chinese who gloated over our abbess's mutilated body at the ruins."

Shan's hand folded, losing the mudra. These were not the gentle words he had hoped for. He rose and straightened his clothes. "I was but the first to mourn her. I closed her eyes."

"You stole her gau."

Something inside Shan sagged. Once he had always been welcomed by nuns and monks. "Public Security likes to open such amulets. They would photograph it and catalog its contents. Often they find evidence that leads to investigation of the owner's friends and family."

The nun glared at him. She seemed ready to shove Shan back down the steps. The oldest of the monks, a man in his late forties, stepped forward as if to intervene. His voice was more level, almost friendly. His face was strong and intelligent. "There are stories of a white-haired uncle who wanders the upper valleys like an ancient yak. They say he has a Chinese companion." The monk wore a pale yellow belt loosely around his robe. Hanging from it was an ornate pen case, a traditional trapping of a Tibetan teacher.

Shan offered a hesitant grin. "I have learned much from that old yak."

"I have heard those two stand in ditches covered with mud sometimes."

"Lokesh says cleaning ditches is purifying. He says the magic of the earth gods begins with soil and water."

The monk turned to the nun, who still studied Shan with cool disapproval. "Surely, Mother," the monk said, "we could all join in some tea."

The nun moved only a single hand, a gesture to Chenmo. The young novice darted toward a door where a brazier stood and disappeared inside.

"My name is Shan," he offered.

"I am called Trisong Norbu."

Shan looked at him in surprise. He recognized the name. "Abbot Norbu," he acknowledged with a slight bow of his head. What was the abbot of Chegar gompa doing at the remote hermitage?

The abbot seemed to have read Shan's mind. "You and I may have different questions but I think perhaps we seek the same answers. The valley will never find peace again until those terrible deaths are reconciled." Norbu gestured to a group of stools in a sunlit corner of the little courtyard, overlooking a vista of jagged ridges and slopes that blushed with flowers. The nun sat silently with them, the reluctant hostess. Another nun appeared and began spinning a heavy prayer wheel mounted on the opposite wall, warily watching as if the hermitage would need protection from Shan.

"The people of the valley say we are their anchors," Norbu explained, "my Chegar at the head of the valley and the convent at its foot. The hermitage," he said, correcting himself. "Our beloved abbess often reminded us that this place was but an outpost of the old convent, a station for nuns on retreat. She said it had been the convent that gave meaning to this place."

"Which is why she was trying to make the old convent live again," Shan said. He glanced at the two other monks, who watched their

abbot like dutiful attendants. "But why now after all these years?"
The question had not occurred to him before.

"She saw it as her sacred duty." Norbu replied, nodding to Chenmo
as she brought tea.

"Even though the restoration had not been approved," Shan ventured.

The abbot paused, studying Shan, as if trying to decide if his
words were a warning. He offered a small smile and gestured to his
companions. "Dakpo, Trinle, and I have to deal with mountains of
forms from Religious Affairs. There is no form for the requisition
of hope and faith. Our valley is a special place, remote enough to
keep traditions alive longer than other parts of Tibet. The government seems jealous of what we have here. With the new town, the
new relocation camp, the abbess and I thought it was time for the
convent to live again."

Shan sipped his tea, weighing not just the abbot's words but his
careful tone. Serving as abbot of any monastery in Tibet was like
navigating a minefield. The inhabitants of the gompa, and all the
devout living nearby, expected spiritual leadership from such a man.
But Beijing expected political leadership. Norbu was no doubt painfully aware that many abbots had been stripped of their rank, often
their robes, for failing to kowtow to Beijing. He offered a respectful
nod of his head and drained his cup.

Chenmo renewed the tea in their cups and the two men spoke as
friends might, of the weather, of the lammergeirs gracefully soaring
overhead, of the probable origins of the little hermitage as a fortress
manned by archers.

"You speak Tibetan better than any Chinese I have ever known,"
the abbot observed.

"I spent a few years living only with Tibetans," Shan replied.
"The solitary Chinese with twenty Tibetans in the same barracks."

Norbu studied him with new interest. "In Lhadrung?"

"The Four hundred and fourth People's Construction Brigade."

Norbu offered a solemn nod. The man of reverence was also a man of the world. He was quiet for a long moment, sipping his tea in silence. "Life can be difficult for former Chinese convicts in Tibet," he observed.

"Life can be difficult for a Tibetan abbot in Tibet," Shan rejoined.

Norbu offered a gentle smile in reply.

"I had a dream," the younger of the two attendants, Dakpo, suddenly declared. "A nightmare really. The ghosts of the abbess and Jamyang were in a deep pit, unable to rise out of it. They were blind. They were weeping, asking me to help."

For a moment Shan saw torment in the abbot's eyes. When Norbu spoke there was a plaintive tone in his voice. "The nuns are very scared. My monks are scared. I am without understanding of these things, of violent killings. It is not part of our world."

"It is not part of the world we wished we had," Shan said. "And for these deaths there is no understanding."

"I don't follow."

"There are people trained to understand such things. They look for motive, for patterns, for evidence of what happened. But all hinges on motive. There could be those with motive to kill a foreigner. There could be motives to kill the leader of a criminal gang. There could be a motive even to kill an abbess. Taking each victim, the police could make a list of suspects. But the lists would all be different. There is nothing linking the three. It is like they were three different murders that just happened at the same place."

Norbu fingered the prayer beads on his belt. "Perhaps when a demon takes over a man," the abbot said looking at his beads with sadness in his eyes, "there is no motive, there is only the demon." He sighed. "But that's not how the government will see it. They will announce a motive, so they can make an arrest," he declared, looking at Shan now.

Shan had no reply.

Dakpo shook his head back and forth. "And how can I tell Jamy-ang and the abbess the truth the next time they come to me?" he asked in despair. "How do I tell them they must wander blind and frightened forever?"

The abbot hung his head a moment. "I want to weep," he said in Chinese, as if the words were only for Shan, "but I am the abbot." He opened his mouth again after a moment, then just shook his head, as if speaking had become too great a burden, and took up his beads with a whispered mantra.

Shan rose and paced along the courtyard, surveying the high slopes again. A demon was loose and Lokesh was unprotected. The knobs were seeking the American woman and Shan's misdirection to Liang would only buy her another day or two. When the major turned his attention back to the valley he would be releasing his hungriest dogs.

He turned to see the abbot speaking in soft tones with Chenmo. Norbu touched his gau, as if offering the woman a blessing, then nodded a farewell to Shan, and with Dakpo and Trinle at his side slowly descended the steep stairs that led down from the hermitage. A great weight seemed to have settled on his shoulders.

Chenmo too had noticed. "He has become a man much loved in this valley since he arrived last year," she said, the worry deep in her voice. "He brought with him a silver dragon bell that had belonged to the monastery for centuries, until it was taken by the government. He persuaded some museum to return it to its true owners. He speaks up when the government pushes too hard, even though he knows the last abbot was sent to prison. He is very troubled by what happened to the abbess, worries the government will use it as an excuse to put more Tibetans in prison. He stays up far into the night praying for her, praying for justice. A man like that is important to this valley if it is to survive. But there is more and more talk about how he might be arrested. If the government's anger builds to a storm he will be the lightning rod." The novice continued to stare down the stairs as the robes of the abbot and his attendants faded into in the shadows.

"The American woman is in great danger," Shan said in a low voice. "She has to be warned. She has to be hidden."

"She is not here," Chenmo replied. "She—"

"Enough!" The stern nun who had greeted him emerged from the shadows, motioning Chenmo toward the tower. The novice swept past Shan with her head down, but not before a long glance toward the slope above the compound, at one of the small stone huts that were used by hermits and those on retreat. The nun stepped between Shan and the tower as though to block any attempt to follow the novice.

"They will come looking for the American," Shan declared to the nun. "They will interrogate. They will search, search very roughly. Is everyone here registered? Do you have documentation that they have all taken loyalty oaths?

"Spoken like a true patriot of Beijing."

"Spoken like one who wishes no more suffering on the nuns of Thousand Steps," Shan shot back. "The knobs probably already know that the abbess was coordinating the restoration at the convent. They know about the foreigners. It will not seem possible to them that the foreigners would be secretly visiting the convent ruins without the abbess knowing."

"I cannot say what knowledge the abbess took to her grave."

"I lived in a hermitage once, Abbess. There were no secrets among the monks. It was like one family."

"I carry no whisk," the nun corrected him, referring to the yak tail whisk that was the traditional sign of office for abbots and abbesses. "The new abbess, Ani Ama, was called away. While she is gone I have responsibility for the others." The nun grew quiet as a dozen others emerged from various buildings and moved into a small building with prayer wheels flanking its door. A nun appeared on the tower and began ringing a handbell.

"If they come," she asked in a whisper, "what will happen?"

"They will separate everyone. Each will be interrogated. The

knobs will seek to divide everyone, turn each against the other. First
will be those who don't present documentation of their loyalty oaths.
If you haven't signed an oath, you do not respect Beijing. A Tibetan
who doesn't respect Beijing is a splittist. A splittist is a traitor. Traitors
have no rights. Imprisonment is the usual punishment, with no right
to be registered as a nun ever again. But you can avoid the punishment
if you just speak about the subversive activities of the abbess or the
names of the traitors who hid the American woman.

"If that doesn't work then they will begin speaking of those
among you from bad families, merchants and landowners, whose
files can always be reopened by political officers. When all else fails
they will find out who harbors secret photos of the Dalai Lama and
prosecute them. These are unsettled times in Tibet. Local law enforcement officers had been given great discretion to inflict punishment. They have but to chant the words 'Dalai Lama splittist' and
they can destroy your life. If the knobs so choose they could arrive
here in the morning and by noon everyone here will be gone, never
to see one another again."

Desolation clouded the woman's face but was slowly replaced
with defiance. She was, Shan could tell, a Khampa, from the old
Tibetan province of Kham, where men and women alike had once
been fierce warriors. "*If* they come," she said.

"There is no *if*, Mother," Shan shot back. "Only *when*."

"But you did not come to warn us away."

Shan looked out over the mountains again. He was not at all certain that the path he was trying to find would bring any less pain to
the nuns. "The only way to change the course of things is to find the
truth."

"We know about Chinese and their truths. We have fifty years of
suffering to show for it."

"I had a teacher when I was in prison. A lama who had helped
train the Dalai Lama when he was a boy. He said the reason Tibetans
remained free in their hearts was because they knew that truth was

more powerful than any law, any prison, any army." The heat in the nun's eyes began to fade. "Why," Shan abruptly asked, "would the abbess be in the company of a Chinese gang leader?"

The nun was looking into her folded hands now, confusion on her face. "I have to lead the prayers," she said, then turned and hurried to the chapel.

Shan followed her and settled onto folded legs near the rear wall of the little chamber. The only light came from the open door and the butter lamps that flickered on the altar below a small bronze Buddha. As the mantras began Shan closed his eyes and tried to push away his nagging fears. The soft chorus of the nuns was a salve to his aching spirit. He found himself beginning to mouth the familiar words, then joined his voice with the others.

He did not move as the nuns filed out, but searched their anxious faces. None of them looked at him. Only the senior nun stayed in the chapel, rising to go to the altar where she added more incense to the censers before turning to him.

"A few months ago some Chinese started appearing at the remote camps and farms, the ones high on the slopes," she suddenly declared, "hitting people with sticks, breaking their tools, stealing whatever they wanted, sometimes burning feed saved for the livestock. It wasn't so much like they were looting, for those people had little of value. More like they were trying to scare people away. They always left a black feather. Chinese, but not in uniform. Shorter and darker than most of those in that Pioneer town. When we heard they had tattoos we thought they must be escapees from prison. The abbess first went to one of the Tibetan constables to report it. The constable said he could do nothing, that it was a matter for those Armed Police."

"You mean the Chinese gang from Baiyun was raiding the farmhouses."

"You heard Abbot Norbu. For centuries the convent and Chegar gompa were the two anchors of the valley, one at each end, assuring its tranquility. It was always the duty of the abbot and the abbess to know of the troubles of the people, and to find ways to ease them. After the convent was destroyed the few nuns who survived came here, and the head of the hermitage became the abbess. We are responsible for the people of the valley. If a farmer's family takes sick in the autumn, we nuns will go and take in the barley for them."

"And so she arranged a meeting with the head of the gang. Lung Ma."

"She just went to that old farm of theirs, with the oldest of our nuns, Ani Ama. The abbess just pushed open the door and went upstairs to see their leader. Ani Ama said his men laughed but not him. He seemed disturbed to see her. He just listened as she berated him and demanded he leave our people alone. Some of his men pulled out knives, but he spoke sharp words and they lowered the weapons."

"You mean just before she was murdered?"

"No. Many weeks ago. Two or three months. Then last month he came for her. All the way up the stairs, gasping for breath when he reached the top."

"To go with her to the convent."

"No. That was later. He came because of his dead son."

Shan looked up in surprise. "The son of the gang chief died?"

The nun nodded. "A driving accident. He wanted her to prepare the body in the old way."

"The Jade Crows had threatened her with knives and she still went?"

"Of course she did. It was for the dead boy. His father was a different man, very shaken. Afterwards all those raids stopped."

Shan considered her words. "So she followed him home that once," he said, "and he followed her again later to the convent where they both died."

The nun shook her head. "You misunderstand. She did not go to the convent for Lung, or Lung for her. They went because of Jamyang. Jamyang told her a demon had crawled out of the earth and had to be destroyed."

CHAPTER SEVEN

Halfway down the worn stone steps, Shan slipped into the steep field of rock outcroppings that flanked the stairs. Using the cover of the rocks, he moved slowly back up the slope, hoping not to attract attention. He could not be certain that Chenmo had deliberately directed him toward the little meditation shelter above the compound, and was even less certain when he reached it.

The hut was empty, devoid of furnishings other than two straw-stuffed pallets, two worn cushions, a low stool, and a bucket. On the wall was a ten-year-old tourist calendar with a glossy photo of Mount Kalais, the most sacred of pilgrimage peaks. He stood in the doorway of the decrepit, windblown structure, finding himself again looking toward the higher slopes, realizing that he would never be able to concentrate on the murders while Lokesh remained missing.

A gust of wind rattled the door on its wooden pintles, then whipped at a line of prayer flags tied to a nail on the corner of the building. Most of the line had blown away. Only half a dozen flags remained, suspended for the moment by the wind. Four of the flags were on faded cotton, but the last two were of a brilliant red material, breaking the traditional pattern of colors. They were not of the same fabric as the other flags.

Shan grabbed the line and pulled in the red flags. They bore the customary mani mantra, the invocation of the compassionate Buddha, inscribed in Tibetan. But on the reverse the mantra had been written out in English, with what looked like a ballpoint pen. *Om mani padme hum,* the letters said. The cloth was nylon, its edges hemmed with narrow strips of medical tape. Someone had cut pieces from a windbreaker or a tent to make prayer flags.

With a new determination he stepped into the hut and began systematically searching it, lifting the pallets and the small bags of yak-hair felt stuffed with fleece that served as cushions. Under one pallet was a tattered pair of leather sandals and a comb, under the other ten pages of Tibetan scripture. He looked back at the first pallet. A comb. Nuns kept their hair close-cropped, if not shorn altogether. He held the small black comb to his nose. It had a strangely cloying scent to it, too vague to be identified. Taking the cushions outside, he unfolded the flaps of cloth covering the stuffing. The first held only the familiar washed wool used in such cushions. The second held wool as well, but at the bottom there was something more, something that sent up an odor of citrus and coconut. He pulled out handfuls of wool, then a long silky skein which he carried into the sunlight. It was dark hair, brunet hair, more than eighteen inches long.

"I thought I could hide it," Chenmo confessed, standing at the corner of the hut.

"You sent me up here to find it," Shan replied.

"I thought you would just find the prayer flags. I didn't know what to do with them. A strong wind blew most of the line away. The mountain god could have taken them then if he wanted to, but he left them. It is not for me to destroy them."

"But you thought I would," Shan replied. He unconsciously lifted the hair to his nose, then felt a flush of embarrassment and quickly lowered it. "Do the others below know?" he asked.

"I don't know. I didn't tell them."

"It's obvious to Public Security that the foreigners were friends of the abbess, that they worked with her at the ruins. There aren't many places foreigners could stay without attracting undue attention. Eventually they will realize that the hermitage must have been their operating base."

"But it wasn't. Rutger and Cora understood the risk that would bring to us. They had a camp higher up, just came here sometimes to join the prayers and speak with the nuns."

"Then why didn't she go to the camp to hide?"

"She didn't think it was safe for some reason. She was terrified."

"Because she was there, at the ruins that day."

Chenmo nodded. "She knew, she saw the killer. I am sure of it. But she wouldn't say anything about what happened. She just kept saying that she had to leave, that it had all been a huge mistake."

"What was a mistake?" Shan pressed. "You mean the ones who died at the convent made a mistake?"

Chenmo shrugged.

"How did you find her after the murders?"

"She knew I often wander on the slopes, looking for herbs, cleaning old pilgrim paths. When she found me the day after the killings she was like some wild animal, nearly out of her mind, covered with brambles, dried blood on her hands. She could barely speak."

"She speaks Tibetan?"

"Not much. She had a little dictionary but she lost it. Rutger spoke it. He usually translated into English for her. She speaks some Chinese, as I do. But when she found me she was too terrified for words. After dark I brought her here. She cried all night. I held her and she cried, until no more tears could come. The next day we spoke and she made me understand she wanted some scissors. After I understood what she intended I got her the right clothes, taught her some of the mantras we say."

"You can't leave the hair here," Shan said. "It has the scent of a foreigner."

Chenmo eyed Shan uneasily. "It is of her body. It must be kept safe."

Shan stared at the woman in confusion a moment, then recalled that Chenmo had been raised among nomads, whose lives were ruled as much by superstition as their religion. Many of them believed that harm could be afflicted on someone by inflicting it on something that had been removed from their body like hair or fingernails.

"Wrap it in a scrap of leather," he suggested, "then bury it under a rock on the high slope. With those two prayer flags."

"She has to have her prayers. More than ever now."

"Then we must move them away from here. I will help do it if you take me to the foreigner's camp."

Chenmo frowned, then looked back at the red nylon flags and nodded.

The foreigners had been shrewd in their selection of a campsite. Chenmo led him for nearly an hour up the rugged slope, stopping only briefly at a high, open ledge for Shan to build a small cairn to cover the hair and affix the flags to the top stone. When she finally stopped by a high outcropping Shan thought she was only resting. Then he saw how she studied the wall of stone. She located a narrow gap and disappeared into its shadows.

The blue nylon tent had seen long use in mountain winds. The equipment around it was that of seasoned trekkers. The campsite looked untouched, as if the two foreigners had just left for a short climb on the rocks above.

Shan bent at the entrance to the tent, pulled down the zipper that secured the covering fly, and stepped inside. On one side two down sleeping bags lay open on foam pads, one with a blanket on top. A nylon stuff sack contained women's clothes, another those of a man. A large backpack held climbing harnesses, pitons, and carabineers. On the other side lay five small, sturdy aluminum cases. He turned to Chenmo, who lingered uneasily at the entrance. "There should be two backpacks. Surely she must have come back."

"No. I kept telling her, kept pointing up here, saying she would be safer, and she refused. She was terrified of coming back."

Three of the metal cases had been designed to hold cameras and lenses. But the compartments shaped of black foam were empty. One camera, he knew, had been destroyed by the killer. The fourth and fifth cases held small plastic containers for miniature videotapes and computer memory cards. He quickly lifted the containers, one by one, opening each. They were all empty.

"She didn't come back because she knew someone else was coming here," Shan declared. "Someone who dumped cameras and the contents of these cases into the second pack." He saw how Chenmo nervously watched the narrow entrance to the campsite. She was frightened.

He probed the sleeping bags and lifted the blanket. It was of cheap grey fabric. He had seen a similar one at Clear Water Camp. "What else is missing?" he asked.

The novice paced slowly around the site. "A little stove that cooked with canisters of gas. Food. Dried food, that they heated with water."

"Who else knew of this place?"

"The abbess came with me to visit Rutger and Cora." The novice gestured toward a circle of flat rocks. "They made a meal there. The abbess asked about their worlds."

Shan studied the rock walls. There were chalk drawings on the stone, some artful, some very primitive. A Buddha. A dog. A yak. A heart. The foreigners had felt safe here. It had been their sanctuary. Pacing along a wall, he saw now a fish and a lotus and realized he knew the artist. "Jamyang was here." It was a statement, not a question.

"Not that I ever knew," Chenmo replied uncertainly.

He lifted a small plastic Buddha from a cleft in the rock. "This was theirs?"

She took the Buddha and studied it with a confused expression. "They give these away at Chegar. But no monks came here. Cora and Rutger were careful to stay hidden from everyone but the nuns and Jamyang."

Shan surveyed the camp with new worry. "The American didn't come back to her secret camp but a thief did."

Chenmo backed against one of the walls, as if suddenly frightened.

"Where is she, Chenmo?" he asked abruptly. "She is in grave danger."

"A message came," the novice said. "The abbess would be waiting for us on the old road behind the ruins."

"You mean her body, after it was stolen from Public Security."

"Stolen? The abbess was ours."

"Public Security considers the body evidence in a criminal investigation."

"Her body is evidence of her saintly life."

"So the nuns went to retrieve it."

Chenmo slowly nodded. "But the old uncle had come the night before. He said—"

Shan's heart leapt. "Lokesh?" he interrupted. "You saw Lokesh?"

"Yes. Uncle Lokesh. He came after dark and asked if he could sleep in our stable. He asked about you, said he was going to Jamyang's shrine the next day and then he would find you. But when he heard about the abbess's body he changed his mind. He said the body must go up the mountain, back with Jamyang, that it would be what she wanted, that it shouldn't be left for the police to find again. He said he would show us a way that would avoid the roads."

"To the flesh cutters."

"The *ragyapa*, yes."

"Ani Ama was the one who was to carry the whisk, to take over for the abbess. She agreed. She said she would go, just four of us. I realized it was Cora's chance. By the time they reached the road there were five."

"You mean the American joined them." Shan let out a sigh of relief. Lokesh and the American were safe. Public Security hated the flesh cutters, loathed even having contact with them.

"A message should go to them," Shan said. "The American should stay there. Lokesh should stay with her."

"Lokesh is with her," Chenmo said in a tight voice. "But not at the flesh cutters."

"What do you mean?"

Pain was filling the novice's eyes. She seemed unable to speak.

Shan studied her and thought he understood. "I am sorry. I ask too much. If you were found to be helping me you would not be cleared to wear a robe."

Chenmo took a long time to answer. "One of those purbas, one of the free Tibetans who came across from India, explained something to me the last time I saw him. The government is not giving robes to those without families. They rely on families as hostages, make them sign guarantees saying they will not allow their son or daughter or brother or sister to engage in disloyal acts. If the monk or nun is disloyal, the families are put in prison. He said an orphan like me will never be given a robe registration."

Shan had no words of comfort. "I ask too much," he said again. "Just tell me where to go to find out what happened."

Chenmo bit her lip. "I don't think I can. I will have to show you."

The novice said nothing as they descended in a more direct path to where Shan had left his truck, then only pointed at intersections, leading him on a narrow gravel track that took them in a wide arc around the convent ruins and into the field of rock outcroppings behind it. He slowed as a line of hoofprints merged with the track, then again as they passed a set of truck tire tracks that swerved onto their road from behind a huge boulder. The route the truck had followed into the rocks was little more than an old farm path. He considered the low hills it disappeared into, realizing he had seen them from the opposite side. The path led to the farm used by Lung and the Jade Crows.

"Here," Chenmo said abruptly as the truck entered a small clearing in the rocks. The tracks he had been following had entered the clearing and gone no farther.

Chenmo seemed to withdraw into herself, and he left her in the truck as he explored the flat circle. He needed no further explanation of what had happened, for the soil told the story. A small horse accompanied by several people had entered the clearing from the south, from the direction of the nun's hermitage. One of the footprints was that of Lokesh, a peculiar barred impression left by strips of rubber glued on the soles of his boots by a cobbler the year before. Two or three figures wearing expensive athletic shoes had emerged from the truck. The horse had gone on to the north side of the clearing, its tracks deeper from a load that had been added.

When he returned to the truck Chenmo was holding his map, biting her lip again. She was pointing to a new destination, a road he did not know that climbed in steep switchbacks out of the valley, cresting the high ridge before continuing over a long plain into the unknown hills of the next county. She looked up expectantly.

"Not until you speak to me," Shan demanded. "I want to know who was in the truck with the body."

"Some of those Chinese men from that farm. Rough men. They scared me. Most of us stayed in the shadows. Ani Ama spoke with them."

"Did Ani Ama know the men? Did she seem acquainted with them?"

"Yes, she knew them. She had been to the farm with the abbess."

"What words were spoken?"

"Not many. Those men were frightened of the body. They had wrapped the abbess in a sheet tied with rope. On the rope they had fastened some kind of a charm with drawings of black birds and snakes on it. Ani Ama started to get angry, saying they should take it off, that it was an evil charm. Then Uncle Lokesh stepped out of the shadows. One of them, the oldest, asked how to clean the body of the dead, and Lokesh explained how we do it. Then he pulled away the charm and just folded it into his pocket and thanked them. He whispered a few more words and they backed away as if scared. I asked him what he had said. He told them they had not brought death with them, but a cocoon from which a beautiful butterfly would emerge. After they left he had us lay the body on a blanket, then he lit incense and led us in prayers. Only then could we tie the abbess to the horse for her journey. He kept patting her as we tightened the ropes, as if to comfort her, speaking the death rites. The abbess may have been close to the deities, he said, but she had not been ready to die that day."

Shan studied the map again, tracing with his finger an alternate route, a detour that would connect with Chenmo's mysterious track farther up the slope. He turned the wheel and followed the tracks left by the truck that had brought the abbess's body.

"No," Chenmo protested. "Please, Shan. Those men scare me."

"Just a quick look, that's all," Shan assured her.

When he pressed on she began saying her rosary.

At last the truck crested a hill overlooking the Jade Crow compound. Chenmo gasped. A column of dark smoke was rising from the farm. He eased the truck back, out of sight from below, and darted to the crest with the binoculars.

A sentry was posted on the road leading to the camp, armed with what looked like a pitchfork. The little stone stable above the compound had something new, a solitary prayer flag fluttering from its roof. The little grain crib Shan had seen in ruin was entirely gone now. Its salvaged timber had been used for a new structure of crossed planks, from which the smoke now rose. At least half a dozen figures were arranged in a circle around the intense fire. The Jade Crows were burning the body of their leader.

The sun was low on the horizon by the time they reached the long grassy plain that straddled the two counties. Shan looked uncomfortably behind him. At the crest of the ridge above them was the county line, where the meager protection he enjoyed would disappear. On the other side he would just be an ex-convict without travel papers.

Chenmo had stopped speaking. She simply pointed onward, toward the crest, more than two miles away.

They had nearly reached the top of the ridge when she signaled for him to stop and jumped out of the truck, running up the slope. She was standing on a ledge that overlooked the wide plain behind them when he caught up with her, looking out over the grassland with fear in her eyes. She pressed a fist against her mouth as if to stifle a cry. A chill began rising up Shan's spine. What was it that so terrified her?

"We climbed quickly, using the road at first," she suddenly explained. She pointed toward the end of the plain where the land rose steeply into more fields of rocks. "We were nearly at the trail that leads to the high country when we saw them. They were running toward us. There was no time to react."

Shan's mouth went dry. "You mean soldiers."

Chenmo shrugged. "They wore uniforms. They had guns. We had so little time. Uncle Lokesh said the abbess had to escape. Three of us went with the horse, running up the trail. When Lokesh ran out into the open to distract the soldiers, the American followed and ran past him as if to help him. Cora was strong, very fast, too fast. She fell. Uncle Lokesh went to her and Ani Ama ran to the two of them. They tried to carry Cora away but the soldiers caught up with them. We watched from the rocks above. When they were gone I was sent back to tell the hermitage."

Shan collapsed onto a rock, holding his head in his hands for a moment. "I don't understand," he said when he looked up. "Where did the soldiers come from? Where did they go? Did they have trucks? A helicopter? What else did you see? Anything that could help me find where they were taken."

"But I know where. I watched. I followed. I had seen it before with Cora and Rutger."

Shan watched, more confused than ever, as the woman hitched up her robe and began to climb over the short, steep slope that led to the crest of the ridge. He did not catch up with her until she was nearly at the top.

"The Chinese think they are so secret," she declared, "as if we are all blind. Rutger and Cora wanted everyone to think they had come to film the restoration of the convent but this is why they came with their cameras, to show the Chinese that not everyone is blind. I helped them sometimes, and they let me look through their long lenses. Old men and women being beaten with sticks. Monks tethered to poles and left outside with no shelter, even in storms. They started digging graves last month." She bit her lip again and looked back down on the plain. "My mother used to tell me of a hell where humans were transformed into animals. This is it." She took the final step to reach the crest and pointed down to the remote valley below.

The sight hit Shan like a physical blow. With a long groan he collapsed to his knees.

The complex lay less than a mile below them, a sprawling labyrinth of crude barracks surrounded by walls of razor wire and short towers that were no doubt equipped with machine guns.

As the numbness left him Shan felt nothing but the desperate, overwhelming need to save Lokesh. The gentle old Tibetan would never survive another term of imprisonment. He had to find him, had to get him away from the wire and the guns. He rose unsteadily and took one step, then another, down the slope, scanning the camp with a prisoner's eye, looking for soft spots in the security.

He became vaguely aware of Chenmo calling to him, protesting, pleading with him. "The soldiers!" she cried. "They were the guard patrol that sweeps the area. They will see us too. No one is allowed this close."

He stumbled on the thick grass and when he rose she was at his side, pulling on his arm.

"No!" he cried as he shrugged her off. "Lokesh will die! Everything I have done will be worthless if I let him die like that!"

She was sobbing now but she did not try to restrain him as he took another step. It was only an internment camp, he told himself. Security would not be as severe as at a gulag prison. It would be dark soon. Surely he could find a way through the wire at the rear of the huge camp.

"I saw him last summer!" Chenmo shouted to his back.

Shan kept moving.

But then she spoke again. "I saw Jamyang on the highway from Golmud! He was not a lama then."

CHAPTER EIGHT

Shan halted and slowly turned toward the nun. "Say that again."

"Some of us went to the Golmud highway to help with those convoys of relocated shepherds. There was a truck station where they stopped for rest." Chenmo cast another worried glance toward the internment camp. "We can't linger here. They will see us and send soldiers."

Shan gazed forlornly back at the camp but let her pull him back over the crest. "Jamyang was helping with the shepherds too, you mean," he said when they were out of sight of the camp.

"No. He was in a big black car, like the government uses. He and others, mostly Chinese, got out and went inside for tea. They were wearing suits, like on a business trip."

He searched her eyes, trying to understand the trick she was playing. "Chenmo, you are mistaken."

"He had that mark on his cheek. The abbess said it was the sign of the lotus flower, a bud of the flower, and that it must mean he was a reincarnated teacher." She spoke of the little birthmark over Jamyang's jaw. The lotus was a symbol of purity. It was believed that those spiritually advanced lamas whose reincarnations could be traced more than hundreds of years, the *tulku*, often had prominent birthmarks to aid their identification as infants.

He struggled to focus on what she said, considering the meaning of her words. "You told the abbess about seeing him?"

"There was no point. She spoke often about how such a tulku had to be treasured by all of us. She would not have believed me. I am just a novice. She liked to say I still had the wildness of my clan in me."

"But you are certain?"

"I was at a water spigot filling some of the cans from the back of the trucks. A can spilled and splashed water on one of the Chinese men, who cursed at me and raised an arm like he was about to strike me. This tall Tibetan with him rushed forward and calmed him, saying it was only an accident, then picked up the can for me. He helped me refill it. He laughed when he got splashed himself, then he squeezed my hand and offered a prayer before he rushed to the others. I saw his face plain, saw that mark. When I looked into my hand there was a folded currency note in it. Ten yuan. I bought incense to put in the back of each of the trucks so the gods would follow and know where those poor shepherds were going. It was Jamyang, Shan, I know it was."

Shan stared at Chenmo, desperately wanting not to believe the tale but seeing in her eyes that the woman spoke the truth. He gestured her back down the hill toward the truck.

He did not bother to speak to the manager of Clear Water Camp, who was affixing a poster to the wall of his building as Shan climbed out of his truck. He felt the man's worried gaze on his back as he marched through the gate.

"This is China's century, Comrade!" the stout man shouted to his back. It was, word for word, the caption on the poster.

The sparse structure that Jigten shared with his mother seemed empty as Shan pulled back the burlap that shuttered the window. He knocked once on the door, then stepped inside before hearing the shallow, raspy breath and saw that what he had taken to be a pile of grey blankets on the pallet was the old woman, curled up like a sleeping cat.

He silently searched the contents of the main room, raising clouds of dust as he probed a basket of clothing, then lifted a crate used as a stool. Inside the crate a cloth bag had been tacked. It held three small hand calculators and two watches that appeared to be broken.

It was the small closet at the back of the kitchen that held Jigten's main inventory. On its top shelf, behind a row of empty water bottles he found what he was looking for. He pulled the blue nylon backpack into the light cast by the open door, examining each of its zippered pockets. As he searched the last of them a shadow appeared in the doorway.

Jigten's expression changed quickly from surprise to resentment as he stepped inside. "You can't just come in and steal things," the shepherd said in a deflated voice.

"I will take the truth where I find it," Shan replied. "Even if it means stealing it." The pockets of the pack were stuffed with freeze-dried food, the main compartment filled with more food, half a dozen carabineers, and a small gas stove wrapped in a windbreaker. On the inside flap was a name in black ink. Cora Michener.

"Truth." Jigten spat the word like a curse. "Like the Chinese who dumped us in this camp said they were just interested in our welfare. I remember one prick who laughed as he shot our sheep. He asked if I could feel my chains dropping away."

Shan extended the pack toward Jigten. "I could take this to Public Security. When they discover it belonged to their dead foreigner they will assume the worst. They are looking for someone to blame the murders on. This would be the only piece of evidence connected to the German."

The color drained from Jigten's face. He leaned against the wall by the door, seeming to lose strength, then slowly slid to the floor. "They were gone," he muttered. "They weren't coming back."

"How did you know that?"

"The German was dead. That American was a frightened mouse in a field of cats. If I hadn't taken the stuff someone else would have." As he spoke Jigten extracted a small bottle of medicine from inside his vest and looked toward his sleeping mother. "I have expenses," he whispered.

"How did you know where their camp was?"

"That girl. Sometimes a few of us would go and help at the old ruins. My mother said I should do it, that I needed to gain merit with the gods," he said with a bitter grin. "Hauling away rubble. Patching and whitewashing that old chorten. She was there sometimes with the nuns. I thought she was a nun at first. She wore an old chuba, a shepherd's coat, and a derby, like some Tibetan girl. I never heard her speak so I thought maybe she was under some kind of vow. But one day we were resting from hauling heavy rocks and she broke up a chocolate bar and gave us all pieces. I saw the wrapper. It was from America. She tried to respond when everyone thanked her, but her Tibetan was terrible."

"So you followed her, like you followed Jamyang to his shrine."

"My grandfather said you always need to know the land. He knew every stream, every rabbit burrow, every wolf den. 'You can't be sure of someone,' he would say, 'until you know where they sleep at night.' " He glanced up at Shan. "I didn't follow from the convent. They were usually given a ride in the truck with the monks, to the bottom of the Thousand Steps. I went to the nun's hermitage and watched. Hell, Westerners like that throw away things that would be worth a month's wages to one of us."

Shan fingered the seams of the nylon pack. "Where are the pictures?"

"I never saw pictures."

"Little cards with cartridges in plastic cases."

Jigten shrugged. "No good to me. A bunch of plastic. Not real things."

"So you saw them, and left them?"

The shepherd slowly nodded. "No good to me," he repeated.

"How many cameras?"

"One for video. One for photographs."

"Where are they?"

"Gone."

"Where exactly? Did they have photos stored in them?"

Jigten's expression hardened. "Who knows? Even if anyone in Clear Water Camp had money to buy such things, no one knows how to use them."

"So you would take them to Baiyun?" Shan studied Jigten a moment. The exiled professors in Baiyun could hardly afford such luxuries. "The Jade Crows. Lung's gang. They would know how to move such things on the black market."

Jigten frowned. "I won't do anything that gets people in more trouble. Everyone in that town made someone in Beijing angry too, like us. That's life in Tibet. Everyone in Tibet has someone in Beijing angry at them. All that matters is who's angry and how deep their anger is."

It was, Shan thought, the wisest thing he had ever heard Jigten say.

The dropka looked up with a desolate expression. "How mad are you?" he asked.

The words hurt more than Jigten could have known. He gazed at the shepherd in silence, not having the strength to tell him that if the police found out about the cameras anyone who had touched them could disappear. He tossed the pack toward Jigten. "You must get that name off the pack," he said, then sat on the doorsill. "Cut it off. Don't just black it out with more ink, for they will have ways to see what's underneath. Don't get caught with it like that."

Jigten looked uncertainly at Shan. "You won't tell the knobs?"

"I won't tell the knobs." Shan hated the fear in the man's eyes.

Had Lokesh been with him, the old Tibetan would have found a way to bring a smile to the man's face. But alone Shan only brought fear.

"Don't go," Jigten said after a brittle silence. "Don't go to Lung today."

"They already burned their leader's body. I saw the pyre yesterday."

"Not that. One of the young ones, that Genghis, was beaten real bad. By knobs working for that Major Liang. The Jade Crows thought the Armed Police would keep them protected as usual. But not this time, not now, not from Liang."

Shan hesitated, searching Jigten's face. "I need to know about the camp on the other side of the mountain, Jigten. The one with razor wire and machine guns. You said you drive supplies there sometimes for the Jade Crows. I want to know about the trucks. I want to know about their schedules."

Jigten shook his head grimly from side to side. "You don't talk about demons. It makes them more powerful."

"I have friends there behind the wire."

"No you don't. Not anymore." Jigten saw the uncertainty on Shan's face, then glanced uneasily toward his sleeping mother. "There was one of our clan, the son of our headman, who carried on the old ways, learned all the tales of the grandfathers and the songs from hearths before time. He was our strength, the one who made us believe in ourselves. He was always telling us the Chinese were just visitors in our land, that we were the true people, just like yaks and sheep were the true animals of the changtang, and no one in Beijing could ever change that. But he spoke too many times in front of caravans and other travelers. One day they came and took him away to a pacification camp like that one on the other side of the mountain. He wrote us at first, said he was fine, that he would be back in a few months. Then the letters stopped coming. We told his mother, who was blind, that the letters still came, even pretended to read some to her. It would have broken the heart of the old ones to know the truth. Two years later his nephew found him begging in some town." Jigten glanced back toward his mother. "He could barely walk. They broke his feet. They broke something in his head. He had no more songs, except those party anthems he kept singing under his breath instead of his mantras. No more laughter, no more light in his eyes."

In the silence that followed Shan realized the steady breathing from the bed had stopped. The old woman had pulled the blanket over her head but Shan could see her hollow eyes, open, staring at them in horror. She had been listening.

"You will have no more friends there," Jigten said, his voice strangely hoarse now. "They will be no more. People go in but only hollow shells come out."

The sun was low in the sky when Shan rose from the tall grass where he had been sitting, watching the Jade Crows compound. There was no sign of sentries. The big trucks were gone. Jigten had explained that twice a week they made long hauls, either to the southern border or up the northern road to Chamdo, Tibet's third biggest city, even sometimes beyond, into Sichuan Province, to pick up supplies for the camps. The compound seemed nearly deserted except for the solitary figure he had seen climbing to the run-down stable on the slope above the farm. He cast a long, worried glance in the direction of Lokesh's new prison, then muttered a prayer and began climbing the hill.

There was no door on the little building. For several moments Shan watched the man at the altar of planks and stones, then extracted a stick of incense from his pocket and lit a match against the wall.

Lung Tso spun about, his eyes flaring as bright as the match. "You have a lot of balls coming here, Old Mao," he spat. His hand drifted toward the dagger Shan knew was in his boot.

"I bring incense to honor your gods."

The words cut through Lung's anger. He glanced back at the altar, seeming uncertain how to respond. On one side of the altar sat a simple sandalwood statue of Buddha, on the other a stout, decorated Buddha of the tropical lands. Beside them were two thick candles, a butter lamp, a glass of wine, and a white *khata* scarf, an offering scarf. At the very edge sat a small toy truck with another khata wrapped around it.

Shan wedged his smoking stick of incense between stones in the wall above the altar, murmuring a quick mantra before turning to the new Jade Crow chieftain. "Tell me something, Lung. Did your brother make this altar before or after his son died?" He half expected Lung to pull out his blade, but then he saw there was no fight in the man before him.

Lung Tso watched the smoke of the smoldering stick as he spoke. "After. Even then he kept it hidden. The night we burned his boy's body he never came back to the house. I found him here, just before dawn, setting out the little statues." He turned to Shan. "When we were young our mother took us to the temple. People would bring little things like images of houses and money and burn them. Should we burn something?"

"That was a temple of the Taoists," Shan explained. "The Buddha does not expect it."

"My brother said he had been having dreams about going to the temple with our mother," Lung continued. "He said maybe we had been wrong to ignore the gods after she died. Maybe it was wrong to have roughed up all those Tibetans in the hills, he said, just because the police said so. He said our mother had warned him about making deals with demons."

"You mean he thought his son's death was some kind of punishment."

"I told him his son died in a truck accident, that our dealing with the police was just good business, that the Jade Crows always made the best of their situation, it's how we survived. But he wouldn't listen. He said bringing the old nun was too late, that he should have done so long before."

Shan paused. "You were here when she came?"

"The first time she came to us with another nun, right up the stairs as we sat at the table playing tiles. She demanded that we stop raiding the farms. My brother made sure she wasn't hurt, even stopped the others from laughing at her, but agreed to nothing. When my nephew died he seemed to reconsider things. Lung Wi was a good boy, very smart, very lively. Always laughing. My brother was devoted to him. If we had stayed in Yunnan some of us might have avoided jail but my brother wouldn't be separated from his son. The others don't know it, but it's why we came here, so my brother and his son would be together.

"When the boy's body was brought back he wept. The only time I ever saw him weep. He pulled out an old box of our mother's things and sat with them a long time. Then he took them and placed them around his son's body. After a couple hours of sitting there in silence he left without a word. When he came back that old nun was with him. They washed the boy's body and they said words together."

"Your brother and the abbess?"

Lung shook his head. "The abbess and that other nun, the older nun. The monk too, though the abbess was in charge."

"A monk? What was his name?"

"That Jamyang."

"The tall lama with the red spot on his jaw?"

As Lung nodded Shan recalled he had seemed to know Jamyang's name on his first visit. "Not as good as the nuns," the gang leader added.

"What do you mean?"

"He disrupted things, stopped the prayers. He ran out like he couldn't bear to be with the dead. What good's a monk who is scared of death?"

Shan stared at the gang leader in confusion. "Where was the boy going when he died?"

"Jade Crow business," was Lung's only reply. He turned back toward the altar. "Do you have more of that incense?"

Shan found himself settling down in front of the altar. He absently handed Lung his last stick of incense. The gang leader lit it and stared at the little Buddha in the exotic garb, his head cocked, as if trying to understand how to speak to it. The last rays of the sun reached into the stable, bathing the altar in a golden glow.

Shan reached into his pocket and extracted the folded piece of paper he had found in Lung Ma's holster. "This is what you wanted. This is what I took from your brother's body."

Lung Tso seemed not to hear for a moment, then he slowly turned and accepted the paper. His brows knitted in confusion as he read it. He looked up at Shan and gestured him closer to the little Buddhas. "My mother said in front of the gods no man can lie. This was it, this was all you took?"

"I swear it to you. These were the words that brought him to the convent that day."

"Just dates and towns?"

"Certain dates. Certain towns, towns on the border, where things get moved out of China. And at the bottom that address in Chamdo. It was written by Jamyang."

"This is why my brother died? I don't think so."

"A man cannot lie in front of the gods, Lung. Were the Jade Crows smuggling things across at those towns? Things like the cameras of those foreigners?"

Lung's nod was so small as to be almost imperceptible.

"Where are they, where are the cameras?"

"Gone. Probably in some Katmandu market by now."

"Look at the last two entries, Lung. One town, with two dates that were in the future when Jamyang gave these to him. One passed a few days ago. You're planning operations there, to smuggle across the Nepali border on those dates. Someone is watching you."

Lung's eyes widened, as realization had finally hit him. "Fuck me."

"Your nephew died," Shan slowly declared. "Your brother and the abbess and Jamyang met here, because of his death. Then they and the German all died."

"Fuck me," Lung murmured again, repeating it several times. It had the tone of a prayer, the Jade Crow mantra.

Wind began to rustle the grass outside. They both stared at the little altar. The candles flickered. A nighthawk called.

"I want you to make a burnt offering after all," Shan said at last. Lung looked up. "I want you to burn a truck for your brother."

CHAPTER NINE

He waited in the shadows for nearly an hour, watching through the windows before walking in the side door of Baiyun's little police post. "The German was an agitator for democracy," he said to Meng's back as she sat at her desk. "You knew that."

Meng went very still, then slowly turned to face him. "He was a foreigner," she replied, as if it were the same thing.

"You knew he was watching the new pacification camp."

"A foreigner known for making documentary films who is traveling illegally in a district with one of the highest concentrations of detention camps in all of China. It would be a reasonable surmise."

"For you."

"And for Major Liang," she shot back.

Shan hesitated a moment, confused at the flicker of uncertainty he saw in her eyes. "I need to get into that camp."

"Don't be a fool. Impossible."

"Arrest me."

Meng brushed a strand of hair from her face. Shan noticed for the first time her disheveled, weary appearance. She gestured toward the computer on her desk. "I spent two hours today trying to figure out who you are, Comrade Shan. Public Security has so many secret operations Beijing can't even keep track of them in any systematic way. And you're not really the Public Security type, are you?"

Shan did not reply.

"One of the green apes from that new pacification camp came in to run a request about a *lao gai* registration number. It was yours, Shan."

He had forgotten that Lung Tso had taken his tattoo number, though not his discovery that the Jade Crows sometimes acted like surrogates for the Armed Police.

"But that's all there was," Meng continued. "Just your name, and an admission date over seven years ago. The Four hundred and fourth People's Construction Brigade. Nothing else. One of Colonel Tan's most famous prisons. Tan doesn't lose records. It has to be a legend, the officer said, a deep cover. I didn't bother to tell the fool that no one creates deep cover with empty files. But on the other hand, no convict would be so clever as to find a way for Tan to destroy his file and then be so foolish as to keep using the same name and stay in Tan's county."

"I could draw you a map of all the roads I helped build with the Four hundred and fourth. Arrest me," he said again.

"Why not change your name?"

He paced along the front of the detention cell that adjoined the office, touching each bar as he passed it. "The Four hundred and fourth People's Construction Brigade. It's how they know me there. It's how I get inside."

"You're making no sense."

Shan gripped the bars of the cell and spoke into its shadows. "I have a son named Ko," he explained after a long moment, "my only flesh and blood. He has nearly ten years left on his sentence. Former inmates are not allowed back, but Tan and I have an arrangement. He lets me see him on the first Sunday of each month, and lets me send one letter a month."

In the long silence that followed they could hear the bleating of sheep in the marketplace paddock.

He turned to her. "I have a friend behind the wire of that new camp. His name is Lokesh."

"There's talk of setting up a visitation program."

"How soon?"

She shrugged. "A few months. By the end of the year if the Tibetans stay quiet. They were blowing that damned horn again last night. Someone made a bonfire of Chinese road signs at one of the crossroads. Another monk burned himself in Sichuan."

"And if they don't?"

She shrugged again. "Then there will be another six camps just like it. There's a new policy. For every Tibetan arrested in a strike or protest two family members will also be arrested."

Shan dropped into the chair across from Meng's desk. "I need to be in there, Lieutenant. All I have in the world is my son and that old Tibetan inside that camp's wire. Please."

Meng grew still again. Somehow the contemplative look on her face unsettled him. "You're lucky to have a son," she said quietly. "I never had a child."

The silence between them took on a strangely awkward air.

"I think I liked it better when you called me a fool. Arrest me," Shan pressed.

"It's administered by the Armed Police. They could arrange for you to slip inside for a few hours."

"Never. The prisoners would smell a plant."

Meng glanced at him, then away, several times, as if not knowing how to react. Finally she looked out the window. "I've been there. It's no hard-labor camp, but the detainees are treated like livestock. Typhus has started. I was being given a tour when a tractor finished digging a wide trench behind the camp. The guards laughed when I asked if they were putting in a foundation for a new building, laughed again when the first bodies were thrown in, said they ran the best camp in all Tibet, because pacification at their camp was permanent."

You're a Public Security officer, Shan almost rejoined, *stop pretending you care.* But then he saw the way she bit her lower lip. There were times when Meng seemed like just another girl adrift in the bitter sea of China.

"Meng, I know how to survive in such places. I speak Tibetan."

When she did not respond he rolled up his sleeve and thrust his forearm in front of her. She stared at the gulag registration number.

"They dig the needle in deep when they do it," he said in a near whisper, "use a scalding needle to cauterize the blood vessels that get severed. I wanted to scream, but I was the only Chinese prisoner and I thought I should set a good example."

She looked away, out the window, as if she didn't want to listen.

"I was never sent in to spy, Meng. I went too far in an investigation, into the top ranks of the Party. Certain ministers in Beijing wanted to bury me alive. They sent me to the prison with the highest fatality rate in China. But I survived, because of Lokesh and men like him. Five years, Meng. I was in five years. I know the diseases. I helped dig mass graves."

When she looked back, her face had hardened. "Do you have any idea how many agencies there are that run secret intelligence agents?" she asked. "At least a dozen that are widely known, as many more that can't be named. Agents routinely invest years in their cover. There are schools run for the purpose. They are dead to their prior lives. They live their cover every hour, every minute, never confiding in anyone, going for months or even years without surfacing for those who run them. There is no sacrifice too great for the motherland."

Shan's mouth went dry.

"An agent could get such a number on his arm, even build a cover no one understands but him and his handlers. The best of those agents could even endure five years in a prison to earn the trust of his targets. If you were such an agent, what would you tell me?"

He looked down into his hands. "That I wasn't sent to spy. That I was truly in prison to be punished."

"Exactly."

Shan opened his mouth to argue but hesitated. He could not fathom why he felt the need to make this woman understand the truth of his life. There was, in the end, no way to refute her. She wanted so badly to believe he was not real, that he was an agent, an informer. In the world she inhabited no one had to be real. There was no truth in her world, only greater and lesser degrees of propaganda. And there was a certain veracity to her words. He did live under cover, he did hide the most important elements of his life, he did keep his most important truths secret.

He rolled his sleeve back over his wrist. "I know how to survive," he repeated in a tight voice.

"You're a fool to think so. Survival in such a place is a cast of the dice. Lose the throw and it's that hole in the ground for you. Not even a shroud. They toss you in the pit and maybe throw some lime on your face. The birds will pick at you until your end of the hole fills and a bulldozer shoves dirt over it. Bodies mean nothing in China," she added as a bitter afterthought.

Shan studied her. She had been sitting in half-darkness, staring at her desk, before he arrived. "What happened, Lieutenant?"

She stared again out the window, into the night. "I wasn't supposed to see. I didn't want to see. There's a shed behind the district headquarters by the cell block. The door was open. There were stacks of ice inside and it made me curious. If I had known the ice was for him I would have stayed away."

"You mean the German. It was only two bodies that were stolen because Liang had already stolen the German's."

The lieutenant nodded. "But they had tortured him."

A chill crept up Shan's spine. "He was already dead, Meng."

"They beat him, crushed the bones in what was left of his face, broke his arms and legs. There was a sledgehammer by the table."

It was Shan's turn to stare at the empty desk. "Has the major left?"

"No. He was gone for a day after his meeting with you. Now he's furious at everyone. He's sending more bulldogs in to stir things up here, says this is the price we pay for giving such a free hand to the Tibetans in the valley. He won't leave until things are resolved."

"You mean until they find the American."

"If she has evidence she should come forward."

"You call me a fool? You know they've decided what to do with the German. He was in an accident, probably a climbing accident, a fall off a thousand-foot cliff. Foreigners are notorious for secretly climbing forbidden mountains. Too bad about his girlfriend. She will probably be roped with him."

"You're making no sense."

"The American girl who saw the murders. She's dead but she doesn't yet know it."

Genghis had the stamina of his Mongol namesake. The youth was in obvious pain, pausing at his work in the park to clutch at his side or adjust the bandage on his head. He was after the big bolts that secured the planks to the benches, and had clearly done it before. With a wrench in one hand and a hammer in the other he moved with mechanical efficiency, leaving every other plank as if to disguise his theft.

Shan saw a motorbike leaning against a tree in the shadows. "The Jade Crows had the cameras of the dead foreigner," he said to the youth's back. "I bet you looked at the photos. "

Genghis spun around, raising the hammer. "You're crazy, Old Mao. Dealing with stolen property is against the law."

Shan grinned and gestured to his bucket of bolts. "A bold statement, all things considered." Genghis waved the hammer as if to threaten him.

Shan pointed toward the darkened houses off the square. "No one in this town can afford to pay what those cameras are worth. Nor could they afford the risk. The cameras left on one of your trucks to Nepal. You drive those trucks sometimes. It must be boring. Surely you looked at the photos."

Genghis's grin revealed teeth stained dark red. Chewing betel nuts was one of the lesser vices of Yunnan natives. "You dumb son of a bitch. You want to take on the Crows over a few photos of Tibetans?"

"Tibetans where?"

Genghis shrugged. "Tibetans making that damned dried cheese. Tibetans blowing big horns. Tibetans on a yak caravan, working at that convent, saying prayers." He raised his hand and mimicked the snap of a shutter. "Like you better pray if you try to fuck with the Crows."

"I'm not the one with cracked ribs, Genghis. You can't just go around stealing bodies and public property."

"Just scrap metal for recycling."

"There's going to be some new police arriving soon. I told the constable outside the police post that someone was vandalizing the statue. They won't be tolerant. At least you could have tried in the middle of the night. You're rather conspicuous."

The youth's eyes flashed. "None of these damned egghead Manchurians are going to say a word about us. I could—" He paused midsentence. "*Cao ni mai!*" he spat.

Shan could see the blinking light of a police sedan reflected in the youth's wide eyes. He forced himself not to turn around, not to evidence his interest. "What color are the uniforms?" he asked. He could hear the crackle of police radios now.

Genghis's face tightened with worry. "Green apes," he replied as he searched the square, looking for an escape route. He glanced back at Shan. "Does it matter?"

"It makes all the difference. Drop your bag and kick it under the

bench." Genghis did as Shan instructed. "Give me your hammer."
Another car pulled up at the opposite end of the square, Meng's grey
utility vehicle.

When the youth froze in indecision, Shan reached out and pulled
the tool from his hand. "Now get your motorbike and walk away
with it. Don't run, don't start the engine until the shouting starts."

"Shouting?"

But Shan had no time to explain. He shoved Genghis toward the
shadows then glanced over his shoulder to see the police moving up
the square, two of the green-uniformed officers on either side, long
batons in their hands. He marched deliberately toward the statue in
the center of the square.

"Shan! No!" Meng called out as he pulled himself up on the
plinth. She began running toward him. The police behind him were
shouting now. He heard the pounding of their boots on the pavement.

Shan held onto the waist of the fiberglass Mao as he edged around
the statue, then steadied himself by throwing his arms around the
short thick neck. The police were cursing at him, running faster. He
nodded into the empty face of the Great Helmsman.

"You did all this, you son of a bitch," he spat at Mao, then lifted
the hammer and smashed in his nose.

CHAPTER TEN

The gentle touch was like cool water over his burning pain. His arms and back throbbed from the beatings, his ears rang from the batons hitting his head. He sensed the trickle of blood from half a dozen cuts. But from the deep pit of his pain a voice called him upward.

"I am not afraid of demons," came the whispered voice. "If I were afraid of demons there would be little profit in knowledge of things as they are." It was not a prayer, but a poem from Milarepa, Tibet's ancient poet-saint, about an encounter with evil gods. "How wonderful it is that you have arrived. Do not leave without making a nuisance of yourself," the gentle voice recited, pulling Shan upward toward the light.

At last, with the gasp of the drowning man reaching air again, he awoke. The leathery, stubbled face that hovered over him smiled. He reached out and grabbed Lokesh's hand.

"If I had known you would miss me so on my holiday I would have written," the old Tibetan quipped.

Shan covered the leathery hand with his other hand, squeezing it as relief flooded over him. He tried to speak but only a parched croak came out of his mouth. Lokesh propped him up and put a wooden ladle of water to his lips.

"Are you well, my friend?" Shan asked after he drank.

"You know these government resorts. They tend to cut corners on meals and bedding."

With painful effort Shan pushed himself back against the wall, leaning there so he could better look about. They were in a corner of what seemed to be a long open-fronted garage. Outside were rows of run-down barracks. "An army base?"

"Built as a camp for summer training," came a soft voice behind Lokesh. A sturdy woman with a stubble of grey hair on her scalp appeared. "Abandoned years ago. Some of the buildings are only good for firewood."

Shan had not worried about finding Lokesh and the nun amid the hundreds in the camp. He had known they would be with the sick and injured.

"My name is Shan," he said to the nun.

The woman offered a hesitant nod.

"Ani Ama knows the healing ways," Lokesh said. "They don't let us have doctors."

Shan turned back to study the building he lay in. The pallets of the sick and injured extended the entire length of the rear wall. A few of the patients, like Shan, wore makeshift bandages over external injuries. Most appeared pale and fevered. Some were shaking uncontrollably. Others wept.

He studied his friend, seeing now the patches of color on his face and forearms where bruises were fading. "Did they . . . are you—"

"I am well enough," Lokesh said with a small grin, fixing Shan with a meaningful gaze. In their gulag barracks Lokesh had often been punished, usually for breaking discipline to aid an ailing prisoner, but he had never spoken of his beatings, never once complained. "You should not have come," he added. "It is too dangerous. You have Ko to think of."

Shan fought a new wave of emotion at the mention of his son. "Ko is not going anywhere. I missed your snoring in the night."

Lokesh's grin, made uneven by a knob boot years earlier, exposed his yellowed, uneven teeth. He gripped Shan's arm tightly for a moment, then rose to help him to his feet.

Shan clenched his jaw against the pain in his shoulders and back, trying to push away the memory of the storm of batons after the police had pulled him off the statue. With Lokesh's help he hobbled into the sunlight.

"There are too many here," Lokesh said. "Twice the number the camp should hold. Not enough food. Not enough pallets and blankets. Not enough latrines."

Shan saw only a few solitary Tibetans wandering around the compound. "Where are they?"

Lokesh gestured toward the largest of the buildings, no doubt originally built as a mess hall. "Classes. You've heard it before. Hours of lectures every day. Duty to the motherland. Beijing's version of the history of Tibet. Learning magical chants from *The Little Red Book*."

Lokesh led Shan toward the nearest barracks, pausing at the warped planks of the stairs leading inside. "Ani Ama convinced them to set up a quarantine, said the soldiers could all get sick otherwise. They aren't real guards, just police." Shan and Lokesh well knew the thugs who ran China's hard-labor prisons. "Like a practice prison. Not even any roll calls. They don't realize the sick rotate in and out every few hours. The worst of those who are really sick are in the old bunkers in the back fields. From there it's a short walk to the graveyard. They're just carried out in wheelbarrows, five or six a day since the typhus started."

An old woman standing on the top step cast them a scolding look, then stepped aside at a murmured syllable from Lokesh. Shan pushed open the door to find more rows of pallets along the walls of the building. Except half the occupants were not lying on them, but sat with legs folded underneath, murmuring prayers as they worked their *malas*, their prayer beads. The end of the long hall was covered with the chalked images of deities.

"Ani Ama organized it the first day we were here. She calls it our secret army," Lokesh explained, then pulled Shan back out of the doorway.

As harsh as it was, the internment camp was indeed not one of the hard-labor prisons Shan was used to, with strict regimens enforced with merciless brutality. He recalled what Jigten had called the place. Not a prison, just a cage with no way out. They paused at a hand pump where Lokesh worked the handle as Shan held his head in the stream of cold water, then found a seat in a decrepit lean-to, out of sight of the guards.

Lokesh spoke of his final journey with the dead lama as if Jamyang had been alive, recounting how the stars had danced overhead as they had climbed at night, how butterflies had often alighted on Jamyang, how the ragyapa, the flesh cutters, had shown him with great reverence a meteorite that had landed, glowing red-hot, in their yard of bones the week before.

Shan explained what he had learned since leaving his friend, though he could not bring himself to repeat Chenmo's strange tale of seeing Jamyang on the highway.

"Did they get away?" he asked, "the ones with the abbess?"

"I am sure of it." Lokesh nodded. "If they had been caught they would be here. The abbess is safe. That meteorite, it was a sign the boneyard is still protected by the deities." He lowered his voice and leaned toward Shan. "Ani Ama told me there is a little hut at the hermitage where there are nuns at all hours, taking turns, always at least two, saying the rites for the full cycle."

The full cycle. Lokesh meant the full forty-nine days that comprised the mourning period of old Tibet. "For Jamyang and the abbess. It will help them find the next step that is destined for them." Lokesh straightened, then cast a faraway look toward the sacred mountain. "Up and down," he said solemnly.

Shan realized after a moment that his friend was referring to the levels of the next existence, the next spiritual stage for the dead.

The fact that Jamyang had taken four, that he was a suicide, weighed heavily on Lokesh. The traditional Tibetans believed suicides and those who killed suffered terrible punishment, then were reincarnated far down the chain of existence. It could take them hundreds of lifetimes to reach the human form again.

"They're going to find the American, Lokesh," Shan said after a long silence. "It won't go well for her when they do. No one outside knows she's here. They don't have to account for her."

"I have been thinking about that, about how many of the people here have not even recognized her as an outsider. Her complexion is dark. She cut her hair." There was an odd pleading in his eyes as Lokesh looked back at Shan. "What if this was meant to be her path, what if she were intended to become a nun in Tibet? How many times have I heard you say you were transformed when you came here. Maybe this is just the passage she must endure to be transformed."

Shan felt a melancholy grin tug at his mouth. He was so tired, so sore. He would like nothing more than to sit and soothe himself with his friend's gentle vision of the world. "They will find her," he said instead. "Someone will tell them. Someone always tells them. You know how it works. A criticism session where prisoners are forced to speak of other inmates. Or she will give herself away. She speaks almost no Tibetan. It is a miracle she has lasted this long. I have to talk with her."

Lokesh smiled, then shrugged. "A miracle, like you say. And what was it that kept you alive in prison, my friend?"

Shan felt a flush of emotion as he returned the old Tibetan's gaze. "A miracle," he whispered. He turned away with a sigh. "I have to get her out."

"She won't speak with you."

"Take me to her. You have to let me try. She could die."

There was pleading in his friend's eyes now. "Don't do it, Shan. Don't take her back to the death, to the blackness of murder. I think she is trying to become a nun. Ani Ama says the deities must have intended it. The abbess dies in an unexpected way, a new nun arrives in an unexpected way."

Shan sighed and gazed out over the camp. "I remember in our prison how one of the old monks found an injured bird. Everyone else would have eaten it but the two of you made a little cage for it out of an old basket. The lama grew very fond of it. But when it was healed you told him he had to keep the door of the cage open. You said it should not decide its fate based on fear. You said it had to follow its true nature. The bird flew away."

Shan saw in his eyes that Lokesh understood. "She can't become a nun out of fear," he continued. "She can only make that decision once she is free."

Lokesh turned to Shan in silence. Shan had seen the gaze before. There was patience and affection in it, but also disappointment.

"Once I was being taken for punishment," Shan said after a moment, shuddering at the memory. The Chinese guards had always singled him out for special punishment for helping the Tibetan prisoners. He had been treated as a traitor for doing so. "You told me the pain would never reach inside as long as I would just act true. She has to act true. She has to let me help her so she can help us."

"What you mean," Lokesh said after a long moment, "is that she can only be a nun if she stops being a nun. But that," he added, "is not something you or I can ask of her."

As he paced along the grounds Shan unsuccessfully tried to convince himself that the pain he felt was that left by the police batons. He cherished Lokesh like a second father and knew the affection was reciprocated. Yet every few months a rift seemed to open between them, a gap that seemed impossible to bridge. Once he had believed it grew out of Lokesh's steadfast belief in allowing fate to take its own course, because the deities would eventually find the solutions to all problems, while Shan constantly wanted to challenge the course of events. But Shan had begun to glimpse something new. The hope of resurrecting the old ways that had nourished men like Lokesh for decades was beginning to die and it was Shan's country that was killing it. Just as Lokesh had once been part of the Dalai Lama's government, Shan had once been part of the government that was destroying Tibet. They were just actors on a stage at the end of time. A great sadness welled within him. Suddenly his fatigue was overpowering.

He sat against one of the only trees in the compound, which had been stripped of bark and lower branches for firewood, and watched life in the camp. Prisoners began pouring out of the mess hall, their catechism for the morning done. A loudspeaker crackled to life and began playing a favorite Party anthem. "The East Is Red."

Shan leaned his head against the dying tree, studying the movements of the guards, the placements of the watchtowers, the intermittent activity at the main gate and the smaller one at the rear of the facility. His eyelids grew heavy, and he was unable to fight his drowsiness.

When he awoke, one of his tattered shoes was off. Lokesh was sitting beside him, mending it with needle and thread. At Shan's side was a tin mug of porridge.

"That's all there is for two meals a day," Lokesh explained as Shan lifted the mug and poked at the thin gruel with a finger. It was pasty and granular.

"Sawdust," he muttered in disgust. The guards were mixing the grain with sawdust.

Lokesh offered a matter-of-fact nod as he continued his task. "There is no shortage of grain this year. Someone is getting rich on the prisoners' empty bellies. Not enough blankets, not enough toilet paper, not enough clothing." It was a common aspect of most Chinese prisons. The guards diverted provisions to sell on the black market.

The old Tibetan pulled a thread tight, then looked up at Shan. "I remember years when there was so much sawdust in the porridge we could burn it. We made little *torma* and lit them for the gods."

Shan offered a melancholy grin in acknowledgment. Winters in their gulag camp had been hellish, with every prisoner just trying to endure the cold and starvation for one more day. Despite their empty bellies Lokesh and several of the older lamas had used their sawdust-laden porridge to shape little offering statues and burned them on makeshift altars, as they would have with the torma butter figures at the temples of their youth. There had been many nights when the lamas had sat with one of their companions as he lay dying of malnutrition or typhus, often clutching his belly in pain, and watched the little flickering deities. The fact that prisoners sometimes died when the last of the flames sputtered out had been taken as a sign that the gods had not forgotten them.

Shan watched Lokesh as he walked back toward the makeshift hospital, reminding himself how much he had missed him. It had taken years to understand that there was an empty place inside him that could only be filled by the old man's presence. For Shan, memories of their sawdust winters in the gulag came back in nightmarish visions of frozen bodies stacked like cordwood, gentle old lamas covered with painful chilblains and work crews dying in avalanches. But when Lokesh reached back to those days, it was to remind him that they had always been able to keep the deities alive.

They sat in silence. Shan forced himself to eat the gruel, studying the prisoners as he did so. Many walked in a circuit inside the wire fence. Some wandered in and out of the decrepit barracks that served as prisoner housing. Others sat alone, working their beads. The structures of the army camp had been laid out in a U-shape, with the mess hall at the base and rows of barracks along each side, facing what had been the parade and training ground. Behind the mess hall, past fields of weeds, along the back wire were rows of dirt mounds that had served as ammunition bunkers. On the doors of half a dozen of the bunkers were yellow rags similar to that of the quaran-

tine barrack. Beyond the wire, down a track that led from the rear
gate, was a dump and a wide, freshly dug trench over which vultures
circled.

Shan followed the worn path along the fence. Sacred mountains
had their pilgrim paths. Inmates always had their prisoner paths. He
well understood the natural instinct of the caged animal to pace
along the barrier that contained it, and the track along the fence was
already worn to a hollow. He fell in line with other solitary prisoners, many of whom looked longingly toward the green slopes of the
surrounding mountains. They were shepherds, and knew they belonged with their flocks on the summer grass.

Banners had been hung over the fence. EMBRACE THE SOCIALIST
MIRACLE said one. Another, part of its adage torn away by the wind,
said only PROGRESS AGAINST. Guards struggled in the breeze to fasten
a new slogan to the wire. ONE PARTY, ONE PEOPLE.

He paused to study the complex outside the wire. A long administration building sat near the main gate, beside the guard barracks.
Beyond them, at the end of the road, were two square buildings with
loading docks, the camp warehouses where Lung's trucks called.

A horn sounded, a screeching air horn that seemed to send a collective shudder through the Tibetans in front of him. A plump Chinese woman in a crisp brown tunic held the horn with its canister of
air over her head, shouting at the prisoners, herding them toward the
mess hall. Shan, not daring to let the woman get closer, lost himself
in the gathering throng and was pushed toward the building. More
brown-clad figures, some carrying batons, appeared on the opposite
flank of the converging prisoners. Shan pressed into the middle of
the crowd and let it carry him into the mess hall.

Rows of plain plank tables and benches were jammed closely together, pads of paper and pencils arranged on each table. More political banners lined three of the walls, large posters bearing the images
of party heroes the fourth. Shan sat and found himself between two
middle-aged Tibetan women who nervously watched the stage at the

front of the hall, where half a dozen young Chinese men and women sat at a table beside a podium. The instructors seemed barely out of their teens. The sons and daughters of the Party elite often took such jobs for a year or two after graduating college. In Beijing they referred to it as missionary work.

The first speaker read a chapter from a book on the heroes of the Revolution, as the Tibetans listened with wooden expressions. Then a woman pulled a cover from a chalkboard and with a ruler pointed to each character of a slogan written there, shouting out the words. CHINA IS MY MOTHERLAND. THE MOTHERLAND PROVIDES FOR ALL. Then she spoke in a squeaky, impatient voice, demanding that the prisoners repeat each word after her. Fearful whispers rose around Shan. He studied his companions at the table, then the others at nearby tables. Some were so frightened their hands trembled. They were farmers and shepherds, rounded up, he suspected, not for something they themselves had done but for the transgressions of someone in their families or neighborhoods. Those who committed overt dissent were sent to hard-labor prisons to be broken. Those in danger of picking up the contagion were sent to be treated by shrill young Chinese in crisp brown tunics.

The woman ordered the prisoners to lift their pencils and write the first character of the slogan. Shan wearily lifted the pencil in front of him, then realized no one else at the table had done so. He suddenly realized they spoke no Chinese.

He quickly translated into Tibetan as other political officers began marching down the aisles with long wooden paddles. Shan wrote the first character on his paper then, as a Tibetan across the room cried out from being struck, quickly grabbed the papers of those around him and inscribed it on theirs as well.

"*Thuchay chay,*" the woman beside him whispered as an officer walked by with an approving nod. "Thank you."

"*Lha gyal lo,*" Shan replied and touched the small amulet box that hung inside his shirt.

Two hours later he stepped out of the building, blinking at the brilliant setting sun. He walked about the prisoners' path, lingering to study the earthen bunkers behind the mess hall and the graveyard beyond the rear gate. Lokesh was not with the sick when he searched for him, but in the shadow of one of the crumbling huts, sitting against a wall. Shan was not sure his friend even noticed when he sat down beside him. Lokesh was gazing at the compound, watching the ranks of gentle, innocent Tibetans being herded by Beijing's hounds. With a wrench of his heart Shan suddenly knew exactly what Lokesh was thinking. This was how the end of the world looked.

Lokesh said nothing as Shan pulled him to his feet and led him to the long line where a watery noodle soup was being served for supper.

After eating he helped Lokesh with the sick in the makeshift hospital until sunset, then they settled onto a pile of straw at the end of the building. Moments later his exhausted friend was snoring. Shan moved to the deep shadows at the edge of the parade yard, watching the guards as they circuited the grounds. They walked slowly, talking to each other, often stopping to light a cigarette. The guard towers were not manned, although the patrols sometimes climbed up them to briefly scan the grounds with searchlights. It was indeed, as Lokesh had said, only a practice prison. Most of the guards avoided the bunkers, turning and retracing their steps when they reached the mess hall, though some patrolled toward the rear wire, lifting their guns from their shoulders. The bunkers held the dying, and were uncomfortably close to the open hole where the dead lay. He waited until a pair of guards passed along the rear of the mess hall, then darted toward the earthen mounds. If he did not find the American in the next few hours he might as well not find her at all.

The sick in the bunkers had no notion of day or night. He stepped down into the fetid air of the first one to a cacaphony of moans and mantras. In the dim light of candles he saw four Tibetans on pallets, the nearest clutching his belly, his face contorted in pain. The others

were shaking with fever. Two women, one a nun, tended them, la-
dling water to their lips and wiping their brows. An old man, his face
covered with sweat, clutched a deep blue stone in his hands. It was
lapis, used to invoke the healing deity.

"How may I help?" he asked the nun. She cast him a quick weary
glance and pointed toward a bucket of night soil in the corner. He
stepped around the pallets, confirming that no one else was in the
shadows before retrieving the bucket and taking it to dump outside.

In the second bunker he helped change a pallet and watched as a
nun and her novice constructed a mandala, a circular sand painting
to invoke the protection of the lapis Buddha. The tiny clockwork
tapping of the narrow sand funnels brought memories of other such
furtive mandalas, in prisons where men Shan had known risked
beatings for making such images.

He was disheartened as he exited the bunker, painfully aware
that he was running out of time. But as he stepped into the moonlight a low whistle rose from behind him. He turned to see a dim
light in the entrance of one of the crumbling bunkers. It was Lokesh,
holding a candle within a tin can into which holes had been punched.
It was a prisoner's lantern, one of the makeshift devices they had
once used to conduct illegal rituals in their gulag barracks. Suddenly
a searchlight in the nearest tower lit the field. Shan ducked and ran.

"When they find you they will beat you," Shan whispered when
he reached his friend. It had been one of their secret greetings for
admission to prison rituals.

"They can only beat my body," came the reflexive reply, with a
flash of a grin. Lokesh gestured him inside and dropped a heavy felt
blanket over the entrance behind Shan.

The bunker was in decay, its roof buckling, its air damp and musty.
A rodent scurried in the darkness. At first Shan thought Lokesh had
only summoned him to speak, but then he saw the low grey shape
huddled in a corner.

They said nothing as they sat beside her, Lokesh on one side and

Shan on the other, the makeshift lantern on the ground before the woman. She clenched a mala in fingers that trembled. "Ani!" she cried in a hoarse voice. "Ani!" "*Nun*," she was saying, "*nun*." Her eyes were wild with fear.

Lokesh reached out and took her hand. With his fingers over hers, he gently moved one bead, then another, slowly reciting the mani mantra, as if he were teaching it to a child, working her fingers in tandem with his own.

The woman, her frightened gaze fixed on the Chinese stranger who had appeared before her, at first seemed unaware of what Lokesh was doing. Then gradually, with nervous glances back at Shan, she began to watch the two hands on the beads. An odd confusion grew on her face, as if she did not understand whose hands they were, and her fingers tightened as if to draw away. Then she focused on the serene face of the old Tibetan and slowly relaxed.

They sat unmoving for several minutes, the only sound that of the quiet mantra and the soft rattle of the beads.

Shan at last spoke, using English. "Lokesh and I would go to the ruins at night sometimes. We would clean up some of the old wall paintings. In the moonlight sometimes it felt like the deities were coming to life."

The woman reacted slowly, as if not certain she had heard correctly. It had been a long time, he realized, since she had heard her native language. She cast a worried glance toward the entry.

"I attacked a statue of Mao just to be able to see you, Cora," Shan ventured.

She looked back at Lokesh, who had not ceased his mantra. Slowly she pulled her hand away. Lokesh produced his own mala and continued the mantra.

"Elves," she whispered. "Rutger and I saw paintings mysteriously cleaned overnight, with little offerings left before them. We joked that there must be magical elves. Once, the abbot and the monks started a sand painting." The American gazed at her beads as she spoke. "The abbess saw it at the end of the day and said part of it was wrong, that some of the deities had been placed in the wrong order. But the next day they were correct. Some of the nuns said it was a miracle, that the deities must have moved themselves."

"The miracle," Shan said with a gesture toward Lokesh, "is that there are those of old Tibet still among us who know the way of the deities."

The American woman looked up from her beads and studied Lokesh as if seeing him for the first time. "Does he speak English?" she asked Shan.

"No. Lokesh says the most important speaking is done without words."

The old Tibetan had his eyes closed as he murmured his mantra. As Cora watched him her expression changed from fascination to melancholy. "He was arrested because of me. I fell down when we were being chased. He could have escaped but he came for me. He saw me in a robe. He thought I was a nun. He's here because of my lie."

Shan was beginning to glimpse the depth of the woman's pain. "No. It had nothing to do with the robe, Cora. You fell. You needed help."

"And he is in this awful prison because of it."

"Lokesh and I know what a prison is. This is more like a retreat for like-minded people."

A spark seemed to flicker in the woman's eyes for a moment, then faded. "People are dying."

Shan nodded. "You and Rutger were right in wanting the world to know about such places."

Cora looked up in alarm, seeming about to deny Shan's suggestion, but then she looked away, back at her beads. A single tear rolled down her cheek. "Rutger was the photographer. I was the artist who sketched faces. I began to do so on scrap paper. I have thirty pages already. I could sketch a whole book of the faces I have seen here."

"You must do so," Shan said. "Give them to the world."

"I was going to wrap them in a cloth and throw them over the wire in the hope someone would find them."

"That's not what Rutger would want."

It was the wrong thing to say. At the mention of Rutger's name the woman's face tightened. She pressed back against the wall, seeming to shrink before his eyes. Her knuckles holding the beads were white.

"You need to let me help you, Cora," Shan said.

She shook her head slowly and began rocking back and forth.

"Please. You don't understand the danger you face. We haven't much time. It will be dawn soon."

She seemed unaware of their presence now. She rocked like a small frightened child. Shan and Lokesh exchanged a worried glance. The risk that they would be discovered by the guards increased every minute.

When the American opened her eyes they seemed to have no focus. Then slowly her rocking stopped and she was looking over the lantern. Lokesh's hand was facing downward, with his thumb and little finger spread, the middle fingers curled toward the thumb.

"It's one of those hand prayers," she said.

"A mudra," Shan confirmed. "It is the sign of giving refuge, Cora. On the long winter nights when we lay shivering and starving in the gulag the old lamas would light a candle. One would walk with it along the bunks while another made a mudra. It was like a holy thing, like a relic brought to life. They would teach us to focus on it, to forget all else but the mudra of the night. It kept some of the prisoners alive."

Cora looked back at Shan. "Gulag?"

"Lokesh spent much of his life in prison, because he had been in the Dalai Lama's government." Lokesh kept looking at the woman with a serene expression, his hand still in the mudra. "These are his words to you," Shan said. "He and I offer you refuge. You can sketch all of his mudras. Chenmo will help. He could tell you of the old days, and of prison. It could be your book."

"Refuge? No one gets out. They just keep adding more and more prisoners."

"I need you to help me find out about the murders. You can't do it here. I need you safe, away from Public Security. Then you can tell me about that day. You were there, weren't you?"

She took so long to answer his question he was not sure she had heard. "I have so many nightmares I don't want to sleep anymore. The abbess calls to me in the night. Sometimes I wonder which is my nightmare and which is my memory. It's like I was there and not there."

"You were there, Cora," Shan assured her. "And you need to remember. For Rutger's sake. You saw the one who did it."

"You mean the monster. The thing."

"The monster. The killer. Yes."

Cora seemed to shrink again. Once more she began rocking back and forth. "Rutger says the colors have to be just right. You can't just paint the old walls red. There's a special shade like maroon, like good Tibetan soil. The Tibetans have pigments they save for such things. Prayer red, he calls it. I painted a gate with the wrong shade and he wants me to redo it. The abbess will help. She teaches me old rhymes for the rhythm of the brush."

Shan's skin crawled. A dry, creaking laugh escaped her throat. "The abbess found a patch of blooming wildflowers above the ruins. We're going to quit early so we can take a meal there. A picnic, I told them. The abbess repeated the word several times like a mantra. Picnic, picnic, picnic. She laughed.

"She wanted to finish painting the cradle of that old wheel. Rutger was going to help her, though she kept telling him to go to the back of the grounds. Someone was coming, and he might scare the man. I said I would go sketch some of the paintings inside the little chapels." Cora's voice trailed away and she began reciting her mantra again.

"A Chinese man named Lung was coming," Shan said. "Who else?"

But Cora did not hear him. She had gone to a distant, terrifying place. Tears were flowing down her cheeks. "I should never have left. I had decided to carry the food out to the place with flowers. I saw the one come on his bicycle but that couldn't be the one they were worried about, I thought. I sat in the flowers, waiting. They were taking so long. I went back down. They were praying by the chorten, I thought. That one didn't see me. He is talking to them now, all angry at them. But they won't speak back. He was bent over Rutger, I thought to help him somehow. He had a red rag in his hand. I thought they must have spilled the red paint on themselves. Then he turned with Rutger's head on his knee and I saw what he had done. It was Rutger's face in his hand. The blood didn't show on that one because of the color.

"I ran. He called out but I was already at the back wall. I ran. I fell. I ran some more. I didn't know where I was going. I must have run for hours."

He did not speak until her tears had dried.

"You have to trust Lokesh and me, Cora. I will get you out. We will take you to a safe place. Not the hermitage, because the nuns are being watched. Perhaps the monks. Lokesh and I will get you to the monastery, to Chegar."

Cora shrank back. Her eyes filled with fear again. "Don't you understand? I told you!"

"Told me what?" Shan asked.

"I didn't see all the blood because it blended with the robe. Take me to the monastery and I will die! The butcher was a monk."

CHAPTER ELEVEN

Ani Ama refused to cooperate with Shan's plan. She raised a hand, cutting him off. "My place is here," the nun said. "There are the sick. Now wounded are being brought in, from riots somewhere." It was the middle of the night. She sat beside a dead woman as two other women worked a canvas shroud around the body.

"What if you could do more for them on the outside?" Shan asked. "What if there was a way to make the world see what was going on here? Once there was even a hint that international representatives may visit you know there would be real medical care, real food."

"No," she insisted. "Do not pretend that I have such power."

"The American and German governments have such power. They will show it, when Cora arrives home with stories of the camp, and the story of a murdered German and a murdered abbess."

The old nun stood up and placed a hand on the dead woman's brow, murmuring a blessing before the shroud was pulled over her head. "Nothing to do with me," she said to Shan.

"The abbess has been calling out to Cora," Shan said to her back. "There is only one way for the abbess to move on to what she deserves."

Ani Ama halted. "You don't think I pray for that every night?"

"One of the young monks of Chegar said he hears her moaning, echoing across the hills in the darkest hours. The abbess is wandering lost, unable to understand what has happened to them." The nun slowly turned toward Shan as he spoke. "A terrible shadow is falling on all those who wear robes in the valley. Help me find the truth. The American was there, at the convent. Leave with us and we will find the killer together."

"The truth about the murders is with those who died."

"If we know how to listen we can still hear it. You have part of it already."

"Nonsense. I wasn't there."

"Jamyang died that day too. It was no coincidence. You went with the abbess to prepare the body of the Lung boy. Jamyang was there. What happened? Why was he frightened by the body?"

"I don't think it was death that frightened him."

"Then tell me, Ani Ama. Why did he flee that day?"

Ani Ama sighed and looked out over the camp. "I didn't want to be abbess. I wanted to spend my last years in some quiet place at a loom. My mother was a weaver, and her mother before." She watched the body as it was carried away, then began explaining. When Lung Tso had arrived to ask the abbess to help, Jamyang had been with her. He had asked questions of Lung Tso, shown great concern that one so young had died. He accepted the invitation of the abbess to join them. "The lama knew about the old ways," Ani Ama explained, "and knew how to receive deities. As soon as we arrived at that old stable he began cleaning it, murmuring the right words, then lit incense for the gods before turning to the body. He was so reverent, so patient in cleansing the boy," the nun said. "But then as he got to the neck he gasped, then frantically worked the skin, pushing it one way and another. The abbess asked what was wrong but he seemed not to hear."

"What was it?" Shan asked. "What was on his neck?"

"Just a mark. A long straight mark like a deep bruise over the throat. The boy had died when his truck went off the road and crashed down a steep hill. His father said the mark was where the steering wheel had smashed against the boy's neck before crushing his ribs. But Jamyang wouldn't listen. It was like he was suddenly possessed. He left without another word to us. We didn't see him for more than a week."

"When was that?"

"He came back one night and sat with the abbess, alone. There were strong words, which was unlike either of them. Voices were raised. A day later she sent messages to the monastery."

"Messages? What messages?"

The nun slowly shook her head. "I didn't understand. She first sent Chenmo, who told me later. Only one word, Dharmasala, to be left on the desk of the monastery office. Later that day she sent another, with a shepherd who was passing through. A day after that she left by herself, saying no one was to follow. But I watched. At the bottom of the stairs the foreigners joined her."

"To the convent," Shan suggested.

"To go to die, yes," Ani Ama said in an anguished voice.

It had begun with the Lung boy, Shan was certain now. But what had happened afterward? What had Jamyang been doing in the days before he returned to the abbess? Why would he have summoned Lung Tso to go to the convent at the same time, but not gone himself?

"That night Jamyang and the abbess spoke," the nun said, "I dream about it. I understand now. The words they spoke were the ending. They didn't know then but they were tying off the knots of the tapestry that had been their lives."

"Only the beginning of the end," Shan said. "Those knots are still untied."

Ani Ama replied with a somber nod. She studied the hills for a long moment as if searching for a sign of the dead abbess. "We can't just walk out of this place," she said, a hint of invitation in her voice.

"No," Shan agreed. He looked back at the shrouded body. "First you have to die."

The guards escorting the burial detail wanted nothing to do with the bodies. They kept their distance, watching with revulsion as Shan and half a dozen others loaded the dead onto the wheelbarrows, then opening the back gate and quickly stepping aside. The dead were infected with disease.

Lokesh had explained that sometimes as many as half a dozen were dying each night. Shan, pushing the last handcart, gave silent thanks that there had been only two deaths that particular night, so that adding three more bodies had not attracted notice. He nervously watched the pair of guards pause to light cigarettes and looked back toward the little warehouse where Lung's trucks were due. He breathed a sigh of relief as one of the guards split away toward the tractor that was used to push earth into the trench. Shan saw the blur of dust that signaled the arrival of Lung's trucks. Then suddenly the second guard lifted his baton and thumped it down on the first body. Shan's heart leapt as the guard approached the second.

"The organs of state must practice democratic centralism!" Shan suddenly shouted as the guard took a step toward the second cart, then darted forward with his cart toward the pit. "Today is chapter seventeen! Quickly! We forgot there is an early review session of Chairman Mao's *Quotations*! We cannot shame the Great Helmsman!" He mouthed a prayer, then hastily pitched his barrow sideways, letting the body he carried roll into the pit. He expected the guard to aim his baton at him, but the few moments of hesitation caused by Shan's outcry had been enough. The man cocked his head toward the road. Lung's trucks were at the warehouse, and someone was frantically shouting from the loading dock. Then suddenly Shan saw the movement on the road. A grey utility vehicle was speeding toward the camp, its red lights flashing. The knobs were coming, the knobs who hated to dirty their hands with the business of the People's Armed Police.

With a sinking heart he watched the knob's car slide to a stop at the front gate. In desperation his gaze shifted back and forth from the knobs climbing out of the vehicle to the warehouse. Dark smoke began pouring out of the engine compartment of the nearest truck. The men at the warehouse shouted, even louder, pointing at the truck, and were running away from it as it suddenly burst into flames.

The guard near Shan shouted for the other prisoners to dump their shrouded loads as the second guard, on the tractor, leapt off the vehicle and ran toward the fire. Shan gestured urgently to his companions, who emptied their carts, dumping the shrouds containing Cora, Ani Ama, and Lokesh onto the ground by sheltering rocks. The three rolled quickly away, pushing off the shrouds, and disappearing into the rocks as Shan threw the shrouds into the pit. The Tibetan who had carried the bucket of lime emptied it into the pit, then took Shan's cart as planned and headed back toward the gate. But Shan stood frozen, watching as the three scrambled out around the nearby outcroppings. He heard Lokesh's urgent whisper, calling him to join them as they had planned. Shan looked back at the knobs. He knew why they were there, knew that if he were missing when they searched for him in the camp that the hills would soon be crawling with troops.

"*Lha gyal lo*," he called in a low voice to the three who watched from the rocks, pointing toward the high ground, then he turned and marched back to the gate.

Major Liang was standing at the window in the interrogation room at the Public Security district headquarters when Shan was shoved inside. He glared at Shan, crushed out his cigarette, took two steps, and slapped Shan in the face with the back of his hand.

"You think you can mock me!" he shouted. "You think you can

interfere with my investigation without my knowing! By the time I am done with you, you will be begging for the bullet I will put in your head!"

Shan lowered himself into a chair at the table and stared out the window.

"You have a hard-labor tattoo on your arm," Liang said to his back. "Do you know how few of those are seen in the reeducation camps? Those who survive hard labor are usually model citizens. If a number shows up in the camps a message is sent to Public Security for follow-up. Except no one can follow up your number. Impossible, I said, there has to be a record. I searched the data myself. It's a Lhadrung registration number but Lhadrung has no record of you. An empty file. When I did a broader search I came up with a famous investigator from Beijing with the same name who disappeared years ago. The only real entry shows you as a ditch inspector for Lhadrung County. A ditch inspector who impersonates a senior investigator. Did you kill the real Shan, the one from Beijing?"

When Shan did not reply Liang stepped to the opposite side of the table and slammed his fist on it. "You're not a mere criminal! You showed your true colors when you attacked that statue in the park. You are a traitor. You mock the motherland! You shame the motherland!"

Shan kept staring at the unfamiliar landscape out the window. The headquarters complex was in a crossroads village miles north of Lhadrung County. "There are three hundred forty miles of ditches in my district," he declared as Liang paced around the table. "I keep the water flowing by removing mud and trash. You'd be surprised how big a job it is."

His only warning was a blur of movement at the corner of his eye. The blow slammed into his cheek with a sharp stinging pain. Liang reappeared at the other side of the table, holding a wooden ruler.

"Who took the bodies?" Liang demanded.

"They did you a favor, Major. The political construct of murder can raise so many dilemmas. With no bodies there can be no murders."

Liang slammed the ruler down again, this time on the back of Shan's hand. "Who took the bodies?" he repeated, his voice shrill now.

Shan blinked away the pain. "I forgot. You have the third body still, the most troublesome one. But you have a plan for that one. A climbing accident. Or is it to be an unfortunate car crash in the mountains? Better have the car explode so you can report the body was destroyed. It might seem negligent to lose a foreigner's face."

Liang's anger was like an evil creature twisting inside him. The knob officer seemed to squirm, his mouth twisting into a snarl, his hands folding and unfolding into fists. He dropped into the chair opposite Shan and opened a shallow drawer. "Do you have any idea what this is?" he growled as he extracted a printed sheet of paper.

A shudder passed through Shan as he recognized the form. An order for imprisonment. He did not reply.

"As a senior Public Security officer I can send you away for a year without any further authority. No messy hearings. No appeal. I have a favorite prison in the Taklamakan Desert where they keep a few bunks reserved for me to fill. So cold in the winter a man can lose an entire foot to frostbite in one night. The sand gets so hot in the summer you can get blisters through your shoes. Last year's mortality rate was nearly twenty-five percent. It will be months before anyone even knows where you are. When your year is up the warden will tell me and I will destroy the original order and I will issue a new one for another prison. And the year after that and the year after that. Every year my new signature. Until I retire. But you won't last that long."

Liang lit a cigarette as he let his words sink in. "You have one night to think it over. I'll instruct them to give you a notepad. Write down everything you know and we can forget the desert. You'll have to be punished for what you did to that statue but I'll just turn you over to the Armed Police for that. You know the system. Have a political epiphany. Confess your sins. Lead a Tibetan choir that sings Party anthems. You could be out in a few months."

As he was led to the cinder block cells at the rear of the compound Shan passed a small storage building. He recognized it from Meng's description as the place where the German's body had been taken, and broken with a hammer. He glanced back at Liang, gloating in the window of the headquarters. Shan began to wonder if Liang's brutal beating of the corpse had just been in spite.

Like every cell block Shan had ever entered, the air was acrid with the scent of urine, vomit, and bleach. His escort led him silently past a table with a chalkboard at its side, and shoved him into the center cell of a row of three empty cells.

It was just another of Liang's lies, Shan tried to tell himself as he stared at the imprisonment order the major had stuffed inside his shirt, one of the tactics Liang used to bully possible informers. But he had seen the hate burning in the major's eyes. There had been no pretense in them. He despised Shan for having deceived him and wanted him to die a slow death in the desert. He sank onto the cell's flimsy cot, elbows on his knees, his face buried in his hands. He tried to think only of Lokesh, of his friend wandering down one of his beloved pilgrim paths but Liang's threats kept echoing in his mind. The Taklamakan. He had spent weeks in one of the desert's prisons before being sent to Tibet. The buildings, and the prisoners, had been etched with the hot blowing sand so that even the newest and youngest had an aged, corroded appearance. Sandstorms kept shifting the dunes, exposing ruins and turning barracks into sand-bound bunkers overnight. In his nightmares he still saw one of the common graves from years past that been gouged out by the wind. Protruding from a wall of sand had been the skeletal feet of a hundred prisoners.

He paced the cell with a prisoner's eye, counting the steps in a circuit, noting a mouse hole under the cot, gleaning a piece of chalk that had rolled across the floor and lodged against the iron bars. Finally he lifted the pad and pencil left on the stool by the cot, staring at the blank paper for a long time. Xiao Ko, he wrote at last. Young Ko. His son. He was due for a visit with Ko in two days, a visit he knew now he would never make. They were both to be in the gulag now, in what the prisoners often called the belly of the dragon. He traced his son's name with trembling fingertips. The wrenching sentences formed in his mind but his hand was unable to move the pencil.

> *I am going away to the Taklamakan. The next time you see me I will be in the row of skeletons emerging from the dune. It wasn't supposed to end this way, Ko. We were going to build a little cabin in the mountains with Lokesh and forget all the miseries of the world below. But the dragon ate me after all.*

A hard black thing seemed to grow inside, until he felt only a cold emptiness. A Tibetan prisoner, a middle-aged man, was shoved into the cell beside him. The man began weeping.

The Tibetan prisoner cried until the middle of the night, then he sat in the center of his cell and stared at the round drain plate in the cement floor.

"*Om mani padme hum,*" the man intoned in a sorrowful voice.

Shan stepped to the bars and extended his prayer beads toward the man. The Tibetan gazed at him in surprise then silently rose and accepted the mala. He returned to his place on the floor, sat down, and slowly began reciting the beads. As he spoke a new strength entered his voice.

Shan watched for a long moment, then turned to the little stool where he had left the paper and began writing.

> *I saw a hawk today flying high overhead, rising in the wind until he was a speck in the southwest sky. I realized at*

that moment that he could see both where I sat and where
you sat. Maybe you saw him too.

Ko, it will be a long time before you hear from me again.
It could be that they will move you to punish me. But know
that as soon as I am able I will start searching for you and I
will not stop until I find you. Meanwhile listen to the guards.
But first, always, listen to the lamas.

He wrote on only half the sheet, so he could fold it twice, making its own envelope. *Shan Ko*, he wrote on the outside. *404th People's Construction Brigade.*

In the early morning hours he awoke. There was no light but the dim reflection cast from the entryway light. A silent shape sat at the interrogation table, masked in shadow, facing Shan. The silhouette, a figure in a stiff uniform with a high-brimmed cap, told him it was one of Liang's lackeys, no doubt there to underscore Liang's message. Shan took the stool to the front of the cell and sat, facing the knob. It was a prisoner's game, and he was alarmed at how readily it came back to him. The fear may ravage your gut, may hollow you out, but you can never let them see it.

He lost track of how long he stared at the shadow figure. Moonlight moved across the floor. The Tibetan prisoner murmured on, his mantra sometimes coming out in sobs. Shan wasn't staring at another knob, he was staring at a wraith, at the dark soulless phantom that was his government.

He was so fatigued, so caught in the spell, that he gasped when he suddenly realized the wraith had risen and was moving toward him. The light was so dim its face was unclear until it stopped in front of him. It was no wraith, it was Lieutenant Meng, a pale and brittle Meng in a starched uniform with her hair tightly tied behind her head.

Meng opened her mouth but her tongue found no words. Shan pulled the folded letter from his pocket and shoved it through the bars. She hesitated, as if scared of the paper, then with a quick motion grabbed it and stuffed it inside her tunic. She did not look at him, but spun about and marched back to the table, where she made a show of opening the drawer and pulling out another paper. She crushed his letter, threw the wad into the trash can, and then walked back, tossing the new paper into his cell before leaving. Another prisoner assignment form.

Shan stared in confusion as Meng disappeared into the compound. He sighed, then turned back to sit on the cot. After a long time he rose, picked up the piece of chalk and whispered to the Tibetan.

He was asleep on the cot when the surprised shout of a guard awakened him. Early morning light filtered through the window. The Tibetan still sat on the floor, though he was singing a quiet song now. The guard ran out of the building and returned moments later with two more guards. All three men began shouting angrily, pointing at Shan, then the Tibetan, then the little creatures placed around their cells and the circle on the Tibetan's floor. Using Shan's chalk and his careful instructions, the Tibetan had created a mandala around the round drain plate in the floor. Using the entire pad of paper meant for his confession Shan had created origami birds. Small flocks roosted on the windowsills of the two cells, others were scattered around the cells. One guard ran back to the doorway, to warn his comrades of any approaching officer as the others opened the cell doors, cursing the two grinning prisoners as they quickly gathered up the birds and scuffed away the prayer circle with their boots.

With angry taps of their batons they pushed Shan against a wall, then fastened manacles to his feet before dragging him to the interrogation table. They disappeared and returned with a tepid cup of tea, which he slowly sipped. He made a show of stretching, ignoring his watchers to better survey the area around the table. His gaze lingered on the chair where Meng had sat for so long, watching him, then he scanned the walls and ceiling.

The small black instrument blended into the shadows of the corner where walls and ceiling met. A camera. Meng had sat in the only

chair that was invisible to the camera that monitored the room, had
kept her back to it and her head bent so she would not have been
identified when she had stepped to his cell.

He drained the cup, then clutched his stomach and convulsed,
spitting up the brown liquid, looking about desperately before leaping
toward the trash basket to spit up more. One of the guards laughed, the
other barked a curse and stepped away from Shan. As he leaned into
the basket he grabbed the wad of paper at the bottom and stuffed it
down his shirt.

A moment later the door opened and Liang marched in. The
guards darted to Shan and heaved him back into the chair. As Liang
silently stepped behind him, his neck exploded in pain. Shan's body
was wracked in a convulsion that slammed his back into the metal
chair, leaving him gasping.

"Excellent," Liang declared as he paused at the opposite side of
the table. "I have your attention." In his hand was a small electronic
taser device. The knobs had once preferred electronic cattle prods. They
were keeping up with technical advances.

A guard dropped one of Shan's little paper cranes in front of
Liang. The major sighed. He picked up the crane, then carefully tore
its wings and head off. A cool grin grew on his face as he tossed the
remains of the bird at Shan, then made a show of increasing the intensity of the taser.

"You got yourself thrown into that reeducation camp to see someone," Liang stated. "I think it was some of those nuns who knew the
dead abbess. What do they know of the murders? Tell me now and
we can be more gentle with them."

Shan spoke first in Tibetan, watching the anger build in Liang's
face, then translated into Chinese. "Nuns are the messengers of the
gods. Be careful what you ask them."

Liang lifted the taser and paced along the table again. "In India I
hear there used to be huge, unnaturally strong men who were kept by
the rajas to conduct torture. They could twist a man's head off. I

read once how they would drive a spike into a man's skull with their bare fists." He lifted the little electronic box in his hand. "When I trained for this device," he explained with a mock fascination in this voice, "they said it sent a spike of lightning into the flesh, said to be sure to only use it on muscle tissue." Shan gripped the arms of the chair as Liang moved back around the table. "But I've always wondered if the skull could block lightning."

The pain was like none Shan had ever known. His back arced, his eyes saw nothing but explosions of light. His body moved involuntarily, convulsing, slamming against the chair, then slamming his head against the table, pounding the table again and again. Tea and stomach acid dribbled down his chin. Liang laughed and pressed the instrument into his scalp again. The spike was in Shan's brain, driving deeper and deeper.

Shan was surely dying. Surely no one could feel such pain and live. His hands on the arms of the chair jerked up and down. His skull was going to explode. The white-hot fire in his head ebbed and flared, ebbed and flared, as if someone kept blowing on its coals. His head slumped onto his chest. He was aware of nothing but the roar of his pain.

He jerked upright, moaning, as cold water was poured over him.

"We will talk about those nuns," Liang growled.

Shan's eyes had difficulty focusing. He made out Liang's hand, adjusting the taser again. He thought of his son, and of Lokesh. This was the end. He was always going to die at the hands of some knob, he had just not known when.

"Anyone who aids that American bitch is a traitor to the motherland!" Liang snarled. "Anyone who—" His words choked away as the door was wrenched open.

A tall thin man with a hatchet face appeared, wearing the field uniform of a senior army officer, flanked by two rock-hard men in the fatigues of mountain commandos. The tall man grabbed the taser and threw it against the wall so hard it shattered.

As a guard moved to protect Liang, the officer gestured and one of his escorts flattened the man with a short, swift chop.

"My name is Colonel Tan," the officer announced. "I am governor of Lhadrung County." His voice was the low growl of a predator ready to spring.

Liang's mouth moved but no one words came out.

Tan pointed to Shan. "That man is mine!"

CHAPTER TWELVE

Tan ordered their car to stop when they crested the ridge that meant they were back in Lhadrung County. He gestured Shan out, then ordered his men to stay with the vehicle as they walked to a ledge that overlooked the valley.

Tan said nothing until he had lit a cigarette. "You're a fucking mess. What did he do to you?"

Shan couldn't stop the tremors in his hand. He stared at it a moment, then gripped it tightly with his other hand. "An experiment. He called it driving lightning into my skull."

The colonel exhaled two sharp columns of smoke from his nostrils. "It has to do with the murders up here."

"I don't think they've been officially recognized as such."

Tan ignored him. "With your unofficial meddling in these unofficial murders. Damn you, you can never leave things alone. It's a Public Security matter. You know I have no authority."

Shan recognized the ice in the colonel's voice, knew the heat of his temper could burn hotter than any taser. He took an unsteady step and lowered himself onto a boulder. "A dead German. A missing American. If you are lucky you have maybe two or three weeks before foreigners are all over your county. First the embassies. Then the reporters."

Tan inhaled deeply on his cigarette. "How many years does he have left?"

Shan's heart sagged. Tan knew ways to torture him that Liang could never dream of. "Ten years. Ko has ten years left."

"With one short message I could have him shipped to another prison. Manchuria. The Gobi. The jungle. If you started right away, you probably wouldn't even locate him in ten years. But then you have no papers so you'd probably be picked up too."

"I have the work papers you gave me."

"Exactly. They would call my office. Everytime I hear your name I will have your son transferred again. When he's released he will have no idea where you are. The two of you will grow old trying to find each other, wandering around China. Like one of those old tragic operas."

Shan struggled to control his pain, and his despair. Liang would invent threats, just to intimidate those he questioned. Tan never made idle threats. He would do it. He would consider it his duty to do so. "The murders happened in Lhadrung County," Shan said. "When the foreigners arrive, they will start with you."

"We will not permit them to come."

"You know those foreign reporters. They will just get in a car and start driving. Refuse them and they just get more persistent. You can't imprison them. Turn one away and two come back. Someone will ask why the locals call the districts in the northern county Tan's Hellhole. How many prisons do you have now? Ten? A dozen? They will discover your penal colony. Better hope some American politician is caught with a mistress that day, or you'll be on every front page in the West."

"Public Security knows how to deal with such things."

"You of all people expect Public Security to find the truth?"

Tan frowned. "I said they would deal with it."

"Liang is one of those who searches for the most convenient solution. You are familiar with the type if I am not mistaken." The year before Shan had saved Tan from another overzealous knob who had jailed him for murder. Tan owed Shan his life, and hated Shan for it.

Tan gazed at him in silence, took a long draw on his cigarette, and flung the butt over the ledge. "I will leave you at the clinic in Baiyun. If you trouble me again I won't even give you a chance to say good-bye to your son."

The nurse who managed the clinic shook her head as she studied Shan's hand. Every time she straightened his fingers they curled back, digging into his palm.

"There's nerve damage," she declared. "You should go to Lhasa for a scan. Who knows what damage there is to your brain." She had cleaned the oozing burn on his scalp where Liang had pressed the taser.

"I thought perhaps a couple of aspirin," Shan said.

"Does it hurt?"

"Like a blade is in my skull, twisting back and forth."

The Chinese woman frowned. "You must rest. Take a week off. You could kill yourself if you push hard."

He heard the door open behind him. The assistant in the office had been furious when Tan's guards had shoved Shan in ahead of the half-dozen patients waiting there.

The nurse frowned and handed him an unlabeled bottle of red pills. "Go home. Let your family nurse you."

"An excellent suggestion," came a voice behind him.

Shan turned to see Professor Yuan at his shoulder. "Shall we go, Xiao Shan?" the professor asked with a sweep of his hand toward the door. Xiao Shan. It was how an uncle might address the younger members of his family.

"I can't . . ." Shan murmured.

"You can," Yuan insisted, and pulled him up from the exam table. "You will. We have a dilemma we need you to resolve."

Shan followed in a fog of pain and fatigue. A quarter hour later he collapsed on a bed in the professor's house, having swallowed a bowl of broth and two of the red pills.

When he awoke it was dark. A candle burned by his bed. He looked out at the moon. He had slept for at least ten hours. The scalding pain in his head was gone, replaced with a dull ache. He extended his fingers. On one hand they stayed straight, on the other they instantly curled back up. He tried to stand, and fell back on the bed. For a long time he stared at the floor as memories of his imprisonment returned, then he reached inside his shirt and straightened the wad of paper he had retrieved from the wastebasket. It was a blank prisoner assignment form. Meng had not thrown out his letter. She had performed a charade for the surveillance camera to save his letter to Ko.

From the sitting room he heard gentle laughter and the sound of several voices speaking in Chinese. With a strange awkwardness he approached the door, then hesitated, looking about the room as if for the first time. There was a dresser with framed photos of a much younger Yuan with his wife and daughter Sansan, several of Sansan alone. There were three sheets of graceful calligraphy pinned to the wall, lines from ancient poems, beside pegs hung with clothing.

He steadied himself on the back of a chair, fighting a new wave of emotion. This was how the home of a family looked. Never in Shan's life had he had such a place, such a home, and he knew that he probably never would. He forced himself to look away, then opened the door, stepped out, and froze.

Four men and a woman, all in their late sixties or seventies, sat around the table. A pall of tobacco smoke hung over the candlelit room. A bottle of cheap rice wine and glasses were on the table, in the center of which were several dice and a bundle of sticks. It was a scene of his youth, when the older inhabitants of his block stayed up into the small hours of the morning, tossing numbers to consult the *I Ching*. It was a timeless scene, a fixture of Chinese villages for centuries.

Professor Yuan looked up from the table. "Xiao Shan! Please come sit with us! We are eager for your advice."

As the professor introduced Shan to his companions Shan realized he had seen most of them before, playing chess or checkers in the town square.

"The hero of the hammer," proclaimed the oldest of the men, a nearly bald man with thick horn-rimmed glasses. "You know, they wrapped a white canvas around the statue afterwards. In the moonlight he is the ghost of Baiyun." He lifted his glass of wine to Shan. "They will replace him eventually. But because of you we will always see it as just another ghost. A noseless ghost," he said with a wheezing laugh. "We salute you for being brave enough to do what each of us has dreamed of doing ever since they put that damned statue up."

Shan silently accepted a glass of wine and sat beside the professor. "You mentioned a dilemma?"

"Our little society strives to better understand the old ways. I know you are well versed in tradition." Yuan gestured to a long scroll of paper opened and weighed down with books at each end. The elderly woman was painting with watercolors on the thick parchment. The images progressed from skyscrapers and city blocks shaded with trees to trains and mountains, then yaks and donkeys. With a flash of excitement he realized she was recording the story of the Harbin exiles in the scroll painting style that had been used to chronicle events during the imperial reigns. He had seen the scroll before, when Yuan had hidden it behind his back to keep the knobs from discovering it. "We have been debating a point of court ceremony," Yuan explained.

Shan looked uncertainly around the table. All of those present were older than him, some of them by decades. He reminded himself that the emigrants forced to move to the village had all been retired professors. "Society?" he asked.

"We call ourselves the Vermilion Society after the color of the ink reserved for the old imperial courts. Keeping old ways alive. Professor Wu," he said, indicating the bald man, "prints up Sung poems and leaves them on doorsteps. Professor Chou," he said, with a gesture to the woman, "organized a production of an old play from the Ming dynasty. We'd sweep old graves if there were any here. We try to remember things from old China and record them. There're so few good history books left, and it's been decades since a true history of China was written. There are wonderful things from the dynasties, things that need to be remembered."

"The truest history," interjected Professor Wu, "is that built on a thousand tales of the common man."

From the kitchen came the sound of low coughing. Sansan stood in the shadows. Shan offered a hesitant nod to Wu. "In the People's Republic that can be dangerous ground."

The old professor's eyes gleamed. "Don't you know we are all here because we are dangerous people? What are they going to do to us? Exile us to Tibet?" Another raspy laugh escaped his throat.

Despite his pain, Shan couldn't suppress the grin that tugged at his mouth.

The woman at the table held up a large sheet of paper bearing small sketches, the first of which was a bird with three legs, a hen in a circle, and a dragon.

Shan cocked his head. "Symbols of the emperor."

Professor Chou's face lit with satisfaction. "Yuan said you knew your history! We are making a collaborative painting of an emperor's robe, then we hope to make an exact replica if we can find the silk. But we can't agree." She pointed to two more symbols, one of three dots connected by lines, one of seven connected dots. "Professor Yuan says there are three and I say seven."

There was something inside Shan that rejoiced at the absurdity of their sitting here in the remote exile community of Tibet debating imperial customs. He paused, venturing into a musty corridor of his memory. "Professor Yuan is from Manchuria, home of the Qing dynasty," he quietly explained. "The Ming emperors used a full seven stars to show the constellation of the Great Bear, though they called it the Bushel then. But when Qing emperors arrived from the north they abbreviated it to three. Apologies, Hsien Sheng," he said to Yuan with a slight bow of his head. "Elder born," it meant, a homage paid to teachers.

Yuan silently smiled, and urged Shan to drink his wine. The woman clapped her hands in triumph.

"You'll have to decide about the beads always worn with such a robe," Shan continued after draining his glass. "They were traditionally red coral beads but late in his reign the Qianlong emperor declared that white Manchurian pearls would henceforth be worn."

The group gave a collective murmur of respect, then quickly followed with a energetic discussion of court ritual. When Shan volunteered that for years he had spent much of his spare time in Beijing exploring every nook of the Forbidden City, they filled his wine cup again and with great enthusiasm fired new queries at him about the proper order of ranks in imperial processions, ceremonies for erecting new temples, archery competitions, and a dozen other aspects of imperial life.

As Sansan brought in fresh tea the talk turned to ancient poetry and the old tales of heroes. "My favorite of all was Sung Chiang," she offered.

Professor Chou, who explained she was a retired professor of literature, nodded. "*The Water Margin,*" she added, referring to the Ming dynasty novel about the rebel Sung Chiang, who forayed out of his marshland lair to defend peasants against injustice.

"History and heroes repeat themselves," Professor Yuan observed.

Shan suddenly realized that everyone was looking at him, grinning. He flushed with color, then, mumbling an excuse, stood and fled out the kitchen door.

He sat on a bench set against the rear wall of the house, watching the moon rise over parched, spindly trees. His mind wandered, toward the mountains, toward the little cottage where he prayed Lokesh and Cora Michener were safely hiding.

"The most enduring myths are all based on fact."

He started at the sudden words and looked up to see the professor's daughter standing beside the bench.

Sansan continued without waiting for his reply. "My father says if you look hard enough in Tibet you can see the myths come to life."

Shan said nothing, just moved to make room for her as she sat beside him.

"Robin Hood, bandit of the forest," she said. "He was the Western equivalent of Sung Chiang, bandit of the marshes. They dared to defy the government, they brought justice when no one else knew how to find it."

"I am no Sung Chiang," Shan whispered.

Sansan seemed not to hear him. "In the city there is so much noise and clutter. Everything moves so quickly. It is easy to miss the important things. Here we have learned to cultivate the quiet, as the old Confucians would say, so there is always time for the important things. Here people speak of deities like they are next-door neighbors. They talk of myths as if they were just family histories."

Shan turned to look at the girl. She had been the ringleader of the dissidents, the reason all the families had been exiled to Tibet. She looked like a young schoolgirl but spoke with the weary wisdom of one far older.

She met his gaze. "You make the people of this valley believe in heroes."

"You confuse me with someone else."

Sansan shrugged. "Then let's just say you inspire them to action. You make me worry for my father."

"I don't understand."

"He says we can't stand by and do nothing." She looked up at the moon with an odd longing. "We have very little money. He's been eating only rice and putting money aside to buy books and ink and brushes for his calligraphy. He offered some of it, enough for a dozen books, to that lame shepherd, Jigten."

A chill ran down Shan's back. "For what purpose?"

"To translate a little journal Jamyang left with my father for safe-keeping. It was like a trade. Jamyang kept our artifacts safe and we kept his writings safe. But it's almost all in Tibetan. Jamyang was a complex man. My father says those murders must have had something to do with Jamyang, that he knows you must think so too." When she turned to Shan there was pleading in her eyes. "He says the journal was meant for Tibetans but if they act on it they will be punished. He says he must understand it, to use the answers it provides. We will not sit back and do nothing when there are wrongs being committed among us. He says you have shown us."

Shan sighed. "I am an example for no one." His throat was dry, his voice hoarse. "He can't . . ." His words drifted away as he recalled the tranquil bedroom he had been in. "He has too much to lose."

"We have nothing to lose. The government liberated us by sending us here."

Shan's heart seemed to sag. "Surely he must understand. He has you. You have each other. You have a home." He could not bear the thought of being responsible for the professor and his daughter being separated and sent into the gulag.

In the silence that followed he could hear the voices from inside, softly reading old verses by candlelight. He did not even realize the girl had left the bench until she stepped back out of the door, holding her laptop computer. She gestured him toward the little toolshed at the back of the yard.

Inside, she unfolded the computer on the workbench. The screen burst to life and she began tapping on the keyboard. A moment later, a scanned document appeared, in Jamyang's familiar handwriting.

"Two dozen pages in all," the woman said, showing him how to scan through the pages. "Some pinned together, some pages of different sizes, like he was just writing on whatever paper was available."

It was not really a journal, Shan saw as he skimmed through the pages, but notes, random entries of life in the valley, of work on his shrine and the deities they uncovered with their cleaning brushes. One page was just a list of Tibetan gods and their protector demons. He pointed to a smudge of color in the top-left corner of the page. "What is this?"

Sansan ran the cursor over the page and tapped another key, magnifying the image. A Tibetan chorten was revealed in pale red ink, with a heavy hammer imposed over it.

A grim silence descended over them.

Shan rubbed the ache at his forehead. "It doesn't mean anything," he whispered uneasily "He was using whatever paper he could find."

"A sacred Tibetan sign under a symbol of the Communist Party. Where would he find such paper?"

Shan did not answer. "What did Jamyang say when he gave this to your father?" he asked.

"Only that it was important. Or more exactly," she said, as if correcting herself, "that one day it might become important. Later he told me I should scan it into my computer, just in case. I wouldn't have thought anything about it, except—"

Shan completed her sentence. "Except he died." He scrolled to the final page. It was a list of artifacts. A ritual dagger with a ruby in its pommel. A bronze trumpet. Three ritual masks with a detailed description of the demons they represented. He knew them. They were from the convent ruins, the very artifacts he and Lokesh had shown to Jamyang, artifacts Jamyang had helped clean and hide.

He slowly searched through the other pages. There were lists of ceremonies conducted by monks and nuns in the valley, with dates for each, as well as lists of shrines, most of them publicly known but some secret. There was a sketch of four young Tibetans blowing a long duncheng horn, with the caption "Sound of Freedom." One page, obviously written in ink and pencil at different times, listed the names of monks and lamas under the heading "Chegar gompa." Years had been written by many of the names, some as far back as three decades, some as recent as the year before. At the bottom of the page were three names with a circle around them. Abbot Norbu and his two attendants Dakpo and Trinle.

One day these pages would become important. "What was it your father and Jamyang spoke of when they were together?" he asked.

"History. Literature. Jamyang would translate some of the old Tibetan poems into Chinese. Sometimes they would speak of their own histories. My father's teaching career. How we were accused and sent here. Jamyang liked to speak of his boyhood on a farm in the mountains north of here."

"Did he ever speak of his recent past?"

"Not that I ever heard. We always understood he was a lama, a senior teacher. So he would have started as a monk at an early age, my father said." She hesitated. "There was one night when a truck filled with Tibetans bound for one of the camps passed by the little grove of trees where we sat. Jamyang was sitting with us outside. He grew very sad. After a long silence he asked my father if he thought a man would be punished in this life for sins of his past life. My father just laughed and said Jamyang was confusing him for another lama."

Shan paused at the last page. It read like a prayer, or a eulogy. "So young to pass," it said, "so confused a spirit that is brought up with violence. You grew up in forests of bamboo and die among trees of flags. One hand on the knife, the other searching for your heart. Beware the prayer that brings poison. Beware the color you see." Shan read it again, and again, each time growing more disturbed. It was about the Lung boy, whose body had scared Jamyang so. *Beware the prayer that brings poison. Beware the color you see.* Jamyang had known the killer was a monk.

They were not the last words on the page. At the very bottom, in a different ink, written later, were four more words. "Kaliyuga," it said. "It has arrived." The grief that surged within Shan as he read them was as real as that he had felt when he had held the lama's dead body. *Kaliyuga* was the Tibetan word for the end of time. Jamyang had known that at least the end of his time had come.

"When was it?" he asked after a long moment, "when did he bring this to you?"

"Two or three weeks ago. He always came in the night. He brought incense sometimes."

"Incense?"

Sansan gave a sad smile. "He knew I was often sick. Sometimes I cough and can't stop for several minutes. He brought things, some from the old convent. I said we couldn't take such things, but he said they were safer with us than in the ruins, that I needed them more."

"Sansan, I don't understand."

She glanced at the door of the little shed, then stepped to the side wall and began lifting away planks. A double wall had been erected, a second row of planks that would be enough for a casual searcher to miss the narrow space they concealed. "Father at first kept his special things here, before entrusting them to Jamyang. The first time Jamyang gave us artifacts we just set them on the little shelf inside the compartment. Later he said he had a better idea. He worked in here alone one night, then brought me in holding a candle, and had me sit on the old rug." She indicated a tattered piece of carpet, that looked like an artifact itself, then pulled away the final planks and held up her light.

Jamyang had built Sansan a shrine. On the lower shelf were offering bowls, several deity figures, and an incense burner. Above them was a faded, but still elegant thangka, a painting of the lapis god Menlha, the deity invoked for healing. In his left hand the blue deity held a bowl of nectar, the universal cure.

"He knew I was having a hard time getting my medicine," Sansan whispered. She wiped a tear from her cheek. "He said this belonged to his uncle, who was a healer and who was known for making special cures out of gemstones and herbs. He said he wished he had such skills but that he did at least know no medicine would work unless the spirit was ready to accept it. He said I should light incense here each day and gaze at the lapis god. He said not to be shy about breathing in the incense, that in smoke and mist were where humans and god meet, that if I could awake the god then some of the nectar would enter my body."

They stood silently in front of the altar. Shan realized he was meditating not so much on the deity as on Jamyang. The only time he had ever heard of the lama speaking of family was to this quiet, spirited Chinese girl. The words he had used echoed of regret. Shan looked back at the workbench. "He told you to scan that journal? He used those words?"

Sansan slowly broke her gaze from the altar. "Yes. It surprised me. I didn't expect him to understand about computers. But that night he showed me differently."

"What else happened?"

"He asked where I could get access to the Internet in town, if there was any place other than my house. I explained that sometimes I connected in the café, that sometimes the owner, another old professor, left the circuits on without controls when he left at night, and that he always kept the shop unlocked." She cast a pointed glance at Shan. Beijing required those who provided public access to the Internet to record the identity of every user.

"Sansan, surely you don't mean Jamyang wanted to use your computer."

"That's exactly what he wanted. And he knew about security controls. He said he would be able to conceal whose computer it was."

Shan stared at the woman in disbelief. He wanted to shake her, to tell her to stop concocting such tales. But he saw her eyes, and knew she understood the weight of her words. Jamyang's ghost was not the lama Shan had known.

"What did he do?"

"It was after midnight. I took him to the tea shop and started to wait outside but he told me to go. Like an order. He was not like a lama for a moment. More like . . . I don't know. A soldier. He said he would leave the computer on the workbench here. I found it the next morning, with one of those khata scarfs wrapped around it, like it had been blessed. The owner of the café found another scarf hanging on his counter, with a little Buddha drawn on a napkin."

The ache in Shan's head was growing again. He had a sense of slipping away. Every truth he clung to was becoming an untruth. "Sansan, the owner of the teahouse was detained by Major Liang, for failing to control Internet usage."

"But he's back, Shan, everything's fine."

He looked at her in alarm. "That only means he cooperated, that he spoke about an unknown user who left a prayer scarf. It means Liang obtained what he was looking for, and it was not about the murders." Shan looked back at the screen, at the disturbing image of the chorten and hammer. Nothing made sense.

There were times, Lokesh had told him, when the only way of knowing was not knowing.

Shan touched the side door of the police post, then withdrew his hand and sat on the step instead. He needed to see Meng, he wanted to see Meng, but didn't know what to say to her. He could not stop worrying about Lokesh and Cora, knowing the grave dangers they faced, knowing how innocent each was in their own way.

He stared into the night sky and suddenly was with Ko again. It was the previous autumn and on arrival he had been taken to the prisoners' infirmary, which was just another barrack lined with single cots instead of double and triple bunks. His son had a fever, an undiagnosed and untreated fever, with a violent nausea that let nothing stay in his stomach. Ko had been too weak to speak, and all Shan could think when he saw him was that this was the last time, that by his next visit the guards would have thrown his son into an unmarked grave and wouldn't even be able to tell him where it was. For the entire visit Shan had just held his son, rocking back and forth with tears streaming down his cheeks.

He became aware that Meng was sitting beside him. He did not know how long she had been there. "If you hadn't called Tan—" he began.

She raised a hand as if to cut him off. "He is not particularly pleasant on the telephone," she said with half a smile as she extended one of her bags of sunflower seeds to Shan.

"The evidence from the murders," Shan asked. "Is it here?"

"Locked in my file cabinet."

"In the pocket of Lung Ma there was a metal object. I want to see it."

"You know there are rules about handling evidence. I would have to make entries in the log."

"Such rules are for taking evidence to trial, Lieutenant. There is never going to be a trial. You know that."

Meng looked into the bag, as if searching for something. "I was a captain once," she said. "I had a driver, access to special facilities for senior officers."

He hesitated, not for the first time wondering about the part of Meng she always kept hidden. "I'm sorry. You're right. I can't ask you to put your career at risk."

His words seemed to hurt Meng. "A triple homicide was committed in my district," she replied. "I have a file."

"You have a file," Shan underscored. "Does Liang? The major came all this way but I am beginning to think the only file he has is on that American woman. You said he took the bullet. But I doubt you've seen a test on it. He doesn't deal in evidence. He deals in fear and manipulation."

"If all he wanted was a political victory," Meng said in a hollow voice, "he could have declared that dead lama the killer, like you suggested. But he didn't. He stayed despite telling us about his urgent business elsewhere."

"He has to stay, because of the American."

"He said he had to go to Rutok."

"He said he had to go because of unrest over another monk who immolated himself. I haven't actually heard of such a suicide. Usually the Tibetans are quick to speak of such things wherever they happen. It wouldn't be hard for you to check."

Meng said nothing. After a long moment she rose and retreated into the building. Shan finished the seeds in his hand before following.

The evidence, scant as it was, lay across her desk. Three bundles of clothing in plastic bags. The severed yak hair necklace of the abbess. The ankle holster worn by Lung, with his keys, cigarettes, and the piece of metal that had been with them. Shan took a pencil and lifted the tapered piece of metal through one of its two holes. He had seen it in the cigarette pack. It had a newly wrought feel to it, though it was clearly made to look old. The edge was tapered but not sharpened as a blade.

"Some old Tibetan thing," Meng suggested. "The Jade Crows sell artifacts on the black market. He must have picked it up in the ruins."

"A Tibetan thing, yes. It is a fire striker. Tibetan shepherds carried these for centuries, to use with flints. Lung Ma brought it with him. But it's not old, not from the ruins."

"You mean it is like a souvenir, something for tourists."

"Something like that," Shan said uncertainly.

"But why would the chief of the Jade Crows carry such a thing?"

Shan grabbed the fire striker and inserted his fingers into the holes. They fit perfectly. He made several strokes with his hand, as if striking a flint. Then he pushed the metal farther down his knuckles and made a different motion, an upward cut with the edge of the striker pointing out. "Did you see the body of the Lung boy who died in the truck?"

"I went out with the constables, for a death report."

"He had taken a severe blow to his windpipe."

Meng nodded. "The steering wheel crushed it, then his ribs."

Shan slowly shook his head as he stared at the striker. "No. Either the windpipe takes the impact or the ribs, not both."

"I saw his neck, Shan. It was crushed. It had a terrible bruise."

Shan spanned the edge of the striker with his fingers then raised them, keeping them spread. "About that long?"

The color drained from Meng's face. "It was an accident. Everyone said it was an accident. Routine. I saw the ruined truck. I just had to—"

"Overlook a murder?"

Anger lit her eyes, but just as quickly it faded into shame.

"They wouldn't let you have the body," Shan said, as if to console her.

"That's no excuse," she snapped. "I could have taken it."

"From the Jade Crows? The Lung brothers would have loathed you for coming that day. They could have planned any number of distractions while they stole the bodies but they decided to assault you in that alley. If I hadn't been there it would have gone even worse for you."

"No excuse," she said again, and lowered herself into her chair. "Why?" she asked. "Why would someone kill that boy?"

"Right now," Shan replied, lifting the striker in his fingers again, "I am more interested in why his father had the murder weapon."

• • •

Lung Tso was sitting at his table with a glass and a bottle of vodka when Genghis escorted Shan up the stairs. "I spent half a day with some damned officer from the internment camp explaining why the trucks they gave us were death traps, how the damned Armed Police had themselves to blame for that truck exploding like that. I told him it was just a matter of luck that the truck was only carrying some bags of rice and not a squad of his thugs."

Shan stared at him in surprise. "You said that?"

"I said it was my patriotic duty to point it out. He wound up providing another truck, a better one he said. Instead of a thirty-year-old piece of shit I have a twenty-year-old piece of shit." Lung studied Shan. "But I could just as easily been thrown inside the wire if someone had seen me ignite the oily rags I put in the engine, or if they had been organized enough for head counts to show they were missing prisoners. We're finished, Shan. No more favors. Get out. Don't make me show you my blade again."

Shan ignored the threat. "You were ready to torture me because you thought I took something from your brother's body. What did you think it was?"

Lung drained his glass. "I don't know. That lama gave him something. I wanted it, to understand what happened. It can't just have been that piece of paper. Sure, it showed someone was tracking our smuggling but that wasn't enough to transform him. It was like the lama worked some kind of damned magic, the way he changed my brother."

"When did Jamyang come back?"

"The day before my brother died. They went up to that shrine of his in the old stable. They were there for an hour or more, then my brother stayed up there another hour after the lama left. When he came back in he had something small wrapped in a piece of felt. He wouldn't show me, wouldn't talk with me."

The fire striker gave a metallic ring when Shan dropped it on the table. "That's what it was. The police had it."

Lung picked the striker up and leaned with it closer to the lantern. "It's some kind of monk thing."

"No, just a Tibetan thing that happens to have prayers on it. It was used to kill your nephew."

Lung Tso went very still. Shan returned his cold, steady gaze until he broke away to pour more vodka. He drained his glass again. "Tell me."

Shan demonstrated how the striker could be used as a weapon to crush a windpipe as he explained. "He was murdered," he concluded. "The killer staged the truck accident afterwards."

"That fucking lama."

"No. Jamyang somehow recognized the killer's blow, somehow identified the killer, somehow got his hands on this striker. Tell me something. Why didn't your brother go to the monks when his son died? Why the nuns?"

"You don't ask a favor of those you do business with." Lung's eyes flared. "That damned lama."

"Jamyang was helping your brother. Jamyang connected everything. He came and told your brother, told him to go to the convent the next day because he arranged for his son's killer to be there. Just like he told the abbess of treachery at Chegar gompa. The killer wore a robe but it was not Jamyang."

A small gasp from the stairway broke the silence. Jigten stood there, carrying a tea thermos, his eyes wide. He backed down slowly, into the shadows.

You don't ask a favor of those you do business with. Like some distant echo, Lung's words came back to Shan as he drove up the mountainside. The dead gang leader, the smuggler, had been doing business with a monk, and a monk had killed him. He pulled the truck into a small grove of trees off a rough, remote track, then sat in the shadows, beginning a half-hour vigil to make sure he was not followed before he ascended the narrow goat trail that led to the small valley above. As he waited the questions came like a flood. The few pieces of the puzzle he had found only seemed to make the puzzle impossibly more complex. What were the favors Lung had done for the monks? Why would Jamyang have sent both Lung and the abbess to confront the killer? How could Jamyang have possibly found the weapon that had killed the Lung boy? He would never know what had happened at the convent on the day of death until he knew the truth about Jamyang.

The American woman was sleeping on a pallet inside the small hut when Shan finally arrived. It was one of the remote, unused shelters that Shan and Lokesh had discovered when looking for lost shrines. The old Tibetan had a mysterious ability to trace what he called the spirit fixtures of such places, pointing out the thin stain along a wall that was the sign of incense having been burned beneath over many years, prying up what looked like random stones along foundations to show Shan the prayers that had been inscribed on them, discovering the rotted ends of twine around a branch or peg that had secured prayer flags in another century. He would clean off the old mani stones and renew such places with new incense and new prayer flags, even if it meant ripping up his shirt to make them. Then he would offer hours of mantras so the deities that dwelled nearby would know they had not been forgotten.

In his uncanny way, Lokesh had seemed to expect Shan. A pot of soup sat at the edge of the small brazier by the door. He did not ask about Shan's imprisonment, did not offer an account of his travails since escaping out of the death pit, but simply handed Shan an old wooden bowl and poured in the soup. The old Tibetan laid another blanket over Cora, then lit a stick of incense in the brazier and stuck it in the stones of the wall above her before sitting beside Shan.

"I know a cave," he said after a long silence.

Shan's chest tightened. It was a conversation they had had before. Lokesh wanted him to leave everything, to go on a meditation retreat.

"I will go with you. We could take the American. Just two or three weeks. You walk too close."

Too close to the edge, Lokesh meant. Other friends might speak of the physical dangers Shan faced, the torment he had endured as Liang's prisoner, but not Lokesh, never Lokesh. He meant Shan was perilously close to tumbling from the true path, the enlightened path, the Buddhist path. Lokesh believed in finding the truth but also fervently believed Shan went too far when he interfered in events, when he became an actor in an unfolding mystery. Rescuing a lamb showed respect for lower animal spirits. Manipulating events and deceiving the government showed disrespect for his own spirit.

"Jamyang told us his story," Lokesh continued. "It is but for us to understand it. He left us the sutra of his life. We simply need to learn how to read it."

"It is what I am doing, old friend, in the only way I know how."

"No. You ride with police. You speak with those who raid our farms. You attack statues. You invite Public Security to beat you. You have learned other ways, Shan. From where you stand if you lose your footing you lose all chance of being human again."

The words tore at Shan's heart. They were the words of a gentle Tibetan father to a son who had become so wayward he was in danger of losing his family. They were perhaps the harshest thing Lokesh had ever said to him. Human existence was a precious thing, won only after thousands of incarnations in lower forms, and those who abused it, for whatever reason, would sink to the bottom of that cycle.

Shan had no reply. He only stared into his now empty bowl.

After a long silence Lokesh gestured outside. "There will be meteors," the old Tibetan said and, seeming to sense Shan's weakness, extended a hand to help him up.

It was a rare evening, with a gentle breeze stirring the fragrant junipers, the stars shimmering in a cloudless sky. Shan lay back on the blanket Lokesh had stretched over the grass for him, longing for a chance to at least share another meteor shower with his friend, but unable to resist the fatigue that wracked his body. As his eyes fluttered closed he heard the faint murmur of a new mantra. He seemed to hover in the warm suspension just before sleep and a sad smile settled onto his face. This time, he knew, Lokesh was praying for him.

CHAPTER THIRTEEN

Lung Tso was strangely subdued when Shan arrived the next day to ask his favor. His question had come not from resentment but confusion.

"Why in hell would you want one of my men to drive along the valley in your truck?"

"Drive, and stop at places I mark on the map, playing with a shovel in the ditches for a while then driving on."

"And where will you be?"

"He is going to drop me off at dawn behind the monk's compound at the end of the valley. With one of your motorbikes. Bring the truck back to the stable in town at the end of the day."

"You're going to spy on monks."

"There's more than meets the eye at that gompa." Shan stared at the smuggler with challenge in his eye. Lung still had not explained what business he conducted with the monks.

"We have a rule we try to follow. Only have one enemy at a time. That way you can keep an eye on him, make sure he is not creeping up behind you. But you, Shan, you just piss off everyone. You have no instinct for self-preservation. Who's following your truck?"

Shan kept staring at him.

"That monk Jamyang. You said he is dead."

"He died the same day as your brother. He convinced your brother to go the convent. He had me stop on the high ridge above there to confirm that your brother's truck was there. Then we went to his shrine and he shot himself in the head as he sat an arm's length from me."

Lung grimaced. "Monks don't kill themselves."

"Monks don't kill themselves," Shan repeated. He gazed steadily at Lung as he extracted the folded paper from his pocket. There were two dates that were yet to arrive when Jamyang gave this paper to your brother. One was last week. What happened when you took your truck to the border last week?"

"Not a thing."

"They have to examine papers, open a few cartons to verify contents."

"They stamped the papers and waved the shipment through."

"Because you bribed them."

Lung said nothing.

"I need to know what you do for the monks, Lung."

"Same thing we always do."

Shan leaned closer. "What exactly are they smuggling?"

"Boxes. Not good business to look inside a customer's goods."

"What size? What did the monks tell you?"

"The monks come to meetings but they don't do the talking. It's those Tibetans from the other side."

"Purbas?"

Lung shrugged. "I don't know the Tibetan name for outlaws. They usually go across the high mountain passes but the army has heavy surveillance there now. They wanted a test run on a new route. That's what happened last week."

"Test run?"

"A couple big boxes."

"How long?"

"Big enough for a cabinet. I figure they have altars and such they want to protect from Beijing."

"The next shipment. Did they say to expect the same kind of shipment?"

"The same, sure."

Shan slowly nodded. "Like I said. I need a favor."

The leader of the Jade Crows frowned then disappeared into one of the farm buildings. As Genghis appeared, pushing a motorbike, Lung returned and stood by Shan, silently looking out over the abandoned barley fields, not turning when he spoke again. "If you don't find the bastard who killed my brother then the Jade Crows will. We'll go through the damned monastery monk by monk. We won't be so subtle."

Chegar gompa was a small, nervous shadow of its former self. It had been built for at least two hundred monks but as he watched from the rocks above Shan estimated it currently held no more than thirty. Half its buildings lay in ruin, still bearing the powder marks from the artillery shells that had destroyed them decades earlier. The little village at its front gate also bore signs of shelling, its structures showing a patchwork of repairs.

The wall that had once enclosed the compound like a fortress was in rubble on the north and east sides, giving Shan a clear view into the courtyard. A chorten, its white surface weathered to grey, sat at the rear center of the yard, allowing room for assemblies of monks and the ritual galas of festival days. But now that space held a new creation, a raised pedestal nearly as high as the base of the stupa, bearing a tall pole with the flag of the People's Republic.

The brush behind him rattled and he turned to see an old woman stepping into the little clearing. She held a sack of grain in one hand, a stone pestle in the other. She began to settle by a worn indentation in the rock when she gasped, startled by his presence.

"I am only passing by," Shan offered.

The woman seemed about to back away, then her gaze fell on the gau that had slipped outside of Shan's shirt. "A pilgrim?" she suggested.

"Just a pilgrim," Shan said.

"A pilgrim in the shadows," the old Tibetan observed.

Shan took the words as an expression of suspicion, but then the woman sighed. "The only way a pilgrim can be safe in these times is to walk in the shadows like the rest of us."

She settled onto the ledge and emptied the grain sack into the bowl in the rock. As she lifted her pestle she looked up at Shan. "It's something my grandmother used to do when she was a cook for the gompa. Every village used to have a rock like this. I come up once a month, to keep the rock alive."

Shan nodded. "My grandmother used to let me work the bellows on her stove when she made dumplings. She would tell me that no one could say they made their own dumplings unless they made the flour themselves."

An uncertain smile crossed the woman's countenance and she silently began grinding the barley kernels. Shan watched her with a strange ache in his heart. The sound of the grinding was like that of a stream flowing over pebbles. A wren lit on the ground and the woman extended a kernel on her palm, which the little bird readily accepted.

"Your grandmother fed many more monks than live here today," he said after turning back toward the compound.

"They have a difficult time. Most of the monks refused to sign those loyalty oaths and the government was going to close it down, finish the demolition they started so many years ago. But Abbot Norbu came. He saved the monks. He saved the gompa."

Shan looked back at the courtyard. "He saved it by raising a Chinese flag?"

The woman shrugged. "He saved it. He saves it every month," she added with a nod toward a nondescript building just outside the gate.

Shan saw monks on the bench by the door of the building, then fought a shudder as a monk emerged from the door, followed by a grey-uniformed officer.

"Public Security comes every month?" he asked as the officer gestured the next monk inside.

"Sometimes the knobs. Sometimes Religious Affairs. Sometimes both."

Gompas were audited. Gompas had periodic fidelity reviews. Gompas were required to certify allegiance and verify registration of all monks, but Shan had never heard of such a small gompa attracting monthly enforcement visits. "Why so often?" he asked. "What is so special about this gompa?"

When the woman looked up there was a perverse grin on her face.

"Perhaps not the gompa," Shan ventured. "The village. What did the village do?"

"Ten years ago there was a farmer here whose children came home one day with Chinese names pinned to their clothes. When they told him the teachers would no longer allow them to use their birth names, he decided to start his own classes, at night, after the Chinese teachers were gone. By the time the Chinese found out about it he had become famous in the valley. When they came looking for him he retreated into the mountains, and they arrested a few who had helped him. He came down to help those in trouble with the government. He began guiding Tibetans across the border, past the army patrols. Public Security put a bounty on his head after he took his family to India. He is in the exile government today, an important official. Public Security knows he has relatives here."

"Any who are monks?"

"One. A nephew named Dakpo."

"Were any in the gompa arrested?"

"One. But he came back."

Shan watched the monks nervously waiting on the bench, saw now how those who finished with Public Security reentered the compound and disappeared into one of the buildings. "Arrested for what exactly?"

"Speaking the way a Tibetan should speak," she replied. Challenge entered her voice. She would speak no more.

Shan murmured his thanks, then slipped down the path toward the village. He stepped into a stable and studied the hamlet through a gap in its plank walls. On the slope behind a farmhouse, out of sight of the knobs, a woman hurried an adolescent girl away with a basket of grain, the reflex of a people used to being harassed by tax collectors. An old man with a wispy beard wearing a black vest sat upright on a chair outside the door of another house, his hand perched on a cane, his head slightly cocked toward the gompa as if listening for something. Two children ran by, chased by a puppy. A woman laughed as a goat pulled a piece of laundry from a clothesline and ran down the street. The old man did not react to any of the movements. He was blind, Shan realized.

He waited as one monk, then another, finished with the knobs, exiting the building without a word to their companions, looking straight ahead, their faces tight with fear. Many such knob squads worked under a quota, so that they would always find someone to be punished. Each of the monks gripped tattered papers in one hand. Examinations always started with a knob scrutinizing identity cards and Religious Affairs registrations, sometimes questioning every line anew.

He saw the despair on the faces of those who sat waiting on the bench. Some of them were young novices but most were old enough to understand that this kind of scrutiny meant the gompa was in grave danger. A few hasty signatures from Religious Affairs and

Public Security and all their hopeful prayers, their reverent memori-
zation of thousands of lines of scriptures, all the flames of their offering lamps, would be snuffed out. Padlocks would be mounted on the
compound doors. Prayers would be spoken no more, forever.

A thin clear note suddenly split the silence. The monk who had
just finished his interview quickened his pace. Another note brought
monks out of several gompa buildings. A monk stood by one of the
inner doors, ringing a ritual bell. Several villagers hurried to the buckets by the entries to their houses, rinsing their hands and faces. Only
the monks on the bench did not move.

The old man rose on shaking legs, leaning on his cane. Shan pulled
his hat low over his brow and darted outside, reaching the man in
time to steady him as he tripped on a stone.

The blind man turned his head only slightly, hesitating. "You're
a stranger," he said in a neutral tone.

"Allow a poor pilgrim to gain favor, Grandfather," Shan replied,
putting his hand lightly on the man's elbow to guide him.

The man sighed, then nodded. "My niece is in the pastures or she
would take me. Just as well when these vultures come to town."

"*Lha gyal lo,*" was Shan's reply.

The little temple was lit only by sputtering butter lamps along
the altar. Incense curled around a simple bronze Buddha. In a voice
as thin as the smoke, a monk below the altar read scripture as
Abbot Norbu stood silently beside him. The assembled monks and
villagers murmured responses then, when the reading was done,
Norbu led them in a long mantra. The words were pronounced softly
at first, in the near whispers Shan usually heard in such rituals but
then to his surprise, the blind man beside him lifted his bowed head
and interrupted, speaking a new mantra, more loudly toward the
ceiling. Shan watched in confusion as the voices of the others faded,
then joined him. As the volume rose, seeming to take on what seemed
almost a defiant tone, a monk rose and pushed a bolt on the door.
Norbu cast a nervous glance toward the door, then pushed aside a

dark swath of felt hanging below from the altar and reached into the shadows, extracting an ornate silver bell with a dragon elegantly worked around its handle. A shiver of excitement coursed through the congregated monks as Norbu bent again and pulled out another deity which he set beside the Buddha. It was a morbid, frightful image of a bull-headed god holding flayed human skins and skulls. The image unmasked by Norbu was one of the most fierce of the protector demons. Norbu reached behind the altar for a cloth that he draped over the figure. It was the flag of free Tibet.

Shan glanced back with worry at the locked door. Not only would the officials outside be livid if they knew of the ritual in the little chapel, they would violently disrupt it and arrest those leading it.

Norbu took up the chant himself now, but not as a leader. He made his way to the rear of the little hall, reached the other side of the blind man, and lowered himself to the stone flags like the rest of the devout, looking up to the blind man.

The old man Shan had helped into the chapel was more than some energetic worshiper. The abbot was paying him homage. The blind man's vest had fallen open and Shan saw now the gau that hung from his neck. A band of maroon cloth was tied around the amulet, the sign of a former monk, or an illegal monk. As he gazed into the man's serene face and listened to the quiet fire in his voice, Shan knew he had been more than a monk. He had been a lama, a teacher, a leader who was now healing the wounds of the monks.

Shan ventured a glance toward Norbu. He understood now the affection, the fierce loyalty, the monks felt toward their abbot. He knew the words to say to appease Public Security, but alone with his flock he dropped his pretense. He nurtured the old ways, kept alive the spark that Beijing tried so hard to extinguish. He did so, moreover, in a village that was obviously under close scrutiny by the knobs. What he did was reckless but it clearly endeared him to his flock. They would tolerate a Chinese flag and loyalty oaths in the open because they knew what happened when the chapel door was locked.

As the ritual concluded the abbot rose, hid the bell, the demon, and the flag, then led the monks outside. Shan lingered until the chamber was nearly empty, then approached the altar where Norbu's attendant Trinle was lighting fresh butter lamps. Shan silently began to help.

"I thought I was leading the blind man," he said after a few moments. "But now I know he was leading me."

Trinle glanced outside before replying. "It is very brave what he does," the monk offered. "Just coming back here was brave."

"Back here?" Shan asked, confused.

The monk kept working as he explained. "He got ten strings for opposing the loyalty oaths. Some would have just lost their robes. But they have to make an example when it's an abbot. They let him out early."

Shan stared at Trinle in confusion. Ten strings. When an imprisoned monk left followers or loved ones behind they would try to send a new rosary each year. But no one got early release for opposing loyalty oaths. "How early?"

"He went blind. It was a grand day for us when Norbu first appeared, with the dragon bell in one hand and old Patrul in the other."

"Patrul was the abbot of this gompa?"

The monk paused and nodded. "It's not enough to just say abbot. Patrul was one of the old ones. One of the original ones," he said, meaning the blind man had been a holy man in old Tibet, before the Chinese came. "The only one most of us have ever met."

There was much more to Chegar gompa than met the eye.

"I am called Shan," he said. "You are Trinle. I met you and Dakpo with Abbot Norbu at Thousand Steps."

The monk nodded again. " I saw you sometimes with Jamyang at the old convent. Is it true he has thrown his face?"

"He died the same day as the abbess and the others."

Trinle gave a small sigh of despair. "Truly the gods were looking elsewhere that day."

"It was a bad day," Shan agreed. "None of those who died were prepared. They are owed the truth about why they died."

Trinle studied Shan a moment. He recognized the invitation in Shan's words. "That is government business. Monks are taught to stay away from government business."

"For a place that stays out of government business you have a lot of government visitors."

Trinle straightened and fixed Shan with a sober expression. "The best way to deal with evil demons is to bring them among demon protectors."

Shan returned his gaze. "The demon who killed the abbess and the others won't come willingly. Help me find him."

Trinle cast a worried glance toward the door. "This is a place of reverence. Why would you look here?"

"Because someone in a monk's robe was there that day. He was the killer."

Trinle stared in disbelief. "No. I could put on one of those grey tunics. It wouldn't make me a knob."

"Fake monk or real monk, all the gompas and convents will take the blame when the government discovers it. It was someone convincing, someone who looked at ease in a robe. A Tibetan with the close-cropped hair of a monk. Tell me, Trinle, has anyone left the gompa in the past year?"

The question seemed to trouble Trinle. "One went across."

"You mean he died?"

"Across to India. He is safe now, has a job in the Dalai Lama's government."

Shan reminded himself that Chenmo had spoken of purbas in the valley, the resistance fighters who came from India. Chegar had a monk now in the exile government. The close scrutiny of Public Security was beginning to make more sense.

Outside, a loudspeaker interrupted the quiet of the courtyard, first with a burst of static, then with a repetitive call for a monk to report to the gatehouse. Shan recognized the name. Dakpo.

Trinle stepped to the entry and edged his head around the doorway to glance furtively into the courtyard. The voice on the speaker grew impatient as it called again for the monk. Trinle's face clouded.

"Dakpo is missing?" Shan asked.

"He isn't here."

Shan considered the monk's worried tone. "You mean he left without permission."

As Trinle watched the activity in the courtyard he gripped the door frame as if to steady himself. Monks were hurrying into buildings. "He has duties elsewhere. If the abbot doesn't calm them down, they will search every room."

"And they will find contraband," Shan asserted.

Trinle turned to Shan with challenge in his eyes. "We of Chegar gompa are true monks."

There was something in his tone that unsettled Shan. Every gompa harbored secret, illegal photos of the Dalai Lama. Now he knew Chegar sometimes even displayed a flag of independent Tibet. Trinle seemed to be speaking of something else.

Shan looked back to where the demon protector was hidden. It was very old, very valuable. "If they come searching, put that protector deity on the altar and drape it with prayer scarves. They won't know what they are looking at."

Trinle considered Shan's words a moment, then nodded. Shan stepped back out into the courtyard.

Norbu was speaking urgently with another monk near the gate. Shan slipped along the shadow of the opposite wall, keeping his head down, mingling with the handful of villagers who were paying homage, pausing as they did at the shrine stations along the wall. He heard only snippets of the abbot's conversation. Norbu was clearly upset.

"How long?" the abbot demanded. "How long has he been missing?"

"He left two nights ago. After midnight."

Shan ventured a glance toward the monk. He was clearly frightened. Norbu kept the gompa safe from Public Security by maintaining tight control. One errant monk could tip the balance.

Shan stepped closer.

"Perhaps he went on a pilgrim's path, to visit the shrines," the monk suggested.

Norbu muttered something like a prayer under his breath. "He is on a mediation retreat in the mountains," the abbot declared more loudly, as if rehearsing the line. "When he returns he will gladly renew his loyalty oath." Norbu straightened his robe and stepped back to the waiting knobs.

Shan kept his head down as the officers converged upon the abbot, slipping out the gate and into the village.

As in many such gompa villages, the old pilgrim paths converged near the gate. Without thinking Shan found himself pausing at the small stations along the main road, many of them nothing more than cairns of mani stones. It was what he and Lokesh would do, and he realized again how much he missed the old Tibetan. The past few months, when they had been together nearly every day, had been a blessing and he guarded himself against expecting he could go back to that simple, peaceful routine when the turmoil in the valley subsided. The troubles might never subside. The valley as it had been for centuries was not going to survive, and its demise would widen the gap between Lokesh and himself.

As he reached the edge of the hamlet he became aware of a low steady rattle coming from the long timber structure that had no doubt once been a barn for the gompa. With cautious steps he entered, following the sound to a stall at the back where the Tibetan woman who had been grinding flour now spun a handheld prayer wheel. She faced the deeper shadows at the rear of the stall. It took Shan a moment to make out the old man. Patrul sat cross-legged on a low table, his sightless eyes cast downward, looking like an altar statue more than a living human. Before him, like an offering, lay an aged brown mastiff.

Shan said nothing, did not move, did not want to cause the woman to break the rhythm of her wheel. Patrul's hand left his mudra long enough for him to gesture Shan to sit.

"Your Tibetan is good," the old man declared. "I have always been able to sense a Chinese. But not you. Why do you suppose that is?"

"I have been immersing myself in good Tibetan mud for the past few months."

The blind man's smile was serene.

"Rinpoche," Shan said. "I had a friend, a hermit who passed over suddenly last month. He needs my help."

Shan knew better than to expect a quick reply. The old man looked down as if studying his fingers with his blind eyes, then rested his hand on the head of the big brown dog, who instantly opened its eyes to stare at Shan. He had the uncanny sensation that the old lama was looking at him through the animal's eyes.

"Jamyang was my friend too," the old teacher said. "First came the news of his death. Then the others. It was a storm of death that day."

"They still need us," Shan said. He found himself addressing the dog.

"We still need them."

Shan paused over the words. They were the perfect words, the exact thing that needed to be said. "I think the deaths were connected," he offered.

"The deities needed them all elsewhere, all at once." It was the old abbot's way of agreeing.

"A monk was at the convent when the abbess and the other two died."

The dog blinked.

"Are you some kind of policeman?" the blind man asked. The woman stopped moving her wheel.

"I am a pilgrim."

"He is the one who digs ditches with Lokesh, Rinpoche," the woman interjected.

The old man's face brightened. "You almost died saving that lamb trapped in quicksand. They say the mud was nearly up to your shoulders." A strange wheezing noise came from his throat. It took a moment for Shan to recognize it as a laugh.

"That lamb and I weren't meant to die that day."

"You gain much merit in doing such things."

"Lokesh said in time I will find that the lamb saved me."

The former abbot slowly nodded. "A man can easily put on a robe. It could mean many things." They were talking about the murders again.

"Where is the monk Dakpo?"

The dog raised its head.

"Dakpo has gone beyond the mountains. He knows he must return before the full moon."

"You mean India?" Dakpo had family with the exile government, Trinle had said.

"The other direction."

Shan puzzled over the words. The other direction was north, or east, deeper into Tibet. The full moon was in five days. Dakpo had confided in Patrul, but not Norbu.

"Why," he asked hesitantly, "would he leave without the abbot's permission?"

"Without the government's permission," Patrul said, as if correcting him. Some monasteries, Shan reminded himself, had to secure government permission for its monks to travel. Dakpo had not wanted the government to know. Or was it that he didn't want Major Liang to know?

"Rinpoche," Shan asked, "you said Jamyang was a friend. Was he a new friend or an old friend?"

"We weren't sure, he and I." It was a very Tibetan answer. "When he came to the valley he traveled all the pilgrim's paths and found me on one up on the mountain. He spent the day with Dakpo and me, praying, cleaning old shrines along the paths, and I invited him to come to the gompa. He declined, said he had become a creature of the high paths, like the wild goats. He said he felt a great affinity for our valley, as if he had been here before. I reminded him that over the centuries many gentle spirits like his had lived at our gompa. He wasn't certain that day but as time went by he seemed to be convinced he had been here previously, that he had some duty from another time that he still owed the gompa."

"He said that? A duty?"

The old man offered another serene smile as he turned to stroke the dog. "I told him the devout owed a duty to all of Tibet."

"To all of Tibet, wherever it is located," Shan ventured after a moment.

Patrul turned back with surprise on his face. It seemed his eyes were alive again. They fixed Shan with an intense gaze, fixed not on his face, it seemed, but something behind his face. "Once in Tibet there were earth-taming temples to subdue the demons that threatened it. They are lost to us today, but there are new ones, secret counterparts to the old." When he leaned forward the woman stopped spinning her wheel. His final words came in a low plaintive whisper. "Are you the demon tamer we have prayed for, Shan?"

Shan left the motorbike hidden among rocks and made the long climb to Jamyang's shrine. The visit to the monastery had been strangely unsettling. Patrul had been trying to tell him that Chegar had a secret connection to Dharamsala. The trail of a murderer had led him to Tibetan freedom fighters. He had no heart for exposing a killer if it meant also exposing more dissidents. But Liang would relish the opportunity. Revealing a killer in a nest of dissidents would earn him another promotion.

He paused at the intersection of two trails, recognizing the old pilgrim's path. His last hours with Jamyang continued to haunt him. Words had been spoken that he had not understood, then or now. From where he stood he could just glimpse the little flat where Jamyang had asked him to stop, where the lama had prostrated himself to the mountain. Shan put his hand on a cairn of mani stones, lingering for a moment as if to consult them, then turned onto the path.

When he reached the flat he stepped to the nearby road, trying to reconstruct each of Jamyang's movements when he had asked Shan to stop his truck there. The lama had warned Shan that he did not understand the dangers of the valley, echoing Shan's own words. He had asked to stop at the cairns where pilgrims communed with the powerful mountain that protected the valley. The old abbot had said Jamyang felt a connection to the valley, as if he owed it something. He had prayed at each of the cairns and . . . Shan froze. As the wind lapsed for a moment he heard a new sound, a low, quick murmuring coming from over the edge of the drop-off.

Shan warily approached, seeing now how one end of the prayer flags Jamyang had left had blown out of its anchor and was dangling over the edge. He stared for a moment in disbelief as he saw the white-haired figure huddled on the steep slope at the end of the strand of flags, then carefully climbed down to join him.

Lokesh was tightly clutching the last of the flags in the strand. He nodded as Shan sat beside him. Shan had come to view the silence that often preceded Lokesh's words as something of a benediction, a way of building reverence before speaking.

"It was always going to be the way of his life," the old Tibetan said at last. "There was never a chance you could change that." He spoke as if Shan needed comforting. "Chenmo and Ani Ama came. They are with the American," he added, acknowledging the question on Shan's face.

Shan looked back at the flag. Lokesh was again doing exactly what Shan was doing, except in a totally different way. The old Tibetan had

gone to the flags to understand Jamyang. Shan had been in a rush
with Jamyang, had not paid attention to the lama's flags, assuming
they were traditional mani mantra flags. Now as he lifted one he saw
something unexpected, an intricately rendered, unfamiliar deity.

"There are thirty-five flags," Lokesh said, as if the number were
significant. "I saw him working on these. I thought it was for the
shrine."

Shan examined another flag, and another. Each of their images
was different, each a painstakingly rendered image of a deity of a
different color or shape. Each would have taken hours to complete.

"This would have been the first one," Lokesh explained, pointing
to the white-bodied, highly ornamented deity at the end of the twine.
"Vajrasattva. This is how it begins," he added, pointing to the words
inscribed below the image.

"*Namo gurubhay, namo Buddhaya,*" Shan read, then looked up
in query.

"Some call it the refuge prayer, others the prayer of remorse. It is
the beginning of the ritual, invoking the first of the Confession Buddhas. There are thirty-five in all. Each must be invoked to purify corruption. Scores of thousands of mantras must be offered to empower
each. I remember in the last month how tired Jamyang always seemed."

Shan nodded. "He was going without sleep to complete this."

Lokesh gazed upon the anchor deity again, as if in silent prayer,
then sighed. "We should go up. We should fasten the flags as Jamyang
intended."

Shan rose and put a hand out to help Lokesh up the slope. They
tied the strand tightly around the biggest stone they could find and
placed it on top of a cairn. He gazed on the flapping flags, ashamed
that he had not paid attention when he had been there with Jamyang,
ashamed too that he not seen the lama's need for confession earlier.
He reached and touched one of the flags. "I have seen this one, or a
bigger one like it. Jamyang kept it by his altar."

Lokesh stretched the flag and examined it. "There are gods for confession of theft, of lying, of sacrilege," he said, pain now entering his voice. "But this one"—he looked up at Shan with a lost expression—"this one is for killing."

After a long moment the old Tibetan settled onto folded legs in the center of the square defined by the cairns, as if to continue the dialogue Jamyang had started with Yangon, the sacred mountain. Shan knew better than to persuade him to come with him. He turned and headed back to Jamyang's shrine.

He was not sure why the shrine drew him, not sure when he arrived why he felt the need to clean the offerings again. Halfway through the task he realized he had stopped and was staring at the carved deities. "I'm sorry," he said. The words came out like a sob. More than ever he felt he had let Jamyang down, had failed the Tibetans. The murders were going to be used to destroy the valley, to sap the essence that made it so important to Tibetans. He looked down the slope. Part of him still seemed to be searching for Jamyang's ghost. He was more confused than ever about who Jamyang was, but knew now that he had felt great anguish in his final days. If Shan had only seen it, perhaps he could have spoken with the lama, helped him find a path other than the day of death.

He finished cleaning the offerings, checked to confirm that Yuan's ancestral tablets were still in the little cave, then found a patch of grass above Jamyang's shrine, where he could gaze on the sacred mountain and let the wind scour his pain. As he closed his eyes memory swept over him.

The visiting chamber was deliberately kept unheated in the winter, to encourage visitors to spend less time with their imprisoned family members. Shan and Ko had shared the room with an aged woman and her skeletal-looking husband, who spent more time coughing than talking, until she had given up and just murmured mantras beside him.

Shan remembered details, every detail of every minute in that room, etched in his memory. They came back unexpectedly, unbidden, often unwelcome.

"We were digging a roadbed when one of the men found a nest of beetles," Ko said. His voice was always very low, conditioned by years in cells. "He tied them in his sock and sold them that night, for men to mix in their porridge the next morning." In his own time Shan had seen many prisoners mix insects into their gruel, for the added protein. "I bought one, a big fat black one, for a purple stone I had found. But that night a lama started talking. He said the souls who had the hardest times as humans sometimes came back as beetles. He took out one of the bugs and began reciting a mantra to it. The thing just looked at him at first, never moved, then damned if it didn't put its front legs up, together, like it was praying. In the morning all the Tibetans went over to the wire and released their beetles. They looked at me and I made like I was going to eat my beetle. They cried out and starting offering me new stones for my big boy. Red stones, yellow stones, blue stones. That lama didn't offer anything. He just came over and touched a finger to my forehead."

"What did you do?" Shan asked.

"I let the little bastard go. All those stones would have just weighed down my pockets."

They stared at each other in silence. Then Ko grinned and Shan grinned back, one prisoner to another.

"I was hoping I might find you here."

Shan stirred from his dream to find Professor Yuan sitting beside him.

"I used to go up on the roof of our apartment building in Harbin when I wanted to contemplate the world in privacy." He gestured to the broad landscape of rich rolling hills, with the majestic Yangon towering behind them. "On the whole I think I prefer this to smoke-stacks and highways."

"Your tablets are safe for now, Professor, but I can't be responsible for them. Others could come."

Professor Yuan ignored Shan's words. He reached inside his shirt and pulled out a rolled-up towel. It was tattered and needed washing but he treated it like a treasure, straightening it on his lap with great care. "He was one of a noble few, our Yuan Yi. A censor, a very senior censor in the court of the Kangxi emperor. You no doubt know about the censors."

"Scores of thousands of officials ran the empire and a few hundred censors watched over the officials to keep them honest." The current government had perverted the term, but once censors had been the elite of government officials.

"Exactly." Yuan lifted the towel in his hands, working his fingers into its seams. "Service in government was a sacred trust to such a man. He used the truth against many corrupt officials and made many enemies in doing so. He was in his twentieth year of service when he was sent to investigate corruption in one of the northeastern provinces, in the emperor's own Manchuria. He discovered the entire province was run as a criminal enterprise, that the governor himself was the ringleader, siphoning off a third of what was supposed to be sent to the emperor. When he returned and made his report to the emperor's counselors in Beijing he was arrested and tried for corruption himself, sentenced to be beheaded. An old eunuch who was favored in the court came to his cell the night before his execution and told him the emperor knew of the governor's corruption but could not act against the governor because the governor was the emperor's strongest supporter in the region. The emperor asked Yuan Yi to withdraw his report. Yuan Yi instead demanded to be executed the next morning to prove he stood by the truth.

"The next morning he was taken to a private temple the emperor used for ceremonies honoring his greatest mandarins, his most trusted advisers. An executioner was there with his sword. Yuan Yi was shoved forward to the block but only to see that his commission as censor was on the block. The executioner cleaved it with his blade."

"Killing the censor," Shan said.

"Yes. The emperor stepped out of the shadows and bowed to Yuan Yi. The gate through which mandarins left after receiving honors from the emperor was thrust open and the emperor escorted him to it. Politics prevented him from arresting the governor but honor prevented him from killing a man for speaking the truth. As Yuan Yi reached the arch he pulled off his badge and handed it to the emperor. Kangxi bowed to him and handed it back. Then Yuan Yi stepped through the gate and fled the capital. He found his way back to Manchuria and formed a group of men who began raiding the caravans carrying the governor's riches. He spread the riches all over the province, to needy families, to temples, to schools. He was an outlaw the rest of his life, but the emperor would never sign the warrants for arrest sent by the governor. For the rest of his years he lived the life of the bandit, helping those who suffered at the hands of the corrupt."

"The years have a way of embellishing stories, Professor."

Yuan only smiled, then gripped the towel and ripped it apart. There had been two towels, sewn together.

Shan's heart stopped beating for a moment when he recognized what was inside. It was impossible.

Yuan held up the secret treasure, a square of silk worked with exquisite embroidery. For hundreds of years, spanning multiple dynasties, there had been nine ranks of official mandarins, each with its own badge of office worn as a square of cloth over dark blue ceremonial robes. The peacock at the center of Yuan's silk was the emblem of the esteemed third rank. Arranged around the bird were the clouds, peonies, and bats that traditionally brought good fortune to the wearer. Yuan was holding the badge of office his ancestor had worn nearly three centuries earlier, the badge touched by an emperor.

"A lesser man would have burned this after what the emperor did," the professor declared. "But Yuan Yi kept it as a token of honor. He said his duty was to the people, that he kept the badge for all those who served the truth no matter what the government said. My family preserved a letter from him, for over two centuries, until the Red Guard burned it. My father used to read it to me. Yuan Yi wrote it as an old man to a grandson. In it he said the most important thing he had ever done was step through that arch, the Mandarin Gate, that the most good he ever did for the people was in leaving the government behind."

Shan's hand trembled as Yuan handed the silk badge to him. "My father would have been speechless to behold such a thing," he said. "As I nearly am." With a racing heart he held the badge closer, examining its intricate artistry, seeing also now butterflies and a sun, and a dark blotch that could have been a very old bloodstain.

"My grandfather would hold this and describe the processions of the court officials before the emperor," Yuan explained. "I could close my eyes and hear the drums and smell the incense." He held up his hand when Shan extended it back to him. "For now this is yours. I loan it to you, until the crisis in the valley is resolved." He cast a pointed gaze at Shan. "It will not be resolved, my friend, except by you." He extended his open hand downwards, toward the earth. "I say this with the mountain as my witness." The professor was learning something of the Tibetan ways.

Shan had no words. "I am just the ditch inspector," he said at last. "A very bad one, since I have neglected my duties for many days."

"You are the one who keeps clear water flowing. Clear water keeps us alive."

"I am the one who is arrested and beaten and tortured. I cannot be trusted with this. Liang would burn it, just to spite me. You think I can walk through that gate but I can't."

"You must understand something," Yuan said in the voice of an old lama. "It isn't valuable because it is so old. It is valuable because of all the risks taken for it, and with it, for so very many years. There are still censors that keep the government in check. We need them more than ever. I think, my friend, you stepped through that gate on the day Jamyang died." Yuan handed the pieces of towel to Shan. "There is so little I can do. Let me at least do this. One of my great-uncles kept it on him in the last war. He said it made him bullet-proof."

"You think too much of me, Yuan. I can't even understand who Jamyang was."

The professor extended a piece of paper to Shan. "Sansan found this. The symbol on Jamyang's paper. A hammer and a chorten."

Shan studied what looked like a printout of a website page, with the hammer and chorten featured prominently at the top. He looked up in confusion. "The Chinese Tibetan Peace Institute?"

"In Chamdo. On the grounds of an old monastery."

Shan shrugged. "He was trying to build bridges between people. The Bureau of Religious Affairs has many such places."

"You misunderstand. Sansan dug deeper. There is no connection to Religious Affairs. The institute is an arm of Public Security."

Lung Tso and Jigten were waiting with his truck at the stable when Shan arrived.

"That last date on the paper Jamyang gave your brother is the night of the full moon," Shan stated.

"What of it?"

"You spoke about a young monk you dealt with at the monastery," Shan said. "Dakpo. He ran away three days ago but he has to be back for the full moon, because that is when you have a truck taking a cargo for India. I think he is party to your secret business with Chegar. Where did you take him?"

"Ah yi," Lung muttered. "You never stop."

"Not until the killer is caught, no."

"Damn it, Shan. My world is based on secrets."

"So is the killer's. Where is he?"

Lung glanced at Jigten, who waited by the truck. "Fine," he spat. "Chamdo. He knew we run to Chamdo twice a week, to the warehouses where shipments arrive from the east. He was desperate to go, said he would help with the loading of the truck if need be. He borrowed some work clothes and rode in the back."

Shan had somehow known. He pressed the badge of Yuan Yi, sewn back into its towels and tucked inside his shirt. "Then I am desperate too. When is your next truck to Chamdo?"

CHAPTER FOURTEEN

They were twenty miles up the highway when Jigten flipped his cigarette out the window and cursed. "They're following us. I slow down,
they slow down. I speed up, they speed up."

Shan leaned to look out the side mirror and his heart sank. The
grey Public Security vehicle was the only car on the empty road but
it was hugging the rear of their big cargo truck. "Pull over," he told
Jigten.

"To hell I will. We're going to Chamdo," the shepherd spat with
unexpected vehemence. Genghis had been scheduled to make the run
to the remote city but at the last minute had been seized with terrible
stomach pains. Jigten, lingering in the garage, had readily volunteered
to replace him.

"I admire your spirit but I doubt they are here for you."

Jigten frowned but began to downshift. The truck eased to a halt
with a hiss of air brakes. As Shan opened his door to confront his
tail, the top of his head felt as it were burning again.

But there was no team sent to retrieve him for Liang. A solitary
figure in a rumpled uniform climbed out of the car.

"Lieutenant Meng, we left your district miles ago," Shan declared.

"I recall that your registration papers don't allow you out of the county," she replied.

"We have already established my scofflaw tendencies. But what's your excuse?"

Something like defiance burned in her eyes. "Three people were murdered in my district. One of the men assigned to Liang says the bullet we took from the murder scene is just sitting on his desk. You were right. He never sent it to the lab. And yesterday there was a general notice, an alert for all Tibetan offices, about an official German delegation arriving in Lhasa to recover the body of a victim in a climbing accident three hundred miles from here. They took Rutger and dropped him off a cliff. The only one who is doing anything about solving those murders is you."

"Those are dangerous words, Lieutenant. Especially for someone who's been broken in rank already. Take my advice and go home. You're only a lieutenant this time. A sergeant's pay is hard to live on."

Meng shrugged. "Less paperwork. More time in the field. I enjoy the fresh air."

"You've been in Tibet too long. I sense a perilous contamination."

"What are you doing?"

"You said it before. I am the only one interested in finding out why Jamyang and the others died." He studied Meng. Behind the weariness on her face was a glint of determination. "Go home," he repeated. "Go back and do whatever it takes to get Major Liang out of your district."

"The highway's being shut down for twelve hours starting at noon. Prisoner convoys. There will be checkpoints and guards everywhere. You'll never make it through without an escort."

"I fear for you, Lieutenant. I sense you are dangerously close to an antisocialist act."

Meng leaned against her car. Her gaze became distant, aimed toward the far horizon. "I have a confession. I was ordered to make sure a canvas was tied around that statue of the Helmsman after you smashed his face. But I went back last night and cut the ropes holding the canvas, let it blow away in the wind. And I didn't even leave. I sat on a bench and stared at him. I remember a story I heard once about an emperor with no clothes. No one would ever call him naked. A dog came up and peed on the pedestal. I laughed out loud. I felt more free than I had in years."

Shan stared at the woman, not understanding the flood of emotion her words released inside him.

"I checked what Liang said about that monk in Rutok," she declared. "There was no report of an immolation in Rutok. He lied to us, like you said. He started asking me about that dead lama, Jamyang. About whether I could find his body, about where he had been living, who his friends were." The wind tugged out a strand of her hair. She let it hang across her face, then turned away as she felt his gaze. "Who was he, Shan? Who was that lama?"

"I don't know. I am following his ghost to Chamdo."

She had no reply.

"What exactly are you proposing to do?" he asked.

"I am going to pull in front of you and escort you to Chamdo. We're going to find his ghost together."

The journey to the northeast was much slower than Shan would have liked but after an hour, when they encountered the first roadblock, he knew they would never have had a chance without Meng. With a knob officer as an escort they were able to crawl past several groups of heavily guarded trucks. In the middle of the afternoon they were forced to stop not for another checkpoint but for a disabled truck that had broken down in the center of the road, blocking both lanes. Two dozen men in threadbare denim had been off-loaded and allowed to sit on the bank at the edge of the road.

Shan's heart lurched as he saw the prisoners. Most were emaciated veterans of years in the gulag, wearing the dull, battered expressions of those without hope. Scattered among them was fresh meat from the east, new prisoners whose faces were tight with fear, not of the guards but of their fellow prisoners, the gaunt reflections of the creatures they would become.

Shan had wondered why so many truckloads were on the move that day, but now he saw the smaller truck behind the first, its open cargo bay piled high with shovels and picks, and stacks of the baskets used for hauling dirt and stones. There were special hard-labor mines for such prisoners, opened only in the summer, some in deep treacherous tunnels prone to cave-ins. Others would go to uranium pits where the radiation would cause every prisoner's hair to fall out by the end of the first month. They were considered the lucky ones, for they would work in the open air and the guards tended to keep their distance for fear of contaminating themselves.

"Buddha's breath," Jigten gasped. "Look at the bastards. Half of them are walking skeletons." He pulled out a cigarette and tossed it to one of the rail-thin prisoners. Another prisoner jerked forward, grabbing it out of the air. With a victorious expression he stuffed it into his mouth and ate it.

The grounds of the former monastery used by the Chinese Tibetan Peace Institute had been lavishly restored. Through the open gate at its entrance, statues of Mao and Buddha stood at either side of the courtyard, staring at each other, an elegant, newly built chorten in between. Shan and Meng, dressed in hastily acquired civilian clothes, watched from an outside table at a café across the street. Monks entered the Institute carrying books. Chinese men and women in business suits moved in and out of the gate. Tibetan townspeople passed through the gate to stand before the Buddha, sometimes draping a traditional prayer scarf over its wrist. At times the compound seemed to convey the air of a traditional monastery, at others it seemed more like a busy government office complex.

They sat in silence, finishing their tea and then accepting a new pot from the waiter. Shan found his gaze drifting toward the street traffic and the flow of urban life. A woman hurried a young girl in pigtails across the street. Two boys teased a puppy with a feather tied to a string. A Tibetan woman hawked hot noodles and *momos,* meat dumplings, from plastic pails covered with towels. A tall Tibetan led a donkey down the street, the black sash woven in his hair marking him as a Khampa.

"You said you had a son," Meng suddenly said. "So you are married?"

It was part of her cover, he told himself at first. They were supposed to be a man and a woman having tea together. Then he saw the shy way she looked at him.

"No," he replied. "Not now. Not ever I guess."

"You guess?"

"My wife had the marriage annulled."

"But you have a son."

"We never spent more than two weeks together. She was in the Party, got an assignment in another city. By the time I was sent to prison she was a vice mayor. After my son was arrested as a drug dealer it was better for her to deny her connections with us."

"So she got a divorce, you mean."

"No. Too messy. My son and I would still be on her record. More politically expedient to get a judge in the Party to issue a decree for the records to be erased. It was as if we never existed in her life."

"That must have been painful."

Shan shrugged. "I was busy building roads and trying to stay alive on corncobs and sawdust gruel. It was years before I even knew."

They sipped tea in silence, forgetting the gate for a long moment.

"Surely you . . ." Shan was not sure how to finish his query.

"Surely I was married? Yes," Meng said matter-of-factly. "He studied literature and drama. He wrote very well but couldn't find a job so he took one in a faceless building where they wrote public scripts for the government. Eulogies for Eighth Route Army veterans. Tales of worker heroes, real and otherwise. He was good at it, good at finding words to tug at the heartstrings of the proletariat. He got noticed. They promoted him. He began writing speeches for officials and news releases for the Party."

"Propaganda." The word slipped out before Shan could stop it.

Meng gave an awkward nod. "I didn't like it. He didn't like it, not at first. He drank. They kept promoting him and he kept drinking. That was the first time I was a lieutenant. When they assigned him to Beijing, they made me a captain, arranging security for officials. I begged him to quit. I said he had sold his soul, that he was better than that. He hit me."

Shan lifted his cup and stared at her over its lip, wondering what it might have been like if he had met Meng like this, not wearing a knob uniform.

"I asked to leave the job, leave Beijing. They broke me and sent me to a stable in Tibet."

"A stable?"

"Public Security jargon. Where officers who have fallen out of favor are sent to be mere workhorses, to plod along without hope of advancement. The jobs no one else wants, in some god-forsaken backwater. Baiyun's a stable, though they told me to consider it rehabilitation, that my record once had been so good I might still might find advancement in four or five years. A few months after I arrived I got the papers saying he had divorced me."

Shan forced himself to look at the gate again, to avoid her eyes. "You didn't have to tell me that," he said. When he looked back she was staring at a pigeon. She looked like a young, lost girl. He looked at her hand on the table and realized he wanted to touch it.

Her face hardened as she felt his stare. "It's an interrogation technique," she said, wincing as if she had bitten something sour. "Let the subject know we are all comrades in the same difficult struggle."

They fell silent again for several minutes, watching the gate again.

"People go in and don't come out," Shan observed.

"There's a chapel. People go in and meditate. They may take an hour or two."

"It's an Institute," Shan replied. "Those carrying briefcases are not going in to meditate."

"There's an official public description," Meng observed, waving a brochure she had picked up in the guesthouse they had registered at, two blocks away. "And there are official private descriptions."

"I don't follow."

The lieutenant unfolded the brochure and began reading. "The Chinese Tibetan Peace Institute is building bridges between the Han and Tibetan ethnic groups that reside in this region of the People's Republic. By teaching the oneness of our great peoples we build happiness and socialist prosperity in every home."

"Socialist prosperity," Shan echoed. "It wasn't written by a Tibetan. And the first Han seen here wore the uniforms of the People's Liberation Army. This is Chamdo, traditional capital of Kham province, where Tibetan warriors using muskets were mown down by Chinese machine guns." He frowned, not understanding why he felt the need to goad her.

Meng ignored him. "There are places on the Internet reserved for the government. They require special passwords." She touched her cell phone and the screen came to life.

Shan cast a nervous glance around the café and leaned forward. "You know passwords for the Institute?"

"Public Security has a new database, like a reference guide to organizations that officers may need to know about." She lowered her voice and read from the little screen. "The Peace Institute in Chamdo is a unique facility," Meng recited, "where Buddhist teachers acquire the perspectives needed to lead their cadres into the future. Those who graduate from the Institute are awarded provisional membership in the Party. Some go on to serve the Motherland in strategic and often heroic capacities."

The words raised a cold knot in Shan's stomach. "Do they have a list of graduates?"

Meng worked at her screen as Shan sipped his tea. "It's classified," she said uncertainly. "A secret even within the Bureau. The screen keeps going back to what the Institute calls its internal manifesto." As she made a movement to turn off the phone Shan grabbed it.

The manifesto was short and to the point: "Tibetans are not born traitors, but taught to live the lie through the influence of ego and prejudice in the religious class. Our goal is to use proven socialist methods to correct the error of their ways, to help them overcome the tyranny of their tradition." He pushed the phone back and looked away.

After a moment he drained his cup, then took off the lid of the little teapot, a sign that it needed refilling. When the waiter ignored it, Meng rose and carried the pot inside. The instant she entered the building he slipped into the crowd. He needed to be alone, needed to be away from Public Security. Jamyang had lived in this town. He needed to find his ghost. He needed to understand the terrible foreboding he felt about the Peace Institute.

Shan found himself at a bus stop, lingering in a crowd of children in school uniforms. He let the crowd push him as a bus approached, did not turn back even as he found himself going up the steps of the bus. He sat at a window, not seeing at first, not feeling anything except impossibly tired.

When he shook himself awake, the bus, nearly empty, was on the outskirts of town. Tracts of shabby houses were giving way to fields and arid pastures. He got out at the next stop, crossed to the stop on the opposite side of the street and sat on its plastic bench. He heard a laugh and turned, seeing the back of a tall Tibetan with shaggy white hair, dressed in tattered clothes, and for a moment felt the ridiculous hope that it was Lokesh. Then the man turned and saw Shan, lowered his head and hurried away.

The hill on which he sat overlooked the town. Chamdo was Tibet's third-largest city but it was isolated, so remote that it was seldom visited by outsiders, and even those were permitted only in organized groups. It was the perfect place for the government to conduct operations out of the public eye. He saw the warehouse complex where Jigten was loading the truck, then located the long block of buildings that comprised the Institute, some of the best-kept structures in the city. Jamyang had been there, at the anonymous complex in the anonymous, remote city. He had left in a suit and reappeared in a robe.

An hour later he was back at the bus stop where he had started, studying its city map, tracing the shaded, anonymous square of land that comprised the Institute. He turned for a moment, and realized that he was looking at the tea shop, unconsciously searching for Meng. Another mystery kept nagging at the edge of his consciousness, the mystery of why she so unsettled him. It was not fear of her he felt when he was with her. It was fear of himself.

Retreating from the corner, he followed the side street along the western wall of the compound. A row of well-manicured houses sharing common walls stretched out in front of the wall. At the end of the first block he crossed and walked slowly, studying the houses. They all had the same hardware on the doors and windows. There was no way through them, no way around them. They were just a buffer, like a moat around a fortress.

He glanced down the street, mindful of two men in spotless coveralls leaning on brooms at either end of the block, then approached the nearest door. It was locked. The window by the door was covered by a curtain but he could see through a narrow opening in the middle. The house was empty. Pressing his head close to the glass he saw through a window at the back. Behind the house was another wall, perhaps eight feet tall, not visible from the street. Strung along its top was razor wire.

Shan hurried on, rounding the next corner, to the back of the compound, where the street was busier. He settled onto a park bench under a tree, studying the buildings at that end of the block. Here too were houses that appeared empty, that seemed to serve as outer barriers to the compound, but in the center of the block was a store of some kind, and across from that a small police station. Monks went in and out of the shop. He searched the faces of each, watching for Dakpo. His hand unconsciously pressed against his chest, touching the badge of Yuan Yi, the mandarin bandit.

"It takes up two city blocks," a voice said over his shoulder. Meng was facing the compound as she spoke. "Nothing but old shops and businesses along the wall on the other side. All with signs saying they were closed for an urban renewal project. Except the paper is all yellowed and dried-up. Like it's been there for years."

"The main gate is the only entry," Shan observed. "Everything else is locked up except for this one shop."

Meng started across the street even before he rose from the bench.

The shop was dedicated to religious literature and memoirs of the Communist struggle. A poster of Mao's calligraphy stood over a stand of little Buddhas holding the flag of the People's Republic. They browsed as if they were a tourist couple, buying a package of the inexpensive prayer scarves that pilgrims left on shrines. At the rear of the store was a room identified by a sign as the library. Inside, a small display case held several artifacts from the original monastery and two larger cases commemorated the Chinese youth brigade that had captured it fifty years before. Their patriotic efforts, the display explained, had liberated more than two hundred monks. It was the uplifting explanation favored by propagandists. It generally meant the monks had been freed of their earthly existence.

A stiff matron sat at a desk at the head of a narrow corridor marked PRIVATE ARCHIVES, tapping the keys of one of the electronic mahjong games that had become so popular in China. During the ten minutes they watched, half a dozen men and women were admitted by the woman after showing identity cards in black leather cases. They were all Chinese, all with cool, arrogant faces.

Meng reached into her pocket and had taken two steps toward the desk when Shan grabbed her hand. "Our bus!" he chided, and pulled her out of the room.

"You fool!" Meng snapped as they reached the street. "I could get in. Those were Public Security identity cards. Somewhere down that corridor is a file with Jamyang's name on it."

"That game she had was for show. There was a keyboard on a shelf below the table top. She was recording every officer's name as they went through. Five minutes after you walked down that hall Liang would have known you were here."

The anger on Meng's face changed to relief. "Ah yi!" she muttered. "Thank you." She looked down and grinned. Shan was still gripping her hand. He flushed and pulled away.

They sat on the bench again. "There's no need to go inside," Meng ventured. "We know what they do."

"Indoctrinate wayward monks." The words were like acid on Shan's tongue.

"They redirect those who have strayed from the ever-correct path of socialism."

Shan would have been repulsed by Meng's words were it not for the bitter tone with which she spoke them.

He watched a group of four men leave the shop, two Chinese and two older Tibetans in robes. "This is not about political calibration," he observed. "There are camps that do that. This is different. This is for very special training." Two limousines pulled up and deposited half a dozen Chinese men near the door.

"It's like a private club," Meng observed. As she spoke the group of four who had left the Institute walked by them. A gasp of surprise left Shan's throat. He shot up and followed, getting closer. The robes of the two Tibetans were loosely belted. Hanging from the belts of each, like trappings of a uniform, were three identical items. A set of red rosary beads, a small ornate pen case, and a bronze wedge-shaped flint striker, identical to that used to kill the Lung boy.

The sun had been down for at an hour when Shan returned to the guesthouse. He had declined the evening meal, leaving Meng alone while he searched the shrines of the town for Dakpo. He climbed the wooden stairs slowly, weary not so much from physical exertion as despair. The monk could have gone on a pilgrimage, Meng had suggested. But not on a moment's notice, Shan had explained, not in a rush to return by the full moon. Dakpo would not have had travel papers. More likely, he had been picked up, and was just a number in some distant detention center by now. The full moon. It was only a few days away now. Shan paused, then pulled out the note on which he had recorded the dates given to Lung Ma by Jamyang. One date, the date for the monk's test run to Nepal, had already transpired. The last date was the date of the full moon.

He washed, then secured Yuan Yi's badge in the bottom of his pack. He settled onto his bed but knew he could not sleep, so he rose and lifted the window, taking in the sounds of urban life. The low rumble of trucks rose from the highway half a mile away. Dogs barked. A child squealed with laughter in a nearby alley. Someone dumped bottles in a trash bin. The scent of fried onions and rice wafted in the night air. Shan was suddenly famished.

"I told them to save our dinner."

Meng stood in the doorway that connected their rooms, holding two tin boxes. She handed Shan the still-warm containers and disappeared back into her room, returned with another chair and a small table that she set below the window. She laid out a towel for a tablecloth and topped it with a candle in a soda bottle. "There's a brownout. The front desk was passing out candles."

"You've been busy," Shan said awkwardly as Meng struck a match and lit the candle.

"Not really. I shopped a little and fell asleep on my bed."

Shan looked away, aware that he had been staring at her. She was not the austere woman he was accustomed to. Her hair hung loose and long over a blouse of red silk. As she opened his box of food and handed him a pair of chopsticks, she offered an uncertain smile. "We're just two travelers tonight, experiencing a strange city together."

Shan did not recognize the flicker of emotion he felt, was not sure why he stared after her when she stepped back into her room for a thermos of tea.

"There was no sign of Dakpo," he said between mouthfuls of dumplings and fried vegetables.

Meng poured him a cup of tea. "I saw a park this evening where a boy was flying a kite with an old man," she said in a quiet voice. "When I was young my uncle used to take me to a park like that every spring. We would leave very early, have to take several buses. I remember getting onto that last bus that took us to the park and how most of the passengers would be children with kites. The kite brigade my uncle called it. I thought it meant we were all going to be soldiers. But I didn't want to be a soldier. Once, I saw a soldier with a kite in the park and I ran and hid because I thought he had come for me."

Shan realized he had stopped eating.

"What is it?" Meng asked.

"I don't . . ." Shan struggled for words. He stared at his food. "I don't know how to do this. I'm sorry."

"This? You don't know how to eat your supper?"

"I mean you and me like this."

"I seem to recall we have sat in more than one teahouse together."

"Not like this. Not talking like a man and a woman."

Meng's face tightened. "You want me to leave?" she asked in a near whisper.

"No," Shan said, too quickly. "I'm sorry. I've done too many things. I've seen too many things."

"I don't understand."

"In the gulag you learn to let scars grow over certain places in your heart."

Meng was quiet for a long time. It was her turn to stare at her food. She bit her lip. "Then we will just practice for a while," she said at last.

The melancholy in her eyes almost took Shan's breath away.

They ate in silence.

"I had two camels when I was a boy," he heard himself say in an oddly parched voice. He drank some tea and tried again. "Little wooden camels. They were my treasures. My uncle had been a trader in Beijing and gave them to me one New Year's. We would light candles and he would speak long into the night about the way Beijing was when he lived there. In the winter there would be long caravans of camels, two humped camels, winding down the streets carrying huge baskets of coal. Sometimes he would go out and the alley he lived on would be entirely blocked by camels waiting to be unloaded. The handlers were all Mongolians, and in those moments he said it was like the great khans who built the city had never left. He expected to see Marco Polo at the next corner. I loved those stories, and I kept those camels even when we were sent to the communes for reeducation. My mother told me to pack my extra shoes but I packed my camels instead."

The words began flowing freely then, and they spoke of tales of their childhood, of schooldays, of youthful visits to the sacred mountains of the east, of anywhere but where they were. It was nearly

midnight when Meng packed up the empty dishes and returned them
to her room. Shan went down the hall to the washroom, then stripped
and lay under his sheet, watching the moon through the window.

She entered so quietly he was not aware of her until she stepped
into a pool of moonlight ten feet from his bed. She was wearing only
a sleeveless undershirt.

"What is it?" he asked, pulling the sheet up over his bare chest.

In reply she pulled the shirt over her head. "I'm not so old, Shan,"
she said as she let the shirt drop on the floor.

"You—you should probably go." He had trouble getting the
words out.

"Do you have any idea, Comrade, how many years go by without
my even meeting a man I respect enough?" She took a step closer.

"Surely not me," Shan whispered. "I'm so much older."

"You're not so old."

"I feel old," he said. "That's gone from my life."

"You told me you couldn't talk like a man with a woman. Then
we talked for hours."

"That was different."

She was at the edge of his bed. "Then we will just practice for
while," she said, and lifted his covers.

"This isn't the way we should . . ." The words died in his throat.
Meng had her own way. His hand trembled as she raised it and
placed it on her body.

Afterwards she lay in the round of his shoulder. "What happened
to them?" she asked. "To those two wooden camels."

"My mother got sick that first winter. We burned them to make
her some tea."

CHAPTER FIFTEEN

The temple at the front of the Institute was already attracting a steady flow of visitors when Shan settled onto the stone flags of its floor the next morning. Tibetans and a few Chinese on the way to work in shops and offices were lighting sticks of incense and lowering themselves in front of altars beside a handful of monks who had been there when Shan arrived. Along a wall half a dozen other monks sat, some twirling handheld prayer wheels. A handful of Tibetans, in the rough clothing of farmers and herders, moved along the shrines that lined the opposite wall.

He glanced toward the door. Meng had been gone when he had awakened, had been all business when he had seen her briefly in the lobby of the guesthouse. She had greeted him with only an awkward smile and he had realized she was feeling the same uncertainty about the night before. He was stunned by the tenderness that had welled up within him, unbidden, unknown for so many years that he had thought he had lost all capacity for it. But as much as he was attracted to who she was, something inside could not help but be repulsed by what she was. He knew too that, for the knob inside her, he was a former convict, a stigma, a chain around her neck, a guarantee that she would never leave her exile within the Bureau. It was no doubt best for both of them to think of the night before as just a fleeting, intimate detour in the crooked paths that were their lives.

Staying in the shadows, he watched the monks at the wall as much as the worshipers, noting the pinched, unsettled expressions on the men in maroon robes. Were they being punished? Were they being brainwashed? Or were they the watchdogs of the temple?

An old man settled nearby and began a mantra in a low, dry voice. The sound invoked fond images of Lokesh and the lamas they knew, and he soon found himself drifting under its spell.

He was so focused on the mantra that the movement did not register at first. It seemed to be just another pilgrim adjusting his position as he paid homage to one more deity. But then the man, wearing a hat low on his head and mumbling a low mantra, seemed to stumble against one of the seated figures in the shadows, a monk. As he bent over the monk his mantra changed to a curse and he slammed his fist into the robed figure. The monk rolled away, trying to escape.

"Bastard! Murderer!" the pilgrim shouted in Tibetan, and leapt over the monk, blocking his path then pummeling him with his fists.

The monk moaned and covered his head with his arms, then pushed up, knocking the pilgrim back. The man staggered forward, landing another blow on the monk, before shoving him down, slamming his head on the stone flags.

"Jigten!" Shan shouted as he recognized the attacker. He shot up and began pushing his way through the crowd of shocked worshipers

The young monk cried out in pain but offered no resistance. "Killer!" Jigten shouted as he began kicking him. As he bent to slam his fist into the monk's jaw, Shan broke free of the crowd and leapt forward to grab his arm.

But other arms reached Jigten first. Four monks were suddenly pulling the two men apart, then a moment later uniformed knobs appeared from the shadows of the corridor. A big man in one of the grey

uniforms viciously kicked Jigten, propelling him across the floor.
As the knobs placed manacles on the shepherd, Shan knelt over the
bruised, whimpering monk, wiping away blood with his sleeve, and
gasped. It was Dakpo.

One of the knobs noticed Shan's reaction and eyed him suspiciously. Shan retreated, joining the throng of frightened worshipers
fleeing the chamber.

He stood in the courtyard, numb with despair. Somehow he had
begun to believe Dakpo knew more than any of them about the murders, that his mysterious quest in the north would hold a key to the
puzzle of the valley and its monastery. But all that was lost. A monk
involved in a civil disturbance was guaranteed incarceration, and
probably loss of his robe.

Police vans with flashing lights rolled up, followed by an ambulance. As he backed away someone gently pulled his arm. He let
Meng guide him across the street to a table in the shadows of the
café. He watched forlornly as uniformed men and women swarmed
into the courtyard. Dakpo was limp as two knobs carried him out of
the temple. Jigten had hit him hard, knocking his head on the stone
flags.

Shan found himself rising from his chair as the officers hauled the
monk into the ambulance. Meng pulled him down. "It's not what you
think," she said, and he watched, confused, as the ambulance drove
away without a police escort.

"I don't understand," he said to Meng, but she was calling the
waiter, ordering tea.

"I bought you something," she said after he had sipped his cup.
He noticed now a small parcel wrapped in brown paper at his elbow.

"Where's the hospital?" he asked.

"It won't be hard to find." She nodded toward the package with
an awkward smile.

"Why wouldn't the police go with Dakpo?"

Meng ignored his question. "I passed a little shop that sells souvenirs. The man said this was an old one. You don't have yours anymore."

Shan studied her a moment. She seemed to have grown younger. There was a light in her eyes he had not seen before. *Leave her,* a voice inside shouted. *She's a knob. She'll always be a knob. You loathe knobs.* He opened the package.

It was a strand of Tibetan prayer beads.

"A mala?" he asked in surprise. He glanced back at the disappearing ambulance, then felt the touch of the beads. It was not simply a mala, it was a very old and rare sandalwood mala, each bead exquisitely carved with the head of a deity. "I can't," he protested. "It's a treasure."

"Don't be silly. They're being sold to tourists."

He watched as his fingers began working the beads as if of their own accord. They had a warm, natural feel, with a patina of long use.

"You wear that well," Meng offered.

Shan looked up. "I'm sorry?"

"Your smile. I haven't seen it before. When's the last time a woman brought you a present?" Her question was as much a surprise as her gift.

His ran his hand over the stubble of his hair, painfully conscious of his shabby clothes. It had been nearly thirty years. "A long time," he answered softly.

She too wore her smile well. For a moment he forgot about Jigten and Dakpo, then his gaze drifted back to the beads. "The shop," he asked, "can you take me there?"

The little store was tucked between a noodle stand and a bicycle repair garage, its front window lined with little plastic busts of Mao labeled in Tibetan and Chinese, soapstone snow leopards and genuine yak tail fly whisks. Inside, at the back, was a display case filled with malas, ritual purba blades, temple bells, and gaus, all of them finely worked antiques. They were being sold as if they were just more cheap trinkets.

Shan glanced in confusion at the shopkeeper, who was busy with a Chinese family. "I don't understand. These should be in museums."

Meng shrugged. "They say the vaults are full. If it's gold or silver it's melted down, but otherwise they allow for disposal locally."

Shan felt a growing unease. "What are you saying?"

"There's bins at the entrance to the camps. We take them. Sell them by the kilogram at auctions." Her grin quickly faded as she saw the pain on Shan's face. "We don't get them all," she offered awkwardly. "Some get hidden."

Shan looked away. The Chinese boy began demanding that his father buy him a temple bell with an elegant tiger engraved around it.

He found himself on the street, strangely short of breath. The crowd buoyed him down the pavement. Minutes later he was standing at the entrance to the temple again, telling himself to forget Meng, that Jigten was somewhere inside the complex, under arrest and needed his help.

Suddenly his arm was pushed down to his side.

"Don't show it," a Tibetan woman warned. It was the noodle vendor he had seen the day before. She gestured him toward her stall.

"Show what?"

The middle-aged woman nodded toward his arm, then stepped between Shan and a passing policeman. He had forgotten about the bloodstains on his sleeve. Dakpo's blood.

"They are looking for you. They think you may have been part of the attack on that monk."

"But I was trying to stop it," he protested. The woman shrugged.

"The other one," Shan said in an urgent whisper. "The Tibetan who jumped on the monk. I have to find him."

The woman shook her head. "You won't see him. Not for a year or two. The knobs will interrogate him, then the police will take him away."

"Where?" Shan pressed.

The woman frowned. "Are you deaf? I said they are looking for you. They will take you away too."

"That police station behind the Institute?"

"They have special treatment for Chinese who help Tibetan hooligans."

Shan clenched his jaw and stepped away from the gate. As he reached the corner another hand pulled him back. "Don't do it, Shan."

When he turned he saw the pain in Meng's eyes. "I'm sorry about those beads. I just thought . . ." Her words trailed away and she took a deep breath. "There's no need for you to go."

"I have to."

"No. I have to." Meng began tying her hair into a bun at the nape of her neck. "Like you said yesterday, I couldn't go into that station or down that corridor because I had no way to account for my visit. Now I am on the trail of a suspected criminal, a known thief, who has to be returned to Lhadrung County." She backed away from Shan and pointed him toward a bench.

Ten minutes later she reappeared in her uniform. She shot him a quick, worried glance as she silently marched past.

The heavy truck pitched and rolled as it sped along the highway. Meng, driving her car in front, seemed as anxious as Jigten to get out of Chamdo. Shan bent over Dakpo, who was in obvious pain, wiping his brow, tapping the dim battery lantern that was their only light in the hollow they had built into the sacks of rice in the cargo compartment

"He can't be moved," the nurse had insisted when Meng and Shan had arrived at the hospital for him. "Cracked ribs," she warned. "A concussion."

"We will accommodate him." Meng had offered.

"Not without a doctor's order," the nurse had snapped and retreated to her workstation. She seemed to be surprised when she turned to find Meng hovering over her.

"I am a lieutenant in the Suppression Brigade," Meng growled, "and I am the most pleasant of all of those in my squad. You don't want me to call my superior. But if I am not out of here in five minutes with this monk I will have no choice. We will start by demanding all the papers of everyone in this unit." She pointed to an image on the wall of a blond couple in a sports car, torn from an American magazine. "When was the last time you were examined for loyalty, Comrade?"

The color drained from the nurse's face and she quickly pulled out a clipboard. "Someone will have to sign," she said. Meng had scrawled an indecipherable character at the bottom of the proffered page and pointed to a wheelchair.

Dakpo moaned as the truck lurched over a pothole. Shan tried to speak with him but he lapsed into unconsciousness. When his eyes were open they seemed unable to focus.

Two hours later the truck stopped and the rear door opened. They were at a crossroads village, parked behind a decrepit stable. An old Tibetan couple, owners of the rundown roadhouse on the corner, helped ease the monk out onto a stack of straw in the stable. The woman brought a small pot of soup and seeing the fatigue on the faces of Shan and Meng, gestured them toward the roadhouse as she sat and began spoon-feeding Dakpo.

The only other customers wandered out as they glimpsed Meng's uniform. She unbuttoned her tunic and hung it on the back of the chair. In her pale grey blouse she almost passed for one more weary traveler. They silently ate the soup brought by the old man, then she reached back into a pocket of the tunic and produced two folded sheets of paper. She pushed the first in front of Shan.

It was a copy of a page from an official Public Security file, marked STATE SECRET. He scanned it quickly, his face clouding in confusion. "It's just a personnel file," he observed. "For some Tibetan named

Pan Xiaofei. Fifty-eight years old. Early assignments with security units. Assigned to special operations, which could mean a hundred different things."

Meng nodded soberly. "He's from a village called Chimpuk, only an hour off the highway. A Tibetan with a Chinese name."

"I don't understand."

"You know what the Peace Institute does."

"It promotes cross-cultural friendship," Shan said in a tight voice.

"Don't be such a damned fool! You know what it does!"

Shan stared at her. He tried to convince himself that the knot in his stomach was from hunger. He looked down at the paper. "They produce politically indoctrinated monks," he said in a hoarse voice.

"And? You damned well know what else they do. They wouldn't need a platoon of senior Public Security officers just to teach quotes from the Chairman."

"You tell me, Lieutenant. I want to hear you say it."

Meng's eyes flared. "There's an inner office there, closely guarded. I waited for an hour for the chance to slip in. They keep a special drawer of files in there, a single copy, one card for each agent. A Tibetan name and a Chinese name. That's how I found this." She tossed another sheet onto the table. It was a photocopy of a card bearing many lines of numerals and personnel codes, with a record of advancement through bureaucratic grades and Party ranks. In the corner there was a photo with the same Chinese name under it. Pan Xiaofei. Except the photo was of Jamyang.

Shan went very still. His hand trembled as he picked up the first sheet again and read the detailed entries. University in Sichuan, then three special government academies in the east, followed by short duty tours at several monasteries in Tibet, marked as training missions, then finally a year at the Institute. The Institute was the finishing school to which only the elite were admitted. He forced himself to read the rest, then looked away out the window for a long moment.

"Why," he asked in a shaking voice, "would they send a highly trained undercover officer to become a hermit in Lhadrung?"

"I don't know. It makes no sense. I don't think he was sent to Lhadrung. At the bottom there is a note that says Drepung. That's the big monastery outside Lhasa. Hundreds of monks. The government would have political watchers there. Agents like that, Shan, would be trained in personal defense, in fighting with improvised weapons, or weapons disguised for other purposes. You saw those monks on the street. That fire striker Lung Ma had when he died, it wasn't the murderer's. Jamyang had an identical one, issued by the Institute. He showed it to Lung Ma to convince him that he told the truth about his son's murder, to help explain who the murderer was. "

He pressed his fist tightly against his forehead, as if he could force out the pain that was rising inside.

"Whatever Jamyang may have been is just a distraction, Shan," Meng said. "We have murders to solve."

He met her worried, earnest gaze, knowing that she had taken a grave risk by venturing into the inner offices of the Institute.

A movement at the corner of the building caught Shan's eye. Jigten, who had been napping in the cab of the truck, was walking toward the stable. As he reached the entry he picked up a pitchfork leaning against the wall. Shan gasped and leapt up, running to the stable.

"This will end!" he shouted as he grabbed the pitchfork from the shepherd.

"When there is justice for the boy it will end!" Jigten snapped. The eyes of the wiry dropka held the same wild gleam Shan had seen when he had first cornered him in Baiyun. Shan paused, not sure if he had heard correctly. "The boy?"

"Lung Wi. He was my friend. He died because of this one!"

"Surely you are mistaken, Jigten. Surely you can't know that."

"I know! It's why I made sure Genghis didn't drive. I heard you say this bastard was in Chamdo."

Dakpo had pushed himself against the wall, his face twisted in pain and fear. Meng appeared as Shan stepped in front of the monk, facing Jigten.

"You are wrong, Jigten. I didn't say it was Dakpo. And this is Tibet. Monks don't kill."

The shepherd greeted the words with a sneer. "This is Chinese Tibet. Everything is backward," he said, and gestured to Shan and Meng as if they somehow proved his point.

"Real monks don't kill," Shan amended, and pointed Jigten to a milking stool. "Sit down. Tell me about the boy."

The shepherd muttered a curse, still glaring at Dakpo, but complied. The Jade Crows had laughed when Jigten had first appeared, he explained, asking if he could help with their trucks. But he had persisted, coming back to the garage again and again, cleaning up, washing trucks, letting them treat him like their slave. The son of the gang's chieftan had taken to lingering in the garage when the others left, and began to take him for rides in the trucks. They had discovered they were only a few years apart in age, discovered a like interest in mahjong and the mechanics of the truck motors. Before long the boy was teaching Jigten how to drive.

"Sometimes we would sneak away and shoot at marmots with his slingshot. That's what happened the day his father told him to drive the small truck to meet with someone, to deliver a message. He picked me up on the other side of the hill and we raced over the road, bouncing in the ruts, laughing. He liked to pretend he was running away from the police, like in some movie. We got to his meeting place early and walked up the ridge to shoot at marmots. We were stalking a big one through some rocks when over the rise we saw two men on the dirt road below. One was a knob and the other was a monk with a bicycle.

"I backed away, and told him to hide but he said it was no problem, that the monk was the one he was doing business with and he stood up and waved at the monk."

Shan shut his eyes a moment. "Genghis was suddenly sick. You did that."

"There's a little red root that grows up on the ridges. I put some in his tea. He's fine by now."

"But why wait all this time?" Meng asked.

"Because he didn't know that the boy was murdered," Shan said heavily. "Not until he eavesdropped on Lung Tso and me."

"A monk did the killing you said. I saw that monk with the bicycle. I went back there," Jigten explained. "I went back to see if I could find something more about that monk and the knob." Jigten pointed at Dakpo. "And I saw him there, on the bicycle again."

Dakpo murmured something, holding his ribs.

Shan stepped closer. "I'm sorry?"

"There's a dozen." The monk's mouth twisted in pain as he spoke. "The gompa has a dozen bicycles. Any monk can take one when he needs it. I borrowed one to go back along that trail where the Lung boy died."

"To do what?"

Dakpo gazed at Jigten. "To find something more about that monk and the knob," he said, repeating the dropka's words.

"It was you I saw that day at the convent," Shan said.

The young monk nodded. "I know Chenmo."

Shan considered his words. "You mean she told you a monk was a killer, because the American had told her."

Dakpo grabbed the gau around his neck and nodded again. "I found a gun," he whispered, glancing fearfully at Meng. Shan looked up at her and she nodded and left the building. "Tell me about it," he said.

It had been hidden inside a prayer wheel on a pilgrim path that was seldom used, the monk explained. But Jamyang had convinced him that all such paths needed clearing, and Dakpo went up the slope to do so whenever he could get away. "The wheel made a terrible clatter when I finally got it moving. I pushed on it, and the top came off. I didn't want to touch it."

"What happened to it?"

"I didn't do anything that day, nothing until Chenmo told me what the American said about the killer. Then I went up in the night and threw it into a crevasse."

"But why go to Chamdo so abruptly?" Shan asked.

"I clean out files all the time in the office at the monastery, because of the auditors who come. I found a message from weeks ago with nothing but a date on it, the date of the full moon next week. It had been sent electronically to an address that said CTPI, with numbers after those letters like a code. The Bureau of Religious Affairs has been trying to train us to use computers better. I was able to investigate on the computer and found the message had been sent to the Institute." There was fear in the monk's voice now. "I had never heard of it. I had to find out what it meant, why it was sent."

In the silence that followed more trucks went by, groaning with full loads. "Tell me this, Dakpo," Shan asked, "who at Chegar does business with the Jade Crows? Who works with the purbas?"

Dakpo would not look at Shan. He gripped his gau tighter. "There are three of us," he said in a hollow voice.

"Who other than you? The purbas knew of the foreigners. Did they tell you about them?"

"There are three of us," Dakpo repeated, and would say no more.

It was nearly midnight before he lowered himself onto a pile of straw opposite Dakpo. Much later he woke to the sound of straining engines. He did not have to rise to know from the repetitive movement of headlights across the back wall that another convoy was passing by. Beside him on the straw was Meng, asleep, nestled against his body.

He turned and through the open door could see the trucks, at least twenty, climbing up the mountain pass. It was another prisoner convoy, curling around the mountain like a serpent. The demon that was eating Tibet.

Meng rolled over, resting her hand on his chest. She had put her tunic on against the chill air and the red enamel star on its collar caught the moonlight. The demon he slept with.

The moon had risen when he stirred again, then abruptly sat up. Jigten sat on the stool staring at Dakpo, asleep on the straw.

The shepherd felt Shan's gaze. "I will take him to Lung Tso. Lung will make him tell us about the killer."

"I don't think he knows. There are three, he said. It's why he went to Chamdo, to try to discover why one of the others would be communicating with the Institute."

"Three, but not him. That leaves two. He can tell us and Lung will get the truth from them."

"With bamboo splints and barbed wire batons? No. That's your anger speaking. You would not torture an innocent monk."

"If I told Lung, he would. One of them killed his nephew and his brother."

"One of them didn't."

Jigten's anger had not faded. It was just directed at Shan now. "I told you," he growled in a low voice. "This is Chinese Tibet. One Tibetan commits a crime and ten get punished."

"No," Shan said. "That is not my Tibet. It not Dakpo's Tibet. It is not the Tibet of your mother, or of your clan."

Jigten hung his head. "My mother would say one of those hailstorms will come again from the mountain and take the killer. Is that what you mean?"

"Something like that."

The shepherd studied Shan in silence, then stepped to Dakpo, pulled up the monk's blanket and left.

There was movement at his side. Meng was also studying him. "You amaze me, Shan. All you have been through and still so innocent. You told me yourself this case will never go to trial. Yet you think somehow justice will be done. There is only one way it gets done in this case."

"I'm not sure what you are suggesting."

"I'm saying there are cases where the only justice is a quick bullet."

Shan spun about to face her. "No! Never! Don't you understand? It would be against everything the old Tibetans believe." Lokesh's admonishment had shaken him, had never been far from his consciousness since they had spoken on the mountainside. "If I killed someone or arranged someone's death there would be a gap between them and me I could never bridge. Lokesh wouldn't live with me. I would never again have the confidence of the lamas. If I couldn't live with them I don't know if I could live with myself. You have to promise me. No bullets. No killing. I will never be involved in another killing, no matter how deserved it might be."

Meng leaned over and traced a finger along his cheek. "You're a complex man, Shan. If you corner the killer he will try to kill you."

"Promise me, Xiao Meng."

She smiled sleepily. "What did you call me?"

He blushed. The affectionate term of address had left his lips unbidden. He had not spoken it to a woman in decades. "Promise me."

She was still smiling. "Of course. I promise. No bullet."

"Never a bullet."

"Never a bullet," she confirmed, then nestled closer to him.

He found her at dawn, studying the road map on the hood of her car. Her cell phone was in her hand. "I called for the convoy schedule," she explained with a worried expression. "There's a steady flow all day." She gazed at the truck. "If a security detail took an interest in the truck there would be no way to explain the injured monk." She pointed to the map. "There's a back road. It will come out on the highway just north of Lhadrung. No military bases. No police stations. Just two little villages. But the old man doesn't know if the bridge at the second town is strong enough for the truck."

"It's gone," came a voice over her shoulder. Jigten stepped between them. "Washed out five months ago." He traced a finger along a dotted line that circled the last town. "There's an old dirt track with a ford across the stream. We just loop around and come back just above Chimpuk."

Shan nodded slowly, then paused, pointing to the second town on the map. "You mean Shijingshan."

"The Chinese renamed it years ago. Chinese maps have to have Chinese names, so for Chinese travelers it's Paradise Hills. Shijingshan. To Tibetans it's still Chimpuk."

Shan reached into his pocket and unfolded the paper Meng had given him the day before. They were going to Jamyang's birthplace.

It was nearly noon when they crossed the shallow ford and pulled the vehicles to the side of the gravel track. The rough ride had been painful for Dakpo, and when the rear door was opened he appeared to have been beaten again. His prayer beads were pressed into his palm, his knuckles white. Without being asked, Jigten went for water as Shan changed the bandage on the monk's head. They washed his wounds and gave him cold soup before leaving him resting peacefully on his makeshift bed.

Half an hour later they stopped on a low hill over Chimpuk village. The rundown little settlement was so remote that it showed little evidence of China other than its signs. On the faded board announcing the town's Chinese name the final character had been scratched out so that it said just Shijing. Paradise.

"Who are we?" Meng asked as they parked the truck by a goat

pen at the edge of town, discomfort obvious in her voice. She had left her car outside of town and changed into civilian clothes. "Not a place that gets many strangers."

Dogs began barking. An old woman cutting the long skirt hairs of a yak, which the Tibetans braided into rope, stopped and stared at them. A man sitting on a stool with a tea churn was stroking a huge black mastiff that bolted toward them, barking. They had no hope of being inconspicuous.

"We are friends of the lama Jamyang," Shan called out, then stood still as the mastiff reached them. It lunged and bit his ankle.

A hearty laugh rose from the man on the stool as Shan grabbed his ankle. "Stay in the truck," he said as he pulled himself up, leaning on a staff. "That's what everyone else does when they're lost. Stay in the truck and yell. Safer that way." He limped forward and dispersed the dog with a shake of his staff.

"We're not lost," Shan ventured. "We're looking for the family of lama Jamyang."

The old man eyed Meng suspiciously before turning to Shan. "Then you're lost and don't even know it." He sighed and pointed with his staff to Shan's ankle. Blood was oozing from the dog bite. Gesturing Shan to his stool, he exposed the wound, rinsed it first with water then, despite Shan's protests, with *chang*, barley beer. Before he spoke he dabbed the wound with some honey and rolled down the pant's leg. "She won't have much to do with strangers," he declared, and pointed to a modest one-story house at the far edge of town that sat back from the others.

It was a well-kept traditional farmhouse, with faded mantras painted under the window and a traditional sun and moon sign over the entry. By the open door stood a small loom where someone had been weaving the heavy fabric used for cargo sacks in yak caravans. An aged woman stepped out of the shadows. Her face was as frayed as the black apron she wore. The reluctant nod she offered shamed

Shan. She did not want them but the traditions of Tibetan hospitality would not allow her to turn them away.

"You are of Jamyang's blood?" he asked as she gestured them to sit on a carpet in the center of her living quarters. The tidy little house had a half wall dividing it. Come autumn her livestock would take shelter on the other side.

"I am his mother's sister. Everyone else."—she made a vague gesture toward the window, or perhaps the sky—"everyone else is gone."

"My companion is Meng," he explained. "I am called Shan."

She tossed a few pieces of dried dung on her brazier and set a kettle on it. "A friend of Jamyang's you said."

Shan hesitated, looking around the chamber. Opposite its small kitchen area was a *kang*, a wide sleeping platform. On one side of the kang was a rolled sleeping pallet. The other side was covered with a faded rug woven to resemble the skin of a tiger, before a small altar that held a bronze Buddha and an old gau.

"I met him when he settled in Lhadrung County last year," Shan explained. "He was teaching shepherds and restoring an old shrine. He was a gentle man, a good teacher."

"No," she shot back. "Never on our rug."

As she bent to pour them tea, Shan strained to make sense of her words. Lokesh would have known how to speak with the woman. His gaze drifted back to the tiger rug and his recollection stirred. Once, Lokesh had told him, tiger skins had been reserved for revered lamas, who sat on them while teaching. "Jamyang taught me things from the old ways," Shan ventured.

The woman ignored him, gesturing to a string of white squares hanging from a rafter. "There's cheese," she stated flatly. Such dried cheese was a staple of many farming households.

"He taught me to look beneath the appearance of people."

The woman gave a snort of derision. "He taught death and betrayal. He taught us about damned appearances well enough."

"Jamyang is dead," Shan declared.

The woman hesitated only a moment. "There's yogurt in a jar in the stream out back."

"I need to know about him. About what happened to him when he was young."

She eyed the teacups as if trying to decide if she had fulfilled her obligation, then fixed him with a hard stare. "What happened to him happened to us all."

Meng tugged on Shan's sleeve, trying to pull him toward the door.

Shan drained his teacup, then pushed the empty cup toward the kettle.

The woman frowned. "If you desire more tea, you will need to get me some more dung," she said icily.

The silence hung heavily about them. Shan was increasingly certain the old woman held a vital piece of the puzzle that was Jamyang, and just as certain she would not share it with two Chinese strangers.

Suddenly a shadow filled the doorway. The woman's eyes went round and with a gasp leaned forward, nearly touching her forehead to the floor.

Dakpo was in the door, his face clenched in pain, blood seeping from the bandage on his head.

"These two were sent by the deities," the monk said. He was breathing heavily. "They saved me. Shan is a friend of the old lamas." He clutched his rib cage and sank to his knees. "They are truth seekers," he moaned, and collapsed in the doorway.

The old woman moved with surprising speed, springing up so quickly she was able to catch Dakpo's head before it hit the stone flags of the floor. For a moment she silently held the monk as if embracing a lost family member.

"His name is Dakpo," Shan explained. "He is from Lhadrung County, from Chegar gompa. He has cracked ribs. He was attacked in Chamdo. We could not leave him there."

It was Meng who broke the silence. "I will get more dung," she said, and disappeared out the door.

Shan and the woman worked wordlessly, unrolling the pallet and laying Dakpo on it as Meng coaxed the brazier into a bright fire. While Shan wiped at the monk's wounds the woman made more tea then put on a pot for soup, which she asked Meng to watch over as she disappeared out the back door. When she returned she carried a wooden box of salves and ointments. A rolled-up piece of cloth was in one hand, a large black dog was at her heels. As Shan relieved her of the box the dog growled. Shan backed away. It was the same bear-like creature that had bit him. The woman leaned over the animal, whispering into his ear. The dog seemed to frown, then turned to examine Dakpo, and began sniffing the monk's body with slow deliberation. Wherever he paused the woman applied salve.

"I am Leshe," the woman declared when she and the dog were done. She unrolled the cloth she had carried in and hung it over Dakpo. It was a small painting of a familiar blue deity, a well-worn thangka that could have been centuries old.

"*Tadyatha om bekhandzye,*" Shan intoned.

He saw the look of disbelief on Leshe's face as he continued the invocation of the Medicine Buddha.

The tension seemed to fall away from the old woman. She nodded, and joined him in the mantra.

When they had finished Shan looked up to see that Jigten had joined them and was quietly helping Meng prepare their meal. As they ate Shan explained how he had met Jamyang, and described his sudden death.

Leshe did not respond until she had lit incense at the little altar and murmured prayers to its bronze Buddha. "We had beautiful farms once," she finally began, "my family and that of Jamyang's father. For as long as memory could reach each generation gave a son who became a great lama. We had many happy years. Even after the Chinese entered Lhasa it was years before they found us. When they did it was just a lot of Chinese teenagers in military trucks. They put all the fathers and mothers on trial, accusing them of being landowners. The Chinese said that was a crime against the people. In some places landowners just lost their lands and became laborers, but here our people were proud. They declared the trial a sham. They said they were free Tibetans who could not be judged by Chinese children. The Chinese laughed and said see if our bullets are a sham. They executed them all. Jamyang's parents. My husband. I was sick in bed or they would have killed me too.

"Jamyang came to live with me then. For a few years we were happy enough. My brother Ugen was a lama at a gompa near Lhasa. When he visited he sat on the tiger skin, as generations before had done, and Jamyang seemed entranced as Ugen spoke of the old ways and of how the Dalai Lama would come back one day. All Jamyang ever wanted to do was be a lama like his uncle. But his Chinese teachers said he was too bright to stay here. They sent him away, gave him a Chinese name. After college he visited, very excited. They were going to let him become a monk after all, to work in the Bureau of Religious Affairs."

Leshe sipped her tea and offered a bitter smile. "I told him to be a monk you have to go to a monastery, have to study many years. He said he would be going to monasteries, to explain about the new order of things. I said he had become a puppet of those who had killed his own parents and he yelled at me, said I was just a backward old hag who knew nothing of the way of the world.

"My brother visited him, tried to get him to leave the Bureau, to go to his gompa and become a real monk. A few weeks later my brother was thrown into prison, one of those gulag camps. They said he was a traitor to China. The Motherland they called it," she added in a melancholy tone.

"It was nearly three years before Jamyang visited again. He was troubled. He kept staring at the tiger rug. He couldn't sleep. I found him up in one of the pastures. We sat in the moonlight and he confessed his shame. Not long after his last visit he had been offered a big promotion, but they had required him to prove his loyalty. So he had turned in his uncle. Jamyang had assumed he would be sent to some reeducation camp for a few months at most. He had only just found out that Ugen had been sentenced to twenty years hard labor." Leshe looked down, wiping at a tear. "He begged my forgiveness but I would not give it to him.

"It was many years before I heard from him again. He had been made administrator of this, director of that, always wearing a robe, always paid by the Chinese. He told me he was corresponding with Ugen, that his uncle was doing well, that his uncle had forgiven him and had become a model prisoner. Jamyang would send me a letter every few weeks then, telling me how he was living in this monastery or that, learning more of the scriptures the way Ugen had taught him from the tiger rug, telling me he was getting reports that Ugen was doing well, that he was being rehabilitated, whatever that meant. I never wrote back. He began sending letters to the headman of the village to make sure I was still alive. He would send gifts for the headman to give to me. Little Chinese cakes and tea. I told the headman to keep the tea. I fed the cakes to the pigs."

Leshe paused and looked at Dakpo. Their patient was awake, and listening intently. Before she continued she braced a cushion behind him so he could sit and drink tea. "Then a few months ago my nephew appeared in my doorway. He wore a lama's robe over a business suit and tie. He said he was traveling to a new assignment and had asked the driver to turn off the highway. A big black car was waiting for him in the village.

"I gave him lunch. We walked up in the pastures. He had a big secret to tell me. He said he had arranged for Ugen to receive light trusty duties two years before, told me how he had been negotiating for his release, that if he performed well in his new assignment his uncle would finally come home. He showed me letters from Ugen, in Chinese, that proved he was in good health and contented. He grew upset with me, asked me why I did not feel joy from the news. I took him inside to the altar," she said with a nod toward the bronze Buddha. "I told him I would sit in front of the Buddha so he would know my words to be true. I explained to him that Ugen did not speak Chinese, did not write Chinese. I lifted the gau, that one you see there on the altar, and told him to study it.

"He stared as if he had seen a ghost. I told him the truth then, for he knew that gau had been in the family for centuries, that it had been Ugen's. It had been sent home to me six years before when Ugen killed himself in prison.

"He stared and stared at the gau, then finally pressed it to his head and wept. I gave him tea. He would not speak with me. He just held the gau and stared at it. His hands trembled like those of an old man.

"Then the car horn started calling him. The other one, his companion, grew impatient, and was standing at the driver's window, pressing the horn."

"The other one?" Dakpo asked in a whisper.

"Another man in a robe over a suit, very tall, carrying what looked like a silver bell. They were being driven like they were Chinese royalty."

An anguished moan escaped Dakpo's throat. He sagged and Leshe helped him lie back on the pallet.

Shan studied Dakpo in confusion, then asked Jigten to bring the truck up. The young monk needed to return to his bed in Chegar gompa, where he could be properly looked after.

"Your foot," Leshe said to Shan. "Pick up your trouser leg."

The Tibetan woman murmured something and the big dog stepped forward. Shan forced himself not to react as the animal sniffed at Shan's ankle. "He apologizes for biting you," Leshe said, then made a clucking sound as she studied the bite. "That old fool put on honey, didn't he?" She made a gesture and the mastiff licked away the honey. She lifted one of her wooden tubes and began applying a salve to the wound. The dog watched with bright, intelligent eyes. "He only bites Chinese," Leshe explained in a matter-of-fact voice, then paused. "He appeared as a pup six years ago, waiting at my door."

Shan offered an awkward grin and touched the dog's head as it turned to contemplate him with its big, moist eyes. "I didn't hear his name."

The old woman cast an impatient glance at Shan, as if he hadn't been listening. "It's Ugen, of course."

CHAPTER SIXTEEN

Brilliant claws of gold reached across the dusk sky, as if a dragon were rising out of the sacred mountain. Shan sat outside the shepherd's hut and arranged sticks on the ground. One six-inch-long stick with two shorter sticks underneath, over another long stick and another short pair, so that they made a square of a solid line, a broken line, a solid line, and another broken line. It was a tetragram, used to identify passages of the *Tao te Ching,* which he had memorized with his father as a boy. With slow, deliberate movements he disassembled the tetragram and built it again, dismantled and built it again, like a meditation practice. It invoked passage eleven, called "Using What Is Not." "Clay is shaped to form a vessel," it said. "What is not there makes the vessel useful. Take advantage of what is there by making use of what is not."

It wasn't simply that Shan had once misunderstood Jamyang. He was misunderstanding him again and again. First, Shan had known him as only a solitary, reverent hermit. Then he had grown to consider him as a lama in some mysterious exile, or a pilgrim doing penance. But he had also been a bureaucrat with a robe, an official who was fluent with computers. One of the agents trained to consume Tibet from the inside out. He had been all and none of those things. Shan had assumed his movements in his last few days had been actions to implement some plan, but they had all been reactions. He had missed the empty place, missed the phantom that gave everything meaning.

The realization had come slowly, a small dark thing gnawing at his gut since leaving Jamyang's village. Some of the old lamas fervently believed that souls made sounds, that old hermits who suddenly found realization howled long syllables that could shake mountains. For Shan, the sound had come first, Dakpo's anguished gasp before Jamyang's aunt. He understood now that the monk's reaction had changed everything. Dakpo had suddenly known, and collapsed, when Leshe had spoken of a man carrying a silver bell.

Shan had missed the phantom, the shadow that was always a step ahead, never there. It was time to use what was not there.

He rose and found the American by the little fire they had made to cook their evening meal. "I understand your need for silence, Cora," he began. "But it must end. I want to help you but now you have to help me."

The American woman struggled with her reply. There were still days, Lokesh said, when she did not speak at all. "There is no way out for me," she said at last. "There is no one I can trust except Lokesh and Chenmo. And we can barely speak with each other," she added with a bitter smile.

"And me, Cora. We can talk together. Together we are going to stop the murderer. Together we will get you home."

"I should have been dead. I know that old Tibetans talk about not arguing with your fate, about embracing it. I was supposed to die that day."

"No. You were supposed to live. You were supposed to become the way we stop the killer, the way word reaches the outside."

"I'm always so afraid."

"There are many things I have learned in Tibet," Shan said to the American. "One is that your life isn't about what others do to you, it is about what you do to yourself."

"The killer wants me dead, doesn't he?"

"I won't lie to you. But Lokesh and his friends have taught me that you can't let your decisions be determined by the cruelty of others."

"I don't know who the killer was. Just a monk."

"It's a puzzle, Cora. I know some of the pieces. You know some of the pieces. We have to fit them together. I should have asked you a question long ago. Did Jamyang come to you and Rutger sometime just before the killings?"

The American woman stirred the dying embers with a stick. "Two weeks before. With Chenmo. It was strange because he had always kept his distance, like he was very shy. Stayed away even from the other monks. Rutger said it must be because he was a hermit, that he had taken some kind of vow of isolation."

"He came to your camp?"

Cora nodded. "He was no hermit that night. He said he understood we had taken pictures of the restoration. He wanted to know if they were the kind he could see on our camera screens. So we showed him. Rutger had been trying to get Chenmo to ask Jamyang to help name some of the old images on the walls and artifacts. A goddess playing a lute. A three-headed Buddha. A lion-headed god. We thought he came for that, and he did answer our questions. But what he wanted to see were photos of the monks who had come to help at the convent. He asked if we knew any of their names, and we explained we did not, that we kept our presence secret."

"What happened? Did he show special interest in any of them?"

"He took the camera and scrolled through the pictures. He stopped at one and went very still. It was like he was scared by something he saw."

"What was it? What photograph scared him?"

Cora shrugged. "Monks. Monks," she repeated. "We came around the world to help monks. But now I know we must fear monks."

"Did Rutger tell the abbess about this?"

"The abbess came to Rutger later. She was excited about what we were doing, about our photographing the internment camp. She encouraged us, gave us information about what went on in the camp, asked if she brought people who had been prisoners whether we would put them in our cameras. That's how she said it. 'Put them in our cameras.' She said we needed to know what happened in those camps." Cora broke off, biting her lips, looking into the embers. For a moment Shan thought she was going to weep again. She had seen for herself what went on in such a camp, had been tied inside one of its death shrouds.

"The day before Rutger died, she came back. She said there was something new, that he could film a different secret of Beijing. Rutger thought she meant he should go to the convent to film someone who had suffered at one of those gulag camps." She pushed the embers and watched the sparks fly into the darkening sky.

"What did Jamyang ask you to do with the photos he saw?"

"He said we must keep them safe."

"Did you?" Shan asked. "Did you keep them safe?"

"Sure. Rutger has special aluminum cases. Waterproof, even fireproof."

Shan recalled the empty cases he had found at the campsite. They had not been demon proof.

"*Om mani padme hum,*" Meng intoned as she gave the prayer wheel a shove. "Isn't that what they say?"

Shan nodded. He was not certain why she had asked him to go with her to the convent ruins. The things they needed to say were not for the police post but they had not needed to drive several miles to find a private place. "It invokes the compassionate Buddha," he explained, and showed her how the words were inscribed in raised script along the rim of the bronze cylinder. "It makes a new prayer each time it spins."

She replied with a strangely somber nod and spun the wheel
again, then again. "I've been in Tibet for years," she said, "and I have
never tried to learn about such things."

The police cleanup squads had been thorough. There were no
more yellow police tapes cordoning off crime scenes, no more red
paint and blood. A pile of fresh sand had been dumped by the front
gate, with buckets and tubs beside it. A trail of footprints showed
where the sand had been hauled and raked around the chorten. Even
the loose stone at the base of the chorten had been pushed back
in, though it seemed to be working its way out again.

"It was here," Meng said, "here was where the abbess was killed.
The first to die that day." The lieutenant ran her hand along the wall,
as if trying to remind herself where the arc of paint had been, then
placed her palm at its center, where the blood had stained the wall.
The surface had been scrubbed clean and painted. Everyone in the
valley was doing their best to eradicate the murders.

"Lung Ma was the first to die," Shan corrected her. "He was the
most dangerous. He carried a gun."

Shan led her to the rear of the compound and positioned himself
at the crumbling gate. "The monk parked his bicycle outside, hidden
in the rocks," he said in a slow voice, considering the landscape as he
spoke. "He took his time, watching at every step. The abbess had
sent him a message, saying she wanted to speak of Dharamsala.
Every Tibetan knows it like a code word. Speaking about it was always in secret. But she had never spoken to this monk about it. This
one thought it was a warning, for he harbored his own secret about
the exile capital. He was suspicious. I think he watched the convent
from the hill and saw Lung's truck arrive. There was no possible
reason for the abbess and Lung to be together. Lung held the secret
of the plan to smuggle the killer across the border. The abbess held
the secret of the strange lama who had been roaming the hills, who
the killer knew now to be a threat to his plans."

Shan let the weight of his words sink in as he led Meng to the little chapel where the farmers had stored tools. "For some reason he suspects the message from the abbess, so he comes from the rear, for the advantage of surprise." Shan stepped inside and showed Meng the brush hook he had found earlier. "He has no weapon but he knows of the heavy blades stored here. Lung was at the front, at ease, having a cigarette, considering his best angle for his target when the man comes in the front gate. On her own the abbess never would want to kill the man, just confront him, shame him. But Jamyang was certain he had caused a killing that day. He knew the leader of the Jade Crows carried a gun, and had told him who had killed his son. Jamyang used the abbess because he knew her message would bring the monk, and used Lung because he knew Lung would kill the man who killed his son." It was the final agony Jamyang had suffered. The lama had been certain he had arranged a killing. He was convinced the killing was necessary, but also convinced he had to take his own life for doing so.

"So the killer has to be careful, ready for anything. He picks up the brush hook and steals along the far wall, using the cover of the buildings. The abbess has her back to him as she works on the prayer wheel, with the German helping her." They walked in silence along the path Shan indicated, to the place by the corner of the front structure where the pool of Lung's blood had been found. "He nearly takes Lung's head off with his first blow. Then he takes Lung's gun."

"Why the front gate?" Meng asked "Why would Lung assume the man was coming in the front gate?"

Shan hesitated. It was point he had overlooked. "Because he didn't expect the bicycle, or a man arriving on foot."

"You mean he expected someone with a vehicle," Meng concluded. "A monk who had access to a vehicle. How many monks in the monastery can even drive?"

"Probably only a handful," Shan admitted. "Maybe just one or two."

Meng set the pace now, back toward the prayer wheel. "He kills Lung, leaves the body to collect later and goes to the abbess. Just a terrible accident for Rutger to be there."

"No. Rutger knew. The abbess invited him. Jamyang told Lung and the abbess because he needed both. The abbess would guarantee the monk would arrive, because no one turns down an abbess. And once there, Lung would exact his revenge. But Jamyang didn't gauge the depth of the abbess's anger. She had her own weapon in mind. She had become a believer in what the foreigners were doing, had grasped how painful it would be for the government's covert plan to be exposed publicly. So she invited Rutger and his camera. Rutger would not have appreciated the risk. A photographer tends to think of his camera as a shield.

"The abbess and Rutger were together. Rutger was probably taking photos of her as she restored the wheel. The killer walked right up to them, immobilized Rutger with a quick shot, then shot the abbess an instant later. When he saw Rutger was not dead he dragged him to the chorten and finished him with the hook then took off his face so he could not be identified."

"And the girl was here the whole time," Meng ventured.

Shan nodded. "Always near Rutger. She was sketching the interior of one of the chapels in the back. She appeared in time to see the killer finishing his work."

As they continued walking they fell into a heavy silence, as if feeling the presence of the killer.

Meng stopped and put her hand on the crumbling stucco of a chapel. "They say these old ruins are filled with ghosts," she said quietly.

Shan hesitated, then realized they were standing exactly where they had first met. "People lived here for centuries," he said, remembering his reply. "Lived and died."

"It wouldn't have been such a bad life," Meng said after a moment, an odd longing in her voice. "Like a big reverent family. I had uncles who always went to the temple," she added after a moment.

He said nothing.

"I've been thinking, Shan," she said abruptly with an awkward glance. "I could get a job as a constable. Lower pay but I would stay in the county. No reassignments a thousand miles away."

He knew how difficult it was for her to have said the words. It had been why she had brought him here. He offered a small, tight smile. "There's still a murderer to catch."

He wasn't sure if Meng had heard. With a finger she traced the dim shape of the eye painted beside the door. "I remember being told by a teacher once about how the eye of the Chairman was always on us. But we knew he was dead. It scared us. This was different, I think."

"This *is* different," he replied.

When she looked up, her expression had become somber. "Is that why I feel we need to be outside if we're going to talk more about killers?"

Shan stared at her, confused, as she stepped away. Then he realized she meant outside the convent, outside the sacred ground.

Five minutes later she unfolded a map on the hood of her car.

"The mystery of the murders is really just the mystery of Jamyang," she said. "I have been thinking about that, about how he got here. He was seen on the Lhasa highway. He was going to Drepung, by Lhasa. Hundreds of monks. Thousands of tourists. A likely place for a graduate of the Peace Institute. But after he saw his aunt he hated himself, hated what he had been turned into."

She ran her fingers along the map to the east and north. "Maybe he was trying to find a way to go home, back to the mountains of his youth. To do penance."

"He was doing his penance here," Shan suggested.

"A route home would take him through Lhadrung. There are buses that run to Baiyun once a week. He could have ridden there and started walking."

Shan bent over the map beside her. "He couldn't risk being stopped by police. The constant convoys and patrols would have driven him up into the hills," he added. It was the likely explanation for Jamyang's arrival on the upper slopes. "He was broken. He just wanted a place to crawl into and hide, where he could begin to heal, to construct a new life, the one his uncle had intended for him. He would never have known about another Institute graduate being assigned to a mission in the valley."

"Of course not. Every assignment would be secret, the agents unknown to one another. But we don't know for certain there was another agent here."

She was trying so hard not to understand. He gazed at her a moment, then pointed to the map. "And what direction did Liang come from?" he asked.

"I'm sorry?"

"It's always the most obvious things that are overlooked in an investigation. You need to find out when Liang arrived at your district headquarters."

"Right after the murders were reported of course."

"No, Meng. He was at the murder scene with the first party of police to arrive. You and I saw him. He was already in the district. His role as some larger-than-life investigator is a cover."

"Nonsense. Liang is just the son of a bitch thug he appears to be."

"Check it. You're going to find he arrived a day or two after Jamyang used a computer in Baiyun to access the Institute's database. It would have been a week before the murders."

Meng went very still.

"He only cares about the murders because his agent is connected to them, and they set into motion events that could threaten that agent's mission. What sent him running to this valley was that threat, not the murders. He's not interested in finding a killer, he is interested in finding the American woman, he's interested in me, and anyone interfering with the mission. You said it yourself. These agents can take years to prepare. The investment in such an agent is huge. Noth-

ing can be allowed to interfere. Liang is a handler, a field troubleshooter for the Institute. No doubt he was once a special investigator
for the Bureau. But like he told us, he was promoted. He knew how
to go through the motions, knew he had to react when the bodies
were stolen. It was perfect pretense for him because he also had to
make sure no one else investigated thoroughly.

"You were the only knob truly probing the murders. He gave you
free rein. He used you because he never thought you were capable
of finding the truth. You became part of his cover. What he does is
the opposite of an investigation. He knew who the killer was from
the beginning. He knew the evidence, and set about to erase or ob-
scure it. He never had tests done on that bullet, he just wanted to be
sure no one else did. He wanted you to believe he was seeking the
American because she might be a witness but he wanted to find her
so he could kill her. From the moment he arrived everything he has
done has been to protect the killer."

Meng staggered backward as if she had been physically struck.
She lowered herself onto a flat boulder. "Impossible," she said. "I
would have—"

"Would have seen it? Been told? Avoided helping him? It's what
he does, Meng, what they do. Manipulate people like you and me.
Cover up. Enlist you to build the lies."

The color was slowly draining from Meng's face. "I don't believe
you, Shan. You mistrust everything. You mistrust yourself. I understand you had a terrible experience. It was all so unjust. But you see
poison everywhere now. I tried to give you a gift and you hated me
for it. Like I had something to do with what happens to these poor
Tibetans."

He returned her stare without speaking. When she broke away,
tears were in her eyes.

"Check the records," he said. "Speak to people at headquarters.
The arrival of Major Liang would not have been missed. There's no

doubt a house for government visitors. They would keep records of who stays overnight. If you can't find the records talk to the house-keepers."

She turned away from him. He waited several minutes, then began walking down the road.

He had gone nearly a mile when he heard the wheels on the gravel behind him. The truck eased by and stopped.

She began shouting before her feet hit the ground. "You think I am just another damned puppet! You think I don't care about anything!" As she pulled her uniform cap from her head hairpins went flying, so that her long tresses whipped about in the wind. She shook the cap at him. "I am tired of your damned self-righteousness! You think no one can see the truth unless they've suffered for it!" She threw her cap on the ground and stomped it into the dust.

Her words came out in sobs now "I am no puppet, Shan Tao Yun! I hate the way Tibetans look at me! I am no animal! I am real! I am—" Tears were streaming down her face. "I just want . . ." Her words broke into sobs.

He laid a finger along his lips, then put his arms around her. She clung to him as if she were drowning. From somewhere in the hills behind them came the deep-throated call of a prayer horn.

Dawn was seeping over the mountains as Shan crept cautiously along the path behind the gompa. When he had taken Dakpo back to Chegar the monk had asked to be left with Patrul, saying he did not wish to disturb the gompa at such a late hour. Only later he real-ized it was more likely that Dakpo feared going back into the mon-astery. He could not shake the feeling that he owed the monk more, and could not forget he had only two days until the full moon.

The former abbot was sitting before his simple altar in the big barn when Shan approached. Shan was standing ten feet away when the blind man raised a hand over his shoulder and gestured for him to come forward and sit.

"It was good what you did for Dakpo," Patrul said. "You have a habit of rescuing creatures in distress."

"With Dakpo, Rinpoche, I am not sure if I rescued him or pulled him deeper into the mud."

"He is young but he has learned enough to know there is no purity without impurity."

"I would like to find a way to speak with him. Did he find his way back to the gompa?"

The old teacher shook his head. "He fears what he would do to it."

Shan turned for a moment to look at the storerooms along the corridor of the long barn, then weighed Patrul's words. "What he might do to it?"

"I think you understand how the truth is the most painful weapon of all. The truth you armed him with would devastate the monks."

Shan gazed up at the Buddha on the makeshift altar. He was the blind man here. He knew how much the monks of the struggling gompa revered their abbot. Norbu was their hero, their savior. Norbu had resurrected Patrul out of the oblivion of the gulag. To tell them the truth would be telling them they had been used, that they were a sham, that they were puppets of Public Security.

When he turned back to Patrul the big shaggy mastiff was by the old lama, gazing at Shan. "You were serving ten strings, Rinpoche," Shan said after a long silence. "No one gets early release when they've opposed loyalty oaths. Trinle said it was because you went blind."

Patrul offered a sad grin. "He's a good boy. Always looks for the best answer, if not the true one. He forgets I was nearly blind when they arrested me."

"Bringing back the silver bell to Chegar would have made Norbu welcome but arranging for you to be at his side made him a hero."

"They called it a humanitarian release," Patrul said with a bitter laugh. There was pain in the teacher's voice. He had already realized that he too had been a puppet.

"But still you are here," Shan replied. "Perhaps there was the hand of a deity in this."

"No matter what happens my Chegar suffers."

"I don't think so. You are its protector. You have always been its protector. No matter what happens there will be no abbot from Beijing here for many months, probably a year or more."

"A gompa needs an abbot."

"They have one, the best they ever could hope for. In a way he never left."

"I am old and blind."

"You are wise and shrewd. If Tibet can have a shadow government, then surely Chegar can have a shadow abbot."

"*Lha gyal lo.*" The words came in a whisper from the shadows.

Shan lifted a butter lamp and stepped to the storage room behind them, the door to which was open. Dakpo sat propped up on a bed of straw. He bent over the monk, feeling his forehead, then his pulse.

"I am well enough, Shan," the monk said bravely. "A few cracked ribs are worth the cure you have given us. But I worry," he added. "Trinle came last night to say Norbu has the monks stirred up, talking about their duty to the Dalai Lama. I can't confront him. I am not sure I would be believed. And now the full moon comes. The tentacles will reach across to Dharamsala. I can't. . . ." The monk's voice faded away.

"I understand, Dakpo. It is nearly over. You need to continue being his student so he does not suspect. Nothing has changed."

"Everything has changed."

Shan grinned. "Exactly."

Suddenly the calm of the dawn was disturbed by the ringing of a bell. It was not a call to worship. Shan stepped to the shadows of the entry to see monks emerging into the courtyard of the gompa, trotting toward the row of bicycles along one wall. He called out a hurried farewell to Patrul and Dakpo, then ran out the back of the barn.

Minutes later he was standing in the back of his truck, watching the monks through his binoculars. They made a thin line of maroon along the flat road, an arrow aimed down the valley. Shan followed the path of the arrow, trying to understand its target. It could be the convent ruins. It could be Baiyun. It could be some pilgrim's path selected for clearing.

By the time he drove back onto the main road he saw that others were traveling toward the center of the valley. Figures on bicycles, on tractors and donkeys, were converging not on the ruins or the town but on a crossroads that marked the intersection of the main road with a dirt track that led to farms in the hills. He sped up as he reached the pavement, soon passing the monks, noting several familiar faces, including Norbu near the front.

A small crowd was already at the intersection as Shan coasted to a stop in front of a newly erected mileage sign. His heart sank as he read it. The sign was only in Chinese. A farmer was standing on the seat of his tractor haranguing the assembled Tibetans about how he didn't live on a Chinese road, he lived on a Tibetan road.

"Just because you call a leopard a mule doesn't make him one!" a man brandishing a scythe shouted.

More vehicles arrived, mostly bicycles and tractors, some pulling wagons with families. A cargo truck approached, blaring its horn at the crowd that blocked its passage. An aged tractor pulling a cart with goats and several more farmers arrived. Shan opened the door of his truck, well aware of the angry stares aimed at him.

The first monks who appeared were younger ones, who began to fuel the anger with calls for Tibetans to remember what it meant to be Tibetan. Sirens rose in the distance. One of the figures with the goats emerged and Shan looked in alarm at the man.

"Yuan!" he called out. The professor and his daughter with three other Baiyun exiles were threading their way through the crowd.

"You should go," Shan said. "These people are furious."

"I promised the goats a trip in the country," Yuan said with a spark in his eyes. Shan looked back at the tractor, the beat-up old community vehicle kept in the Baiyun market ground, then saw the defiant glint in Yuan's eyes. They were more than five miles from the town. The professor had not come in reaction to the disturbance, he had set out before it had started. "You knew about this?"

"Jigten drove past the police crew that was installing this last night. Each one that's been installed in the past three months has brought a demonstration by Tibetans. The valley doesn't need more disturbances."

"Police crew? Not a road crew. Are you sure he said that?"

Yuan offered a pointed nod as Norbu mounted one of the wagons.

"We must not give them cause to make more arrests," the abbot implored the Tibetans. The police cars were visible now, an Armed Police troop truck led by two grey vehicles. The driver of the cargo truck, now stopped, got out and stood on the hood. It was one of Lung's men.

While the attention of the Tibetans was fixed on Norbu, Yuan moved through the throng, his daughter close behind, holding a small pail. The professor extracted a brush from his jacket, dipped it in the pail and began writing with yellow paint on the blank back of the sign, carefully consulting a piece of paper held up by his daughter. The letters were in Tibetan and though his hand was unsteady the letters were legible.

Shan gasped. A Tibetan boy gave a startled laugh. At the end of the word Yuan painted an arrow, pointing south.

As Norbu climbed down he called on the Tibetans to rally behind him, so he could be their shield against the police, now climbing out of their vehicles. But another Tibetan, and another, stepped behind the sign to look at Yuan's handiwork. Each gazed for a moment then laughed. *"Lha gyal lo,"* a woman called, smiling at Yuan. Shan's alarm changed to fear as a bullhorn crackled.

"Unless you have a permit to assemble," came Liang's voice, "you are committing a crime. Disperse now or you will be arrested." Shan studied the major, and the uneasy way the police looked at him. There was no official reason the special officer from outside the district should be supervising what for them was a routine security detail.

Norbu's voice at first rang out clearly. "We are but farmers going about our business," he called back. "The police have nothing to fear from us. We seek only your respect as the original inhabitants of this valley."

A woman beside Shan groaned. "No, he mustn't," she cried. "Not our blessed abbot. We can't let them throw another abbot in prison."

Norbu spoke again but the growing murmur of the Tibetans who hurried to look at the back of the sign swelled over the abbot's words. Yuan stepped back so all could see his work.

Dharamsala, he had written by the arrow, first in Tibetan then in Chinese. He had pointed the way to the capital of the free Tibetans in India.

An old Tibetan woman grabbed Yuan as he tried to go to Shan and embraced him. Shan could not hear Liang's words but the anger in his tone was unmistakable. Four policemen with truncheons left the major's side. A Tibetan farmer grabbed Sansan and pulled her into the crowd. The Tibetans were in trouble enough, but if Liang grasped what had happened his venom would be directed at the exiles.

Shan eased back into his truck. He turned on the ignition and pressed the accelerator so that the old engine sputtered loudly, then he fumbled with the shifter and clutch, noisily grinding the gears. Those around the truck cleared away. Liang roared out angry orders. Truncheons were being raised. Shan caught Norbu's gaze and held it with cool intensity. Then he shoved the truck into gear and shot forward.

The sign exploded as he hit it, sending splinters into the air. The post was thick and well set. It bent his bumper and knocked the radiator ajar before snapping. He climbed out, staring in mock confusion at the steam rising from his damaged truck, casting furtive glances to confirm that the Tibetans, now satisfied, were leaving.

Norbu studied Shan a moment uncertainly, then trotted to his side. "We pray you were not hurt, Comrade," the abbot offered loudly, then turned to the police. "Once again the gods have intervened for Tibetans," he called out defiantly.

Liang's eyes stabbed at Shan. After Tan's intervention he knew he could not arrest Shan, not with so many witnesses, not for what could be characterized as an accident. He raised his bullhorn to his lips, turning to point at Norbu.

"Chegar monastery is behind this!" the major shouted, then in an uncertain tone he spoke again. "Those who refuse the embrace of the Motherland must suffer the consequences!" It was the sound of a seasoned actor trying to salvage a disrupted script.

For the first time the little café in Baiyun had a light, almost cheerful atmosphere. Tables had been carried outside into the golden afternoon sun.

Shan had looked for Professor Yuan at his house but found only his daughter working at her computer on the kitchen table. "It was a reckless thing you did this morning," he told Sansan.

"I tried to talk him out of it. He had found a quote from Mao that he decided to embrace. 'The only way to have a true government of the people is to engage in constant revolution.' When Jigten came to pick up medicine and mentioned the sign, the Vermilion Society was here. My father suggested it as a joke but one of them said he knew where to find paint. They were like boys planning an adventure. They are still celebrating at the teahouse. I'll go with you."

To Shan's surprise there were Tibetans sitting with the usual patrons at the little café. They cast uncertain glances about the street. One of the professors was trying to cajole the Tibetan waitress into joining him for a game of checkers. Shan found a seat at a rear table and tea was brought to him. It was a rare hour of camaraderie between Tibetan and Chinese. They had enjoyed the tiniest of victories over the government and though it would not last it was worth savoring. But for Shan the taste was sour.

He had managed to drive his crippled truck to Lung's garage but the repairs would take more than a day. Lokesh knew enough about his unpredictable life in the valley not to worry if he did not reach their little hut that night. But tomorrow was Sunday, the first Sunday of the month. For the past week the voice inside his head had been growing louder and more insistent. *Ko is waiting for you. Ko needs you. He can't think you've given up on him. Nothing must prevent you from seeing your son.*

For a few moments as he stared at the southern horizon he told himself he would walk. More than a few Tibetan families walked two or three days to visit loved ones in prison. But even if he walked all night he would not make it over the steep mountain roads before the visiting hours ended the next morning. He would have to sleep in the stable and write a letter, praying it would reach his son.

The cheerful banter suddenly died. He looked up. A public security car was parking on the opposite side of the road. Liang and Meng climbed out with two knob soldiers behind them.

As Shan saw the glint in Liang's eye his gut tightened. The major had been defeated at the crossroads but now he strutted across the street with a smug, satisfied air. Liang seemed to make a show of searching the tables, then he nodded to Shan.

Shan pushed back his chair, thinking of slipping away, but Liang had anticipated him. One of the soldiers had circuited to the rear of the tables, behind Shan. Meng held back, looking at him with pain in her eyes.

"Comrade Shan!" Liang called out loudly as he reached Shan's side. "At last we have found you! Good news! Everything about that splittist Jamyang has been confirmed! Your payment is approved!" The major reached into his tunic and extracted a stack of currency notes, bound with a rubber band. "One thousand is the going rate. A rare bargain for the body of another outlaw lama."

Liang dropped the money on Shan's table, offered a stiff bow, then spun about and marched back to the car.

There was no more jesting, no more talking at all. Every person at every table stared in shock at Shan, some with hatred in their eyes, others with disgust. Shan had just been publicly declared a bonecatcher.

All but one of the tables were quickly vacated. The thin grey-haired man who remained slowly rose and stepped to Shan's side, placing a hand on his shoulder as his daughter appeared at his side. "Come with us," Yuan said.

Shan said nothing but stood and followed the professor. His daughter picked up the money where Shan had left it, untouched.

"It is just Liang's way," Yuan said as he poured tea for Shan in his kitchen. "Those in Baiyun will soon realize it. They know you better."

Shan had trouble speaking. Liang had tried, and failed, to imprison Shan. It had been parry and thrust since the two men had met. Now Liang had inflicted the crippling blow. When he finally spoke his voice was hoarse. "By this time tomorrow," he said, "there won't be a Tibetan in the valley who will speak with me."

CHAPTER SEVENTEEN

Shan awoke abruptly, his nightmare so real he flinched, thinking the touch on his shoulder was that of another prison guard's baton.

"Shan," Yuan whispered, shaking him. "She's here, been parked outside for two hours. She's at the door."

He groggily followed the professor, tucking in his shirt, to the entry.

Meng stood in the dim predawn light. "We need to be going," she declared.

"Going?" Shan asked through his fog.

"Have you truly forgotten what day it is? It's the first Sunday of the month."

Whether from fatigue or disbelief, he could find no words. He followed the lieutenant to her car and obediently climbed in, then stared out the window, strangely ashamed.

They had left the sleeping town far behind before he turned toward Meng. Her uniform was disheveled. "Did you sleep in your car?" he asked.

"Not much."

"You don't have to do this."

"It's Sunday. Isn't this what couples do on Sunday, take carefree drives in the country?"

"Meng Linmei, you really don't. It won't be pleasant."

As if in response she tossed a paper into his lap. He slowly, painfully opened it. It was the letter he had written to Ko in Liang's cell. "It was good of you to—"

"You look like hell," she interrupted. "Get some sleep."

He stuffed the letter inside his shirt and leaned his head on the window, watching the sky. Stars were blinking out as dawn spread across the sky. He watched the shadows retreat across the mountains.

Much later, he stirred at the sound of voices outside the car. Meng was speaking to soldiers. A security gate that blocked the road was being lifted. Suddenly he was wide awake, rubbing his eyes, then reflexively looked down as a patrol drove by. They had entered a penal zone. Arrows pointed the way to each of Colonel Tan's hard-labor camps.

His mouth went dry as the 404th People's Construction Brigade came into view. His eyes were unable to move from the long, decrepit barracks where he had lived for years, where he had met Lokesh and the lamas who had built him anew out of the broken, drug-dazed body that had been dumped there by Public Security. The shabby structures had become chapels to him. Many good and innocent men had died in them, and on the execution ground outside, men who still visited him in his dreams and nightmares.

Meng shook his shoulder. They were at the main gate, a guard leaning inside the window with a clipboard. "Your son's name, Shan. They need his name."

"Shan Ko," he said, his voice breaking. "Barracks fourteen."

The guard paused as he heard the name, then glanced pointedly at Meng and lowered the clipboard without looking at it. "Don't waste your time," he muttered.

"Is he or isn't he a prisoner in the Four hundred and fourth?" Meng demanded.

"Of course he is. But he is in solitary. Locked up this past week. No visitors for those in solitary."

Only when Meng cast a worried glance at him did Shan realize a moan had escaped his throat.

"We are coming in," the lieutenant stated.

The guard shrugged and pointed to a strip of gravel inside the gate.

Shan did not argue when she told him to stay in the car. He watched the compound behind the razor wire, saw the rail-thin prisoners shuffling around the perimeter, saw old men too weak to walk being carried out into pools of sunlight, the Sunday rituals of the camp. This was no reeducation camp, this was where Beijing ground its enemies into dust. Shan found himself clutching the seat, as if part of him expected to be seized and thrown back inside the wire at any moment. It was always like this when he waited on visiting days. Some days he would pace back and forth in front of the gate, calming himself before going through. Once a prisoner always a prisoner.

It was nearly an hour before Meng finally returned, a guard at her side. "Only fifteen minutes," she announced. "I'm sorry."

As he climbed out he shot a confused glance toward her, knowing he should thank her. Here in the prison, with her standing by him in her uniform, he could not forget that more than once he had been interrogated, even beaten by women like her. But getting a prisoner out of the special punishment lockup, however briefly, was nothing short of a miracle.

They left him alone in the sterile, drafty chamber reserved for visits, with barred windows and four heavy metal chairs bolted to the cement floor, each with two stools in front of it. He stared out a window, looking for familiar faces among the prisoners until he heard the closing of the metal door at the end of the long corridor leading to the isolated room, then quickly sat on a stool, facing a chair. He knew better than to watch.

The rattle of the chains down the hall was always a slow torture for Shan. They seemed to wrap around his heart and wrench it with each step. He forced himself to stare at the metal chair, not looking up even when he realized the rattle was different this time, not the usual sound of Ko's foot manacles.

Then suddenly they were beside him, two beefy guards flanking their slender prisoner. Shan clenched his jaw to keep from crying out. A heavy leather collar had been placed around Ko's neck, with a link through which a chain was fastened. The chain was wrapped around hand manacles and connected to a link on his foot chains. The guards shoved him into the chair and looped still another chain to bind him to a metal ring on the chair before retreating.

When he looked up his son was grinning. "They seem to think I am the wildest tiger in their cage."

Shan opened his mouth to speak and found he couldn't. He swallowed and tried again. "What happened?"

"When I didn't get your letter I was worried. But then they pulled me out of the barracks one night and dragged me to the lockup. Then I knew everything was all right."

"But why, Ko? What was it?"

"Nothing. That's what I mean," Ko said, still grinning. "I didn't do a thing this time. That's when I realized you must be okay, that you had just done something that really pissed them off."

Ko had been a handsome youth but his years in prison had aged him prematurely. He was hard and thin and scarred. Two fingers, once broken, had never healed properly and were permanently crooked. His grin revealed teeth chipped from beatings. He smelled of urine.

"Do they feed you?" Shan asked.

"Sure. Piles of beef and chicken. So much I had to go on a diet."

Shan offered a hollow smile. He fought the compulsion to leap up and embrace his son for fear of bringing the guards from the back of the chamber. "I had a dream the other night," he said to his son. "A memory really, but so vivid. I was visiting you when you were five or six. I took you to the cricket market in Beijing. There were hundreds of crickets, fighting crickets, singing crickets, crickets bred just to be beautiful, each in its own cage. I couldn't drag you away.

We stayed for hours, talking to the old men who sold them. Even the cages were amazing, intricate little things of bamboo and rosewood and molded gourds with carved ivory caps. One of them let you take his cricket for a walk on a leash of braided silk thread. You couldn't stop laughing. I told you about my grandfather, who had a green cricket with a funny name that always sang at midnight. You kept laughing at the name, kept repeating it all the way home."

Ko was staring at him now with an empty expression, as if he did not hear. Sometimes he would stay like that for Shan's entire visit. For several months he had been confined to a hospital for the criminally insane, where experimental drugs had been used.

Shan kept speaking, about the weather, about Lokesh, about how he had made some friends in the new Pioneer town. He always kept talking when Ko blanked out, though he didn't know if he did so for Ko, for himself, or for the guards.

"There's an owl who comes," Ko suddenly said.

Shan cocked his head.

"I have one of those tiny windows near the top of my cell. He comes in the middle of the night. He spits out fur and bones from his prey and I eat them." Ko's voice dropped to a whisper. "He dropped a feather the other night. I have to keep it hidden because they would confiscate it. But when the guards aren't near I take it out and study it. It's a miracle, you know, a feather."

"I know what Lokesh will say. A deity has sought you out in owl form."

Ko grinned again. "Five years ago I would have laughed at that. Now I am not so sure."

"Then there is hope for you yet, Son."

They both smiled. Despite where they were, despite the tortured paths their lives had taken, when they were together they smiled a lot. But Ko had seen something in his father's eyes. "You have to push it down," his son declared.

"I'm sorry?"

"You taught me that. The greatest power of a prisoner lies in pushing down his fear."

The words made Shan's throat constrict. He offered a small, slow nod.

Ko kept smiling as his face drifted back into the vacant, unfocused expression.

Shan became aware that the guards were at his side, releasing Ko from his chair. "Be well, Son," he said quietly. *"Lha gyal lo."*

When he turned he saw Meng waiting, staring at the two of them from the back of the room. She too was silent as his son was escorted past her into the corridor. Halfway down the hall Ko's voice rang out. "Thunder Dragon!" he shouted. "Grandfather's cricket was called Thunder Dragon!" He staggered as a guard pounded his shoulder, then slowly straightened and marched on.

Shan kept watching until the heavy metal door slammed behind his son.

It was Meng who broke the long silence on the drive back to the valley. "He's going to survive," she said in a tight voice. "I can see it in his eyes. They burn like yours."

He pointed to a family of partridges crossing the road. He had no stomach for talk of prisons and prisoners. The visit with Ko had been more painful than most. He knew he would relive it, every second of it, the next time he tried to sleep.

Meng dropped him off where she had found him that morning. No one answered, however, when he knocked on Yuan's door. He considered walking the miles to Lung's compound for his truck but knew the repairs would not have been completed. In the square he sat on a bench across from the plinth. The statue that had been on it was gone. Someone had placed a little souvenir Buddha there instead, looking ridiculously small on the big stone base. It stood on its own plinth, a red book of Mao's quotations.

He could not remember when he had felt so powerless. The valley, which for so long had been a stronghold of Tibetan tradition, was falling, soon to become another landscape of internment camps and immigrant settlements. Jamyang and the abbess, Lung Ma and the German, had died for nothing. No, a despairing voice said, they had died because of Beijing, had died to fuel the machine that was grinding up Tibet.

It was no longer the truth that was eluding him, it was what to do with the truth. Extracting the truth usually felt like pulling some shiny bauble out of a quagmire. But this time the truth had claimed him, pulling him down into the murk. He was suffocating in it. There was no path open to him. No Tibetan would believe him now if he tried to confront the killer. Shan would just be another bitter bone-catcher, resentful of a Tibetan hero. He rose and walked the streets, walked around every block of the small town. Those he passed turned away from him.

Finally he found himself at the side door of the police post, and sat on the step. The world was closing in around him. Liang and those he served had won. Shan and Jamyang had lost. The only real mystery had been why he had ever thought he could change things. He stared at the night sky a long time, until suddenly he heard his son's words again. *Push down your fear. It is the greatest power a prisoner can have.*

He stepped inside and found Meng staring at two papers on her desk. She raised one. "I am ordered to initiate a process against Professor Yuan and his daughter to revoke their Pioneer status."

"Meaning what?"

"They will be given a chance to provide evidence of their loyalty. Meaning they will have ten days to inform on unpatriotic activity known to them. Or they will be revoked and sent back to face their original charges. Certain prison for the girl."

She shook the paper and laid it on the desk. "That one came to me over the Public Security computer." She raised the other paper.

"This one I found on the old fax machine in the outer office they use for messages to the constables. An arrest order for Abbot Norbu. Not to me," she said pointedly, "to the local Tibetan constables. They are supposed to join Armed Police at Chegar tomorrow night to make the arrest, at the monks' evening assembly."

"The charges?"

"Political activity by a registered monk. Organizing unauthorized public assemblies. Suspicion of conspiracy against the government."

"The constables," he observed. "Do you ever wonder why those who blow their horns are never caught?"

"Only why we would trouble over them."

"Liang never intends to arrest Norbu. It's why the order went only to the constables."

"I don't understand."

"Liang is gone. Call headquarters and ask. He is done here. This order is his farewell gesture." He saw Meng's uncertain expression. "Call now," Shan insisted. "Ask for him."

The lieutenant frowned and picked up the phone. She spoke to one office at headquarters, then another, before hanging up. "He packed up the office they loaned him," Meng reported. "Officially he is gone, on to his next posting. They say he may be at that guesthouse. It's still the weekend. He probably won't leave until tomorrow." She looked back at the papers on her desk. "Why issue the order now?"

"He wants the word out to the Tibetans, and sending the order to the constables is how he achieves that. Did they see it?"

"One of them read it and left."

Shan nodded, as if it proved his point. "He wants everyone to believe Norbu is in grave danger, so there is no hesitation in the plans for his flight from Tibet. It's the endgame," Shan said. "The final act of their drama, to ensure he doesn't arrive in India as just another refugee, but as a hero. We've run out of time. The full moon is tomorrow night. By the time the police arrive for him he will have disappeared in the smuggler's truck."

"I don't understand."

He pulled a slip of paper from his pocket and handed it to her.

"What's this?"

"Me and Ko. Our registration numbers."

Her face tightened. "Why do I want this?"

"I have to get Liang back here. I can't go to the monks and tell them their abbot is a spy and a murderer. They will never believe me now. It has to be a secret they steal from Major Liang."

She raised the slip of paper again. "Why do I want this?" she asked once more.

"Liang only has authority to imprison me for a year. I can take a year. It will be like a meditation retreat enforced with chains. But there's a chance he will make good on the threat he made the last time he arrested me. Keep me for years, keep me invisible by moving me around. If that happens, I ask a small favor. Every few months, maybe once a year, just check the central records. It's important to me, Xiao Meng, a great favor to me. One I will never forget. Then get word to each of us where the other is. Public Security can get messages to prisoners. Otherwise . . ." he was having difficulty getting the words out. "Otherwise I will never find him. Otherwise today will have been the last day I ever see my son."

Her face drained of color. "What are you going to do?"

"Lokesh once told me that words are just hollow things. Truth can only be found in the heart, and in actions."

"Please, Shan. No more riddles."

"The Tibetans will not accept the truth from my lips, or yours. It has to be shown to them. I will force Liang back here so Tibetan ears will hear what I have to say, so the constables will grasp the truth by Liang's reaction and get the word to the monastery. It's a great risk to his mission for him to appear again in the valley. He had to take things to a boiling point, then back away. Otherwise he risks everything. He could frighten away the purbas, the ones waiting to escort Norbu to India. There are only two things that would make him ignore the risk. A chance to complete his vengeance on me and a way to correct his failure to capture the American woman. I will give him both. Everyone already knows me as the bonecatcher who killed a lama. It will come as no surprise when I demand more bounties for killing those who were going to expose his agent and delivering Cora Michener."

CHAPTER EIGHTEEN

Tears welled in Meng's eyes. "You fool," she whispered. "You damned fool. You can't beat Liang."

"I am not going to beat him. I am going to use him. I will not let all of them die in vain. I will not let the poison spread across the border. There has to be an end to it."

"He will kill you if he can."

"Probably not. Too many people know about me. But he will have to put me away. He has a prison he uses in the desert."

Meng was silent a long time. "Why does it have to be you?" she asked at last.

He ignored the question. "Will he bring other knobs when he comes?"

Meng looked down at her desk. "He no longer has an official role here. Those assigned to him will have been given new duties."

"Bring the Tibetan constables. They're the audience. We'll do it at the marketplace, by the old stable."

"Audience?"

"For my confession. Liang announced I killed Jamyang. Half the people here suspect I am some sort of secret operative. Liang himself demonstrated that I was one of those clandestine bonecatchers everyone hates. He showed me he has bounty money. Now I want payment in full. I killed a nun who conspired against the state and I want my reward. I will give them the gun I took from Jamyang as proof. I will say I killed them all for the Motherland. Liang knew Norbu had killed the Lung boy, because of the risk the boy represented to his secret mission, because the boy saw Norbu secretly conferring with Public Security. A bonecatcher relies on the government for his living, and therefore owes it a duty. He keeps watch, keeps alert for trouble. I had to kill the others because they were going to expose Norbu as an agent of Public Security, prevent him from his mission of infiltrating the government in exile. The major will cut me off for fear I give away too much. But they will hear enough. Don't give the constables any assignments afterwards. Give them plenty of time to warn those in the monastery before the end of the day. In time to stop the purbas from putting Norbu on that truck to Nepal."

"Liang can't imprison you for protecting Public Security."

"Not for the killings. For knowing his secrets."

"But Colonel Tan—"

"Will do nothing if I am declared a threat to national security. He will be powerless."

"It's madness, Shan. It will never work."

"It is all that *will* work now. I can't just go to the monks or any other Tibetan. They will never believe me after what Liang did."

"It doesn't get Cora Michener out of danger."

"I will see the girl gets to the purbas. They can put her on that truck, instead of Norbu."

Shan turned at the sound of movement in the darkened holding cell. Sansan appeared in the pool of light at the front, her hands gripping the bars.

He sagged. The world indeed was closing in about him. He had to give himself up to stop Norbu but it meant giving up the possibility of helping the exiles and the dropka. "Meng. You have to give her a chance. You can't just—"

"Shan!" Sansan called out in a strangely scolding voice. "You have to give *her* a chance." As she echoed his words she pushed open the cell door. "Lieutenant Meng is helping me."

"I told her if she stayed at her house she would be picked up by police out of district headquarters," Meng explained. "Suspicion of stealing state secrets is a serious charge. For now she is safer here."

Sansan offered Shan a sad smile as she stepped out of the cell. She poured them each a cup of tea from the thermos on a side table.

"Stealing state secrets?" Shan asked. "I thought you were just another dissident."

Sansan cast a sidelong glance toward Meng, then shrugged. "When I was in college I was noticed for the first time by Public Security. Not for my political activities but for my skills with computer systems. They targeted me for a career with them, running and designing such systems, breaking into systems elsewhere, outside of China. I took special courses at school. That was before someone else noticed my antisocialist leanings," she added.

"What state secrets could you steal in Baiyun?" he pressed.

"On my computer I was looking into the management systems for the dropka relocation camps. They need more medicine than they're getting at Clear Water."

Shan gazed at her with new interest. "Show me," he said, indicating Meng's computer.

"No!" Meng gasped. "You can't . . ." Her protest died away. Sansan fingers were already flying over the keyboard.

Minutes later Sansan was scrolling through pages of data showing the camps throughout Tibet, with lists of inhabitants and management plans for moving the dropka into factory jobs. She stopped at the entries for Clear Water Camp.

"What if some official wants to send orders? Like to the manager of Clear Water Camp?"

"It would require special security codes."

Shan frowned in disappointment.

"Which will take a few more minutes," Sansan added with a new glint in her eyes.

Shan watched in confused awe as the woman sped through screens of numbers and symbols. At last she looked up expectantly. "What do you want to say to him?"

Shan looked up and saw the warning in Meng's eyes. He held her gaze as he spoke to Sansan. "What I want to say is that the granddaughter of the headman Rapeche is to be immediately recalled from her factory in Guangdong."

Meng muttered a curse but did not move.

When Sansan had finished he turned to Meng. "Dakpo told me the monastery has a computer," he said, query in his eyes.

"I wouldn't know," the lieutenant said, then paused. "Yes. Actually they do. In the administrative office. The Bureau of Religious Affairs requires it now, so that decrees and orders can be efficiently transmitted."

Shan nodded. "Every police laptop computer I've ever seen looks the same. Do you have others here?" he asked Meng.

"A couple were sent for the constables. They never use them. The drives are empty."

Shan filled his cup and paced around the room, pausing to study the outer office and the cell beyond the desk. "I've changed my mind. We will invite Liang here. But first get one of those other computers. Put it under the pallet in the cell. Sansan will need it tomorrow."

Shan felt closer to Jamyang than ever as he drove up the rugged track toward the lama's hut. Lung's men had finished repairing his truck as Shan and the leader of the Jade Crows had spoken of his plans. Shan had left Lung with a packet of incense sticks and made him promise that he would stay with the American girl all the way to Nepal. Lung had been quiet when Shan had stated he probably would be leaving the valley. "Wait here," the gang leader had said, then disappeared into his house. When he returned he handed Shan a small clay deity figure. "That first day," he said. "I smashed that one of yours. I shouldn't have. . . ." He shrugged, not finishing the sentence, and shook Shan's hand.

Shan took care of his main task at the shrine first, finding the decorated pistol and Yuan's spirit tablets, then stowing them in his truck before returning to the shrine. The offering objects were still on the lama's makeshift altar, along with sprigs of heather and hearth-baked effigy figures left by Tibetans who lived in the hills. Shan lit some incense, then picked up a little bronze figure and began cleaning it. He had finished nearly half the altar objects when he heard footsteps behind him.

Meng was at the cairn by the edge of the shrine, holding a weathered mani stone. "I found this by the side of the highway," she said in a self-conscious tone. "All by itself. It was going to be broken under some truck. I picked it up and put it in my car. It seemed like it needed to be somewhere else." She looked inquiringly at Shan as she set it on top of the cairn. "Will this do?"

He nodded slowly.

She moved hesitantly toward him, as if uncertain of his reaction. She had replaced her uniform top with a bright red blouse and one of the rough felt vests sold by Tibetans in the market.

"You look like a Tibetan farmer going out for her herd."

"Is that good?" She seemed to be struggling to put a smile on her face.

"It's fine, Meng. More than fine."

She reached his side and gestured to the other offerings. "Show me what to do."

Shan handed her one of the rags he was using.

They worked in silence. Meng had the air of a novice nun as she handled the little deities. Shan explained the deities carved in the rock, showing her the little skulls underneath depicting the frailty of human existence.

When they finished, they walked on the slope above and spoke of little things, of stories from their youth and the larks that flitted about them. "I've heard it's a magic mountain," Meng said, pointing to snow-capped Yangon as it came into view.

"They say," Shan added, "that at least the people who dwell in its shadow find magic sometimes."

She looked at him, searching his eyes, as if longing to say something, then she turned away. They were not to speak of things below, they each seemed to have decided, not to talk of the treachery and death, not to speak of the disaster that Shan was about to bring on himself the next day. From Meng's car they brought a blanket and a sack of cold dumplings she had brought from town, then laid under the summer stars. They listened to the cries of nighthawks and watched a meteor streaking toward the massive mountain.

He stirred her at dawn. "I have to go," he said as he picked grass from her hair. "I have to ready things."

For a moment she lay without moving, her eyes wide and unknowing. Then she shut them and sighed and when she opened they were heavy with the world.

They folded the blanket in silence and descended the slope. His truck had come into sight when they encountered a small cairn with a tangled strand of prayer flags wrapped around its base. They straightened the rope and anchored it anew at the top. Meng began straightening and wiping the tattered, dirty flags. "I hear there are words to say, to put power in the flags," she said.

He taught her the mantra. "I must go make arrangements," he said.

She held his arm a moment. "We can't just let the murderer leave, Shan, can't let him go unpunished."

Shan saw the torment in her eyes. "He will be punished, Meng. He will be punished by the truth. He will be pushed out of the valley and marked by all monks, never allowed to accomplish his mission. The Institute will be exposed, unable to send out agents again. That is the way of Tibet. His crime was a crime against Tibet. There will be an accounting, in this life or the next."

She stared at him as if about to argue. "You would trade yourself for that?"

"If it is the only way, yes. It's not prison I fear, it's standing in the way of the truth."

She broke from his gaze and looked back toward the mountain. "*Yan que yong you hong hu zhi,*" she murmured.

Shan touched her. "I'm sorry?"

Meng gave a tiny, sad smile. "Nothing. It's something my mother used to say about me. The story of my life, she would say. I was speaking to the mountain, not to you."

But Shan had heard. "Little sparrow who dreams of swans," she had said.

Meng suddenly embraced him, very tightly, very quickly, then turned to the first flag and recited the mantra as she kneaded the dirt off the cotton.

"I have to go," he reminded her.

"I know. I want to finish this."

He left her there. When he reached his truck he looked up. In the distance she was just another peasant, wringing blessings out of the old cloth.

The constable at the Baiyun post had to invoke Meng's name to convince the headquarters office to transfer the call to the guesthouse. "He is loading bags into his car," the Tibetan nervously reported. He kept looking over Shan's shoulder. Sansan watched from the holding cell.

"Tell him Shan demands to speak with him."

Two minutes later the constable handed the phone to Shan, then hurried out of the room. Shan did not give Liang a chance to complain. "Major, you are going to meet me in Baiyun this afternoon," he began.

He had three hours to wait, and no stomach for the condemning stares of those on the streets of Baiyun. He retrieved Yuan Yi's tablets from the truck and took them to the little shed behind the professor's house. He murmured a little prayer as he left them, and the ancient mandarin's badge, inside the secret shrine, then drove to the empty marketplace. He left the truck and began climbing the trail that wound up the steep ridge above the town. At the top he found the outcropping where he had been with Jamyang as they confronted Jigten. It seemed a lifetime ago. He sat on a flat boulder and gazed down the valley, then noticed a deposit of white sand at the base of a rock. He sifted it in his fingers, making a circle on the flat surface of the rock, then within it the outlines of temples. It was the simplest of mandalas, the kind young boys had once been taught when they first entered monasteries. Lokesh would make such a shape and gaze upon it for hours, envisioning the deities that dwelled in each chamber.

As he stared at the sand image he recalled Chenmo's description of how the abbot had made a mandala at the convent but had mistakenly arranged the deities on it. One of the nuns had seen Lokesh walk toward the convent to work there that night and had spoken with him, out of Shan's earshot. Lokesh had gone right to the mandala and spent hours correcting the mistakes. He recalled how melancholy had seeped into Lokesh's wise, gentle eyes after he had examined the abbot's work. Lokesh's way of seeing the world often cut closer, and quicker, to the truth than Shan's. At that moment, Shan knew now, his old friend had sensed something wrong, something out of balance at Chegar.

He gazed in the direction of the shrine where Jamyang had died and murmured an apology. Shan had been too blind, too slow, to understand the path Jamyang had left for him. The lama had raced to save the tablets from Jigten because they were the first clue on the path. He had wanted Shan to investigate, to know why he had had to take such terrible steps, perhaps even to assure the truth came out if somehow his plans went awry. The ribbon had been left on the altar to lead Shan to the tablets, the tablets had been meant to lead Shan to Yuan and his daughter, who had the journal that connected Jamyang to the Peace Institute.

He was halfway down the slope when he saw the grey car speeding toward Baiyun. The demon sent by Beijing was making one last appearance in the valley.

"You were supposed to bring me the American!" Liang roared as Shan entered Meng's office alone.

"I did not say I would deliver her in person. I said I could sell her to you. Worth more than some outlaw lama surely. Then there's the abbess and that Chinese criminal Lung." Shan fought the temptation to turn to confirm that the constables were still in the outer office.

Liang's hatred for Shan was a living thing, a serpent that seemed to writhe inside before the major opened his mouth. "I will see you dead before I am done!"

"Just a business transaction," Shan replied in a level voice. "A thousand for my patriotic killings. Another thousand and I'll tell you where to find the American."

Liang glanced into the outer office. All he had for backup was Meng and the taciturn Tibetan constables. Liang gave a nod, as if acknowledging the constables, then Shan heard the sound of the main door opening and shutting behind him. Meng probably had no stomach for the scene.

The major spat a curse. "You didn't kill them."

"You mean to argue against my petition?" Shan shot back. "By all means. There are procedures, committees who hear such disputes. I will write everything down, explain how I had to act to protect the glorious work of the Peace Institute. I have the pistol," he said, setting Jamyang's weapon on Meng's desk. "You threw away the killer's bullet so no one can say otherwise. They were at the convent that day to stop the abbot of Chegar from infiltrating the exile government so I did the work of any good patriot."

Liang did not react at first. His face remained impassive as he studied Shan. "I see now you are dead inside, Comrade. You have no political consciousness. I don't have to kill you. You are killing yourself." He dropped a bundle of currency on the desk.

Shan pocketed the money.

"And the American?" Liang seemed to struggle to keep from striking Shan. His eyes narrowed to thin slits as he tossed a second bundle of money in front of Shan.

"There's a field of rock formations a mile south of the monastery. You can't miss it. On the top of a hill just off the highway, with a view in all directions. She will be there at sundown, waiting to meet some of the purbas."

Liang hesitated, as if confused by Shan's words. He had not expected Shan to speak of purbas, or the rendezvous point with the smugglers. His gaze drifted down to the top of the desk, his eyes working back and forth until at last his lips curled into a thin, lightless grin. He gestured Shan to the far side of the office then sat, opened his computer, and began rapidly tapping the keys. He could not risk going to the monastery, Shan knew, but he had to get word to his agent about the gift Shan had just given them.

"She's yours to deal with as you wish then," Shan said as Liang shut his computer with a victorious gleam. "Unless the American consulate calls."

"What are you talking about?" Liang snarled.

"I took a photograph of her," Shan lied. "With a copy of yesterday's *Lhasa Times*. If anything happens to me the photo gets mailed to the embassy."

The rage quickly rekindled in the major's eyes, then burst into flame.

Shan jumped an instant before Liang leapt for him.

"Seize him!" the major roared as he grabbed the truncheon Shan had earlier placed on the desk. Shan swerved away from a violent blow, then darted into the outer office. With a groan of sudden despair, he saw that the office was empty. Through the window he caught a glimpse of Meng and the constables standing at the back of the parking lot and froze in panic. *No! They had misunderstood! They had not been inside! The constables had not heard!*

He regained his senses in time to swerve as Liang took another vicious swing with the stick.

Liang's fury raged like a bonfire. Chairs fell over, files were knocked on the floor in his frenzy. One slam of his baton broke the back of a chair, another left a long scar on a desktop. He wanted nothing more than to lay a skull-shattering blow on Shan. "This time no one will see your name in the record!" Liang roared.

Shan glanced at the clock on the wall and parried another furious downstroke.

"The manacles!" Liang shouted. "Chain him!" Shan sensed movement in the doorway. The constables must be coming back. They could at least witness Liang's fury and they could learn the reason afterwards. He glanced at the clock again, then ran around Liang into Meng's office. As the major gained on him he grabbed Liang's computer on the desk and held it like a shield.

"Bastard!" Liang hissed. The serpent inside had full control of him.

The first hammer blow of the truncheon split the top of the laptop, the second tore the top away, the third split the keyboard and spilled electronic shards onto the floor. Liang hesitated only a moment as he saw what he had done, then kept smashing at the machine, desperately trying to reach Shan's head. Shan retreated backward toward the door until suddenly strong arms seized him. As Shan's hands were being cuffed behind him, Liang slammed the baton into his belly, dropping him to his knees.

"You saw him! He attacked an officer!" Liang screeched, kicking Shan now.

To Shan's horror he saw the grey uniforms of the men who had grabbed him. They were not the Tibetan constables who were supposed to have witnessed his performance. They were knobs. Liang had found soldiers to help him after all. They had kept Meng and the constables outside. No one had heard. No one had seen anything. His desperate plan had failed. He had given up his freedom for nothing.

Shan shut his eyes against the pain in his gut as he was thrown into the backseat of a car. He lay on the seat, his head reeling, trying to catch his breath after having the wind knocked out of him, trying to think only of the next moment and the next, anything to keep his mind off the cell that waited, the prison far away. In another day he would be hundreds of miles from Ko.

Moments before it stopped he realized the car was driving on gravel, not the paved highway. It was a constable who pulled him out of the car, and another who turned it around. Suddenly his hands were released. The Tibetan constable wiped at the blood on his face. "*Lha gyal lo*," he whispered to Shan, then tossed something to his feet.

"What are you doing?" Shan shouted in confusion as they drove away. He was standing at the gate to the Jade Crow compound. Jamyang's gun lay at his feet.

Lung Tso leaned against a post, smoking a cigarette, as if waiting for him. As Shan took a staggering step toward him another car drove up.

Meng was alone. "I told you Liang had officially departed," she explained. "But I left a message for him at headquarters that they relayed to his car. I said Colonel Tan was looking for him, had questions about something called the Peace Institute. He didn't dare take any more official action here, in Tan's county, for fear of compromising what goes on in Chamdo."

"You lied to him." As his pain subsided he began to grasp the cleverness of her ploy. Liang knew Tan as the powerful bully who hated Public Security, but he was also experienced enough to know how furious an old veteran like Tan would be to learn of covert operations inside his territory that had been kept hidden from him.

"Words are such hollow things," Meng reminded him. "He knew he never should have come here today. Like you said, it was too big a risk to his mission, too big a risk to him personally. He has to disappear. He's gone. He is convinced his work is done, that his agent will take the American woman. That was enough for him, that and being able to rough you up."

"But the soldiers . . ."

"You were wrong, Shan. He never would have spoken openly in front of Tibetan constables. Those soldiers were here to help me with traffic duties, because of the convoys. They had no idea what was going on." Meng gestured to Lung and with a short bow of her head left him with the gang leader.

Lung Tso stomped out his cigarette as Meng drove away. "The girl won't go any farther, says she won't go near a monk without you."

Shan followed Lung's gaze toward the entry of the house, where Cora Michener stood with Ani Ama, watching him with a frightened expression. He had no words to comfort her. The only way for her to escape was for Shan to take her to the one man left in the county who wanted her dead.

CHAPTER NINETEEN

Lung Tso eased the truck to a stop behind the long rock formation that flanked the highway, below a knoll that was surrounded by boulders on all sides like a natural fortress. A strange mist was building on the valley floor, its fingers reaching up into the rocks. At the top a monk appeared and gestured for them to join him. When Cora saw the man in the robe she shrank back, gripping Shan's arm tightly as he led her forward.

Dakpo moved slowly. Although he was clearly still in pain, his serene expression had returned. He stepped into the evening light so that Cora could see his face.

The American cautiously studied him, then relaxed her grip as Dakpo stepped aside, pointing them down a short passage between the rocks. Trinle was in the clearing they entered but Cora stepped ahead of Shan as she saw Chenmo at his side, helping him tie off the top of a large backpack. As Cora and the novice embraced, a third man in a robe emerged from behind a rock.

As Cora looked up from her friend's shoulder, a startled gasp left her throat. She began backing away, the color draining from her face.

"Cora, no!" Chenmo said to her friend. "Norbu, Norbu. The abbot!"

The lama snapped out an order for the monks to return to the gompa, then as they disappeared into the shadows he turned to Shan and sighed. "She was supposed to come alone," he said in Chinese. He cast a puzzled glance at Dakpo as the monk disappeared into the rocks. "Dakpo was supposed to intercept her and leave her alone with me so I could console her."

The American backed into one of the rock walls that enclosed the clearing, her face clenched in fear.

Shan replied in Tibetan. "She saw the monk who killed the three at the convent. But she couldn't describe him in detail. She said she would recognize him if she ever saw him again." Chenmo gasped and moved to Cora's side.

Norbu sighed. "It's not exactly courtroom testimony."

"I was never expecting a courtroom," Shan said. He inched forward, trying to get between Cora and the abbot.

"It could make for an awkward journey," Norbu said conversationally.

He glanced at Jamyang's pistol, now tucked into Shan's belt, then back at Cora. Shan watched his hands move toward his own belt. A pen case hung there, and one of the bronze fire strikers issued to Peace Institute graduates. Not any fire striker, Shan knew, but the one that had killed the Lung boy.

"Major Liang had you in custody," the abbot said with a peevish expression. "That makes you a fugitive."

"The only one who could have told you that was the major himself," Shan observed. "I do recall seeing him send a message. A secret message from a handler of undercover agents."

Shan's words brought a groan of despair from Chenmo. She tried to shield Cora with her body.

Suddenly there was movement at the back of the small clearing. Meng stepped into the light, the two Tibetan constables at her side. The lieutenant had a scrubbed, well-polished look about her. Her cap was cleaned, her uniform freshly pressed, her hair pinned back in a severe knot. She had become the knob Shan had first met at the convent.

Shan stared at her in disbelief. She would ruin everything. Purbas were nearby, probably approaching this very moment, ready for their passenger to India. They would flee at the first sight of her, taking Cora's only hope of escape with them, leaving the killer in a desperate rage that he would turn against those left in the clearing. Shan tried to get her attention, to warn her away, but she would not acknowledge him.

Norbu too gazed at her in confusion for a moment, but quickly recovered. "Lieutenant Meng!" he greeted her. "For once you are a welcome sight." He pointed at Shan. "This man is a fugitive criminal. He must have escaped from Major Liang."

"Major Liang," Meng explained, "has departed the region, back to his Peace Institute." Norbu shot a chastising glance at Meng, then moved with surprising agility, feigning a move toward Meng before lunging at Shan and grabbing the pistol from his belt. "Lieutenant Meng," Norbu said, speaking like a senior officer now, "you must take these two"—he gestured to Shan and Chenmo—"into custody. Contact Major Liang. Secure accommodations must be arranged for them. One of those institutions for the criminally insane would do nicely."

Chenmo began a low, fearful mantra.

Meng dutifully stepped around Norbu and pulled the dazed novice from Cora, back to one of the constables. Shan stood frozen as he realized that Meng indeed was just a knob again. He had seen her changing, had seen her struggling with something inside. She had scared herself with her lies to Liang, had recognized the dangerous ground she had been treading and was retreating, making her amends to the government.

Norbu seemed to be enjoying himself. He examined the pistol with an amused expression. "Jamyang's handiwork," he said of the little symbols painted on it. "Even in our training classes he was always doodling, drawing these things. He spent too long building his cover, succumbed to it in the end," he declared to Shan, speaking as if one professional to another. "We must recalibrate the training."

Shan cast another worried glance at Meng. She could correct all she had done, could become a hero, even attain her former rank, by arresting them all. Shan the traitorous convict, the purbas who were no doubt lingering nearby, Chenmo the splittist, the American woman whom Public Security so desperately wanted to disappear. He pushed down his fears and turned back to Norbu. "It's what happens when you train people to ignore their true selves."

Norbu gave a hollow laugh. "True self, Comrade? We are all but clay to be shaped by the Motherland."

"And what shape do you assume, Norbu, once you get across to India?" Shan asked. "Just a spy? Or is it to be assassin? The way you dealt with the Lung boy and those at the convent showed a natural talent."

"No training is complete unless it is both mental and physical. The opportunities are endless. I am but an instrument to be aimed by the people's will."

"The instrument of a gang of old men in Beijing who lost touch with the people years ago," Shan shot back.

"Spoken like the unrepentant criminal you are," Norbu sneered. "Liang will find a cure for you." He glanced back at Meng, standing behind him, and lifted the gun again. "Possession of a firearm by a former convict, Lieutenant. Make a note. Ten strings at least." He noticed Chenmo, who had collapsed, sobbing, against a rock. "And search that damned hermitage of the nuns. The place reeks of splittism. Should have leveled it years ago."

At last he turned to the American. Cora seemed to have lost all her strength. She had collapsed to the ground and was on her knees now, as if in supplication. But there was no surrender in her face. "You killed them," she declared to Norbu in English in a quiet but steady voice. "You butchered them. I watched. You arranged the bodies like you were stacking wood. You enjoyed it."

Shan had no notion whether Norbu understood. But then the abbot laughed and replied in perfect English. "When risks are presented I am taught to eliminate them. The deaths were an affirmation of my mission, a sign that I am destined to succeed. Even those photos I worried about, they were just waiting for me in those little cases, not even hidden, ready for me to destroy them. It's my destiny," he said, with a gesture to those gathered before him.

"What I never understood," Shan said in Tibetan, "was how you knew, who warned you so that you suspected you would be confronted that day?"

Norbu was enjoying himself. "Loyal Dakpo of course. He told me how the old abbot was meeting some tall solitary lama who had begun asking questions about me. He was excited because the lama had a little lotus mark on his neck, called it an auspicious sign. But I knew that mark. Our wayward agent. Liang made a special trip all the way from Chamdo just to warn me that Jamyang was missing. It was just bad luck that fool Lung boy saw us together. I told Liang we should never have let Jamyang stop to see his elderly aunt. And the abbess was so straightforward, no sense of subterfuge. What did she expect when she asked me to come to the convent?" He shrugged. "I actually think she thought I would weep on her shoulder and ask forgiveness."

"Murder!" Chenmo spat.

"No, my dear. Casualties in our glorious war." Norbu cocked his head at the novice. "Look at you. You must have been pretty once. The Bureau could have found a good use for you. Now"—he shrugged—"after five or ten years they may trust you to scrub the toilets in their barracks."

He suddenly swiveled, cocking the pistol and raising it in one swift motion, aiming at Cora's head. "You should have stayed home," he said in English, and pulled the trigger.

There was less than a second between the metallic click on the empty chamber and the sharp crack of a shot. Norbu looked in confusion at the pistol in his hand, then down at the swelling crimson blossom on his chest. He looked at Shan, opening his mouth as if in question, then collapsed to the ground.

In the awful silence that followed there was no movement except that of Meng as she returned her pistol to her belt. Shan was aware of nothing but her gaze. For an instant he saw desolation in her eyes, the look of one being swept out to sea without hope of rescue. Then she clenched her jaw and took command.

"Now," she murmured to the constables. One of them whistled and two young Tibetan men materialized out of the shadows, followed a moment later by Dakpo and Trinle. They had been listening. She had been wiser than Shan, had known the audience had to be those most directly affected by Norbu's violence. She turned to the two strangers. They were, Shan suddenly realized, the purbas who were to escort Norbu to Dharamsala. "You are going to take the American across the border," Meng commanded, "but on the way, somewhere in the high mountains, you will lose Norbu's body in a crevasse. As far as his superiors will know he went across to India. Take his identity cards. Find someone who can use them to check into a hotel in Macau or Hong Kong. In a few weeks when he doesn't show up in Dharamsala they will begin a search and find the record. They will assume he has fled to the West. They will have to assume everything he touched is compromised, that no graduate of their Institute will ever be trusted again. They will have to roll up the operations at Chamdo and start over somewhere else."

Another figure stepped out of the shadows as Meng backed away. Sansan clutched a flat black box to her breast. "It worked," she said to Shan, excitement in her eyes. "We have a computer with all the knob clearances embedded in it." Shan breathed a sigh of relief. He had not been certain if Sansan had had the time to dart out of the shadows of the holding cell and switch the computers when he had lured Liang into the outer office.

"She says we have to destroy it in two or three days but until then we—"

Shan did not hear the rest of the sentence, for Sansan had nodded toward the path that led to the road. He darted into the shadows and out onto the open slope. Meng was already at her car. She paused, seeing him, and for a long moment they silently gazed at each other. Then she climbed inside and drove away.

EPILOGUE

The long trail of dust gleamed silver in the moonlight, a cloud that seemed to be pushing them ever on, deeper into the new land. Shan and Lokesh stood on the ridge to watch as the three heavy vehicles that had been following them climbed the steep dirt track below. Like scouts in the wilderness Jigten and Rapeche the headman had stood in the back of Shan's truck, guiding them for hours through the vast grassland, their night passage lit only by dim parking lights and the hand lanterns used when rocks had to be cleared from their path.

They turned at the sound of a low whistle from Jigten and climbed back into their own truck. Jigten and the old shepherd insisted now on walking in front of the weary column, leading the vehicles along the narrow track between tall, narrow stone formations that loomed like ghostly sentinels in the night. Half an hour later they stopped as Jigten and the old man conferred excitedly. Rapeche dropped to one knee and plucked some of the grass at his feet and chewed on it, then tasted the soil. As the headman turned his face was full of joy. He seemed to have discovered a long-lost friend.

When the clan patriarch had proclaimed that Shan had performed a miracle, Shan had quickly corrected the old man, insisting that the magic had all been in the young Chinese woman, explaining how Sansan had used the Public Security computer to confuse the government. Rapeche had listened patiently, then proclaimed again that Shan had performed a miracle. Not even Shan and Yuan had fully grasped Sansan's passion when she first tried to explain the opportunities presented by having Liang's computer but after several hours at their dining table, running through programs on the little machine, learning how the populations of the dropka camps were managed and assigned, they had begun to share her excitement. When Jigten had reported an unexpected, joyful reunion between Rapeche and his granddaughter, they had invited the headman to Yuan's house and spent most of the night consulting maps and devising the plan. At dawn they had gone to see Lung and the Jade Crows.

Now, four days later, Shan was still in awe at the boldness of their plan. The manager at Clear Water Camp had expected his residents to be relocated, and although it had been sooner than he had anticipated Shan had seen the relief on his face as the trucks were being loaded with his unruly charges. Sansan had simply altered relocation schedules, vehicle records, and destinations. In fact, at her father's urging, the destination of the clan was changed repeatedly in the system, then the last destination was linked back to the first so that the record would seem to disappear into a loop of reassignments. The administration of relocation and internment programs was notoriously inefficient. No one had time to reconcile the records and if they tried they would find neither the real destination of the missing shepherds nor the vehicles that had transported them.

Shan and Lokesh climbed out to join Jigten and the old headman in a clearing on what appeared to be one more rise in the endless hills. Before them the landscape was unknown, shrouded in fog. But as the trucks pulled up side by side, Rapeche threw up his arms and shouted what sounded like a mantra.

"Truly the gods shine on us this night!" Lokesh exclaimed. Shan turned to his friend in confusion then followed his gaze toward an increasingly bright patch of light ahead of them. The fog was shifting, quickly blowing away, leaving the landscape washed in moon-light.

Jigten dropped to his knees. They were not on just another hill-top, they were on the crest of a ridge that rose like a wall to protect a vast basin of grassland below. Small lakes dotted the land, patches of silver in a rolling sea.

"They say there is no paved road for nearly four hundred miles in that direction." Professor Yuan spoke over Shan's shoulder. "Not even the army has reliable maps. It's a wilderness of grass."

Lung Tso jumped out of the cab of the first truck and began shouting orders to the drivers, who backed their trucks to the edge of the ridge. From the last truck came eager bleats. The animals too seemed to sense where they were. The sheep had been the Jade Crows' payment for joining their scheme. Sansan had provided the gang with the schedules of trucks traveling the central highway with cargos of livestock for the government abattoirs in the north. The smugglers had done the rest. By the end of the night the Jade Crows would be gone on the eastern highway, to some city in a distant province where they could buy false registrations for their trucks and themselves and start anew. All the bounty money left after out-fitting the dropka for the trip Shan had given to Lung. When the police finally went to the Jade Crow compound they would find it abandoned, with a little Buddha sitting on the gatepost.

The excited cries of the sheep began to stir the passengers who had been sleeping in the bays of the other trucks. The rear flaps were flung open and bright faces appeared. Cries of joy and prayers of thanks rippled through the dropka as they began unloading packs of supplies. One of the first to jump down was Chenmo, her face beam-ing. She gave Shan a shy embrace. "Uncle Lokesh says I will be the clan's nun now. I told him I could never get a robe and he said it is what is in your heart that makes you a nun, not what you wear." She touched the abbess's gau, now hanging from her neck, and turned to help a young boy out of the truck.

As Shan helped empty the first truck, the professor and Sansan appeared, hoisting packs on their backs.

"I'm sorry," Shan said, "but there is no time for you to help them find a camp. We have to be back in the valley by daybreak."

Yuan's smile was as wide as the landscape. "In the spring come and find us," he said. "There is a festival for the lambing."

Shan stared at his friend in disbelief. "Think this through, Yuan. You have no idea of the hardship."

"Someone needs to record all their stories. The world needs to know. The shepherds who have been forced to towns need to know. There used to be an honored profession among the nomads, that of the traveling letter writer, who would write messages to share among the clans. Maybe that will be my new job."

"Do you have any idea how harsh the winter will be?"

"Jigten's mother has promised to show us how to make thick felt blankets. She has been steadily recovering since learning she was returning home. She says once she is back in her homelands she can make proper medicines for Sansan and her."

Sansan grabbed Shan's hand, squeezing it tightly, then darted away to help another child out of the truck.

"Please," Shan said to Yuan. "You are too old."

The professor gazed after his daughter. "Meng came by our house. She told us the arrest order could not be avoided for much longer. If they took Sansan it would be at least five years, more likely ten. At my age I would never see her again. This way we are together, living a new adventure, making a difference for these people. Meng made it possible, my friend," Yuan added.

Shan looked away, into the night sky, fighting another wave of emotion. He had not seen Meng again. When he had gone to the police post the constables had reported she had abruptly taken a new assignment on the Mongolian border. She had left a report with them, that stated that she and Shan had found that Major Liang and Norbu were engaged in smuggling. Once Norbu's disappearance was discovered it would be enough to protect Shan from Liang if the major tried to find him.

Yuan reached into the truck one last time and hoisted out a familiar bundle. Shan helped him balance the bound ancestral tablets onto his shoulder. "This one has done more traveling than any of us," he said with a laugh.

"The old bandit is ready for a new adventure," Shan said.

"All of us old bandits," Yuan replied with a shine in his eyes.

At last came the sheep, leaping to the ground the moment Lung Tso and Genghis lowered the tailgate, some running among the shepherds as if by instinct, others darting into the night, toward the rich grass below.

From somewhere in the distance the deep voice of an owl echoed, sounding like a prayer horn.

Shan did not know if it was the flight of their animals or the growing spell of the vast moonlit land before them but he saw a new wildness enter the eyes of the dropka, a feral skittishness. As they began filing down the path Lokesh stood at the side, touching each one, blessing each with a quick, joyful prayer. Chenmo led several in song as they descended the slope.

The professor and Rapeche paused, waiting for the last of the party to pass before finally raising their hands to Shan in farewell. Then they turned and became two more of the wary shadows that merged with the night, leaving the world behind.

AUTHOR'S NOTE

The dismantling of Tibet by the Chinese government over the past two generations is one of the darkest chapters of Asia's long, rich history. While examples of more technically advanced, militarized nations overwhelming smaller countries can be found in nearly every century, the scope of Beijing's conduct in Tibet, and the scale of the damage inflicted, has few parallels in any age. Tibet didn't just have a vibrant spiritually centered culture, it had what by any objective criteria must be characterized as an entirely separate civilization, with vital centuries-old frameworks of medicine, literature, education, government, and religion that were unlike any in the world. Our entire planet lost something very important in the battles in which mountain warriors fought with muskets and swords against machine guns, and monks resisted with prayers against aerial bombs and artillery shells.

The suffering of the Tibetan people didn't end with the loss of a million lives and thousands of temples in the original occupation of their country. I am sometimes asked whether in my Shan novels I exaggerate Beijing's behavior in Tibet for dramatic effect. The answer is a steadfast no. The reality is dramatic enough. Armies of soldiers and police still crush every hint of political resistance. Armies of bureaucrats are dedicated to dismantling Tibetan society, teaching Tibetan children to chant only Beijing's mantras, monitoring political usage of the Internet, regulating monks, and seizing the religious artifacts that were once fixtures of Tibetan life. These pages reflect how Beijing has in recent years turned up the heat, sharply swelling the ranks of Tibetans in remote internment camps, in part by arresting the family members of those suspected of engaging in dissidence. Monasteries that were once surrounded by shrines are now ringed by surveillance cameras. Undercover agents trained to pose as monks were introduced years ago, and are routinely employed to detect disloyal behavior in monasteries. The government has also launched a program to relocate over a million nomad shepherds into what it calls "productive" lives far from their ancestral lands.

For those who wish to learn more about the tragedies, and heroism, arising out of the modern Tibetan experience there are several excellent overviews, including John Avedon's *In Exile from the Land of the Snows*, David Patt's *Tibetan Lives in Chinese Hands*, Tsering Shakya's *The Dragon in the Land of the Snows* and Mary Craig's *Tears of Blood: A Cry for Tibet*, as well as poignant personal chronicles such as *Born in Lhasa* by Namgyal Lhamo Taklha, *The Autobiography of a Tibetan Monk* by Palden Gyatso with Tsering Shakya, *In the Presence of My Enemies* by Sumner Carnahan, and *Ama Adhe: The Voice That Remembers* by Adhe Tapontsang and Joy Blakeslee. For those who wish to play a more active role, the International Campaign for Tibet offers many opportunities.

One of the great paradoxes of Beijing's role in Tibet is that the traditional culture of the Chinese people themselves was built on a family-centered spiritualistic life that was similar in many ways to that of Tibetans. Many Chinese, in fact, remain active practitioners of Buddhism, or follow the spiritual traditions of Confucianism and Taoism. Their government's treatment of Tibetan and other ethnic groups often weighs heavily on the conscience of individual Chinese.

In a very real sense that conscience was once collectively expressed in the mandarin censors alluded to in *Mandarin Gate*. Attaining the rank of a mandarin official in imperial China required years of study and examination, so rigorous that many did not attain office until well advanced in age. The censors were a highly ethical, elite subset of these mandarins, charged with watching over the government. It was in their nature, and inherent in their office, to confront other officials over injustice and corruption and, like other mandarins who fell out of favor, they were sometimes banished to remote mountainous regions for their efforts.

Internal exiles like the professors of Baiyun therefore do not just have real-life counterparts in the remote western lands of modern China, they share their fate with many others who historically ran afoul of the government. Chinese culture was enriched in the process, since more than a few of these outcasts took up lives as hermit poets. The bittersweet verses of such exiles as Su tung-po, an official banished for criticizing the emperor in 1097, can still wrench the heart and would certainly resonate with Shan and the professors of the Vermilion Society.

Tales of those who have been thus abandoned by history are so plentiful at the roof of the world that they almost seem ingrained in the landscape. While there is much ugliness to be found in the behavior of the government in today's Tibet, the power of that rugged landscape sometimes seems to eclipse it—and certainly the stark beauty of their land is only enhanced by the enduring strength of the Tibetan people.